Celestial Dogs

Celestial Dogs

A Novel

J. S. Russell

St. Martin's Press
New York

CELESTIAL DOGS. Copyright © 199 ´ 1997 by Jay Russell. All rights
reserved. Printed in the United St   ˋ merica. No part of this
book may be used or reproduced   ..iy manner whatsoever without
written permission except in the case of brief quotations embodied
in critical articles or reviews. For information, address St. Martin's
Press, 175 Fifth Avenue, New York, N.Y. 10010.

Book design by Ellen R. Sasahara
Edited by Gordon Van Gelder

First published by Raven Books, London.

Library of Congress Cataloging-in-Publication Data

Russell, J. S. (Jay S.).
    Celestial dogs : a novel / by J. S. Russell.—1st U.S. ed.
       p.   cm.
    ISBN 0-312-15076-8
    I. Title.
    PS3568.U76667C45   1997
    813'.54—dc20   96-34065
                               CIP

First U.S. Edition: March 1997

10 9 8 7 6 5 4 3 2 1

For Florence Schechter,
who gave me the words
&
For Jane Stokes,
who teaches me the meaning

Acknowledgments

O kay, acknowledgment pages can sometimes be a little bit dull. So just try to imagine this as if it were one of those eye-popping Saul Bass credit sequences. And dig that crazy Elmer Bernstein score!

Many thanks to:

Jessica Horsting and Paul M. Sammon for believing in and supporting new writers just because they like the work.

Steve Jones for thoughtful editorial advice and especially for recklessly wading through the slush.

Louis Schechter for a lifetime of support and belief far beyond the call of duty.

And Jane for . . . well, just about everything else!

Celestial Dogs

Prologue

Winter

The flesh is failing.

It always does—as it must—but on this sojourn to *Naka-Tsu-Kuni,* the realm of men, his adopted, fragile flesh has given way sooner than planned. It has *all* given way sooner than planned.

The kimono hangs from the damaged human host in silky shreds, its once resplendent pattern indecipherable amid the rips and bloodstains. The chain of sacred ideograms, an intricate spiral tattooed upon the amber skin, has been broken, the delicate characters also smeared by blood that leaks from a score of cuts and slashes. Shards of bone, still wrapped in glistening pink bands of sinews, poke like broken teeth through tattered flaps of blackened skin. Tortured breath comes, open-mouthed, in labored rasps as fractured ribs scrape against lung in the wrack and ruin of the perfectly proportioned torso. The right eye has been reduced to a bloody red hole, the soft orb carelessly lost to the point of an enemy arrow, but the left eye takes in the view of the carnage with superhuman clarity.

The battlefield spread before him is as much a ruin as the dying flesh he wears. Mutilated bodies litter the face of Mt. Ōe for as far as the eye—the remaining eye—can see. Some of the defeated warriors writhe and scream in agony, waiting and praying for death's teasing release, but most are already as cold as the frozen ground on which they lay. The pale stone walls of the great castle are veined with trickles of red, the thin rivulets of blood merging at the bottom and cascading down the steep slope toward the corpse-strewn river below. The cold February air is choked with grimy smoke as flames dervish-dance from tree to denuded tree, fiery orange tongues hotly lapping away at the blanket of tainted snow covering the mountain peak. The fighting goes on, but the battle, Shuten Dōji knows, has been lost. His *Goryō-dō* soldiers fought as well as could be expected, but it was he who squandered their devotion, miscalculating the enemy's resources and fanatical resolve. Yet another in a very long series of lessons to add to his experience.

A hideous black shape swoops down with the wind from on high: the last of the winged demons, black ichor dripping from its wounds, attacks an enemy flank with beak and talon and thrice-cursed steel. A full dozen of the *Kakure* warriors fall before the sheer savagery of the demon's assault; two dozen more quickly pour through a gap in the wall to take their place. A line of archers release a volley of silver-tipped arrows, and the demon, wailing its anger and pain, comes crashing to earth. The cadre of warriors rush to smother it. The demon extends a broken claw and rips open a fat belly, unleashing a coil of intestine. Another desperate swipe of its talons removes a surprised head, before the monster loses its own misshapen skull and is hacked to bits in a flurry of flashing steel. The demon fell too easily, but then it drew much of its strength from Shuten Dōji, a strength that, with the tattered flesh, is failing.

A tiny three-eyed creature, among the lesser—and manifestly *stupider*—of Shuten Dōji's legion of *oni,* stops to lap greedily at the open throat of a fallen *Kakure* priest. The demon lord could shout a warning to the witless creature, but decides that the foolish imp deserves what it is about to receive. A *Kakure* warrior approaches from behind and pinions the demon through the back with a *katana* and hefts it off the ground. The creature screeches with dismay and tries to spit acid venom at its attacker, but cannot twist its head around far enough to reach. The warrior draws a second sword and hacks off the demon's tail, followed by each of its limbs until all eight lie in a twitching pile at his feet. The warrior jerks the sword and the tiny *oni* slides farther down the blade, howling in agony as it flails its stumps. A final, neat slice separates the ugly head from the dismembered torso. The warrior scrapes the body off his sword with his boot and smiles as he picks the demon's head up by an ivory horn. It is Shuten Dōji's turn to smile when the severed head spits one last gob of bile into the warrior's face and the *Kakure* fool's flesh ignites and burns, running off the skull like hot wax beneath the flame.

The demon lord's smile fades, then broadens again as two of the *Kakure* warriors, each wearing *o-fuda* charms to ward away evil, approach him from opposite sides. The first expertly hurls a pair of jeweled daggers—one low, one high—as the other screams and charges with swords extended. Shuten Dōji lets the first dagger penetrate the meaty flesh of his thigh, but knocks the other away with the flat of his massive blade, using the backswing to parry the thrusts of the charging warrior. He drops to the ground and in one clean movement tugs the dagger from the thigh wound and reverses it into the oncoming swordsman's heart. Springing back to his feet, he grabs his already dead foe before the body can fall to the ground and single-handedly hurls the corpse at his comrade. Before the knife-thrower can push his way out from under the body, the demon lord is upon him. He yanks a long jade charm from around the warrior's neck and plunges its sharp end deep into the man's ear. Then Shuten Dōji reaches under the downed warrior's kimono and castrates him with a flick of his wrist.

He devours the dripping prize in a swallow, leaving the *Kakure* soldier to die slowly.

The time is almost come. He can feel it as a tugging from beyond. His stay in *Naka-Tsu-Kuni* is almost done. The irresistible pull comes from the gateway between the realms: a wind where there is no wind. And from that nowhere beyond, he begins to hear the toll of bells.

He will miss all this, he knows, when he is back in-between. There is nothing in the many realms above or below quite like human flesh, either to wear or to taste. It is perverse, he thinks, that so frail and pathetic a form should yield such rich pleasures. More perverse still that the awesome likes of Shuten Dōji should be compelled to endure it.

But more than just endure, *enjoy* it, revel in it:

The delight of steel in his borrowed hands, hate in his stolen heart.

The taste of raw meat ripped fresh off the bone with sharpened teeth.

The heavy, rich scent of fresh-spilled blood filling his lungs.

The explosion of manly pleasure between the legs or the warm, wet lips of a practiced geisha.

Muscles and ligaments. Skin and bone. Sound and vision. Taste and smell.

Human flesh, living and dying.

He *will* miss it.

Until the next time, whenever that may be. Though he knows, if nothing else—perhaps, above all else—that his time will come again. It always has. It always will.

The thigh wound bleeds profusely and the vision in his remaining eye shifts in and out of focus. But he takes pleasure even now in the unadulterated pain of this dying flesh. He plunges a finger into the hole in the leg to stanch the flow of blood as he limps back up toward the castle keep. The stairs are difficult for the injured flesh to mount now, and he is subjected to several fresh attacks by energetic if none-too-clever *Kakure* warriors as he goes. Their feeble assaults are easily fended off—a thrust of sword, a twist of neck—as he passes up through the levels of the mountain fortress.

Even in his weakened state, this close to the end, there is only one who will best him.

Shuten Dōji will wait for his foe at the very top of the mountain.

He is all alone on the castle roof. The wind has grown fierce, carrying with it the heady, copper malodor of blood and death. The last of the magical *oni* are slain or have fled, returned to their dens and hidey-holes in this realm and beyond. His few remaining human forces have been captured, and the ritual torture and victory celebrations will soon begin. The laughter of the *Kakure* warriors drifts up to him on the wind along with the mournful screams of his defeated *Goryō-dō*. He watches as several of the *Kakure* fighters kick a severed human head back and forth across the bloody snow in some improvised game. He is even able to chuckle along as one of the soldiers slips and falls on the ice when his foot gets caught between the dead man's gaping jaws.

A sound comes from behind him: a blade dragged across stone.

The Other has come.

The Other's skin, like his own, is adorned with a dense labyrinth of interlaced tattoos, a looping spiral of scarlet and black characters of purification and invocation: the *hannya-shinkyo*. His enemy of old has chosen a fine body this time, Shuten Dōji thinks: lithe, muscular, even (uncharacteristically) handsome. If the Other has been engaged in the battle, it does not show on the flesh. There is not a mark on him, nor so much as a rent in his beautiful crimson kimono. The demon lord himself might have chosen such a body as this, and he nods his approval. The Other ever so slightly dips his chin in acknowledgment, then raises his

4

sword. Shuten Dōji recognizes the flawless blade, with the sacred characters etched into the steel and the gold and mother-of-pearl hilt. He recognizes this sword, knows its name for it, too, is an ancient and venerated enemy.

Shuten Dōji glances back over the rampart. Below them, the *Kakure* faithful gather to watch the final confrontation. The demon lord has half a notion to leap down and wreak havoc among them, just to teach the smug fools a lesson, but the whimsy passes.

He turns back to his adversary and raises his sword.

The two foes face each other in silence, eyes locked. The wind kicks up, swirling ash and cinders around them, but neither combatant so much as blinks. Shuten Dōji feels the tensed muscles in his damaged leg begin to spasm as the blood pours down his thigh, but his blade does not waver. He hears the rough breathing of the men watching from below, the shuffling of their feet, the rise and fall of their gorges as the tension builds. He smells excitement and fear rising from their flesh, off the human shell of his enemy.

Off his own wracked body.

From somewhere out in the forest beyond the castle walls a raven caws a lonely, piercing cry. As if on cue, the two figures atop the castle have at each other, screaming death curses as they charge.

Their blades meet in a fountain of sparks. The mountain itself all but quakes from the resounding clang of steel on perfect steel.

The two enemies turn and face each other and freeze once more.

Shuten Dōji exults in the thrill of the moment, the literal knife-edge excitement of life and death. His hands and arms still pulse with the reverberation of the clash. Blood courses through the body, injuries forgotten, lost in the magical ecstasy of sheer *being*. Pain and pleasure are one in these moments. Sensation is the only thing that matters: the wonder of the flesh.

He allows himself a grin when he sees that his opponent feels it—revels in the thrill—as well.

Below, many of the warriors cannot bear to watch. They cover their eyes or abase themselves on the ground as the priests chant a discordant, singsong prayer. There are some who believe that such sights as this are not meant for human eyes. Who is to say that they are wrong?

The ancient foes prepare themselves again for confrontation. Each shifts his blade slightly, every gesture and movement a calculated response to the other's pose and position. An incline of neck breeds a turn of the wrist; a hair's tilt of blade evokes a bend of the knee; a raised eyebrow brings a flick of the tongue.

They freeze.

They charge.

It is the moment Shuten Dōji has known must come. He knows it with the first fraction of a step taken toward his nemesis. He turns his entire consciousness to the study of the unfolding:

He memorizes the way the winter air freezes and tickles the hairs in his nose.

He marvels at the rumble of his stomach, begging to be fed even as death prepares to put an end to all mortal hungers.

He sheds a tear at the feeling of blood rushing to his sex as if to make possible one last engorgement and spewing of seed before the end.

He simply and purely—as ever he does—marvels at the ways and joys of the flesh.

Even as his enemy's blade bites into the tender skin of his neck, Shuten Dōji is recording in his ancient and evil mind every movement and feeling, every detail: his enemy's precise sword-grip, the color of the sky through with smoke, an itch between his toes. Perhaps it will help him next time, proving the difference between victory and defeat. Perhaps it will be him delivering the death blow in their next encounter.

Or perhaps it will simply be pleasurable to think back on such things.

He allows himself, for the briefest moment, to savor the feel of his enemy's sword as it tears through his throat, severing the carotid, the jugular, the windpipe.

Then Shuten Dōji, darkest and most feared of the demon lords, flees his human shell as his host's smiling head is rendered completely from the body.

Sound and vision, taste and smell, begin to fade. The wind-from-between draws him back in its iron embrace. There will be only the blackness now, though for how long it will last, even Shuten Dōji cannot know.

Darkness and memory are all that remain.

And the promise—always the promise—of another, distant day.

*O*ne

Los Angeles, California
A.D. 1997

Endless Summer

"Hot enough for you?"
The beer was almost in my mouth. I flinched, sending a luke-warm, amber wave sloshing over the lip of the glass and down my wrist. With a sigh, I completed the all-too-familiar motion, draining the flat Budweiser in a gulp.

I looked over at the sweaty, grinning face of the fat man to my right. His flesh was doughy and discolored, flushed red with heat and alcohol. His mud-brown eyes gaped wide with expectation, his thin lips curled in a cheap salesman's smirk that screamed "Gotcha!"

"Fuck off," I told him.

His smile jerked into a twitch and he snorted something green out one nostril. He quickly wiped it with the back of his hand, then turned away from me, back to his drink.

"Turd," I muttered.

I rapped on the bar for another beer. The Formica was tacky with the indelible residue of countless spilled drinks. I reached behind the counter for a stack of cocktail napkins. They featured crude cartoon sketches of big-tittied women engaged in oral sex, captioned "Summer of '69, Summer of Love." I wiped the beer off my wrist and tossed the crumpled napkins to the floor as the bartender dropped a more-or-less full glass of beer in front of me.

"Nice place," I said.

The bartender's nose was bent as a West Hollywood hustler. He hocked a lugey onto the floor behind the bar.

"Two-fifty," he said.

I dropped a five on the counter. I started to inspect the glass, then thought better of the idea. Downing half the warm beer in a swallow, I glanced again at my watch. I'd give my would-be client another ten minutes and then bail. Not that I had any place else to go, but I've always thought it best not to look as desperate as you really are. Bored, I surveyed the premises again.

The bar was long and narrow, fronting on Hollywood Boulevard just up the street from the theater with the footprints. I always want to call it Grumman's, but it's just another multiplex now and I can never remember the right name. A rusty old air conditioner sputtered weakly in the transom over the front door, but the hot September day was way too much for it. The place reeked of pine disinfectant. The actual bar ran three-quarters the length of the room. A couple of cockeyed pool tables with worn red felt stood in the back, wads of folded newspaper wedged under the table legs to foster the illusion of level play. A pair of Latino junkies, thin as Mexican dogs, cheated each other at eight ball on one table while a mocha-colored hooker of indeterminate ethnicity—just L.A. third-world, I suppose—lay passed out on the other. One of the junkies had wedged a pool ball into the V of her crotch and jammed one of her gaudy red pumps (right) into a side pocket (left).

My fat friend was the only other early afternoon customer, and he'd slid a couple of stools down the bar after our delightful tête-à-tête. I stared at the corpulent little fuck and saw him furtively eye me back.

My name is Marty Burns, and once, a million or so years ago, I was a minor celebrity. Sometimes I think there isn't any other kind. At the ripe age of sixteen I'd starred in a situation comedy called *Salt & Pepper.* You probably remember. It was one of those god-awful sixties atrocities about two white-bread suburban families with apple-pie-perfect moms and zany, feuding dads. It's best remembered as the answer to a Trivial Pursuit question: What show did Russell Johnson star in after *Gilligan's Island?*

I played Sandy Salt, the teenage son who was secretly in love—à la Romeo and Juliet; ain't TV writers clever?—with Penny, the ever-so-perky Pepper daughter. There was a precocious little sister, a fat baby brother, a grumpy old grandpa—Gale Gordon, no less—and more pratfalls than you could shake a Keystone Kop at.

At least once every episode I was obliged to shriek the line "Hot enough for you?" to the howling delight of a goosed laugh track. It became a catchphrase, like Mork's "Nanu-nanu," or Maxwell Smart's "Sorry about that, Chief." It caught on with the public for a while, too, at least until Judy Carne and "Sock it to me" came along. I even got to say it to Carson on the *Tonight Show* once, during my brief tenure as a teen heartthrob, but then *Salt & Pepper* was sent to its proper resting place in sitcom hell by *All in the Family.* And before you could say "receding hairline," David Cassidy took my place on the cover of *Tiger Beat.*

The show did last almost three full seasons. Along with my personal nine hundred seconds in the kliegs, *Salt & Pepper* netted me a spiffy Jaguar XKE and more teenage twat than any horny American boy could ever have dreamed about. But the money had been blown before the last episode even aired, and my acting career pretty well took to the skids thereafter. I made a passel of low-budget flicks and a couple of dreadful network pilots before my scumbag agent ditched me. I gave up the life for good one day when I found myself playing yet another pizza-faced high school virgin in a woeful titty movie opposite one of the girls from *The Brady Bunch.* Or was it *Family Affair?* In any case, I walked off the set halfway through the shoot and swore I'd never work in front of a camera again.

I hoped and thought that I'd slipped into comfortable obscurity only to find *Salt & Pepper* cursed with eternal life in cable syndication. I still look pretty young for my age, and thanks to the lovely folks at Nickelodeon, who run the show every damn night, I still get recognized all these years after the fact. It's the only residual I do get. Hardly a week goes by that I don't run into some pathetic simp thinking he's God's gift to the art of wit demanding to know if it's "hot enough for me." I've been busted twice for assault as a result, though I was pretty drunk each time and neither case went to trial.

I usually drink for good reason—Immanuel Kant's birthday, the anniversary of my third paternity suit—but I was just trying to pass the time while I waited for the client. I generally feel obliged to maintain the illusion of sobriety on such auspicious occasions, at least until I have a cash retainer in hand. After all, who'd want to hire a private investigator who *wasn't* hard-drinking? God bless that Raymond Chandler for making it easy for all the woeful sots who've come into the racket since *The Big Sleep.*

Most of my work these days consists of serving subpoenas for the kind of law firms that advertise on local TV before noon and after midnight. They use old ballplayers as spokesmen and always *habla español.* Sometimes I do sub-rosa work as well—that's surveillance, for you civilians—mostly worker's compensation cases, tracking down the Mexicans filing false claims with the medical and law mills before they hightail it back south of the border. But every second or third blue moon I manage to turn up an outside client. Generally it's surveillance work and it's always through word of mouth. I've long since pulled my ad from the yellow pages: I learned, through very much heartache, that people who hire detectives out of the phone book usually can't or won't pay for what they need and never like the results when they get them. Also, the yellow page people won't take my checks anymore.

I glanced up at the harsh sound of a skittering pool ball. The hooker sat up on the table as an eight ball rolled to a stop beneath my stool. Not a good omen, I thought. The whore yawned broadly, flashing a mouthful of sharp yellow teeth, and scratched her crotch.

One of the junkies mumbled something to her in Spanish, and she smiled back at him and flipped him the bird. She caught me looking her way and rolled off the table with sluglike grace. She sidled over to the bar, pulling on her orange spandex tights until I could see the outline of her cunt through the shiny material. She was bald down below and walked a tad unsteadily with only the one shoe on.

As she approached, I leaned an elbow on the sticky bar, resting my cheek on a curled fist. The shy little thing came right up and pressed her meaty breasts against me. She ran a hand through her scraggly hair and licked her chapped lips. Her tongue was coated with white film and she smelled like Thunderbird.

"Buy me a drink, baby?" she wheezed. She dropped a hand onto my thigh. Her red fingernails had been chewed raw.

A cool voice answered from behind my back: "Better make it a Massengil cocktail."

I pushed the hooker away and turned around. Standing beside me was a tall, very pale white man in a neat linen suit. He had a round face and two weak double chins. His nose was sharp as his trouser crease, and his silver eyes flashed liked a cat's in moonlight. His fine, dirty-blond hair was pulled back into a tight ponytail fastened with curved bands of thick silver. He held his hand out to me.

"Marty Burns! I always thought you got fragged in the 'Nam," he said.

"I wish," I said shaking hands, "but that was Eddie Haskell."

"No, man, it was the Beaver."

" 'Fraid not. But if it makes you feel any better, Walt Disney really is on ice down in Anaheim. He's planted in a chamber deep beneath Mr. Toad's Wild Ride." I motioned for the man to sit down. "You'd be Long John."

The hooker snorted. "Ain't *so* long from what I hear," she said.

Faster than I could follow, the pimp snaked his left arm out and slapped the whore across the face. Her head snapped back and she let out a cry that was all the more affecting for its frailty.

Her cheek started to bleed below the eye from a cut made by Long John's silver pinky ring. I could see she wanted to say something, but one look into the pimp's hard eyes convinced her that it wouldn't be a good idea. Pressing a hand to the side of her face, she went back to the pool table to retrieve her shoe. She slipped it on and walked out the door with what small dignity she could muster. I watched her leave, then glanced back at Long John, who beamed broadly at me. The bartender hacked another lugey onto the floor. The little fat man had scampered off.

The pimp called Long John sat down next to me and held up a finger to the bartender, who poured him a shot of Grand Marnier—on the rocks, yet—before strolling back to the far end of the bar.

"I love this shit," Long John said, taking a sip. "Like licking an orange's pussy."

"I look forward to hearing your opinion of banana daiquiris sometime," I said.

Long John cocked his head, then laughed, patting me on the arm. He had long, thin fingers with finely manicured nails, but his knuckles were cracked and swollen, and the thumb had once been broken and badly set.

"Hey, I like you, man. The Jar said you were all right."

"I'm not sure I can take that as a compliment."

Joey the Jar worked as muscle for a local shylock who I'd once pulled from some switches. Joey got his nickname on account of a jar rumored to sit in his refrigerator which held the genitalia of recalcitrant debtors. I hadn't actually ever seen the conversation piece, but reputable sources assured me of its existence.

"Aaahhhh, Joey's okay. A little spooky sometimes, but then who ain't? You know what I'm saying?"

I smiled and nodded. The pimp drained the last of his drink and started chewing on the ice cubes.

"What'd the Jar tell you?" he asked.

"Not much. You're looking for someone to look for someone."

"That's right, that's the ticket. Let me tell you what I need," he began. "I got five, six girls I'm running at any one time, you know what I'm saying? It's not a big operation, but it's manageable and very satisfactory from your fiduciary point of view. The ladies do their thing, I treat 'em good. I keep 'em in line, you understand, but I don't mess 'em up. Not my style. If I gotta knock 'em around, it's not gonna leave any marks. I keep 'em supplied with rubbers and I make sure they get clean works if they got the jones. But I don't push. You know what I'm saying? It's not my thing."

"You can't be too careful these days," I said, but the pimp didn't have an ear for sarcasm.

"You fuckin' said it, my man, you know the score." Long John waved at the bartender, who brought him another shot and a freshly warmed beer for me.

"Anyways, there's a lot of what-you-call turnover in this trade. The girls, they come and they go."

"But mostly come," I interrupted.

Long John narrowed his eyes at me, then started to laugh. "Hey, you're still a pretty funny guy, huh? I like that. A sense of humor's an important thing. It's something you don't see enough of these days."

I was already disgusted with the pimp. I knew that any job that came by way of Joey the Jar was bound to be ugly, but it had been a long time since I had seriously worked the street. I'd almost forgotten the attitude it demanded, the cold apathy you had to embrace to survive here. I'd listen to the pimp's story, drink his flat beer, but whatever the hell he wanted would have to be done by somebody else. No matter how bad I needed the money.

Which was pretty bad, actually.

"So anyway, I'm lately playing a string of five very attractive young ladies when fing-fang-foom one of 'em decides she's had enough of the life and is going back to Pittsburgh, which is a hell of a thing if you ask me, but if they're gonna go, they're gonna go, that's one thing I learned. Then two days later my redhead—a natural, no bullshit, tits like a cow and ass like a teakettle—she disappears without a word. She was a squirrelly little bitch, Nina was, but she could suck the barnacles off a steamship and polish the keel at the same time, if you know what I'm saying. Pussy like a Mack truck."

I had absolutely no idea what the hell that last bit meant, and frankly, I was afraid to ask.

"Naturally I'm a little pissed that she takes off without a word, but what the fuck can I do? I check the 'vine, but nobody knows nothing from her.

"So I'm down to three ladies and things are looking like your grandma's cunt, no offense, and I mean bad. Then like a gift from the fucking gods I'm sittin' in the pancake house over Cahuenga when this little piece of juice with mambos from here to Catalina and a smile like a sunny day walks in. Says her name is Jenny. She's this blond heartbreaker from like South Nebraska or one of those fucking states and she is oh so ripe for the plucking, if you know what I mean. So I give her the rap and fing-fang-foom you know how it goes."

"You turned her," I said, looking into my glass. I didn't really want to hear this.

"No," Long John whispered.

I looked up. Long John turned away from me and stared at himself in the grimy mirror behind the bar. The two junkies had gone out via the back door, and the bartender stood stolid and quiet as a bottle of Beefeater by the front window. The only sound was the terminal hack of the straining air conditioner. Long John turned back and looked me in the eye.

"I meant to, man, I won't lie to you about the plan. But I didn't . . . couldn't do it." He closed his eyes and ground his fists into them like a baby who needs a nap.

"She was so fine and so ready for the play. And man, those tits. Her stepdaddy tried to fuck her and she came to L.A. to make it as an actress and blah, blah, blah. You know the song, man. It's old as 'Happy Birthday' and twice as dull. So I brought her in and you know what? She's fuckin' cherry. A virgin, man, right here in L.A.

"I tell you, I done some stuff in my life and I mean serious shit. I done things I wouldn't tell the devil if he buried me up to my nose in monkey shit. But you know what? I ain't never had no virgin before."

Long John took his hands from his eyes and looked at me again. For the first time I saw something like a human being sitting there.

"I took her, man. I did. And she cried it sounded like a little cat or a baby getting hungry for its mama's tit. But it was sweet, you know? And I looked at her and thought about all the things I had ready for her. I thought about how I was gonna teach her to make like she loved it while three scumbags fucked her up every hole. And how her soft skin was gonna look after six months of jabbin' needles in her arm. Or hitting on a rock pipe.

"And I couldn't do it, man. *Me.* Long fucking John. I couldn't do it. It would've been like shitting on a clean sheet, or pissing on new snow. Like, what do you call it, corrupt."

I couldn't believe what I was hearing. Poetry from a pimp was like darkness from the sun: a contradiction in terms. And I thought I saw a tear forming in Long John's eye.

"You love her," I said, not quite believing my own words.

Long John looked away and then down. He nodded.

"I love her. I ain't never loved nothing in my life, man. Not my whore of a mother, not a goddamn cat or dog or gold fucking fish, and sure as shit not none of my girls. But this little thing from Cornhole, Nebraska, turned me inside out. She made me feel like a new way."

He looked back up at me and now there *were* tears in his eyes. "But she's gone."

I was embarrassed as hell. I looked past the pimp toward the view onto Hollywood Boulevard.

"Another sugar daddy?"

"No, man. No way. She loves me, too. She wouldn't have just run off. We was talking about making a life together, a clean life. I was even working on getting her into the business."

I raised an eyebrow.

"I know, man, it sounds like a load of horseshit, another rap, but it's true. I been around town, you know. I got some connections with agents. Some of 'em legit, nearly. I got her some readings. Even a couple of parts. Titty work, but legit."

Everybody in L.A. is in—or *thinks* they're in—*The Business.* Every bag lady's got a screenplay, is what they say in this town, and that may or may not be true. But they *do* all have agents. Long John clearly saw the doubt on my face.

"It's no shit, man. I'm talking for real. She's pretty good, too. It's the tits that sell her, no denying, but she's got some talent. Believe me, I know a thing or two about acting."

He handed me a couple of photos, a color candid shot and a standard studio glossy. She had the requisite blue eyes and corn-silk blond hair, the inviting lips. And, oh yeah, a rack Betty Page would have envied. Posed glossies all look the same—kind of like dummies in wax museums if you ask me—but I had to admit, even in wallet size, Long John's girl radiated something. Freshness and vitality; that all-American, girl-next-door look that's pure bullshit, but somehow still works on the screen after all these years. Looking at her, I could almost smell the breeze of a summer night in the country.

"She know anyone else in the city? Friends, relatives?"

"Uh-uh. Just me. I didn't even introduce her to any of my other girls. She was stayin' with me, but not in my fuck pad."

I thought for a minute. It was just insane. A pathetic pimp who had probably been taken in at his own game. Or a scared little girl who went running back to the farm when she realized what her supposed savior really was. Finding one tiny blonde on the run in Southern California was like sifting Death Valley for a particular grain of sand.

"She's my out, man. Can you understand that? Out of the life. Out of the shit and the junk. My chance."

I still hesitated.

"Please. She's everything."

I looked into the pimp's pleading eyes and back down at the photo. I saw something I hadn't seen in my own mirror for a very long time: I think it's called hope.

"Okay," I said, shaking my head. "Okay."

*t*wo

O nly the existence of a bawdily mirthful deity could explain the fact that Hollywood Vice operates out of the 69th Precinct in Los Feliz. Two bums slept like low-rent lions on opposite sides of the stone stairs leading to the front entrance of the station house. I saw a squat, ebony black man going round and around like a carousel pony in the revolving front door. He wore high-voltage lime-green shorts without a shirt. I winced at the skull-and-crossbones ring dangling from a pierced nipple. He wasn't moving very quickly, so I timed my steps and dashed into an empty door, letting him propel me into the building. The doorman mumbled to himself as he went, but I couldn't quite make out what he was saying.

I glanced back over my shoulder at him as I approached the desk. The man kept at his slow circles. I pointed a thumb at the door and raised an eyebrow when the desk sergeant looked up, but the cop just shrugged.

"Yeah." He nodded. "We call him Little Black Sambo. Keep hoping he'll turn himself into butter sooner or later. K-Y's more likely."

"What the hell is he mumbling about?" I asked.

"I dunno. He's always going on some shit about cougars in the dark and the pandemonium shadow show, whatever that means. He comes up every day, but he's harmless. He'll go away. Can I help you?"

"I'm looking for Lieutenant Teitlebaum."

"Sid the Yid? Yeah, I think he's around. You know where his office is?"

I nodded. The sergeant handed me a visitor's pass and pointed toward the stairs. I climbed the two flights to Vice and found myself puffing just a little as I reached the top. My exercise regimen had gone to shit, and I vowed, yet again, to do something about it. Real soon, now.

Virtually the entire third floor of the building was reserved for the Vice Squad. Two dozen or more gray steel desks were lined up across from each other in the big, open squad room. Detectives sat around taking statements, drinking coffee, and reading newspapers. A steady stream of uniforms trudged in and out of the room, picking up and depositing suspects, trading foul mouthed barbs with the detectives, and keeping the perps down. I marched up the long aisle toward the glassed-in offices at the far end of the room, past the hookers and snitches and junkies, nodding at a couple of cops I vaguely knew and hadn't seen in a dead dog's age.

The opaque glass door with the names Teitlebaum and Straczynski in peeling stencil was slightly open. I peered in, saw Sid hunched over his desk alternately taking bites from a gooey tuna fish sandwich and filling in the squares of the *L.A. Times* crossword. I rapped on the door, entering the office as I announced myself.

"I hear you need some help with seventeen across," I said.

Teitlebaum looked up and leaned back in his swivel chair. He licked a dollop of mayonnaise off his lower lip.

"Yeah," he said, "a four-letter word for private eye. Any ideas?"

I started to smile, but Teitlebaum kept a straight face. He was tall and lean with a thick shock of kinky black hair. His plump, Semitic nose and bushy eyebrows sat on his face like a dimestore novelty, and his droopy eyelids lent him an almost dopey appearance. Many a suspect, I knew, had been lulled by Teitlebaum's dull looks, only to betray themselves under his fierce interrogation.

"How's it hanging, Sidney?" I asked as we shook hands.

"Like a duck in a Chinatown window. Jesus H., what brings you to this little corner of the underworld?"

"I'm thinking maybe I want to join the force, become one of the finest. I want to protect and serve."

"Yeah, like maybe I want to join your ass with my dick. So what's shaking, Marty, how's business?"

I plopped down on the hard wooden chair beside Teitlebaum's desk. I picked up the paper, glanced idly at the puzzle, and tossed it back down: an acrostic. The cop was chewing on his messy sandwich again.

"Fuck me," a voice at the door said, "here I thought I musta stepped in dog shit and all the time the stink's coming from my own goddamn office."

Peter Straczynski walked into the cubicle holding his nose. Teitlebaum's partner was smallish and pudgy with greasy, thinning hair and a shiny seventies-vintage suit. He wore amber-tinted aviator glasses and thick gold chains around his neck and wrist. The first time we'd met I assumed the pseudo pimp look was part of his cover; I quickly learned that Straczynski was just an asshole.

We'd had a run-in several years before when I accused Straczynski of hitting up underage hookers for blow jobs. Everybody, Teitlebaum included, knew it was true, but no one would break the cop code of silence. My fifteen-year-old witness died of a smack overdose before the departmental hearing, so Straczynski got off clean. But both of us remembered the incident all too well.

"See that?" I said to Teitlebaum. "Just talk about taking it up the ass and he appears. It's like rubbing Aladdin's dick."

Straczynski seemed to be debating whether or not to haul off on me when Teitlebaum interrupted. He looked up at his partner, warning him away with a glance.

"There something I can do for you, Marty, or are you just here for the floor show?"

Straczynski grunted, then sat down behind his desk and studied a day-old racing form. He glowered over at me from time to time and spat the odd profanity.

I dropped the photo of Long John's girl in front of Teitlebaum. The detective wiped his hands on the desk blotter before picking it up.

"Runaway?" he asked.

I nodded. "I think she's on the street, probably in Hollywood, but maybe up in the Valley. Hell, maybe even down in Orange County. I'm not all that sure. She's cherry to the life as far as I know."

"I didn't think you did this kind of shit anymore," Teitlebaum said. "I thought you had more sense." He looked the picture over carefully, shaking his head as he memorized her features. He tossed the photo to Straczynski, who took a grudging look at it and threw it back.

"Nice lips," he said.

"Forget it, Strac. She graduated junior high."

Teitlebaum broke in before his partner could respond. "I don't know her, Marty, but I'll keep an eye out. For what it's worth."

"No, I didn't expect you to know her. But I thought you might be able to help me track down T.J. I've been prowling around all morning, but I can't seem to find him."

"Jake the Snake?" Teitlebaum asked incredulously. Straczynski snorted in the background.

"Yeah, he always kept track of the action better than anyone. I figured he'd be a good place to start, but I can't sniff him out."

"Jesus, Marty, you *have* been out of it," Teitlebaum said. He looked over at Straczynski. "T.J.'s dead must be what, two months?"

Straczynski looked up almost wistfully and nodded. "Fuckin' Jake, the one-eyed trouser snake. Wormed into one hole too many."

"T.J. died of AIDS, Marty. I saw him right before the end and it wasn't pretty. Thin as an old dog and all covered in purple blotches. Ugghhh. The snake deserved better."

"Hung like a bear," Straczynski eulogized.

"Shit," I said, and we all observed a moment of silence.

"You might try talking to Rosa Mendez," Sid said. "She works out of a storefront on Santa Monica over by Virgil. She runs a kind of a halfway house for girls who want out of the life, even just for a night or two. Night Haven, the place is called. She knows most of what's happening on the street."

"Religioso?" I asked.

"No, no, she's all right. I don't think she even knows why she does it, she just does. She's some kind of journalist or writer or something, but she's real down to earth. She's really something else, like you don't see too often."

"She's a piece, too," Straczynski offered. "Face like a La-Z-Boy recliner."

I looked over at him, Teitlebaum just groaned. Straczynski smiled big and ugly, waiting to deliver the punch line.

"I could sit on it all the do-dah-day."

Bodegas and schlock discount stores lined the block, along with a boarded-up nudie house with a tattered marquee advertising CHER Y PIE + COCK T LES. Rosa Mendez's place was directly across from the theater in what must have once been an old furniture store. Dirty venetian blinds hung crookedly in the big windows, and the front door was locked. The only identification was a small hand-lettered sign over the door that simply read "Night Haven," and beneath that, "Press buzzer for entry." A shade was pulled down over the glass, and though I tried to peer around the edges, I couldn't see anything inside.

I leaned on the buzzer and heard a muffled yell from within. I took a step back from the door and waited. After a minute someone fumbled with the shade and a gray eye in a black face peered out at me.

"Whatchoo want?"

I smiled and tried to look harmless. "Hi. I'm looking for Rosa Mendez."

"Whatchoo want with Rosa?"

I leaned forward a little, but could only see a crescent of the woman's face through the small crack between the shade and the door.

"Uhh, my name is Marty Burns. Lieutenant Teitlebaum of the 69th Precinct sent me over. Is Ms. Mendez here?"

The woman turned briefly away and said something to someone inside, then turned back to me.

"You a cop?"

"I'm a private detective, miss."

"You don't look like no cop. But you good-lookin' for a white boy."

"We aim to please."

I stood there for a moment, grinning stupidly at the disembodied eye that continued to study me, with apparently not entirely satisfactory results. I was about to try another tack when the eye vanished and I heard someone turning open the locks. The door opened and I looked into the face of drop-dead beauty.

"I'm Rosa Mendez," she said. "Can I help you?"

She wore a long denim skirt and a sky-blue T-shirt with an upside-down pink triangle in the center above the words TOTALLY QUEER NATION. She was thirtyish, of average height and trim. Her hair was light brown and fine as spring rain. She had high, strong cheekbones and a thin, delicate nose. Her lips were full and pink and more than validated Straczynski's rating. Her eyes sparkled like the city at night.

"Hi," I said.

"Hello," she said, and glanced back over her shoulder. She had the look of someone for whom there was never enough time in a day.

"My name is Marty Burns. Sid Teitlebaum thought you might be able to help me out."

"The Kotex are in the closet," she said to someone inside. "No, the other one. Yeah, that's it." She turned back to me. "Yeah, so?"

"Well, I'm looking for . . ."

"A runaway girl from Iowa who's hooking on the strip. You're screwing her parents for two grand a week until you track her down and screw *her* in exchange for which you promise not to send her back."

"Yeah, but what's my favorite color?" I asked.

She was just about to dismiss me when that look came over her face. I've seen the look a thousand times. More. She smiled and I heard my watch crystal shatter.

"Danny Partridge," she said, wagging a finger at me.

"Right night, wrong network."

"Here Come the Brides?"

"No, but I once got tanked with Bobby Sherman. He can't hold his liquor, you know."

Then it hit her. "Hot enough for you?" she said, and I took an exaggerated bow. "Marty Burns. Wow, I had the biggest crush on you when I was a kid."

I felt myself shrivel and die. When she invited me in I just slithered under the crack at the base of the door.

The place was big with a high ceiling. Portable room dividers were set up throughout, separating out living and office spaces. The desks and couches were old and battered, and the tile floor cracked and discolored. Though fans lazily turned everywhere, the ventilation was poor, and the air hot and thick with the stench of cheap perfume.

As I followed Rosa to her office I passed several cubicles with cots and throw rugs and lots of teenaged girls sleeping or eating or watching TV. They all eyed me nervously as I passed, responding not at all to my smiles. I realized as I entered Rosa's office that I was the only man in the place, and felt as though I had crashed a big slumber party.

Rosa sat on her desk, smoothing the skirt over her long legs. She waved me to the couch and leaned her arms behind her on the desktop. Her skin was the color of wheat, smooth and perfect as a crystal swan.

"Sandy Salt," she said, shaking her head. "Man, oh, man. I guess Hollywood's a tough town for everyone."

"It's no worse than anyplace else. And the name's Marty."

"Bullshit, Marty. L.A.'s the cesspool's cesspool."

"City of angels," I said, and smiled.

"So tell me who you're working for."

"That's privileged information."

"So's mine, sweetie," she said, swinging her legs like a little girl.

I looked her straight in the eye, but couldn't stare her down. She suppressed a giggle as I glanced away and sighed.

"Her old boyfriend hired me," I said, stretching the truth slightly.

"How much you really taking him for?"

I looked up at her again, actually offended. I hadn't wanted this case to begin with.

"I may be an asshole, but like our former and blessedly deceased president, I am not a crook. I'm charging exactly what's fair. I don't normally do this kind of shit 'cause I *used to* do it for a living and I know where

I'm going to find her and I know it'll suck. I promised myself I'd give this case three days before I told the client it was hopeless. I wouldn't even be doing this much except the jerk really seems to be in love with her. I already can't remember why I thought that might mean something."

Rosa slid off the edge of the desk and walked over to me. She put a hand on my shoulder, but I looked away, embarrassed by my dishonestly self-righteous outburst. She interpreted it as something else.

"I'm sorry," she said. "What's her name?"

"Jenny Leo," I told her, and handed her the candid photo Long John had given me. I watched her green eyes carefully scan the silvered lines until she shook her head.

"No. She hasn't been here," she said with certainty. "Do you know who was running her?"

I hesitated. I was afraid she might question me about where I came by my information. "I think she may have had a pimp called Long John, but the information is sketchy. Sound familiar?"

Rosa nodded and twisted her perfect mouth into a grimace. "Yeah, Long John Silver, he calls himself. The man with the wire coat hanger."

I felt myself flush, but Rosa had turned toward the door and called out a girl's name. Even if I found the girl, I didn't know if I could return her to a pimp with that rep. I regained my composure as Rosa sat back down on the desk.

"Rosa Mendez," I said, studying her face.

"What?"

"Sorry. It's just, well, this probably makes me sound like a racist Anglo . . ."

"You probably are one."

"Probably." I nodded. "But . . . you don't look like a Rosa Mendez."

"And how, pray tell, should a Rosa Mendez look? Short and dumpy and in a maid's uniform?"

"I didn't mean that . . . I . . . Help me out of this. Please?"

She actually smiled a bit. "I'm just giving you a hard time. Actually my mom is half-Scottish, but my dad was all Mexican. She used to say I inherited her cheekbones and his temper."

"You could have done worse," I said.

She was about to reply when a lanky black girl in shorts and a halter walked in the room. She wore an Angels cap sideways on her head. I saw track marks on her arms. Rosa handed her Jenny's picture.

"Do you know this girl, Debby?"

Debby looked at the picture and I saw the recognition flare in her eyes. I leaned forward, but the girl was instantly suspicious.

"What for you want to know?"

"This man is trying to find her. It's okay, Debby, I trust him."

I practically choked on her words. "Have you seen her?" I asked.

"That Julie Something," she said. "Ain't seen her for maybe a few weeks, but yeah, I know'd her."

"Julie?" I asked. "Are you sure you don't mean Jenny?"

"If I meant Jenny, I'd a say so, wouldn't I, mister? No, that be Julie."

Something was wrong here. Long John claimed that the girl hadn't been around the scene at all. And nothing about her using more than one name.

"Do you know where she lives? Where I might be able to find her?"

"She fuckin' that Long John last I know. Prob'ly find her sucking on his long john."

"Do you know anything else about her, Debby?" Rosa asked.

The girl thought for a minute, her expression as blank as a freshly washed chalkboard. Finally she nodded.

"Yeah. Girl had a thing for them Johnny Rockets hamburgers. She over on Melrose all the time, but they always be throwing her whore ass out. Sometimes she go around the back and blow the manager for a take-out. And she don't even get fries or no shake. That plain crazy."

"Anything else?" I said. "Any idea who her friends are? Who she might hang with?"

Debby just shook her head.

"Thanks, honey." Rosa smiled. "Why don't you go on back to your show."

The girl shrugged and started to walk out, then turned back toward me.

"You her daddy?" she said.

Startled, I quickly shook my head. "No," I rasped.

The girl shrugged again. "Too bad. She just looking for her daddy. Just another dumb cunt looking for her fucking daddy."

As she walked away I noticed that her shorts were torn in the back, exposing the fleshy cheek of her butt. A tiny blue rose was tattooed on her deep black skin.

I watched it disappear down the hall.

Three

Following a somewhat reluctant departure from Night Haven and Rosa Mendez, I decided to take a little afternoon spin around town just for the hell of it.

I cruised west up Santa Monica Boulevard. It was a little too early for any serious action, but the more pathetic of the baby pimps were already staking out the best doorways, and the seemingly endless parade of penny-ante hustlers, Kaposi-blotched transsexuals, and twitchy chicken hawks were starting to emerge for their daily sleaze prowl. At every corner not claimed by a fruit-vending Mexican, bums—I mean homeless people, of course—came up to the car window holding out shaky palms. I gave them each a quarter to keep them from spitting on my dirty-enough windshield.

I headed up to Hollywood Boulevard and stopped at a phone booth to call Long John. I was more than a little disturbed by the discrepancies between his story about the missing girl and what the young hooker at Night Haven told me. It was possible that the black girl made a mistake about Jenny's picture, but I had a bad feeling that she knew exactly what she was talking about. In which case Long John had fed me a line and I went for it like a dopey old halibut. Depending on what he had to say for himself, I'd have to decide about keeping the case, not to mention his money. I already felt fouled by it from having spun some seriously off-white lies to Rosa Mendez.

I dug Long John's phone number out of my wallet, but I got his voice mail system. I tried his cellular number, but it routed me back to the same recorded response. I left a message that I wanted to see him pronto and said I'd call back later.

I suppose I really should have my own cellular phone, but I can't bear the thought. Everyone in L.A. seems to have one—like the bag ladies with their screenplays—and every second asshole on the road seems to be talking into his hand as he obliviously cuts you off on the freeway. The last thing I want to do is answer phone calls in my goddamn car, not that that many people ring. Next to the crapper, it's the only place you can get any real solitude. A man's home may be his castle everywhere else in the world, but in Los Angeles all the best castles have four wheels, fuel injection, and a fax.

As I opened the door to my portable palace, a little Japanese man with a portacam—is there any other kind?—came running toward me. He held the tiny Sony camera pressed to his eye and waved furiously at me with his free hand. A heavy Nikon still camera dangled around his neck over a rainbow-colored Hawaiian shirt adorned with smiling Don Hos floating in tiny bubbles. Twenty paces behind him, also running, was an even shorter Japanese woman. She had her own video camera to hand and tugged at a little boy who, at least, wasn't filming anything.

As the man approached, he stopped waving long enough to clutch at the battered porkpie hat that threatened to fly off the top of his round head. His wife—I assumed it was his wife—was screeching at him from down the street in Japanese, but he ignored her in his feverish efforts to capture a bit of my soul on tape. He came right up to me, then danced a slow circle around my car, taping all the while. He nearly got clipped by an RTD bus as he wandered out into the street, and I had to grab him by a camera strap to avert disaster. The woman, breathless, drew to a stop on the sidewalk and taped her husband while he taped me. The little boy picked his nose and ate it.

"Ummm . . . can I help you?" I said, grabbing at him again as he heedlessly tracked backward into the street for a wide shot.

Finally he stopped shooting, though I noted that his wife kept her finger on her record button. He lowered the camera and smiled broadly at me.

"Ho' eno' fo' you?" he said, and tipped his hat. Then he clapped his hands merrily and did a kind of jig.

"Hot enough," the little boy repeated in perfect English, and clapped like his father. The woman kept the tape rolling: she was a pro.

I wanted to be annoyed, but it was just too damn ridiculous. The man was so obviously delighted to have recognized me that I simply couldn't be mad. Hell, I was probably the first celebrity—one should pardon the expression—they'd seen on their visit to Hollywood. Likely the only one they would see unless they ventured out to the Palisades. I figured: What the hell?

"Hot enough for *you?"* I said, summoning my most enthusiastic imitation of former glory.

The man literally jumped into the air with glee. Even his wife cracked a smile behind her camera, and the little boy laughed hysterically. The man bowed and, like a sleight-of-hand artist snatching nickels out of thin air, presented me with a business card. Pathetically, I don't have any business cards, so I merely bowed extra deeply in return. We stood there staring at each other for a minute, then he bowed again and scampered off down the street, once again raising his camera, clutching his hat, and leaving his wife and child half a block behind. The woman immediately began tracking him with her camera as she sped off after him. She really could have used a Steadicam.

I shook my head and laughed out loud at their parade.

Back in the car and headed west again, I cut south on La Brea. I felt so good that I stopped at Pinks and treated myself to a pair of chili dogs and a diet 7 UP. I ate standing up, using my roof as a table, then got back in the car and turned west on Melrose, slowing and pulling over to the curb as I cruised past Johnny Rockets. A handful of obvious tourist types and make-believe punks in four-hundred-dollar leather jackets sat around the counter chewing the overpriced, undercooked burgers, but the restaurant was pretty quiet. I sure didn't see any hookers lurking in the alley.

I zipped back out onto Melrose, then headed north on Fairfax, up toward Laurel Canyon. The traffic started to pick up heading into the Valley with the afternoon rush. I tailed a bronze, blond goddess in a blood-red convertible through the winding canyon pass. Her long hair shimmered brighter than the car's lacquered paint, but her obsessive preening in the rearview mirror and consequent swerves in and out of lane started to make me nervous. I finally passed her where the road widens out on the Valley side of the Hollywood Hills. I glanced over just long enough to catch a glimpse of the kind of collagened lips and gravity-defying, impossibly perky tits that make Hollywood everything it is.

Such as it is. I fear sometimes for my little city by the sea. Every year it seems to become more of a cliché, like a bad film version of itself. There's some famous old quote to the effect that all art aspires to the condition of music; I think maybe Los Angeles aspires to the condition of daytime television.

Once in the Valley, I got on the freeway and briefly accelerated my ancient Japanese beast up to eighty, where the DTs start to set in, then eased it back to sixty-five and slipped into the slow lane. Within a mile the traffic started backing up and I had to crawl all the way to Sherman Oaks. I popped a Warren Zevon tape into the cassette deck and tried to enjoy the ride as crazy Warren serenaded me on the subject of lawyers, guns, and money. I admired the scenery as cars inched along in both directions. It was another perfect Los Angeles day: seventy-two degrees in the sun and the Valley sky the color of Gulden's spicy brown mustard. I was free, white, and twenty-one with nothing to do but scout up a teenage hooker for her hanger-wielding pimp and enjoy life's rich pageant and the rush-hour traffic.

I got off at Sepulveda and rode the great Boulevard north. Sepulveda is my favorite street in all of L.A., the one New Yorkers invariably garble in pronunciation the first time they visit and then joke about forever after. Supple-veeda, they always call it, though *supple* is the last word to describe the tar and traffic. I passed through Sherman Oaks with its endless panoply of prefab corner mini-malls, discount gas stations, and absurdly rococo, but effectively identical, apartment blocks. On cassette, good old Warren sang the sad story of a headless Thompson gunner named Roland. As I approached the fringe of the bustling Van Nuys redlight district, the sun started to vanish into Ventura and the tape ran out to a soft hiss, like burgers on a grill.

I made a slow circuit of the Boulevard along with a dozen or so other browsers, but didn't see anything or one of particular interest. Most of the spandex crowd in this part of the Valley are white, though I spotted a couple-three Hispanic faces mixed in as well. The neighborhood's always changing, I suppose. A sheriff's car cruised past, but the cops showed little interest in either the girls or the johns. They save it for the bimonthly rousts when the local TV news cameras tag dutifully behind, recording for six-o'clock posterity the eternal vigilance of L.A.'s finest. The cop car pulled right on in to a Yum-Yum Donut Shop. Two others were already parked there.

I don't know exactly what I was looking for. I didn't really expect to spot Long John's honey walking the street—hell, I really didn't even believe she was still in L.A. After Night Haven, I couldn't be sure if Long John had fed me a line about the girl or she had fed one to him. I wouldn't have taken him for that big a sap, but who knows? The heart is a funny goddamn muscle, not that anyone ever gets to laugh. Maybe the girl had just played Long John at his own game and moved on to the next grift while the getting was still good.

I had planned to head back to the freeway and maybe take another run at the Hollywood scene, but the sight of all those bars on Sepulveda got the better of me. I've always gone for neon beer signs the way mosquitoes go for those purple bug lights. ZAAAPPP!!! I parked in front of a relatively inoffensive-looking place called Valente's and slipped inside for a cold one.

It was meat city.

An anorexic blonde with mismatched tits and electric-red pubic hair shook like a geriatric epileptic beneath some dim track lighting on a small stage. She kept her eyes squeezed closed and her fists clenched tight. A thin red line ran down one thigh. It was either blood or hair dye and sweat, but either way, I didn't want to get close enough to check.

I was surprised by the number of people inside. The booths were all taken, with only a couple of empty stools at the bar. A bunch of construction workers, grimy and pungent from a day working in the sun, laughed raucously at a big table in the corner. No one else in the place looked like they could conceivably hold a job.

I ordered up a beer and a shot of Jack Daniel's from a bartender who looked remarkably like William Frawley. I half feared that Vivian Vance would come out and shake her wrinkled booty under the spotlight. The Jack was watered down and the beer lines hadn't been cleaned since Carter was president, but the happy-hour prices were a deal, which explained the crowd. I ordered another round when Fred Mertz worked his way back down the bar. By the time I was ready for a third, I asked for a bottle of Guinness, which old Fred seemed shocked to find in his fridge. He stood around to watch me pour it into a glass—I got the feeling it wasn't a common sight round these parts—so for the hell of it, I showed him the photo of Long John's hooker.

"Know her?" I asked.

He glanced quickly at her face. "Cunt," he said.

I leaned forward, suddenly excited. "You do know her?"

"Cunt is cunt," Fred said, and walked away.

Cunt is cunt.

That might as well have been the name of the place and all the others like it on the strip. It was the mantra chanted by the customers, what brought them in the door. I felt like I should be disgusted or appalled, but I couldn't raise the energy.

They came in to stare at saggy tits and crab-infested snatch and dream that maybe there was hope of escape in a pair of track-marked arms. I looked around the bar at the sad, ugly faces. The balding heads and ill-fitting suits. The half-shaved chins and the hairy ears. The place was a shrine to wash-and-wear polyester. Most of the customers looked middle-aged, but I saw a few young men, too. I was overwhelmed by the loneliness, the desperation and morbidity of it all. I felt like I was in one of those zombie movies where the hapless, brain-dead creatures go through the motions and routines of living because they can't quite grasp the fact that they're dead. They just do what few things they remember over and over, without reason and without even the semblance of joy.

I felt glad there wasn't a mirror over the bar.

I stared down at the hooker's picture, the candid shot. She just looked so . . . *pure*. However unlikely that really was. Putting the picture back in my pocket, I shuddered. I polished off my beer and decided to get the hell out. I stopped at the pay phone by the men's room and tried Long John again, but got the same recorded message. I repeated that I needed to see him and told him to call me at home. Just then the bathroom door swung open and I saw one of the dancers blowing a construction worker in a doorless stall while a couple of his buddies looked on and waited their turn.

I couldn't face a tour of more of the same on Hollywood Boulevard just then, so I got right on the freeway and drove straight back to my place in Silver Lake. I nuked a microwave chicken-something in an ever-so-delicate gray sauce and forced it down while I watched a Bruce Willis picture I'd seen five times before on cable. I polished off a sixer of Samuel Adams while Bruce blew away the bad guys and cracked wise. What a card. And Demi Moore to boot.

I found myself thinking about Rosa Mendez's denim skirt and tan legs as I jerked off into the toilet. It was pretty good as those things go, but I felt sort of bad about it afterward.

I fell asleep still waiting for Long John to return my call.

*I*nvocation (I)

One eye watches.

Even in sleep—as deep and cold as the Pit—a million eyes closed, one eye watches.

In-between. The nether-realms. Darkness profound and silence painful. No touch, no scent, no taste. Only emptiness. Sensation is just a memory, a dream of a dream in the vast and forever fabric of black that enfolds him.

One eye watches.

Times drifts: Crawls, runs. Scratches, claws. Slows, stops. Moves on.

And on.

And on.

And one eye watches.

Dreams fade. Memories, too. The darkness consumes everything within it, before it. Inhuman breath grows shallow with the cascade of years. The dark ichor thickens, pulses flicker. But, but . . .

A distant rumble. Oh-so-faint in the deafening silence. A sound: a cry of pain.

A pinprick flash of light in the ebon cloak. There for a moment and just as quickly gone. A vision: death.

A crack in the hermetic void. A foul, sweet zephyr to carry the bouquet. A scent: blood.

A sacrifice.

A summons.

Breath deepens, ichor flows, pulses quicken as darkness, at last, begins to recede.

A million eyes open.

One eye blinks.

Four

The cops showed up just before six the next morning. A pair of plain-clothes who did everything they could to live up to the sobriquet. I didn't recognize either of them—no great surprise—but they both knew me. Or of me, at least. They didn't pound on the door or draw their guns or even make much noise at all. They actually can behave like that when they're in middle-class, white neighborhoods. They rang the bell twice and waited patiently on the porch. It was more than enough to wake me, though. I'm a woefully light sleeper.

The sun was only just up, but well hidden by the early morning overcast. The result was a dismal, very un-California-like gray of the sort that brings tears to surfer dudes' eyes and makes even the HOLLYWOOD sign look like an old Burma Shave billboard. The thick, summer marine layer usually burns off by eight or nine in my part of town, and I couldn't remember the last time I'd been up early enough to catch a glimpse of it. I hate mornings and always have. If only because of the hangovers.

Mornings belong to those who wear suits and ties and have kids and real jobs. That awful multitude who not only insist on taking responsibility for their lives, but expect everyone else to do the same. The kind that get into high dudgeon over those of us who choose not to follow their dull leads. Usually, when you peel back their outer layer of haughtiness, you find a core of molten resentment because they hate their fucking lives, too.

I used to loathe early morning shoots back in the bad old days. I had trouble remembering my lines at the best of times, and at eight in the morning it just wasn't a possibility. In my whole career I don't think I ever hit a mark on a first take before noon. The best thing about *Salt & Pepper*—well, next to the flow of babes—was that we always taped late in the afternoon. Good old Papa Pepper had it written into his contract. God bless him, Pops had a more than occasional problem with the morning headache himself.

"Martin Burns?" the cop said as if he didn't already know. A black guy in his fifties, with big teeth and little eyes. He looked tough as a brick firehouse. His partner was white and maybe ten years younger, but twice as doughy. He looked like a boozer.

I nodded and yawned at them.

"I'm Dickens, he's Fenster," the white cop said, and smiled broadly. His partner grinned.

"Yeah?" I said.

Cops love morning rousts. They have to be up anyway, and live for spreading the misery of their own awful lives. It's something they learn early on because of having to wear those blue uniforms and square black shoes. It's also a distinct psychological advantage for them to show up at your doorstep with the sun, all fresh and clean in jackets and ties while you're padding around barefoot with your hair mussed, trying not to smell your own morning breath while you scrape whatever the hell that white stuff is off your tongue with your front teeth.

"Don't you get it? I'm Dickens, he's Fenster."

I stared back at them.

"The show. Don't you remember? It was on right after *Salt and Pepper*. With the guy from *The Addams Family*. What's his name?"

"John Huston," the black cop said. "His daughter played Morticia in the movie. Isabella."

"Uhh . . . I don't think so," I said. I dopily wondered why we were having this conversation. Then I reminded myself yet again that absolutely *everyone* in Los Angeles thinks they're in The Business. At least they talk like they are.

"No, that's right," the white cop said. "I'm surprised you don't remember."

"It was a long time ago," I said.

"Yeah," the cop said, and they both nodded. The white cop was still smiling, no doubt fantasizing about the beautiful Isabella Huston. We stood there like that for a while, in blissful nostalgic reverie.

"Is there something I can do for you guys?"

The black cop straightened up. "Actually, I'm Detective Rowan."

"So this would be Sergeant Martin?" I asked.

Blank stares. You can't win.

"Holloway," the partner said, his smile fading. "Lieutenant. Homicide."

"We have a few questions we'd like to ask you. Would it be all right if we went inside?"

I shrugged and led them into the living room. I cleared a pile of newspapers off the couch and pulled another chair in from the dining room. I set it opposite the couch across a small coffee table strewn with books and magazines and sat down. As I gestured toward the couch, I saw Rowan touch his tie knot—real subtle—to signal his partner. He sat right down, but Holloway started to pace around behind me. I could hear him picking things up off my desk, trying to distract me, but I kept my eyes locked on the black detective.

"Who died?" I asked.

Rowan cop-smiled at me, the corners of his lips rising like a theater curtain while the rest of his face remained inanimate.

"Holy fuck!" Holloway said behind me. It was enough to turn me around. The detective had found my Golden Globe award. I use it as a bookend and it was dusty as hell. I should have pawned it years ago, but I'm not entirely unsentimental. Holloway cradled it like a newborn baby.

"What'd you get this for?" he asked. The little inscription plaque fell off sometime in the eighties.

"Most Promising Male Newcomer of 1967. In television," I said. The words felt uncomfortable in my mouth, like undercooked chicken. "Leonard Whiting won the newby award for movies that year."

"Who?" Rowan asked.

"Exactly," I said.

"No shit," Holloway whispered. He marveled at the award some more, then glanced around my tired little apartment. He looked back at the award, tracing a swath in the dust with his thumb. He glanced back at me, looking almost sad. "No shit," he repeated softly.

"Do you know a young woman named Janine Lassiter?" Rowan said. I turned back to him and suddenly he was all business. "Also known as Jenny Leo."

Rowan's eyes widened as he read my expression. I'll never get rich playing poker.

"She's dead?" I asked. Stupid question.

Rowan pulled a photograph out of his pocket and tossed it on the table. It landed on a paperback copy of an Andrew Vachss novel. It was a square Polaroid of Long John's hooker. Her pretty, farm-girl features hadn't been touched, but a gaping hole had been cut from her abdomen to a point midway between her breasts. The skin had been peeled back in what looked to be a very deliberate manner. Fortunately I couldn't make out any further details. I looked at her face again. It seemed impossibly tranquil.

"We understand you've been looking for her," Holloway said. He sauntered over behind my shoulder and glared down. He rolled the dust from my Golden Globe into a tiny black ball between his thumb and forefinger, then flicked it away like a booger. "Your pal Straczynski over in Vice says you were asking around after her. He said some other things about you, too, but I promised my mommy I wouldn't use that kind of language. I think maybe he don't like you so much."

I ignored Holloway and continued to stare at the picture. I tried just to look at her face, but found my eyes drawn to the awful wound. I couldn't help but think that she had been stretched into an enormous cunt. Her body violently transformed into a mockery of what she did. I handed the picture back to Rowan.

"Yeah," I said. "I never actually caught up with her, though. Till now. Where'd you find her?"

Holloway started to say something behind me, but Rowan cut him off. "She was discovered in a ditch on a little canyon road between Coldwater and Laurel. A Mex gardener spotted her yesterday afternoon. Seems that all the folks up there water their grass about the same time of day. The body blocked up a drain and flooded a couple lawns. But it doesn't look to me like she drowned."

I nodded and stared down at the photo again. I realized that I had more or less driven right past that spot the previous afternoon on my way to Van Nuys. For all I know she might have been screaming for her life behind a bush at the side of the road while I was ogling the tits on the blonde in the convertible. I shook my head.

"No?" Rowan asked. "Is that some sort of denial you're indicating there?"

"I drove right past there yesterday," I said, regretting the words even as they escaped my lips.

"Is that a fact?" Rowan said.

"Maybe you want to tell us about it?" Holloway said. He was leaning over my shoulder now, hands tightly gripping the back of my chair. I could feel his knuckles against my back.

"Nothing to tell. I drove up to the Valley yesterday to look for her. I cut across via Laurel Canyon on the way. Obviously I didn't know she was there."

Rowan's turn: "Obviously. And what time was this?"

"About four, four-thirty."

"And the reason you were looking for her?"

"I have a client," I said, and shrugged.

"And," Rowan prompted.

I took a deep breath. "I have a client who's been looking for her. He's . . . her boyfriend. Or ex. She disappeared a few days ago and he's worried about her. He hired me to sniff around for her."

"Hell of a smell," Holloway growled.

"You maybe want to tell us the name of this client?" Rowan asked. Holloway leaned over until I could feel his breath on the back of my neck. He slid his hands along the chair, digging his knuckles into my back. I hunched forward, leaning my elbows on my thighs. I realized that Rowan could see my balls through the slit in my robe. I uncrossed my legs and cinched the robe.

"You know I can't tell you that," I said.

Holloway snorted behind me. "What are you? A fucking priest?"

"The Lord and the Jackson family move in mysterious ways," I said over my shoulder. Holloway growled and Rowan's eyes narrowed.

"So you're a smart guy now?" Rowan asked.

"No," I said, thinking about my situation. "Not hardly."

"Damn straight. 'Cause there's a long list of people I gotta take grief from, and believe you me, you couldn't be much further from the top. You know, Straczynski really gave us an earful about you. I know what a grade-A asshole he is, so I took it with a grain or two of salt. The Yid pretty well vouched for you, but you're making me wonder here."

"Straczynski ain't so bad," Holloway said. I might have figured.

"Look, Lieutenant," I said, "the last thing I'm looking to do here is bust your balls. But you know I can't give up a client's name, and you also know my ass is covered by my license."

"Licenses can get revoked," Holloway said.

"Not retroactively, they can't. Listen: The girl's a runaway, but she's over age." I wasn't so sure about that, but Rowan didn't react. "I've only been on this for a day or two—not even, really—so I don't have much. Less than that, even. The boyfriend's a local and they shacked up. He's not exactly the cleanest Joe in the world—" I damn near choked on those words "—but he says he's worried about her. I don't have any reason to doubt that. She was maybe working the street, but he didn't think so. Me? I'm not so sure. The little I've been able to find out is that she was probably into the life a little heavier than the schmuck thought. Maybe playing him for a sucker. He was pretty broken up that she took off on him."

"Broken up like to cap her if he found her?" Rowan asked.

"No. Not that way at all. He was practically bawling like a baby because she left him. I sure don't see him doing *that* to her." I pointed my chin at the photograph.

"He don't see, Stanley," Holloway said. He smiled broadly. Rowan nodded and smiled at me again, and I knew for sure this was going to be the start of a very long day.

"You don't see," Rowan repeated. "Well, let me tell you what I see. I see a dead girl, gutted like a trout and left in a ditch in a very nice part of town. I see a chief of detectives who's already taken half a dozen phone calls from the rich taxpayers who pay big bucks to live in that nice part of town just so's they *don't* have to find bodies in their pretty ditches. Now I see a pencil-dick, penny-ante, washed-up asshole who just so happens to be looking for this cunt the day she's iced. This washed-up fuck now tells me maybe she's a hooker, but he won't tell me who hired him to find her. This asshole—that's you, in case you're having any trouble following me here—wants me to take *his* word about the saintliness of his client, who is also, what did you say? Not the cleanest Jake in the world? Now, you know what else I see?"

"I see it," Holloway barked. They both waited for a response.

"What do you see, Lieutenant?" I said with a sigh.

"I see you taking a little trip with us. Unless you care to be more forthcoming."

"Sorry," I said, meaning it. "I can't."

"Well, then I see it all too clear in those crystal balls of yours."

Rowan pointed a weathered finger at me. My robe had come open again and my constricted genitals dangled freely. I tried to muster some dignity as I drew the terry cloth back over my crotch.

Holloway followed me into the bedroom and watched while I quickly dressed. He wouldn't let me close the bathroom door to take a piss, but at least he didn't trail me inside. He studied the pictures hanging over the dresser and whistled at a framed glossy of a very youthful me standing next to a playfully squinting Clint Eastwood.

"What's this from?" he asked when I came out of the can.

"I had a part in *Coogan's Bluff,*" I said. "Microscopic, but credited. The still guy on the shoot gave that to me as a souvenir."

"Don Siegel, right?"

I glanced at the cop in surprise. He apparently knew his directors. "Yeah. Nice guy."

"Directed a mean action scene. I love *Madigan.*"

Christ, I thought, even the fucking cops in Hollywood are auteurists!

"Hey, you ever bang anybody famous?"

I peered up at him and frowned.

"What? Is that privileged information, too? Criminy!"

I shook my head and went back into the living room to put on my shoes. Rowan hadn't stirred from the couch. He watched me tie my laces, only getting up after I stood and stared at him. I followed him out the door, with Holloway bringing up the rear.

Rowan went right to the driver's side as Holloway opened the back door of their unmarked car. As I ducked my head to get in, he slapped a meaty hand on my shoulder.

"Hey!" he said. "You ever do what's-her-name? The Partridge babe? You know, the anorexic one. Became a lawyer."

"Susan Dey?" I asked. He nodded enthusiastically. I sighed and shook my head. He grunted with disappointment and shoved me into the back of the car.

"I'd still like to do her," he said. "I *likes* 'em thin."

And we were off.

Rowan and Holloway sweated me for most of the day. They ran the usual routines, but I wasn't buying. I sort of got the feeling that for some reason, their hearts weren't really in it. I'm not sure why, maybe Sid Teitlebaum's word carried some weight with them. Maybe they saw it was a waste of time; Rowan struck me as a smarter than average cop. Hell, maybe Holloway just liked the picture of me and Clint. Who knows how cops think? The worst of it was that they wouldn't let me go to the bathroom again until midafternoon. It's a tactic—you'd be surprised how often it works—but anyone who's been drinking as long as I have develops something of a hollow leg.

Before they cut me loose, Rowan tried to threaten my state investigator's license again, but that rang even hollower than my leg. The cops can fuck with your license if they really want, but the bureaucracy is so out of control and the process so involved that with hearings and appeals, it can take months or even years for any action. The DA can make it move a little faster, but I didn't see where I merited that kind of attention, and I doubted that Rowan would be willing to tug that important a pant leg over me. He *could* have my carry permit suspended, that's pure PD territory, except the cops refuse to issue carry permits in L.A., so I don't have one. The policy doesn't stop half the populace from packing artillery, but it sounds good around election time.

In the end, Rowan and Holloway had to let me go with little more than a full bladder and some nasty looks. I made as nice with them as I could, then made a beeline for the men's room. It stank of piss and vomit, and something brown was encrusted on the handle of the urinal, so I didn't flush. I wanted to wash my face, but the sinks were equally gross and there weren't any paper towels, just those goddamn hand blowers. One of the taps was running slowly, so I gingerly stuck my hands under the light stream and wiped them on the front of my shirt.

I stopped at the vending machine in the front lobby and bought a Coke. It took my dollar and spat out a can of soda, but kept the change. You'd think you wouldn't get ripped off right there in a police station. I considered complaining to the desk sergeant but decided that it might fit the operational definition of pressing one's luck. I held the cold can against my forehead and exhaled. I popped open the top, downed half the soda in a swallow, and stepped out into the warm afternoon sunlight.

Long John was waiting for me across the street.

He leaned against the front fender of a new Lexus. The car was silver and shiny as a fresh-minted quarter. The vanity plate read SILVER J, and a yellow placard in the rear window warned "Bitches Beware!" Real classy. Long John wore a white suit with a peach silk shirt open at the collar. A thumb-sized silver crucifix dangled in the thick forest of his chest hair.

He stood up when he saw me and raised a hand in salute. I paused at the top of the precinct steps and looked up and down the street. I considered ignoring him and walking the other way, but decided I'd have to face him sooner or later and might as well get it over with now. Besides, I needed a ride home, and cabs don't cruise the streets in L.A.

"Yo, chief," he said. He smiled and opened the passenger door for me as I approached, gesturing me in with a bow. I didn't answer, but I got into the car. The interior still smelled new and the dash looked like the cockpit of the space shuttle. Long John ran around the front and got in behind the wheel. He started the engine, which purred like a fat kitten, and pulled out into the street.

"Effie and Silver Lake," I said. "You know the way?"

"Aw, man! Don't be that way. Let me buy you a drink."

"I don't think I want to drink with you," I said. "I *know* I don't want anything to do with you."

Long John looked at me, but kept driving. I wanted to stare him down but couldn't help peering back and forth from his eyes to the windshield. Large steel objects were looming ahead, but Long John never looked away.

"Umm," I said.

He continued to glare at me. A parked mail truck was coming up fast.

"Long John . . ."

More of the same.

"Okay," I shouted, "we'll have a drink."

He turned his head and slammed on the breaks. The Lexus jerked to a stop half a foot from the rear of the truck. Long John backed up and pulled around the truck as the driver stuck his head out the window and flipped us the bird.

"You'll feel better after a beer," Long John said.

We drove on in silence for a while, then Long John poked at a number pad on the console between the seats. A digital display flashed a couple of times, and a few seconds later a heavy-metal CD screeched through the speakers. The sound quality was great—better than what I had in my house—but the music sucked. Metallica, I think, but God only knows. I looked for the volume knob, but there wasn't a prayer.

"You want to turn that down a little?" I yelled. He nodded and punched a button on the console.

"They sweat you bad?" Long asked after a while. He had turned east onto Sunset and was at least heading in my general direction.

"You mean as opposed to did they sweat me good?"

Long John nodded briskly and smiled. He was pounding the leather steering wheel along with the music. "I hear you, chief. We all been there."

I punched the same button Long John had touched, but it only made the music louder, so I slammed my fist against the keypad until the music abruptly cut out.

"Hey!" Long John complained.

"Fucking hey yourself! I just spent the whole goddamn day sitting on a steel chair in an interrogation room because of you, and the last thing I need is your fucking headache music."

"You're getting paid," Long John said.

"Not enough for this shit. Not enough for your fucking lies."

"Say what? What lies?"

"Please. No more of your pimp-ass bullshit. All that 'I love her' and 'She's my out' shit that you laid on me the other day. Man, I must have 'sap' flashing in big neon letters over my head. Just tell me, Mr. Pimp Stick: Did you do her yourself or did you have her done? FUUUUCCCKK!!!"

Long John hit the brakes so hard that my head smacked against the front window before the belt jerked me back into the seat. Horns screamed at us from behind, but incredibly, the car didn't get rear-ended. I touched my fingers to my forehead and came away with some blood.

"Fuck me," I said.

"Fuck you, yeah," Long John said. He grabbed the front of my shirt and twisted it in his fist, pulling me toward him. "No way I did her, man. No. Way."

I grabbed his wrist, but he wouldn't loosen his grip. I dug my nails into his hard skin until he finally relented with a squeal. Blood poured down into my eye faster than I could wipe it away. Long John snorted in disgust, then pulled a silk handkerchief out of his pocket and handed it to me. I pressed it to my forehead and winced as Long John finally responded to the blaring horns behind us and pulled over.

"You didn't do her?" I said, turning the handkerchief inside out.

"Fuck no!"

"So, what? She fell into a threshing machine or something out there?"

Long John didn't respond. The flow of blood was tapering off, though I suspected I could use a stitch or two. I glanced over at him and saw that he was staring blankly out through the side window.

"What?" I asked.

"Was it that bad?" he asked.

"Fuck," I said. "You didn't see her?"

He shook his head. "I can't claim the body, man. It would raise some eyebrows."

"Right," I said. "Heaven forbid."

"Tell me," he said.

I leaned back against the headrest and continued to press the sodden piece of silk to my forehead. I noticed that a tiny question mark of red marked the inside of the windshield.

"Please," he said.

I looked back over at the pimp, who was staring down at the floor. His hands were braced against the wheel, the bony knuckles white with tension. Could he really be that good an actor? I wondered.

"She was hacked up pretty bad," I said, watching him closely. "I only saw the one picture, but it was major violence. Like maybe someone dug her guts out with a trowel. They threw what was left in a ditch."

Long John closed his eyes, but didn't otherwise move. He breathed loudly through his nose. His hands clutched the wheel so tightly that his arms began to quiver.

"For what it's worth, they didn't touch her face," I said. It didn't sound too good when I said it, either.

Long John just sat there with his eyes closed. I didn't know what the hell to say. A Mexican lady wandered up to the window and held up a bag of peanuts, but I waved her off with the bloody handkerchief. She moved fast.

"You didn't do her," I said, accepting the inevitable. It wasn't a question, but Long John shook his head anyway. When he opened his eyes, I saw the tears.

"Oh, Christ," I said. "My luck: I get the Betsy Wetsy pimp." I regretted the words as soon as I said them, but Long John didn't seem to notice.

"You gotta help me," he said.

I sighed.

"Listen, Long John. Maybe you didn't do her. Maybe you don't know about it. *I* don't know. But you did fucking lie to me."

"How?" he said, anger filling his eyes. "What did I lie?"

"Come on," I half laughed. "You told me she was cherry to the life, that she wasn't on the street. You know that's a crock. Half a day on the job I find out she used to blow the manager of a burger joint for free lunches."

"You fuck!" Long John yelled, and grabbed my shirt again. I lashed out with my left and caught him solidly under the nose and he let go.

"Fucking maniac!" I said, and started to get out of the car.

"Wait. I'm sorry. Wait."

"What? What should I wait for?"

Long John grabbed me lightly by the elbow and pulled me back inside. "Please," he said.

I shook him off, but sat back down in the car. He didn't say anything, and I started to get mad again. "I'm losing precious bodily fluids here . . ."

"I . . . I didn't completely tell you the truth," Long John sputtered.

"Oh. Which is different from lying."

"I didn't exactly lie," he insisted. "I told you Jenny was cherry to the life, and I swear to God I thought that was true. I didn't know she worked the streets. I . . . I guess I have to believe it, now, but I didn't know then."

He looked right into my eyes as he spoke, but I was still uncertain about his trustworthiness. He *looked* pretty sincere, at least.

"You *told* me she was a goddamn virgin, Long John."

"She was!"

"Phtttpptt."

"I *thought* she was. She told me and . . . maybe I wanted to believe it. I don't know. Maybe I knew it was a line, but it was something to believe. Something nice. Didn't you ever want nothing like that? Wish for something to believe in like that?"

I swallowed hard.

"It was really special. I mean I thought it was. But maybe I knew it wasn't all what it seemed."

"How so?"

"The acting stuff, I told you about. The gigs I got her. Some of it was on the level, but some of it was, you know . . ."

"Porno?"

"It was . . . it was edgy stuff. And she went along with it, so maybe I started to guess that she wasn't all sunshine and fresh air."

"So why'd you feed me that shit?"

"I didn't think you'd take the case otherwise."

"Who am I? Pope fucking Pious? You could have got anybody to take this case."

Long John started to look uncomfortable. "I heard stuff about you. I wanted *you* to take it. You know, the Jar really likes you, so I figured you could be trusted. You proved that today when you didn't give me up."

"Jesus!" I said, thinking again about the Jar's collection. "All customers should be so loyal. So what kind of shoots was she doing? Kids? Animals? What?"

"No. Nothing like that. Straightforward stuff. Pretty good production values. Film-school brats directing. U.S.C., they said."

"They? Was it mob stuff? Tell me it's wise guys, Long John, make the day complete."

"No way. I ain't that stupid. It was pretty legit as these things go. For foreign markets. It even got her some straight work."

"Bullshit," I said.

"Serious. It's a Jap outfit. Celestial Dog. They do some commercial stuff, too. The fucking Nips go apeshit for white pussy. It's 'cause their own broads got them nasty little Jap tits."

That was a conversation killer, so we sat there silently for a while. The blood had stopped oozing from my head, but it hurt like a son of a bitch. Long John's handkerchief was soaked red with blood, but I didn't have the heart to toss it on the fancy carpeting, so I clutched it in my hand. Long John seemed to be waiting for me to say something.

"Take me home," I said.

"You bailing on me?"

"What do you want me to do, Long John? She's dead. The cops'll show you the pictures."

"I want to know who killed her," he said.

I exhaled loudly and shook my head. "You say you loved her and maybe you did. It's not my place to say who was scamming who here. And to tell you the truth: I don't care. I didn't want this case to begin with, and now that the cops are chewing my ass, I sure as hell don't need any more of it. And even if I did, murder investigations are *way* out of my league. It may be pathetic, but I'm strictly small time. I take what little pride I still possess in knowing my own very severe limitations."

"You could do it," he said, somewhat petulantly.

"I don't *want* to do it, Long John. Is that plain enough? Can you understand that?"

The pimp looked up at himself in the rearview, then looked at me. He started at the top of my head and ran his gaze down my body all the way to the tips of my scuffed shoes. Then he reached over and opened the glove compartment. He pulled out a white envelope and dropped it in my lap.

"Open it," he said.

I knew right then and there I should just get out of the car and walk home. I knew, like old Pandora, that I shouldn't open up that envelope, shouldn't look inside.

It was stuffed with hundreds.

"Ten thou, Small Time," Long John said. "Cash in your hand. Take it now. If it's not enough, you say when it runs out."

I thumbed through the wad of bills. Some were crisp and new, others faded and old. It looked as dirty as it had to be, but it represented six months of scut work for me. I glanced over at Long John, but he was carefully facing the other way, looking out the side window. You should never take money from someone who looks the other way.

"Okay," I said. I was another one of his whores now.

Long John turned back my way and nodded, then started the car and pulled out into traffic. He reached for the CD button, but I caught his hand an inch from the keypad.

"As God is my witness, Long John," I said, "I don't know which of us is the bigger chump."

*F*ive

I took a long, hot shower when I got home, nuked a frozen pot pie, and spent the rest of the night with the Dodgers and a six of Henry Weinhart's. Henry's is the best cheap beer around short of crossing the border and stocking up on quarter-apiece Mexican piss in Ensenada. The pot pie was full of stringy, dark-meat chicken and way too many carrots, so I ended up tossing most of it. I chomped a bag of unsalted Bavarian pretzels for dessert. When I fell asleep on the sofa, the Dodgers were up 6–3 on the Giants, but in the morning paper I saw that the bullpen blew the lead in the ninth.

My forehead still felt a little tender the next day. The cut oozed something brown in the shower, but I dabbed on a little antiseptic and it stopped by itself after a while. I could have done with another Henry's to brace the day, but I'd drunk it all the night before. I considered snorting just a finger or two of chilled vodka, but a look in the mirror convinced me that it wasn't such a great idea and maybe that wasn't the kind of drunk I was ready to be just yet. Screwing up some courage, I chugged two mugs of stale coffee and set out to face a bright new day.

By the time I made it out the door, it was nearly eleven-thirty.

The sun was up to full bake and a mean Santa Ana—a demon wind—swept down from the hills, fluttering trash across the streets and scratching skin with its toasty sandpaper edge. Sweat stains took bold Rorschach form under my armpits before I walked halfway across the street to my car. Thursday was street-cleaning day, and my brave little Subaru was the only car left along the curb. Miraculously, the Parking Enforcement clown car hadn't come by yet, so I was spared the indignity of having to not pay yet another twenty-seven-dollar ticket. I had half expected the homicide dicks to nail me for the fistful of citations already moldering in my glove compartment when they took me in, but none of them were for moving violations, so maybe it didn't kick out when they ran my sheet. Or maybe my film buff buddy Holloway couldn't bring himself to press a penny-ante scofflaw beef against someone who'd once been directed by Don Siegel. In a city where the cops actually write tickets for jaywalking, who the fuck knows?

The car's air conditioner was sort of working, which I took to be a good omen. I was tempted to stop and grab a quick lunch at the Burrito King on Hyperion, but I was afraid the air conditioner would quit if I killed the engine, and I couldn't face the monstrous midday heat of the Valley without it. Instead I cruised into the drive-through of a Taco Bell and chowed down on a couple of their thirty-nine-cent specials, praying that they'd cooked the beef (if that's what it was) at the appropriate temperature as I headed up the Glendale Freeway.

The address for Celestial Dog, the company that Long John's hooker supposedly worked for, was up in Burbank. As near as I could tell from the map in my Thomas Guide, it wasn't too far from the big Warner Studio lot, but far enough that you'd never confuse the two. I'd never heard of Celestial Dog before—and it's the kind of screwy name you wouldn't likely forget—but there're a million little outfits around town, and everyone and their brother-in-law claims to be a producer. Everyone who isn't a screenwriter, that is (of course, there are those talented few—no more than, say, every second putz—who claim to be both). Most of these "offices" are just post office boxes listed as suite numbers to look good on letterhead. Or, if it's a Beverly Hills or Marina address, a closet-sized cubicle in some run-down office building. The fact that Celestial Dog was shooting fuck films, whatever legitimate business they may or may not also do, led me to assume that the address would turn out to be a cubbyhole in a "Mailboxes 'R Us." Long John said he'd never visited the offices, had only dealt with the company via phone and fax. I still don't own a fax. There's no one I know who'd want to send me something that badly.

I figured it for a long shot that anything would pan out at Celestial Dog, but for Long John's ten large, I had to check it out.

My knack for being wrong is genuinely uncanny.

The spanking new office block, five floors of gleaming mirrored walls and goofy, postmodern angles, was actually in the good part of Burbank (to the extent that such a thing can be said to exist). A small but subtle and elegant rock garden greeted visitors in front, and a cantilevered fountain, in which the water appeared to flow uphill in impossible, Escher-like ways, occupied the center of an immaculately clean concrete courtyard. A long row of delicate and beautiful bonsai trees in polished jade planters lined the walkway leading to the main entrance. As always, it was a good ten degrees hotter in the Valley than down in the L.A. basin, and the Santa Ana bit with slightly sharper teeth. Still, the wind kicked some cooling mist off the gushing fountain, and I stood for a moment, smiling like a kid dancing under a garden sprinkler, as the tiny droplets tickled my skin.

Stepping inside the building was like taking a high dive into a pool of ice water. The air-conditioning blew with arctic intensity, and I felt goose pimples break out down my exposed arms. The vast, sparkling lobby was empty, but for an elderly black man in a dark brown uniform at an information kiosk. He briefly peered up at me from his newspaper and smiled when I nodded in his direction. Crossing my arms over my chest, I strolled to the building directory and ran my finger up and down the board twice without finding any listing for Celestial Dog. An awful lot of the names on the directory seemed to be foreign, but I didn't think much of it. The way of the world. I glanced back at the building number, checking it again against the slip of paper with the address Long John had given me. This definitely should have been the place. I carefully scanned the whole directory again, then walked over to the information guy.

"How y'all doing?" he said as I approached the desk.

"Pretty good." I smiled. "Little cold, maybe."

"Tell me 'bout it," he said, shaking his head. "Man could catch his death in this place." He furtively peered up and down the lobby. There was no one else around. "See here?"

He flipped his paisley tie over his shoulder and unfastened a button on his starched white shirt. Underneath he wore a thermal undershirt. "S'only way I can stand it," he said.

"Little bit hot when you go out, though, ain't it?" I asked.

"Got no choice," he said, refastening the button. "Sweat or starve."

"I know that feeling," I said.

The old man suddenly seemed to remember where he was and what he was supposed to be doing. He straightened his tie and squared his shoulders. "Can I help you with something, sir?"

"Yeah. I'm looking for Celestial Dog Productions. I was given this address, but I can't find them listed on the board. Did they move?"

"No, sir. Ain't never been nobody listed here by that name."

"Damn," I said. I looked back across the empty lobby, and the old man cleared his throat at me. "What?"

The old man fought a tiny smile. "Said ain't never been nobody *listed*. Didn't say ain't never been nobody here."

"Aha," I said, and peeled a twenty out of my wallet, sliding it across the counter. It nimbly disappeared into the old man's pocket.

"They sometime used to get deliveries to that name, but only once in a great while. It's supposed to get marked return to sender, so they leaves it with me. Then I'd put it aside and bring it on upstairs after hours."

"Upstairs to who?"

The old man struggled with that smile again until a second twenty vanished into his pocket. I realized he had more than just the thermal vest to keep him warm.

"Laughing Boy Pictures. They got a big suite up on the third floor. Number 305 over in the west wing." He pointed at a far bank of elevators.

I nodded at him and started toward the elevator bank when he cleared his throat at me again. I started to reach for my wallet, but he held up his hand.

"This one's for free," he said. "It may be chilly down here, but it be *cold* up there. You got to keep the brass monkeys inside round them folks. You hear what I'm saying?"

No trace of a smile was left on the old man's face. His puffy eyes had narrowed with concern.

"I always try to look after my brass monkeys," I said. "But thanks."

I rode the elevator up to the third floor. I still hadn't seen another soul in the building, and wondered what kind of businesses rented space here. Just up the hall was a large double door with the name LAUGHING BOY PICTURES in bold block letters stenciled in gold. Below it was the image of a cackling harlequin dancing in the cone of a spotlight. There was something annoyingly familiar about the harlequin's face, but I couldn't quite place it. Probably some TV or commercial actor had served as the model for the logo.

I reached for the knob when the door jerked open in front of me. A small, bald man with thick glasses and an umber complexion was yelling over his shoulder at someone I couldn't see. Prodding him from behind was a very large, very severe-looking fellow who looked like he could have eaten two of the little man with plenty of room left for dessert.

"You fucks!" the bald man screamed. "You tell that rat bastard I won't be treated this way. We got history, and Mickey Marvin's got a memory like an elephant. You tell that cheating fuck that Mickey Marvin knows things. Mickey Marvin just might start to talk."

The big guy continued to poke the little man in the small of the back. His square face looked like it was screwed up for murder until he saw me standing there, then it melted like an ice cream cone in the sun. He stopped poking the little man and took a step back.

"Yeah, that's right," the bald guy said. "You keep your fucking fingers off Mickey Marvin. You miserable bastards are all the same."

The little man suddenly noticed me standing there and started. He adjusted his shiny sport coat and tugged at the knot on his too wide tie, then pushed past me.

"Rat bastards," I heard him mutter.

I looked up at the big man, who shrugged, then half smiled, then shrugged again, and finally looked down and scratched his forehead. It was a curiously awkward gesture from a man who had just looked so tough, but it somehow managed to communicate: "It's the goddamn Movie Business and it's full of schmucks like that who talk about themselves in the third person and jeez, what the hell can you do anyway?"

That's what it communicated to me, anyway. Maybe you have to have been in The Business to appreciate it.

The big man stepped back out of the doorway and gestured me inside. He had the good grace not to follow me into the reception area. He stuck his head out into the hall, peering after the bald man, then loudly shut the door and disappeared into the suite.

Two Asian men, in identical gray suits, sat on opposite ends of a plush couch across from the receptionist. Each had his hands folded over his lap, and neither wasted a look at me as I walked in. The lobby had the pristine feel of a big-money operation: simple and tasteful, but unmistakably expensive. The color scheme was all muted, soothing pastels, and the furnishings all silver and glass. Harpsichord music played lightly in the background, emanating from hidden speakers.

The receptionist was speaking on the phone as I approached. She smiled formally and gestured with a finger for me to wait. I nodded back at her and stood there for a little while, but the call seemed sort of complicated. I glanced down at the papers on her desk and scanned the open page of an appointment calendar. The receptionist caught me peeking and closed the book, offering me an awkward smile as she continued with her conversation.

I wandered over to inspect a colorful painting on the far wall. It was

Japanese and showed several vile-looking creatures converging on what I took to be three geisha. One of the creatures in the painting wore a human mask, but the other monsters glared at the white-faced women with undisguised and hungry lust. The geisha were portrayed as more submissive than scared or upset, and I had a feeling that they were supposed to be prostitutes. After a minute I spotted a small card plastered to the wall below the painting identifying the artist as Utagawa Yoshi-iku. Never heard of him. Big surprise.

"How can I help you?"

The receptionist was off the phone and looking my way. The Asian men on the couch continued to sit as stiff and silently as bookends. I walked back over to the desk and mustered up as much of the old Burns charm as I could manage.

"Hi," I said, and smiled. "I'm a friend of Mickey Marvin's."

The receptionist didn't have a sense of humor. I saw that right away.

"Joke," I said. "Just a joke."

No sense of humor at all. So much for the old Burns charm.

"Actually," I said, smiling broadly, "I'm here in reference to a matter regarding Celestial Dog Productions."

"You've got the wrong office," she said coldly. "This is Laughing Boy Pictures."

"I know that. But I understand that Celestial Dog is also run out of this office."

"I can't help with your understandings." As she said it, the bruiser who'd ushered out the bald man reappeared behind her. Pretty slick.

"Problem," the bruiser said. No question.

"I was just telling this gentleman that he appears to be in the wrong office," the receptionist told him.

"The door's that way, bub," Bruiser said. I think the last time anyone called me "bub" was in an episode of *McMillan and Wife* I did back in 1972. I tried the charm bit again.

"I'm sure I can find the door," I said, "I'm clever like that, but I don't think Mr. Aldus would appreciate your showing it to me."

The big guy took a step back, seeming to reconsider, and the receptionist narrowed her eyes at me. "You a friend of Mr. Aldus?" the bruiser said.

I'd actually pulled Aldus's name off the appointment book when I glanced at it before. The receptionist looked down at the closed book, then back up at me, and seemed to guess that was the case. But she wasn't sure.

"You don't have an appointment," she said.

"How do you know? You haven't even asked my name."

"Mr. Aldus isn't in . . ." she caught herself. "What was the name?"

"The name is Silver," I told her. "Just tell Mr. A that I stopped by to discuss new terms for the Celestial Dog project."

"Well, I'm sure he won't know what you're talking about," she said, but it wasn't convincing. She looked up at the bruiser, who was coming out from behind the desk. I took the hint and headed for the door. The two men on the couch were now watching me intently. One of them had unfolded his hands and splayed them on his thighs, as if preparing to stand. I noticed that the top joints of two of his fingers were missing.

"Tell him we'll do lunch," I told the receptionist, and darted back out into the hall. I started toward the elevators when the door opened behind me. The big man watched me walk down the hall, closing the door only when I turned the corner toward the bank of elevators.

I was still peering back behind me and practically walked right into the little bald man who'd been leaving Laughing Boy when I arrived. I wondered just how many people got thrown out of that office a day. The little man was standing between the rows of elevators, smoking a cheap cigar in front of a big NO SMOKING UNDER PENALTY OF LAW sign. He looked pretty ashen.

"You work with those rat bastards?" he asked me.

"Who?" I said, playing dumb.

"Who. Laughing Boy. Cocksuckers!"

"No," I said. "I work with Celestial Dog. You?"

"I don't know that name. But they got a million scams. Every one a limited partnership, and none of them ever turn a dime in the black on the books. Gonifs!"

"Actually, we're just in negotiation right now."

"Yeah, well, watch your fucking balls, 'cause he'll slice 'em right off and then try and sell 'em back to you less fifteen percent. You can take that to the bank and tell 'em Mickey Marvin sent you." He tapped his cigar ash on the carpet and smeared it with his toe. Nice.

"You talking about Aldus?" I asked. What the hell, it worked once.

"Who?"

"Mr. Aldus."

"Fucking hell!" Mickey Marvin barked. "I'm talking about the Ripper. What are you, goofy?"

"The Ripper?"

"The Ripper! Jack 'the Ripper' Rippen. What are there? Two Rippers in this town?"

"Jack Rippen?" I said, stunned. "Are you telling me that Jack Rippen runs Laughing Boy?"

The little man had started to finger his foul cigar, but stopped and stared at me. The stogie drooped off his wet lower lip, Bogart style, as he took me in.

"Mickey Marvin don't suffer fools," he said, and turned the other way. I punched the elevator button, and though it took a minute for a car to come, Mickey Marvin didn't look my way again. Watching the little man puff away on his cigar while he stood alone in the hall, I guessed that, in fact, Mickey Marvin probably suffered quite a lot.

The information guy in the lobby was talking to someone as I came off the elevator, so I went on out into the courtyard and sat by the fountain. A group of secretaries stood just outside the front door, hurriedly smoking cigarettes and exchanging laughter as they nervously looked back and forth at their watches. I waited for the nicotine exiles to finish and go back inside, then checked that the lobby was again clear before returning to the information desk. The old man watched me and licked his lips as I approached, perhaps anticipating what I had to say.

"Find your way?" he asked.

"More or less. You were right about the temperature up there." He smiled but didn't say anything. "I thought maybe you might hear things now and again."

"Ain't nothing wrong with my ears," he said. He stuck his pinky in his right ear to clean it out, as if to demonstrate.

"Maybe you could give me a call if you should hear anything about Celestial Dog," I said, and slid a fifty across the counter along with a scrap of paper with my phone number. David Copperfield couldn't have made it disappear any quicker.

"Maybe," he said.

I nodded at the counter where the money had briefly lain. "There'll be more on the other end if it's anything at all."

"I surely will remember that."

Just then the elevator doors whooshed open and Mickey Marvin came walking out. He glanced over our way, snorting when he saw me.

He tossed his cigar butt on the floor and strode out in something like a huff.

"Goddamn," the information guy said. "Who's he think got to clean that up?"

"My guess," I said, "is that Mickey Marvin just don't care."

Six

The air conditioner sputtered when I got back into the car, but I was still so cold from being in the Laughing Boy building that I managed to survive the ride back down to Hollywood. Besides, I had a lot to think about.

It was clear that Celestial Dog was being run on the sly out of Laughing Boy Pictures. Probably held through one or more dummy corporations, but that all could be checked out. I didn't know how Long John ever made the connection between Celestial Dog and Laughing Boy, but I'd be willing to bet that he wasn't supposed to know and that someone had screwed up, but good. Laughing Boy's offices were way too swank for any kind of fuck-film outfit.

And then there was the Jack Rippen connection. My buddy Mickey Marvin—and based on his personality, I guessed he was either a low-rent agent or low-rent talent manager; the only thing I was certain about was the low-rent part—seemed awfully sure that Rippen ran Laughing Boy, and though I'd have to check that out, too, there was no real reason to doubt him. Rippen Entertainment had gobbled up dozens of small and not-so-small film, record, and publishing companies over the last ten years or so and become one of the major players in The Business. At one time or another Rippen had worked with everyone from Merchant-Ivory to Arnold Schwarzenegger, and Rippen Entertainment had been on an incredible roll for years. Whether it was Rippen's doing or not—and no one in Hollywood is ever willing to attribute other people's success to anything but the dumbest of luck—his company always seemed to be in the right place at the right time with the hot product. In fact, I thought I recalled reading that Rippen had recently sold out to one of the really big boys in one of those billions-with-a-B deals that seem to go down every other week.

Rippen himself had started out as a smarmy, hyperactive personal manager and made himself into the archetypical Hollywood baby mogul. Along the way he picked up the nickname "the Ripper," though no one dared use it to his face these days. *The Reporter* and *Variety* could still get away with calling him Ripper in pieces that weren't bylined, but no one who wanted to continue to eat lunch in town had the temerity to remind Rippen of how he got where he was. Part of his transformation from creep to mogul involved a re-creation of his personality. Or of his image anyway. The Ripper was replaced by Mr. Benefit, who feted any cause that got his puss in the pages of the *L.A. Times.* From saving Santa Monica Bay to teddy bears for African orphans, Jack Rippen was always there with a check, a smile, and a photog.

The funny thing is that I actually knew Rippen from the old days, though I couldn't imagine that he'd remember me. He was just coming up as a personal rep, and was still known by his real name of J.J. Ripowitz, when my star started to sputter. He represented a gaggle of pneumatic starlets back when that term was still politically correct. I remember him as nervous and fluttery, all jerky hand movements and eye blinks, thin and jumpy as a speed freak. I met him after *Salt & Pepper* bit the big one, but when I still had enough residual heat that CBS planned to build another series around me. We were casting—that's the Hollywood *we,* by the way, meaning I sat there and ogled tits while an associate producer did all the work—and Rippen née Ripowitz was pushing some kid for the part. I can't remember the starlet's name, but I do remember that Rippen's management technique consisted of pimping the girl around to anyone who might do her—or more accurately, *him*—some good. I remember that the girl was maybe seventeen, and I quickly marked Rippen as among the more repulsive of Hollywood bottom feeders.

I'm also pretty sure I balled the girl once or twice. I *know* she didn't get the part.

Fortunes sure enough change in Hollywood, but personality is another story. Rippen soared from the bottom to the top while my career took the tumble, but here I was involved with pimps and whores, and Rippen's name turned up again. Of course, Rippen ran a billion-dollar company with subsidiaries up the wazoo. Chances were he didn't even know he owned Laughing Boy, much less Celestial Dog. It wouldn't take much to run a little porno operation out of a big production house, especially if all the product got sent abroad. Rippen would have to be nuts to allow an operation like that to take place. If it ever got out, his picture would make the paper, but not in the way he liked it. He had way too much to lose to be that dumb, didn't he?

Still, fortunes may change in this business. But personalities . . .

I decided to head for the offices of the Screen Actor's Guild in Hollywood. I stopped first at The Cat and Fiddle on Sunset for a late lunch and opted for the shepherd's pie along with a couple of pints of Bass Ale. Los Angeles may be the world's worst city for people-watching, ironic given the effort Angelinos put into being seen, but there are a few places where it's fun: Melrose for the fakes, Venice for the freaks, and Hollywood for the fucks. The Cat and Fiddle is ostensibly a British-style pub, but based on a strictly movieland dream of jolly olde England. The food's not bad, though, and the beer is cold—so you know it's not really British—and the crowd that sits in the courtyard, lots of heavy-metal-hair types, are a hoot to behold. I debated ordering a third pint of ale, but the afternoon was moving right along. I couldn't find a parking spot near SAG headquarters and had to walk half a dozen blocks to the building: L.A. apostasy!

I worked up a good sweat making the trek and luxuriated for a moment in the blissful cool of SAG's air-conditioning. I went over to the front desk and told the receptionist I was seeking information about the credentials of a production company that had offered me a job. The receptionist was a bloated little queen with a bad tuck job. He asked to see my union card, which has a twenty-year-old picture. He looked dubiously between the photo on the card and my current face, then ran my name by his computer. Fortunately, I've continued to pay my dues all these years, though I've never been sure why. Once in The Business, always in, I suppose. I belong to the motion picture academy, too. I'm one of the miserable fucks responsible for the crappy nominees who win the Oscars every year. The academy is full of old farts like me who can't bear to vote for anyone successful who's younger than they are.

The receptionist grunted with surprise when his database spat up an approving response, and he directed me to an office on the second floor. I had to wait for the elevator, but felt like I'd already done more than my share of walking for a single day, and besides, I had to pace myself for the hike back to the car. I took a wrong turn off the elevator, but wandered around till I found the right office.

The door was open, so I rapped lightly on it and stuck my head inside. A young woman—Christ, she looked like a high school cheer-leader—was typing away in front of a monitor, with a telephone wedged between her ear and shoulder. She had short, dirty-blond hair cut into a wedge, with something that could only be described as a spoiler in the back. She kind of bounced as she typed and she looked perky as hell. A tiny name plaque on the desk identified her as B. Arthur. She half-glanced my way and waved me in, continuing to talk on the phone.

I sat down across from her desk and studied the office while she finished her business. A couple of dozen framed stills haphazardly graced the beige walls. They were all studio publicity shots from the thirties and forties: Carole Lombard, Lupe Velez, Thelma Todd, Virginia Hill. A whole bunch more I didn't recognize, but beauties all, captured in their youthful, forever-radiant glamour.

"Wow!" the young woman said. She looked me up and down as she hung up the phone.

"Huh?"

"Marty Burns! Holy moly!" A broad smile stretched across her pretty face. I decided maybe she was a *college* junior.

"Yeah. Have we met?"

"Oh, no. But jeez, I'd know you anywhere. I just love *Salt and Pep-per.*"

"Nickelodeon, huh?" I said. No way she had been born when the show originally aired.

"Uh-huh. I've got every episode on tape. Indexed and cross-referenced."

"No kidding," I said. "Why?"

"Oh, it's brilliant. I mean, people go on and on about Paul Henning and Sherwood Schwartz and Norman Lear, but Manny Stiles? If you ask me, he is *the* unsung genius of the sixties sitcom. *Beverly Hillbillies* and *Gilligan's Island* are okay and all, but they don't belong on the same set with *Salt and Pepper* or *Doggs and Katz.*"

"You ever meet Manny?" I asked her. The mere mention of Stiles's name set off an involuntary tic in my cheek. He'd created and produced *Salt & Pepper* (regarding *Doggs & Katz,* one can say two words only: Doodles Weaver), and he made Jack Rippen look like Joan of Arc. When I was sixteen he offered me my own series if I'd moo like a cow and crap on his willy. "You ever meet anybody who *met* Manny?"

"Alas, no," she said with a sigh. "I would have loved to interview him for my dissertation, but unfortunately he died."

I'd never heard anyone actually use the word "alas" in simple conversation, and prudently decided to let the "unfortunately" pass without comment. "Dissertation?" I asked, eyebrows arching, still suppressing the tic. "You mean like in Ph.D.?"

"Uh-huh. From the Annenberg School at U.S.C. In communications. The title was *Real Estates, Fantasy Islands: The American Situation Comedy, 1951–1981.* Duke University Press is maybe going to publish it next year. Pretty good, huh?"

"Congratulations," I said. "So you're *Dr.* Arthur?"

She looked puzzled for a moment, then tapped the name plaque and smiled. "Doctor, yes. Arthur, no. My name's Kendall. Kendall Arlo."

She stuck out her hand, so I shook it, though it felt a little silly at that point. "So who's B. Arthur?"

"Well, she's best known as the star of *Maude,* which was actually a spin-off from *All in the Family.* In *The Golden Girls*—"

"No, I mean . . ." And I pointed at the plaque on her desk. She shrugged mysteriously. She smiled, and though she continued to examine me almost dreamily, it made me feel like something stuffed and musty in a glass museum case. *Sitcom Man* or something equally Pliocene. "Umm, they told me downstairs that you could maybe help me with some information I need."

"Oh, hey! That's my job. Anything I can do for Sandy Salt would be a pleasure."

I cringed a little and she must have noticed, because her light skin blushed pink. I smiled at her to put the matter aside. "I'm looking for any information you might have about a small film company called Celestial Dog Productions."

"What kind of information?" she asked. She suddenly looked a lot more serious.

"Anything, really. You know, are they legit? Any grievances on file? Any problems? Hell, I'd settle for some gossip."

The young woman leaned back in her chair and bent her elbows back behind her, arching her chest and staring at the ceiling. From anyone else the gesture would have been provocative, but from her it seemed entirely innocent and unconscious. She hunched forward and leaned over the desk, looking very serious.

"Can I ask you a question, Marty?"

"Sure," I said, leaning in closer.

"Were they thinking of adding you as a regular after you did that guest shot on *Room 222*?"

I leaned back and sighed. "Yeah," I said blankly, "but my agent couldn't come to terms."

Arlo nodded thoughtfully. I started to get up when she said: "Stay away from Celestial Dog."

I sat back down and saw she looked nervous. "Why? What do you know?"

"They're bad news, Marty. Celestial Dog isn't going to get you back into The Business."

"Why do you say that? They seem to have some real money."

Arlo crossed her arms over her chest and shook her head. "Just trust me here. There's nothing on file about them, not even a listing, but I hear things, you know? Nothing that could be proved, nothing I would say on the record, but . . ."

"It's okay," I prompted, "this conversation never happened." She still hesitated. "Please. I need to know."

"Hardly anybody would even have heard of them. But I, you know, I make it my business."

"And?"

"And they're maybe into some ugly stuff. They shoot commercials for overseas markets, mostly Pacific Rim, I think. There's a big call for commercials with American faces and bodies. The Japanese, especially, are into American cheesecake and beefcake. They really love American celebrities—people do commercials there who wouldn't dream of doing them here—but there's work even for nobodies, assuming those bodies have the right shape."

She paused and I nodded, encouraging her.

"Word is," she went on, "that they shoot some other stuff, too. Maybe even with the same actors. It's . . . well, it's not the kind of thing I imagine Sandy Salt would want to be a part of."

"Porno," I said. She nodded and lowered her voice.

"I knew someone at U.S.C. A guy on the production side in the film school. He was hitting on me one time at a party and bragged about some freelance work he got with a company called Celestial Dog. Like he was gonna get into my pants because he was directing pornography. He was a little drunk and told me the gory details. It sounded pretty nasty. I saw him a couple days after and he told me to forget about what he said. That it was all bullshit. But I got the feeling he was worried about telling secrets out of school, you know? He's got a three-picture deal with Disney now."

"Any idea who runs Celestial Dog?"

She vigorously shook her head. "No idea. I really only know that much 'cause of this guy from film school. But if they're incorporated, there'll be some paperwork on file with the county."

"What can you tell me about Laughing Boy Pictures?"

Arlo did a genuine take at me, then held her head between her hands. "What?" I asked.

"You trying to give me whiplash or something?"

"What do you mean?"

"It's just that you couldn't ask about something more different than Celestial Dog. Laughing Boy is a Jack Rippen outfit. Very fru-fru."

"And what exactly does that mean?"

"Just that it's Rippen's personal baby. Laughing Boy's not much more than a name, but Rippen uses it to develop the projects that are nearest and dearest to his heart." She lowered her voice again. "I mean, if he actually has a heart. Anyway, it's more than just another subsidiary of Rippen Entertainment. Rippen keeps a pretty active hand in Laughing Boy. In fact, rumor is that one of the terms of the buyout deal on Rippen Entertainment is that Rippen keeps complete control over Laughing Boy."

"Who bought Rippen out?" I asked.

"The Japanese, of course. Yoshitoshi International. One of the real monsters. It's not actually a done deal yet, but good as. Or so they say. There's some government approval still to come, but they'll rubber-stamp it through. Rippen's supposed to get a cool billion out of the deal."

"Huh!" I said.

" 'Huh' what? Does Laughing Boy have something to do with Celestial Dog?"

"No," I said, perhaps a little too quickly. I smiled. "I'm just considering all my options."

"Listen, Marty. If you've got a shot at something with Laughing Boy, go for it. Go for it as hard as you run away from Celestial Dog. I mean, if you're looking for a break someplace, it couldn't get any bigger than Laughing Boy."

"No, I don't think I'll be acting again anytime soon."

"If there's anything I can do," she said. I looked over at her with some surprise. "I know some people who I'm sure would be thrilled to, you know, throw some work your way. I'd really be happy to help."

She looked so goddamn sincere that I couldn't help but be flattered. "It's okay." I smiled. "But I appreciate the thought." She blushed again and looked away. "And I appreciate your time."

She shook her head to say it was nothing. I shook her hand and started to leave when I thought of something else.

"Hey. Do you have any idea why they're called Celestial Dog?"

"No," she said. "I remember asking my, ummm, 'friend,' but he didn't know. It's a name that sticks with you, though, isn't it?"

"It is indeed. Well, thanks again."

"Any time."

I again started to leave, but got stopped by one of the photos on the wall: a particularly affecting still of a pouting Veronica Lake at her peek-aboo best. Something about the pictures had been bothering me from the first, and it suddenly dawned on me what it was.

"These stills," I said, pointing. "They're all of them actresses who came to bad ends. Suicides, accidents, busted careers."

Arlo nodded at me and smiled sweetly. "I call it the wall of tears."

"Why would you want to look at this every day?"

"It's a reminder," she said. "Whenever I get too exuberant or gung ho about The Business, or think I've got the world by the tail, I look up that their faces. At all that beauty and talent and what it meant in the end. They remind me what that's all really worth in this town. What's really valued. It helps keep my feet on the ground, you know?"

I nodded. "That's why you have the Ph.D. and not me," I said.

It was almost five o'clock when I came out of the SAG building. As I walked back to my car I passed a cozy little tavern with a big HAPPY HOUR sign in the front window. The Santa Ana was still gusting and I felt a tad parched after all that talking, so I dropped in for a quick beer. It was cool and quiet inside and the Dodgers were on the big screen, so I stayed for half a dozen drafts and a couple of tiny shots of Jack. I watched the game and in between innings mused some on the pretty faces and perky breasts of young women who felt pity for old actors. There did seem to be a lot of them. *Too* goddamn many, if you ask me. By the time I found my way back to the car, the sun had set, the winds had waned, and under the influence of beer and bourbon, all was well with the world.

I buckled myself in—I'm nothing if not a *safe* drunk driver—and headed back toward my place in Silver Lake. I took Melrose east just for the hell of it and slowed, for no good reason, as I cruised past Johnny Rockets. There must have been about a dozen polished Harleys parked out in front, but the bikers draped around them were all fakes. They'd never allow a real biker scene to flourish amidst the trendoid capitalism of the Melrose district.

I took a left on La Brea and then a right down Santa Monica. I slowed again as I drove past Night Haven. I could see lights on inside, but the blinds were drawn and there was no activity out on the street. I sighed as I thought about Rosa Mendez, and decided that maybe I was attracted to the brainy type after all.

I spotted the car as soon as I turned up my block. I could have hung a U-turn or zipped right past them—it was dark enough that they wouldn't have noticed me—but I didn't see the point. I did turn around before I parked, so I wouldn't get stuck with a street-cleaning ticket the next morning. I didn't even bother to walk towards my front door. Rowan and Holloway took their time getting out of their unmarked car and met me in the middle of the street.

"Officers," I said.

"We've been sitting here for three goddamn hours!" Holloway complained.

"Well, you should have made an appointment," I told him. "What are you doing here anyway?"

"Found us another body," Rowan said. There was no trace of friendliness in his voice.

"That's pretty much your stock-in-trade, isn't it?"

"Yup. Yup," Rowan said. "But this one had your address and phone number in his pocket."

"Uh-oh," I said.

"On a little piece of paper with the number ten thousand circled in red just below it."

"With a dollar sign in front," Holloway added.

"And there's more."

I looked at Rowan. He stood with his hands on his hips, under his suit jacket. His shirt was drenched with perspiration, but his tie was firmly knotted at his collar. Holloway wasn't wearing his coat, and his tie was pulled loose, his top two shirt buttons open.

"Who is it?" I capitulated. Cops love these games.

"He had this on him." Rowan handed me a photograph. It was Long

John and Jenny camping it up for the camera in one of those stupid photo booths. Long John had pulled Jenny's shirt up and she was aiming a luscious tit at the lens. She had her eyes closed and stuck her tongue out, but there was no mistaking who it was.

"What happened to him?"

"Nothing much." Holloway grinned. "Someone pulled his liver out through his asshole is all. I didn't even know you could do that."

"Very creative," Rowan concurred.

"Fuck," I said.

"Maybe you want to read the man his rights," Rowan told his partner.

"What's the charge?" I demanded.

"Withholding evidence. Obstruction. Maybe more. We'll decide after we all have a little chat back at the station. This is just to be safe."

Holloway mumbled the Miranda at me as he slipped on the handcuffs. I nodded and mumbled back when he asked me if I understood my rights.

They escorted me back to their car, and Holloway opened up the back door. As he pushed me down onto the seat his eyes lit up.

"Hey!" he said. "I looked up that Leonard Whiting guy."

"What?" I asked.

"You know, the guy what won the Golden Globe with you."

"Oh, right."

"He won it for *Romeo and Juliet*. I never saw it's why I didn't know his name. Can't stand Zeffirelli."

"I thought he won it for *Bonnie and Clyde*," I said, but I was thinking about lawyers I might call.

"No, it was definitely *Romeo and Juliet*." Holloway nodded.

"Huh," was all I could think to say.

"Course," Holloway said, scratching his cheek, "they're pretty much the same fucking story when you come right down to it."

I didn't argue the point. I never much liked either film.

Seven

At least the cops let me use the toilet this time.

Actually, that just made it seem serious and all the more scary. The whole night was played strictly by the book, and though Holloway occasionally tried to pry the dark secrets of aging Hollywood starlets out of me—like I really know whether Sally Field wore panties under her flying nun get-up—Rowan was all business. They didn't actually book me when we got to the station, but Rowan did tell me I could call a lawyer if I wanted. I said no, deciding to play it by ear for the time being and tell them what I knew. Other than neglecting to mention Long John's name during the last interrogation, I couldn't see where I had significantly stepped outside the law. I hadn't actually lied and was probably covered on refusing to reveal the name of my client. I didn't see the DA's office really pushing an obstruction or withholding-evidence charge against me for what amounted to unsworn, voluntary testimony anyway.

Rowan and Holloway gave me a couple of hours by myself in the interrogation room to think things over before they trooped in with a tape recorder. Rowan bitched about not being able to find a stenographer after five o'clock and fumbled with the cassette for a while, reciting "one-two-three-testings" before getting the machine to work. The interrogation was straightforward—no funny stuff, no good cop/bad cop foolishness—and I answered their questions as simply and honestly as I could. I told them everything that had happened, from my first delightful meeting with Long John in the bar to my conversations with Sid Teitlebaum and Rosa Mendez, right on up to when they picked me up again.

Well, I told them *almost* everything.

I didn't mention the ten thousand in cash Long John bribed me with to stay on the case, and I didn't say anything about either Celestial Dog or Laughing Boy. As to the cash, I figured there was no reason to put on my permanent record anything that could later be used against me by the tax man. And Celestial Dog? I kept close to the truth, telling the cops

I'd spent a day looking for a fuck-film outfit that the dead hooker had supposedly worked for. I made up a name and told them I couldn't track it down. I wasn't sure why I didn't mention Celestial Dog. A certain piqued interest and unease about what was going on there that I'd garnered during my visit, perhaps; an unease that had been further exacerbated by my conversation with Kendall Arlo. Something about Laughing Boy and Jack Rippen that I'd been chewing on like old gum, or had been chewing on me, that I wasn't ready to spit out yet.

Or just old-fashioned muleheadedness, maybe.

The two detectives poked and prodded at parts of my explanation—they had a hard time believing that I felt sorry for Long John; who could blame them?—but they more or less seemed to buy what I had to say. Rowan didn't look very happy about it, but I knew that he knew there was nothing he could do. He stared at me for a while after they seemed to run out of questions. His mud-brown eyes were tiny but bright, and his five-o'clock shadow had long since stretched into night. Holloway, beside him, was breathing loudly through his nose. Deviated septum, I made it.

"And the ten thousand?" Rowan suddenly asked.

"What ten thousand?" I said, clearing my throat.

"The ten thousand the pimp scrawled in red next to your name. When did he give it to you?"

I shrugged and tried to meet Rowan's gaze. It was much easier to look at Holloway. "Long John talked about some big money, but it was supposed to be waiting on the other end."

"End of what?"

I shrugged and tried to look nonchalant, but Rowan could tell I was lying. He smiled dully at me while Holloway shook his head ever so slightly from side to side. I saw that the question about the money had been a test and I'd failed. Or passed. Confirmed Rowan's judgment of me, anyway, and probably discounted most of my story in his eyes. I knew that there'd be no slack left for me in any future dealings with the detective, and decided then and there that no such dealings could be in order.

Was I supposed to give up the ten large?

They gave me the fishbowl treatment for a few more minutes, staring at me in silence until the tape ran out and the machine clicked itself off. Holloway popped the cassette out and dropped it into an envelope. He scribbled my name on the label and glanced at his watch. It must have stopped, 'cause he grabbed his partner's wrist and read the time off Rowan's cheap digital watch.

"Okay," Rowan said. "Don't *ever* let me see your face again." He got up without another word. And that was it. Holloway looked at me for a few seconds longer, then got up himself, gesturing for me to follow.

"Don fucking Siegel," he muttered, shaking his head and his stopped watch. The way he said it made me feel like I'd been excommunicated.

They hadn't bothered to print me, but they did take my stuff before sitting me down in interrogation. I had to sign to get it back from the desk sergeant. I was checking to see how much cash had been lifted from my wallet when I heard my name called.

Sid Teitlebaum charged across the lobby at me. "C'mere," he said, grabbing me by the elbow and pulling me off down a hall. He threw open an office door, glanced inside, then tugged me in after him.

"What the hell are you doing?" he spat.

"Christ, Sid, it's"—I glanced at my watch—"it's three-thirty in the goddamn morning and I'm all done in. And then some. What are you doing here, anyway?"

"Hooker sweep," he said. "Never mind. What the fuck were you doing working for that piece of shit Long John? Where do you get off coming to me for help with that kind of shit? Fucking pimp scumbag. I vouched for you, motherfucker, and you burned me."

Sid was still clutching my arm. Hard. I squirmed out of his grasp and plopped down on an empty desk. Sid continued to glare daggers at me.

"Fuck," I said.

"Is that your explanation?"

I took a long, deep breath and exhaled. I tried to put on a pathetic face, but Sid wasn't in the mood for it. "Look, I'm sorry about that. That I didn't tell you who I was working for. I . . . I didn't think, to tell you the truth. I didn't think this was what it was, what it would turn out to be, and I didn't think about . . . using you."

Sid shook his head, but looked no less angry. "Jesus, Marty! Is that all you have to say? You didn't think? You telling me you didn't know who you were dealing with here? That if you look up 'scumbag' in the dictionary, you find two pictures of Long John? Front and profile? I have a hard time buying that from you. If I need stupid, I've got Straczynski.

It leaves me wondering what else you aren't saying. What else you aren't telling me here."

"Long John . . . told me a story, okay? It . . . I believed him. I think I still do, actually. I thought he was looking for something that he'd lost. And not just a good whore. Crazy, huh?"

Some of the anger had drained from Sid's features. His eyes narrowed in puzzlement. "What the hell are you talking about, Marty?"

"I'm too tired, Sid. If you want, Holloway and Rowan have it all on tape. Hell, you can probably get them to make a copy for Straczynski for his birthday. I'll even autograph it: 'from one asshole to another.' "

"NG," he said, shaking his head. "Tell me!"

"I know it's hard to believe," I said with a sigh, "but I thought I was doing something . . . worthwhile. I mean, I did it for the money, I ain't gonna lie about that, but it seemed like there was something more, too." I felt like a fool saying it out loud. "I thought he really loved this girl and that maybe I could save her for him. Like I could maybe give them a chance. I . . . I tried to believe in it. Sounds pretty stupid now. Even to me. I don't know, I guess you had to be there."

Even the puzzlement was gone from the cop's face now. What was left was either disbelief or raw pity. I prefer to believe the former, but that may be wishful thinking.

"Get off the street, Marty," Sid said. His voice was soft and cold. "And stay there. Go flip burgers or sell insurance or used cars. Anything. Hell, go back to acting. 'Cause you surely must be living in some world of make-believe. Just stay off the fucking street and keep out of my face."

I wanted to say something to him, but for the life of me, I couldn't find the words. I thought he might even be right. Sid opened the door and started out toward the hall. He stopped in the doorway and let the doorknob hit him in the back. He didn't turn around but over his shoulder said: "You can still send me a Chanukah card if you want."

Then he was gone.

I sat there for a while, staring at the dirty floor. I'd always liked Sid, thought of him as a friend. I doubted he'd ever feel quite the same way about me again. I cursed Long John and Joey the Jar and all the pimps and hookers and lowlifes who made my existence the joyful thing it was.

"Fuck," I said, cursing myself most of all.

I slunk back down the hall toward the pay phones in the lobby. I'd have to call a cab to get back home.

I never saw the punch coming.

"You cocksucking bastard!"

"Whuh?" I groaned.

Rosa Mendez glared gleaming steel scimitars at me, her lips drawn back over her perfect teeth, her pretty face flushed a shade between umber and livid. Her manicured fingers were curled in a tight fist, and she drew back her arm to deliver a knockout jab to follow the upper cut. I took—stumbled, really—two quick steps away from her and pressed the back of my hand to my nose. It came away bloody. A couple of uniforms looked on in amusement, but neither of them made any move to intervene.

"You lying sack of dog shit!" Rosa screamed. "You walking piece of vomit! You used me. While you were working for that killer pimp bastard you used me *and* my girls. I'd like to rip your fucking heart out and piss on it. If you even have one, you dickless cocksucker."

She was still winding up to deliver the coup de grâce. I glanced over toward the cops, but they just continued to laugh. I reckoned they were waiting for the knockout punch.

"Rosa," I said.

"Don't you dare say my name," she warned, and poked me in the chest with her fist. Hard. "Every word is just garbage in your mouth. You stay away from Night Haven and stay the hell away from my girls. If I hear you go anywhere near one of them, I *will* have your tiny balls, shithead. I know people who'd do it for laughs. You keep your fucking distance."

She poked me again, pushing me back another step. She raised her hand, open palm, as if to slap me, then thought better of it. She looked me up and down, top to bottom, then spit on my shoes and stormed off. The cops looked at me, shaking their heads.

"Nine point three," the first one said.

"You're too easy," his partner chided. "Eight-nine, tops."

"She drew blood," the first offered.

"Yeah, but the nose ain't broke. And no follow-through. She didn't kick him in the nuts."

"Point," the first one said, and they walked off.

I leaned back against the wall and slid to the floor. I touched my nose, which felt a little raw, but the cop was right: the blood had more or less stopped flowing.

I felt about as low as I could remember feeling since I'd given up acting. First Sid, then Rosa. Not to mention the murders. The pisser was,

I couldn't blame either one of them. I wished I could have blamed Long John or his dead hooker or anyone else at all. But I'd brought everything down on myself. I knew what I was getting into when I agreed to work for the pimp; I just decided not to worry about it. I knew what I was doing when I hit Sid up for information, when I pumped Rosa.

I reckoned that I wouldn't be pumping her in any other manner anytime soon. And I'd have to find someone else to fantasize about for masturbation purposes.

I forced myself to get up and shuffled on out of the station house. I should have cleaned myself up a little, but I couldn't be bothered. I should have called a cab, but I didn't have the energy.

I walked for a while down the quiet streets. Eventually I caught an RTD bus with one other passenger. The driver didn't so much as blink at the bloodstains on my shirt. He just watched to see that I deposited the full fare, then closed the doors and drove on. He sang a wretched old Harry Nilson tune to himself as he went.

The saddest thing was, I knew all the words.

𝓘nvocation (II)

The contact is weak, the images so strange:

An alien landscape, populated by multitudes beyond counting, swarming like bugs. Their skins are pale, like the belly of a slug, their eyes round as stones from the sea. And big, so big, they seem, in size and manner. Big, like everything around them.

It is a city he takes in, but such a city! More expansive than kingdoms he has known, laid with an infinite crisscross of roads, smooth and hard and wider than the great rivers. Bold towers of crystal and steel sprout from the ground like planted swords. Machines dominate the earth and soar through the air—through the air, like demons!—and roar with the voice of a storm god.

How long has it been?

A long time, he kens. Long enough for a major turning. Long enough for the birth of another, a whole new world.

To see and explore.

To conquer and exploit.

To rule as his own.

The images wink in and out, flickering like candles in the wind with every strained effort to solidify the link. Each brief connection brings with it a drip of knowledge, a dollop of understanding. The alien becomes familiar as he picks scabs from the minds of his summoners. However much time may run ahead, he is reminded, little truly changes. The essence of human nature is constant: hunger, sex, domination.

Evil is eternal. And it, too, hungers.

The contact sputters, breaks.

Blackness returns.

A brilliant flash arcs through the darkness. He hears, distant at first but growing in strength, the worshipful voices of invocation and summoning. A new contact, the most solid yet. A surge of electricity crackles through him and he sees through new eyes, but they are not human. It is, he understands, too soon for that; the way must slowly be paved for his full return to human flesh. He will have to be patient.

He reaches out with his ancient mind and touches this other. Recognition sets in like a fondly remembered scent. The link has been established through one of the Lesser Ones: soulless and stupid, but loyal and with great physical strength. He immerses himself inside the creature at once, exulting in the almost forgotten sensation of corporeality. Muscles ripple beneath scaled limbs. Claws extend and rape the air. A forked tongue emerges from a lipless mouth to taste the chill of the night.

He reaches between his legs and is briefly disappointed to find only an unmarked expanse of leathery skin. The Lesser Ones are sexless, of course, and he spares a moment for regret. Still, there will be time for that later. A great deal of time. The indulgent pleasures of human flesh will have to wait, anticipation making realization that much the greater.

A ceremonial bowl with an offering of warm blood sits at his feet. He crouches and laps up the contents like a dog, batting away the empty vessel with his snout when he is done.

He wants, needs, must have more.

The voices of invocation continue to sing and echo around him and in his mind. The summoners—knowing the bloodlust that would be upon him—have wisely secluded themselves from the Lesser One, though their song continues.

But he is not alone in the chamber.

One of the pale ones has been chained to the top of a makeshift altar: a sacrifice. A female, young and cowlike and braying with fear. He raises his head and sniffs in its direction. He can smell its tasty sex—though it is not a virgin—and the blood that races beneath its white skin. He can hear its heartbeat. Above all he can smell its terror: his favorite fragrance.

With a thought he urges the Lesser One's massive body to the human's side and the smell grows richer, thicker. The sacrifice opens its mouth and screams, but it is like music to him. He runs a claw across the naked flesh of its belly. Blood bubbles up from the wound, the intoxicating scent inciting his desire. Forgetfully he again reaches down to grasp for an organ that isn't there, and laughs at his own folly. The noise that emerges from the Lesser One's deformed mouth is the sound of a rat being swallowed by a snake.

The music of the sacrifice's screams grows louder as he ferociously sucks blood from the skin he has rent. The improvised recital drives him on as he *tears the flesh off its bones with his spiked teeth, devouring his way toward the meaty organs within. Offal first—tripe, kidneys, liver—saving the heart as the symphony reaches its crescendo. Moving up, he sucks out an eye, swallows it whole, and digs a dirty talon deep into the emptied socket to scoop out a soupçon of gray.*

Before the body can cool, he returns to the hole in the belly, tearing further at the flayed skin until he exposes the ovaries. He rips the tiny organs out and pinches them between his claws, releasing an eggy paste which he smears over the exposed ribs. He licks the goo off like so much caviar, then cracks the ribs with his teeth to suck out the juicy marrow. Finally he removes the still heart, holding it above his head in a taloned hand. He squeezes the cold blood of the sacrifice into his waiting mouth and straight down his gullet, then tosses aside the drained muscle. He picks briefly at the bones, but there is nothing good left to savor.

A jolt of blackness suddenly shocks him. The summoners' chant begins to fade as the contact stutters. He feels himself pulling away from the body of the Lesser One as the creature's own animal-like soul retakes possession of its form. The creature slumps to the floor and spews up a steaming mess of blood and meat. His own appetite is far greater than that which even the demon can abide. It is an appetite that knows no bounds: he wants more, *and he longs to retain even this limited physicality.*

Nonetheless, even as the darkness returns and the connection fails, he feels stronger, more solid and substantial than before. Though reduced again to no more than a disembodied force, he can still taste the blood of the sacrifice, feel the weight of its devoured organs where he should—and will again— have a belly. For the briefest of moments, he can even sense arousal in an organ that is, for the time being, nothing more than a wisp of dream and desire.

As the last filament of the contact collapses, he knows his moment is still to come.

He can't wait.

Eight

The rest of the week slipped by like a pretty girl on a city sidewalk. I drank a bit—well, more than a bit, truth be known—and wallowed in a funk of admittedly undeserved self-pity for a couple of days. I couldn't even bring myself to go *out* and get drunk. I just sat around the apartment guzzling bourbon and beer, watching ball games, Court TV, and Oprah. I think I may have ordered a juicer at one point.

Or was it a Thigh Master?

I got a couple of calls from lowlife attorneys for the usual scut work, but turned it all down. I didn't especially feel like working, and what with Long John's ten thousand sitting in my fridge, I didn't really need to. I took the money out several times that week and spread it on the floor to stare at it. I knew I should feel guilty about having it, but looking at it just made me smile. *That* made me feel a little cheap—as in easily bought—but what the hell. I yam what I yam, as the sailor with the spinach used to say. In the end, I used the money to buy myself out of the funk.

There's no better cure for the blues than a wad of green.

I decided to assuage any latent guilt that might be lying in wait by sending off a thousand in cash to the Los Angeles AIDS Research Foundation in memory of Jake the Snake. They run a hospice in Hollywood and seemed an appropriate charity given the source of Long John's assets. I'd never given anyone a gift that big before, and I was surprised at how good it felt.

Then I spent a chunk of change on myself.

Which felt even better.

I took a drive over to the west side. I stopped in at Dutton's Books in Brentwood and dropped a sizable amount on some new hardcover fiction, then zipped back toward Westwood and bought myself a real treat at Vagabond Books: a signed first edition of W. P. Kinsella's *Shoeless Joe*. It's one of my favorite novels, but it's been obscenely overpriced ever since they filmed it as *Field of Dreams*. I've wanted a copy for a long time, and who knew if I'd ever have money to burn like this again.

From there I diddled around a couple of malls—hardly my native terrain—and bought just about anything that struck my fancy. I got myself a Speed Racer wristwatch in a place that sold official cartoon stuff and a Humphrey Bogart fedora in a place that supposedly didn't. I hadn't been on such a shopping spree since the salad days of *Salt & Pepper*, and it reminded me, oh yeah, how nice it was to have cash. That thought started to depress me again, but I headed it off with a quick tequila shooter and Corona chaser that only set me back eight and a half bucks in a Santa Monica sports bar. I suppose the maintenance costs on those felt Dodger pennants must be pretty high. I sure as hell didn't leave a tip.

The Santa Anas had blown themselves out during my in-house drinking bout, making way for a streak of cliché-perfect Southern California weather. I felt like taking a walk on the beach, but I can't bear the crowds of tourists at Santa Monica or Venice. I headed south on Lincoln, then detoured east to stop for lunch at Johnny's in Culver City. I had one of their jumbo, artery-hardening pastrami sandwiches with fries and a whole bucket of their wonderful pickles, sour as an old man and crisp as a fall day. I washed it all down with a pair of icy cold Millers and felt mighty fine as I got back in my shopping-bag-laden Subaru and drove west on Culver down to the ocean.

I parked along the beach at Playa Del Rey and strolled across the sand toward the man-made breakwaters that mark the edge of the marina. A couple of sleepy sunbathers shared the beach with a flock of dirty terns picking through the shells and Styrofoam cups along the shore. It looks pretty as hell (if you overlook the Styrofoam), but the water is too filthy to swim in. A half dozen fishermen, all either black or Mexican and most with families in tow, dotted the nearest jetty, trawling for God knows what in fierce competition with the diving gulls and pelicans. I know I wouldn't want to eat anything that survived those waters, though the pelicans seem healthy enough. Fishermen are always lined up along the breakwater, but in all the times I've walked there, I've yet to see anyone land a catch. Sometimes I wonder if they don't get paid by some civic group to stand there and look picturesque.

I took off my shoes and socks and followed the bicycle path south towards Dockweiler Beach. It's pretty nice, at least until dark when the drug dealers come out. Jets taking off from LAX roared just overhead, close enough to block out the sun intermittently. I sat down in the sand and watched the planes and the surf for a while, thinking that it had been a long time since I'd even been out of L.A., much less gone anyplace exotic. I'd made it over to Vegas a couple of times on business in the last year or so, but didn't even stay long enough to lose any money or catch Elvis on Ice. Back when I was rolling in *Salt & Pepper* money, I'd sometimes grab a bunch of friends and cling-ons and fly them to Europe on a whim. We'd go to Amsterdam for the drugs or Nice for the topless beaches and party like the animals that we were. Watching an Air France jumbo jet scream by above me, I thought maybe I'd use some of Long John's dough for an overseas romp. Maybe a titty beach at Cannes for old times' sake.

Did I still own a passport?

Realizing that I had to head back if I wanted to avoid the afternoon rush hour, I started walking toward my car. I saw a crowd milling about near a set of basketball courts in a little park just across from the beach. Always easily entertained, especially by some good two-on-two, I drifted over that way until I saw the trucks and trailers parked along a side street. By the time I approached the court, I was not at all surprised to see a film crew scurrying around, tearing up the park grass beneath their dolly tracks and heavy equipment. The crowd seemed to be abuzz and broke out into applause as I got close enough to see who was on the court.

A pair of well-proportioned, shirtless young men waved at the crowd as they whispered in each other's ear. They seemed to be sizing up a group of scantily attired teenaged girls who watched them with visible awe. A bronzed blonde in a tube top and shorts stood just behind the pair, arms framing her silicone tits, a sour pout on her puss. I didn't recognize any of the actors, but I seemed to be alone in that regard. A couple of the crew members wore Fox Network T-shirts, which explained why they were mysteries to me. As near as I could tell, you had to be under twenty-one to have a clue about any show on Fox.

I walked away from the basketball court as quickly as I could, leaving with it much of the lingering pleasantness of my day. I didn't glance back, but I couldn't get out of my mind's eye the looks on the faces of those admiring young girls. I envisioned them going down on the two actors after the shoot and thanking them for the chance to swallow their cum.

Once upon a time it had happened to me.

Am I bitter? Damn straight I am. And why not? That old saying that it's better to have loved and lost is the biggest crock of all time, no doubt coined by someone who still had everything. It's much worse to have possessed something—something wondrous—that you know you can never have again than to have never known the pleasure at all. There's another saying that has it much closer to right: Ignorance is bliss.

I could hear the crowd applauding again in the background as I got to my car. Thankfully it was drowned out by the roar of another departing plane. I looked up at it and glumly knew I wouldn't be visiting the south of France anytime soon.

I hit the road instead.

The San Diego Freeway was a parking lot, and the car's AC was acting wonky again. I cranked down the windows and tried to distract myself with some talk radio—when exactly did the brown shirts take over this country?—but it was nothing doing. The sight of that film crew set me thinking again about Celestial Dog and Laughing Boy. I didn't *want* to think about it, any of it, but like the song goes, we can't always get what we want. But does that *really* mean that we get what we need?

It nagged at me that Celestial Dog might be connected with Jack Rippen. What possible motivation could a man in his position have to hold on to an operation that was clearly known to be shady? The fuck-film business was good—though not what it used to be—but hardly good enough to interest a man with a billion-dollar bank account. Especially since any public tie to such an operation would kill his reputation in town. But then even my friend Kendall at SAG who knew about Celestial Dog—and she seemed to know virtually everything that happened in The Business—had no idea there was a link between Celestial Dog and Laughing Boy. The old black guy who worked the lobby at Laughing Boy knew, but pretty much by accident. And it was doubtful he knew anything more about Celestial Dog than its name.

So how in hell had Long John made the connection?

I had been trying to avoid thinking about the pimp. He was a sleaze-ball and a scumbag, everyone seemed to agree, but he was also my client. I'd never had a client murdered on me before. Truth be known, I'd never had the kind of client likely to *be* murdered. I took his money and now spent it freely enough, but did I have any lasting obligation to him? Rowan and Holloway—not to mention Sid Teitlebaum—had warned me in no uncertain terms to keep clear of anything that looked like it even smelled of something related to the two murders. I readily agreed at the time, but glancing now at my mint copy of *Shoeless Joe* on the passenger seat, I had some doubts.

I definitely got the impression that Long John's murder was going to be something less than top priority for the homicide boys. Holloway had more or less intimated that they believed that Long John had killed the girl and that someone associated with the girl, a former pimp maybe, had whacked him in return. Once they cleared me in their minds, and I believe that they did, there were no obvious suspects. Dead hooker. Dead pimp. Closed case.

I knew—well, I was pretty sure—that Long John hadn't killed the girl. Regardless of any scams he was running, including whatever it was he had going down with Celestial Dog, I think Long John really did care for her. Rowan and Holloway, even Sid, could sneer all they wanted, but I couldn't shake the belief that Long John loved her. That belief had drawn me into this mess to begin with, and I was still left with it here at the end of things. That is, if this was the end.

I thought I could hear *Shoeless Joe* whispering to me that I still owed Long John. Owed him not for the ten thousand, but for my belief in his love for the girl. My belief in something other than just making it through another day, another week, another scummy skip trace. I stuck the book in a bag and shoved it on the backseat, but I still heard the whisper.

I told it to shut up, turned up the radio, and got off the goddamn freeway.

I'd been home for about an hour before I noticed that the light was blinking on my answering machine. I usually know if there's a beer in the fridge, but I'm always forgetting to check phone messages. A consequence of being such a social leper, no doubt.

The only message that could have surprised me more would have been one from Long John himself.

"This is Rosa Mendez," Rosa Mendez said. Then a very long pause, as if a major decision was being made. "I'd like to talk to you." *Zowie,* I thought during another pause. "I'm on campus at U.C.L.A., in the University Research Library. It's a big building in the middle of campus. You can ask anyone where it is. I'll be working here all day in the reference reading room on the first floor. Please meet me here if you can. The library's open until ten tonight." A pause so long, I waited for the beep indicating the end of the message. Then: "It's important."

The call came in at two in the afternoon, almost three hours earlier. I played it back twice more, wondering what in the world it could be about. Maybe she'd been taking boxing lessons.

My first instinct was to hop in the car and head for the campus in Westwood. I pulled a beer out of the fridge to stop myself and take a little time to think. Did I really want any more involvement with Rosa or anything else connected with Long John and his hooker? Was it worth the risk of crossing the cops to wade any deeper into this disaster than I already had?

The beer was gone before I knew it. I whistled across the top of the empty bottle, making childish foghorn noises, and stared at the wall. I drummed my fingers against my thigh.

I thought about the cops and their warning to me. About Long John and his dead whore and what I owed them. About Celestial Dog and Laughing Boy and Jack Rippen.

About Rosa's long legs and high cheekbones.

I ran to the car and sped across town.

It cost me six bucks to park at U.C.L.A., and at that they stuck me in a lot clear across campus from the library. I got lost a couple times wandering around the university's lush grounds, but eventually found my way to the Research Library.

I'm always sort of awed by colleges. I never had the chance to go, being too busy working when I was college age. Though opinions differ, I like to think of myself as a fairly bright guy and I have a high school degree, but it's not worth the fake sheepskin it's printed on. I always had tutors on the set during the *Salt & Pepper* years, which, as any kid actor will tell you, is less than a joke. You'd go to a trailer to do a little history or algebra between takes, and likely as not, end up doing the tutor instead. Valuable lessons, to be sure, but nothing you could put on a transcript. It was for exactly that reason that the network tried hiring older women as tutors, except they were every bit as randy and ready as the young ones.

They usually knew more, too.

I like the feeling of walking into libraries, especially big ones. Maybe it's because I'm a book lover myself, but I just like the musty pulp smell and the reverent quiet. Of course, the lobby of the U.C.L.A. library looks more like the checkout stand at a Wal-Mart, but really it's the idea of the thing that matters.

I followed the signs to the reference section and snooped up and down the aisles for Rosa. Tiny carrels, like monks' cells, were secreted among the stacks, and I thought I spotted a likely turn of calf at one point, only to intrude on a pair of snogging freshmen. I walked through the reference room twice without finding her and thought maybe she'd gone home when I noticed a door leading to the microdocuments room. I checked inside and sure enough saw Rosa hunched over a whirring microfilm reader, her strong features aglow with the machine's reflected light.

I came up behind her and glanced at what she was reading on the screen. It was a feature article from an old issue of *The Los Angeles Times* about the porn industry in Southern California.

"Hey," I said.

She jumped about a foot.

"Jesus Christ!" she yelled, then looked around her and lowered her voice to a whisper. "What the hell's the matter with you?"

"Sorry," I said, but couldn't suppress a smile. "I got your message. What's up?"

The micro clerk, an old man with yellow, Yasser Arafat beard stubble, glowered at us from behind his desk. "Not here," Rosa said. "Give me a minute to finish up."

I nodded and pulled over a chair, straddling it backward. That seemed to earn me another dirty look from the PLO chief. Rosa wound the microfilm reel back and forth a bit and dropped a couple of quarters into the top of the machine. A few seconds later it spat out a dark and smudged reproduction of the newspaper page. She quickly copied several more pages, then rewound the reel and returned it to the counter. The old guy smiled at *her*. He had bad teeth.

Rosa came back and gathered her stuff, stashing it in a red knapsack and throwing it over her shoulder.

"Carry your books?" I offered.

She smiled sarcastically and shook her head. She walked out of the room without waiting to see if I'd follow. I did.

I caught up with her in the lobby. "There's a little cafeteria next door," she said, and started walking again. I shrugged and followed. We didn't say a word as we walked out of the building and across a courtyard to a small snack bar. The place was quiet, no more than half a dozen students, a couple of them sleeping, spread out around the dining room. They were all Asian. A staticky classic rock station—hah! don't get me started on that subject—played dimly in the background, accompanied by random blips, bleeps, and samples from a row of video games set along one wall.

Rosa got herself a cup of black coffee and a bran muffin. I trawled around for a beer, settled for a large Coke and a chocolate chip cookie. Rosa was already fishing through her knapsack at the register when I came up behind her.

"My treat," I said, paying with one of Long John's twenties. She put her bag away, but didn't say thank you.

She looked around the room and settled on a round table in the corner. There was no one else in that section. I sat down across from her, put my feet up on another chair, and took a bite out of my cookie. It was stale and had walnuts in it. I hate walnuts.

"I don't know about this," Rosa said. She had yet to meet my gaze fully.

"That pretty much makes two of us. Why don't you tell me what 'this' is."

She took a big slug of coffee and made a bitter face. I reckoned it wasn't any fresher than my cookie. I took a sip of Coke. It was flat.

"I'm worried about a couple of my girls," she said.

"I'll bet there's a lot to worry about. What specifically?"

She continued to stare down into her coffee. I could tell that she was clearly in conflict about talking to me, and I had the feeling that she might bolt from the table at any second. Still, *I* was the one who had schlepped clear across town to answer *her* call.

"Listen," I said, "I've got very few rules with regard to business. You've probably figured that out for yourself. But there's one rule I've religiously adhered to since my Hollywood days, and it seems to hold for any serious transaction."

"And what's that?" she asked, still divining from her coffee.

"Don't do business with someone who won't look you in the eye."

She didn't look up right away, but seemed to consider the gesture. When she did raise her eyes away from the coffee cup and looked into mine, I was taken slightly aback; for what I saw wasn't conflict or hesitation, but seething anger. Her full lips had gone thin and white from being pressed too tightly shut, and her jaw practically quivered with tension. She took deep, noisy breaths through her nose—not a very attractive sound, I have to say—and shredded the rim of the Styrofoam cup.

"Zowie," I said.

She exhaled loudly—through her mouth—then took a deep breath.

Some of the tension went out of her as she dropped the square of her shoulders.

"I don't know about this," she said again.

"Oy," I said. "Listen: I understand that you're pissed at me . . ."

"Ohhhh," she said, shaking her head, "I don't think you do."

"But you called me. You didn't have to. And, I might note, I didn't have to come." At least she was looking at me now. "But I'm here. I'm sorry that I misled you—" She snorted. "Okay, that I lied to you about working for Long John. I have an explanation, though I admit it's not a great one. And you already got a couple free shots at me the other day. So why don't we just leave all that in the past for the time being and you tell me why you're worried about your girls."

She ran her thumbnail along the edge of her lips as she sized me up. It was obviously an "I'm thinking" gesture, but I found it sexy as hell.

"A couple of them are missing," she said at last. She was visibly more relaxed having made the decision to talk. She picked at her muffin, tearing little chunks off the top and nibbling at them like a squirrel. A cute squirrel. *Stop that,* I told myself.

"That can't be too unusual," I said.

"No, it's not. But these two, Cheri and Sydney are their names—I know, I know—they're pretty together girls. And they're regulars at Night Haven. Every Wednesday night we do this big sort of potluck thing that's a cross between a party and group therapy. It's . . . well, it's a lot of fun. And Cheri and Syd never miss it. But they didn't show the other night."

"Doesn't sound like anything to panic about," I said.

"I wouldn't. But I haven't seen either of them around anyplace for the last week or so. They're a real team. Where one goes, the other follows."

I conjured visions of the two hookers working in tandem. Rosa must have guessed what I was thinking, because the anger flashed in her eyes again. I blushed and tried to look coy.

"Maybe they just moved on. Took a trip. Went to Disneyland."

"The girls do move around, but not unless they have to," Rosa said. "And definitely not without saying something to me. Just good-bye."

"Pimp trouble?" I asked.

Rosa shook her head. "No, they've been freelancing."

"That can be pretty dangerous, no? Maybe they stepped on somebody's toes."

"It's always possible, but I doubt it. Everybody knows which territory is marked. And these girls are pretty smart. And careful. Well, Syd is.

Cheri can get herself in some trouble, but Syd's usually on top of things."

That summoned another mental image, but I tried to ignore it. "I'm still not sure why you called me."

"I'm worried, you know, so I've been asking around. No one has seen either of them for about a week now. Like I say, the girls move in loose circles, but they don't wander too far. *Somebody* should have seen them."

"It's a big city," I said.

"Not for girls like this, it isn't. Trust me. And there's something else." She paused long enough to slip the last big chunk of muffin in her mouth. She chewed it carefully before swallowing. I'd wager she was a thorough brusher, too.

"Yeah?" I said.

"In asking around I heard that Cheri also used to hang around some with Long John's girl. The one you were looking for."

"Jenny," I said. A bad feeling crawled up my trouser leg.

"Yeah. I found this other girl who knew her. Jenny, that is. She said she thought that Jenny was doing some film work and that maybe Cheri was in on it, too. She said she didn't know who they were working for, though."

I didn't say a word, but visions of Celestial Dog danced through my brain.

"It just got me scared," Rosa said. "Not that the cops really give a damn, but I get the feeling they don't think Long John killed Jenny. I think it makes a tidy case for them, so that's what they're happy to call it. I'm worried that someone else killed her and that if Cheri and Syd were working with her for whoever, that they're caught up in it, too. I thought maybe you might have a handle on what the dead girl was doing. Who she was working for."

"That's why you're here doing research into the porn business?" I asked.

"Just trying to follow up some leads," she said. "Isn't that what detectives do?"

"You're not a detective."

She shrugged. "I know how to follow a paper trail. I've done plenty of research as a reporter."

"That's well and fine," I said, "except newspaper editors don't tear your liver out through your asshole when they don't like what you find."

"You've obviously never worked for the *Times,*" she said, and smiled. I didn't respond in kind.

"These are some very bad people," I told her. "They make Long John look like a choir boy."

"So you do know who Jenny was working for?"

"I didn't say that."

"Well, do you?"

I tried to maintain a noncommittal expression, but my antipoker face always trips me up.

"Tell me!" she demanded.

"I don't know precisely who she was working for, though I have some ideas," I told her. "I was just starting to follow up some leads when Long John got whacked. I gave it up when my client did, and the cops told me to keep my nose out of it."

"Do you think you would have found out?" Rosa asked. I shrugged and tried to look bored.

"Jesus!" she hissed. "You actually make a living doing this?"

"Not much of one."

We sat there in silence for a while, Rosa shaking her head, me playing with my cookie crumbs and jiggling the melting ice in my soda.

"I'll hire you," she finally said.

"What?"

"You need a client? I'll be your client. I want you to follow up the leads you were chasing."

"Listen, Rosa: I really don't need to get in Homicide's face any more than I already have. My ass—"

"Fuck that! You owe me, you son of a bitch. You took advantage of me and you used me and my girls. For all I know, Syd and Cheri are in trouble because of how I helped you . . ."

"I really don't see how that could be," I said.

"I do. I'm not asking you for any charity work here. I'll pay you your thirty pieces. I just want to know what's happening to my girls."

I covered my face with my hands and rubbed at my eyes. On the one hand, I really didn't want to get in the way of the cops, give Rowan and Holloway an excuse to go after me or pull my license. I had all the cash I'd need for a few months and no desire to stir up any hornets' nests. Especially those perched in the branches of the porn industry.

On the other hand, I couldn't deny that I was bothered and intrigued by the whole Celestial Dog/Laughing Boy connection. I was curious as hell about why Jack Rippen would be involved in any way with such nasty business. And truth be known, I did feel just the tiniest pang of guilt over what had happened to Long John. However creepy, he was a client who got iced while I was on his clock.

And then there was Rosa.

"Okay," I said, "but on one condition."

She turned her head and eyed me suspiciously. "Yeah?"

"No charge," I said. "I'll follow up a few things, see where it leads, if it does. And if it goes anyplace too nasty, we let it drop."

"You don't want any money," she said dubiously.

I shook my head. "Maybe I do owe you," I said.

Maybe I've got enough debts, I thought.

Nine

I got up bright and early the next morning—the very crack of nine-thirty—and set out to conduct some research of my own. I drove downtown, paid a small fortune to park, and walked over to the county clerk's office. Anybody doing business in Los Angeles under any name other than their own is obliged to file a fictitious business statement form, known as a DBA, with the clerk and fork over their eighty-six bits to the county. I had to fill in three blurry forms of my own and sit around on a wobbly plastic chair for about two hours, but finally the grumpy prole at the desk called my number and handed over a couple of pages of computer printout from the county record on Celestial Dog Productions and Laughing Boy Pictures.

The Laughing Boy information looked straightforward enough. The company was registered as an independent subsidiary of Rippen Entertainment, with Jack Rippen identified as corporate president and the name and address of a former mayor's high-powered Century City law firm stamped right underneath. The incorporation papers had been filed and validated in March of 1988.

The Celestial Dog record was considerably shorter: I got a single white sheet with faint dot-matrix type reporting that there is no DBA listing for Celestial Dog in the L.A. County record.

I had more or less expected that would prove to be the case, but I was still pissed off at having had to waste two hours for the confirmation.

From the clerk's office, I meandered over to the main public library. People love to say that L.A. is a city of pictures and not words, and I tend to agree, but you wouldn't know it from the central library, which is a pip. I wanted to see if I could find out anything more about Night Haven. Well, about Rosa Mendez, to be honest. It's not just that she intrigued me at a personal level, but all I knew about Night Haven was the little bit Sid Teitlebaum had told me. I wondered how an attractive lady like that ended up riding herd over a hostel full of hookers. Given that she'd been a reporter, I figured one of the local papers must have glommed on to her story at some point.

Sure enough, I found several references to Night Haven in the *Los Angeles Times* index, along with a bunch of older articles with Rosa's by-line. Apparently, Rosa had worked a Hollywood beat for a couple of years and got to know some of the working girls on the street. She was so disturbed and angered by the awfulness of their lives that she decided someone had to do something about it. The city and county were no help, so she took the job on herself.

It wasn't easy, but a year later, she had established Night Haven in an old storefront, convincing a host of donors to kick in some cash. One of the stories reported how the original Night Haven location had been burned down by an irate pimp. Rosa just dug her heels in, started over, and rebuilt it.

Wow, I thought.

Since I was downtown anyway, I stopped in for lunch at The Pantry. The place has been there since the dawn of time (that's Los Angeles–speak for more than twenty-five years), and they dish up the meanest, greasiest plate of hash browns this side of the muddy Mississippi. I ordered myself up a three-egg, heart-attack omelette to go with the spuds—which were pleasantly light on the thirty-weight for once—washed it down with half a dozen cups of their Charles Manson coffee, and felt like I'd eaten enough for a week.

Next stop was the Mid-Wilshire district and the offices of everybody's favorite trade paper, *Daily Variety.* The city's been digging up the streets under and around Wilshire Boulevard for what seems like years now to make way for a subway.

A goddamn subway in Los Angeles. They've only got a little stretch of it open so far, but no one seems too thrilled to ride it. They say it'll be the safest place in town, but I know that underground is not where I want to be when the Big One hits. They've spent about umpteen billion dollars on the system already, but so far it doesn't go much of anywhere. At least, not anyplace anyone *wants* to go. The city claims it's going to be great when it's finished—in something like the year 2007—but one way or another, I don't figure I'll be around to see it. In the meantime, the construction crews continue to screw up the traffic and make it that much harder to find a parking spot. As if it wasn't hard enough already. I eventually found a spot on a side street and even inherited an hour and a half on the meter. What with the hash browns and all, this was turning out to be a regular "Dear Diary" kind of day.

I asked at the security desk for Doug Hughes and was handed a visitor's pass and directions to an office on the fourth floor. Hughes wrote a twice-weekly business column for *Variety* and knew every deal in town that was going down or going up in flames. Unlike lots of other industry reporters, he also seemed to be a pretty regular guy and, so far as I knew, wasn't trying break in as a screenwriter, though I wouldn't bet cash on the latter. I probably should have called before stopping in, but figured that would only give him a chance to blow me off. Hughes had interviewed me at length a couple of years earlier for a book about the adult lives of ex–child actors, so I figured he owed me. I don't know if he ever finished the book or if it was published. I know I never got a copy if it was.

Hughes's office door was open, but there was no one inside. Most of the office was taken up by a big oak desk buried under an avalanche of paper. A couple of promotional posters from Nielsen and Arbitron had been tacked up on the walls. There was also a small framed picture of Hughes wearing a goofy fishing hat and a smile big as Alaska, holding up the Saddam Hussein of rainbow trout.

"Ahhh, excuse me . . ." As I turned around, Hughes's expression flowed from irritation to I-know-this-guy-who-the-hell-is-he to sudden recognition. I was pleased when it didn't appear to revert to irritation.

"Hey, Marty Burns," he said, and stuck out his hand.

"How you doing, Douglas?"

"Not too shabby, not too shabby. How's by you?"

"Hanging in there," I said. "How goes the book-writing business?"

"Nest of vipers. That's show biz. They're all motherfuckers, but that's half the fun." He squeezed past me and sat down behind his desk. I almost couldn't see him over the papers until he shoved a stack aside and gestured for me to sit. "What brings you around these lonesome parts?"

"I apologize for just dropping in like this—" Hughes waved his hand to dismiss the thought "—but I'm looking for some information, and I thought you were the man who could help me out. Can you spare a few minutes?"

"Hey, no problem," Hughes said. "I'm a columnist, remember? No deadlines for this boy. You on a case on something?"

"Sort of," I said. Back when he interviewed me, Hughes had been fascinated by the fact that I was a PI. Even after I explained my low-grade status and boring routine to him, I got the feeling that he somehow saw me as Thomas Magnum or Jim Rockford or the like. "I'm wondering what the lowdown is on the takeover of Rippen Entertainment."

"Hooo doggies!" Hughes said, and rocked back in his chair. "I may not be on deadline, but I am hoping to retire in ten years. That's a big old mess, son. What exactly do you want to know?"

"To tell you the truth, I haven't followed any of it all that closely. If you could give me a quick rundown on the big picture, I'd be obliged. I'm especially interested in anything concerning Laughing Boy Pictures."

Hughes narrowed his gaze at me. "Laughing Boy, huh? That's Rippen's private little playpen, you know. You working on something involving big, bad Jack?"

"Look, Doug. I was sort of hoping this could be off the record. I'm not really sure what I'm looking for just yet, and it probably has nothing at all to do with Rippen. I don't want to rouse any sleeping dogs with this. That okay with you?"

Hughes briefly drummed his fingers on a stack of reports, then smiled. "Sure," he said, "but how about anything interesting shakes out, you give me a buzz."

"Deal," I said. "Now tell me about Rippen Entertainment."

Hughes laced his fingers behind his head and leaned back in his chair again. Then he darted forward and dug through the stack of papers, pulling out a very slick annual report, thick as the San Diego phone book. "That tells it all," he said.

I grabbed the report. The glossy cover featured a montage of photos of smiling Japanese and American workers. In the upper left-hand corner was a Japanese rising sun. In the lower right the good old stars and bars. In small, elegant type across the middle was stenciled "Yoshitoshi International." I thumbed through it, then tossed it back on the desk with a shrug.

" 'Splain, please," I said.

"You probably know the story already," Hughes began. "It's a rerun, really. Or a sequel. Yoshitoshi's another Japanese giant that decided it wants in on the media biz. Just like Matsushita with MCA, and Sony with Columbia/Tri-Star. Yoshitoshi actually got beat out on the MCA deal and then got burned by the eye-ties on that MGM fiasco. Then they lost MCA again to Seagrams when Matsushita bailed and blew MGM again on the last go-round. They decided they weren't about to get beat again, so they made a monster bid on Rippen Entertainment. All that razzmatazz about software being the future of the business, vertical integration and all. Some people never learn. They started in steel, I believe, but now they're into everything. You see those commercials for that new car line, Mistral? With what's-her-tits? Sharon Stone. That's a Yoshitoshi subsidiary."

"So we're talking big time."

"Very big. There've been a few stories about the company's unsavory past, but I mean hell, all the Japanese companies are dirty. That's just the system there, not that it's any less true of Exxon or any of the American big boys if you look hard enough."

"What kind of stories?" I asked. "Unsavory how?"

"This is all rumor, mind you . . ." Hughes said. I nodded for him to continue. "All the corporations there are into dirty politics, but Yoshitoshi supposedly used Korean slave labor in its steel mills during the Second World War."

"Charming," I muttered. Hughes shrugged.

"They've also been linked with Yakuza—Japanese mafia?—both in the past and more recently. The Yaks are different from our bad boys, though. A little more legit. The fact that a Japanese company might have some Yakuza connections in its past—if they are in the past—isn't all that damning."

"You mean to say they can still come in and buy an American company with that background?"

"Hey, I told you it was just rumor. And technically the Rippen deal is still pending SEC approval, though that should be easy as apple pie. Really, it was a straightforward deal: Rippen himself controls fifty-plus percent of the shares, so in the end it was all his call. But any shareholder with an ounce of sense would have voted for the deal in a Tokyo minute."

"Why's that?"

"It's crazy like a weasel. Yoshitoshi is paying way over market value for the shares. I mean, Ripen's been a solid enough performer, but why pay twice what the company's worth?"

"I give up," I said. "Why?"

"Hey, that's the billion-dollar question. Look at the reaming Sony took on their deal. They're still writing off the losses. Not only did they pay too much, but they didn't have the management techniques for creative product. Matsushita would have committed hari-kari to lose MCA. Movies ain't cars, you know. Everybody talks about the value of software, but it's a risky game. Especially for outsiders, which the yellow peril most definitely are. Christ, Marty, you know what The Business is like. It never changes. Nothing ever shows a profit on the books, and everybody gets rich but the investors and Jim Garner. Granted, it's a little different on the corporate end, but all the Jap companies have taken it on the chin since they bought in. Not that I've got any sympathy for the little yellow fuckers."

"So why do you think Yoshitoshi wants the deal?"

"Pee-pee envy, my friend. It's all Freudian, which is to say crazy. They want what the other guy's got. Maybe Yoshitoshi feels left out. Or they're afraid they're missing out on something. Or they just want to prove they can succeed where their competitors failed."

"Doesn't sound like very smart business to me," I said. "I thought the Japanese were cleverer than that."

"Don't believe everything you read," Hughes explained. "You know the story: Everybody gets stardust in their eyes when it comes to the movies. Every dentist who socks five grand into a limited partnership suddenly thinks he's Sam fucking Goldwyn. Though Yoshitoshi did extract one major concession in the deal."

"How's that?"

"They get Rippen along with Rippen Entertainment. For seven years, exclusive."

"Who the fuck would want him?" I said.

"I know, I know," Hughes laughed. "But Rippen *is* the company. The Ripper's a bastard to be sure—and I'll swear on my daughter's cherry that I never said that—but he's a smart bastard. Give the sum-bitch credit: he and he alone made Rippen Entertainment the giant that it is. A whole lot of bigger fish have floundered while he's swum merrily along in milky white waters."

I picked the annual report up and again tried to browse it. The rows of numbers quickly made my eyes glaze over.

"What about Laughing Boy?" I asked.

"What about it?"

"I don't know. What kind of operation is it?"

Hughes pursed his mouth and rubbed his upper lip against the tip of his nose. It made him look like Gabby Hayes. "It's Rippen's baby," he said. "He uses it for personal, prestige projects. That crazy horror musical he did with David Lynch, remember? Or that ultraviolent John Woo western: *Fort Da.* And that cable miniseries set in Sarajevo with Tom Hanks and Winona Ryder. Laughing Boy stuff doesn't always make money, but it usually wins awards. Truth be known, it usually ends up making money, too."

"How does the Yoshitoshi deal affect it?" I asked.

"Hmmmph! I'm not sure," Hughes muttered. I could see he didn't like saying that. "Probably not at all would be my guess. I can't see Rippen giving up control of Laughing Boy. Let me see what I can find out, though."

"Thanks."

"Okay, spit it out," Hughes said.

"What?"

"I can see there's something else you want to ask," Hughes said with a smirk. "So ask."

I tapped my fingers against my mouth, then folded my hands in my lap. "Off the record," I repeated. Hughes nodded again. "You ever hear anything . . . unsavory about Laughing Boy?"

"In what sense?" Hughes asked.

"Any," I said. "Anything at all that might tickle your nose hairs. Allegations, rumors, pencil scrawls on the men's room wall. Whatever."

Hughes leaned forward on his desk and stared at me for a moment. He self-consciously ran a finger under his nose. There weren't really any hairs sticking out.

"You know what this town is like, Marty," Hughes finally said. "There are always stories. About everyone and everything. If Mother Teresa turned up in Spago, someone would whisper that she had a gerbil up her ass. Jack Rippen has a *lot* of enemies. Maybe he *deserves* a lot of enemies. Probably he does. If you ask enough people, you will hear stories about him and maybe some about Laughing Boy. *I* won't repeat any of them here. Not even shooting the shit, off the record with you. Whatever my personal feelings about Rippen—and as I am a normal, moral human being, I think you can guess those—I wouldn't feel right repeating those stories. Does that answer your question?"

Hughes had an odd gleam in his eye. I couldn't tell if he was taking a stand on an ethical point or just teasing me to pique my interest. In either case, it did answer my question.

"I guess it'll have to do," I replied. I glanced at my watch and saw that I'd taken up too much of his time. I stood up and thanked him. I promised again to drop any tidbits I might stumble upon his way, and he said he'd find out what he could about the status of Laughing Boy in the Yoshitoshi deal. I started out the door, but before I crossed the threshold I snapped my fingers and turned around.

"Oh, yeah," I said, "one other thing." Hughes raised a bushy eyebrow at me. "You know anything about an outfit called, uh, Celestial Dog Productions?"

I was fishing for a reaction, I suppose, thinking maybe Celestial Dog tied into one of the rumors about Laughing Boy that Hughes didn't want to repeat, but the reporter didn't blink. He just thought for a minute, then shook his head. "Doesn't ring any bells," he said. "Is it connected with Rippen?"

I shrugged and smiled, then waved myself out the door. I hoped maybe I'd piqued his interest a little bit myself.

I cruised back to Hollywood and stopped in at Night Haven. Rosa told me she'd try and rustle up a couple of pictures of the missing hookers. She wasn't in when I got there, but one of the girls handed me a Manila envelope with my name neatly typed on a stick-on label across the front. I unsealed it and slipped out a pair of fuzzy snapshots that looked like they'd been taken at a Christmas party at the shelter. They were group shots, but in each picture one girl's face was circled in red with a name written on the back. Cheri, no surprise, was an extravagant redhead, with enormous tits and a mile-wide smile; Syd was a brunette, with short-cropped hair and a boyish, almost bookish look. She seemed discomfited by the camera. Both photos were badly taken, leaving all the subjects with varying degrees of pinkeye. In both snaps, Rosa dangled at the edge of the frame wearing a crooked smile and a Santa cap and white beard.

There was no note to accompany the pictures.

"Was you really famous once?"

I looked up at the girl, who examined me like I was in a cage at the zoo. She looked about thirteen except for her hair, which had been dyed shocking pink, and the line of needle marks down her arm. She twisted back and forth on the toes of her bare right foot. She pressed the sole of her left foot against her right calf, like a dancer. Her short shorts exposed spindly legs and more track marks. She didn't look very graceful, but it made her look very much like a little girl.

"I reckon so," I said. I slipped the photos back into the envelope and shoved it in my pocket. She probably knew what they were about, but I didn't want to have to discuss it if she didn't.

"What's it like?" she asked dreamily.

"Being famous or being famous once?" I asked.

A potato chip crumb dangled off her cheek by the corner of her mouth. I reached up and gently brushed it away with my thumb. It made her giggle.

"Silly," she said.

I took the pictures out of my pocket when I got back to the car and stared at them for a while. I tried to memorize Syd and Cheri's faces, but truth be known, they looked like every other hooker I'd ever seen and faded from memory as soon as my eyes wandered off them. I stared more intently at Rosa's face. Hers was one I had no problem remembering.

On a whim I decided to drive back up to the Laughing Boy offices in Burbank. I thought maybe I'd stake out the place until closing time just to see who came and went. It's a low-percentage play, but it never hurts to check out exactly who you're dealing with, and frankly I didn't have anything better to do. I stopped at a convenience store for a six of Henry's and a pound bag of peanut M&Ms, figuring I needed something to keep me company during the lonely hours of surveillance. I grabbed a copy of *Premiere,* too. I keep a mini cooler in the car at all times just in case. The Korean behind the counter only charged me twice what the sixer should have cost, so I figured I actually did all right.

The first bottle was already a goner by the time I pulled up across the street from the Laughing Boy building. I listened to a ball game on the radio for a while, thumbed the magazine—that Johnny Depp is just a devil—and kept an eye on the front door. The spot also afforded me a view of the gated entrance to the building's underground parking lot. For a big office complex, there was surprisingly little foot traffic. I sat there long enough to polish off two more bottles of beer, then decided I needed a whiz. I thought about wandering into a nearby alley, but decided there was no harm in using the men's room in the Laughing Boy building. It's not like anyone knew me or had any reason to suspect any kind of surveillance. I thought maybe I'd stop and check in with my buddy at the information desk, too. Maybe slip him another deuce to keep his eyes open. I had the presence of mind to pop a breath mint in my mouth before leaving the car.

The arctic cold again sent a wave of gooseflesh up my exposed arms as I entered the building. Sooner or later I was going to catch pneumonia this way. A pair of men in identical gray business suits came off the elevator, but otherwise the lobby was deserted. The information desk was unmanned, so I headed straight for the men's room at the opposite end of the lobby. The door whooshed open in front of me as a young man in a dark blue jacket emerged from the bathroom. We both started, then nodded slightly at each other, and he held the door open for me. Tacky elevator music played dimly from a tiny speaker in the corner of the john. I felt almost patriotic peeing to the strains of 101 Strings playing Neil Diamond's "Coming to America."

I washed my hands and splashed some water on my face before noticing that there weren't any paper towels, only those miserable hot-air blowers. Water dripped down my neck and I tried contorting under the machine to dry my face. Just then a guy walked in and saw me. I straightened up and forced a smile, but he took a wide step around me and made quickly for a stall. He fiddled with the lock for a while, no doubt wanting to make sure to keep the weirdos out where they belonged with the hot-air dryers. By that point my face had pretty well dried on its own. I sighed and went back out into the lobby.

The young man who I'd tangoed with going into the can stood behind the information kiosk. He sat on a high stool and stared dumbly out the tinted windows. I had a vision that he was dreaming of surfboards and volleyballs and girls in French bikinis. It's what I would have been doing. He turned and nodded again at me as I approached the desk.

"Can I help you, sir?" he asked.

"Yeah," I said. "Actually, I was looking for the gentleman who usually works here."

"That's me," he said.

"No. I mean the elderly black gentleman. I'm slightly embarrassed to admit that I don't know his name, but we've had a number of pleasant conversations over the years. I just wanted to say hello."

Of course, I had no idea how long the black man had been working there. I got the feeling, from our brief chat, that he'd been there for some time.

"I'm the only one who works here days," the kid said.

"But you haven't been working here long."

"Third day," he said, forcing a smile. Maybe he thought I was someone important.

"And you don't know what became of the other fellow?"

"Probably quit," the kid said. "Or got fired. Lot of movement in this line of work. I'm studying data processing and computers myself. Information superhighway, you know."

"Sounds good," I said. I doubted the kid would know from computers if he swallowed eight megs of RAM. "Too bad about the old guy, though. He told some great stories."

The kid shrugged. I think he decided I was nobody, and lost interest.

"Say," I tried, "the old guy was supposed to get an address for me. It was a forwarding address for a former tenant. Celestial Dog Productions?"

The kid sighed, obviously put out that I was going to make him do some work after all. He fished through several drawers below the counter until he found a clipboard with a list of names and addresses. "What's the name again?"

"Celestial Dog Productions. I think they used to share the Laughing Boy offices."

I had to spell "celestial" for him twice. He went through his list several times, but came up empty.

"Sorry," he said. "If they were here, they must have moved more than a year ago."

"You never heard the name?" I prompted. The kid just shook his head.

"You could go up to Laughing Boy and ask there," he suggested.

It was a higher-order thought process than I would have given him credit for. I said that it was okay and thanked him. I walked back out to my car, got in, and popped open another beer. Even in the cooler they were starting to get warm.

I sucked down the draft and tapped my fingers against the hot steering wheel. I was troubled by the fact that the old black guy was gone. I had no good reason to worry—for all I knew, he'd put in his twenty-five years and they threw him a big retirement party and gave him a gold watch—but somehow I didn't think so. I couldn't help but wonder if maybe he mentioned our conversation about Celestial Dog to someone and landed himself in some trouble. It hadn't exactly escaped me that Long John's murder occurred shortly *after* I had introduced myself as "Mr. Silver" at the Laughing Boy offices. I assumed it was merely coincidental, but with the disappearance of two more hookers and now the old man at the desk, I was starting to feel a little nervous.

I decided that if I had to pee again, I'd settle for an alley and keep my face in the shadows.

. . .

It was dumb luck that brought me the lead. It usually is.

There was nothing but warm backwash left in the last bottle of beer, and my shirt was soaked through with sweat. The Dodgers had lost and the elastic had given way in my underwear. I had to shift around on the hot car seat to keep my shorts out of my ass. I'd kept watch through the late afternoon, saw the throngs file out of the office building promptly at five o'clock, but I didn't see anyone I recognized, and certainly no sign of Jack Rippen. By six o'clock the number of people exiting the building had dwindled to a trickle and I was ready to pack it in. Then I considered the traffic I'd have to contend with driving back via one of the canyon passes to Silver Lake. The thought of dealing with it, what with my shorts up my butt and all, was too much for me. I decided I'd been sitting in the car this long, another hour or so wouldn't kill me.

The white van pulled out just after six-thirty. I'd been keeping an eye on all the vehicles exiting the underground garage, but none had made an impression. I would have ignored this one, too, except the driver stopped and got out of the van right after he cleared the automatic gate arm. Someone had stuck something under his windshield wiper—one of those pink rectangular flyers that are supposed to resemble parking tickets, but are really take-out menus or the like—and he couldn't remove it from inside the cab. As he turned his back to me to snatch the flyer off the windshield, I was able to read the lettering stenciled on the back of his jacket. It was one of those satin baseball affairs that once upon a time were worn only by teenaged thugs with greasy hair and zip guns, but which have become de rigueur for crew members on every film production in town. *Why* he was wearing a jacket in this heat, I couldn't begin to imagine, except that your typical union crew member would rather look good than feel good (or work good, but then why should they be different from anyone else?). The flowing script letters were bold enough, though: Laughing Boy Pictures. The dancing harlequin was outlined in Day-Glo colors just underneath.

The driver jumped back into the unmarked van and took a left, heading in the direction opposite from which my car pointed. Glare reflected back off the windshield, so I couldn't tell if there was anyone else riding up front. I quickly turned the key and promptly stalled the car out. I started it up again and traced a wide U-turn across the boulevard, nearly sideswiping two vastly more expensive cars in the process. I heard a stream of epithets unleashed behind me, but cranked up the window and hit the AC as I set off in pursuit. Wonder of wonders, cold air blasted out.

I almost lost the van a couple of times as it wound its way through Burbank. Mobile surveillance looks so easy in movies and on television, but unless you're willing to risk racking up some serious moving violations, it's damned hard to keep up with someone in city traffic. Especially if the other driver is at all reckless, as the van driver proved to be, seeing every yellow light like a red cape to a bull and darting across lanes like Damon fucking Hill. Fortunately, traffic was heavy enough that he never got too far ahead of me, even when I got caught at red lights he'd already driven through. I was no more than six car lengths behind him when he turned up the entrance ramp to the northbound Golden State Freeway.

The son of a bitch punched it once he got on the freeway, which was shockingly traffic-free, and I feared my trusty Subaru couldn't keep up with him. As the speedometer crept up on eighty, I was even more scared that we'd both get ticketed, especially as we approached a speed trap that's often set up near the Lankershim Boulevard exit. Fortunately, the highway patrol were off eating doughnuts or beating a black motorist or something, and traffic started to back up again another mile or so up the road. I was able to keep the van in sight for a long stretch until the traffic thinned again where the Golden State joins up with the San Diego Freeway.

I had no idea where the van might be headed and only a slightly greater notion as to why I was following it. For all I knew, he was making a simple delivery and would head straight back to Burbank, but it seemed a funny time of day to be carrying out such mundane business in an unmarked van. The van driver floored it again as he turned off onto the eastbound Antelope Valley Freeway in the direction of Canyon Country. I had to struggle to keep up, but hardly any other cars were heading out in that direction, so there wasn't much chance of losing him. There's not a whole lot out that way other than rocks and scrub brush. My interest was further piqued.

The sun had more or less gone down, but I waited for the van driver to turn on his headlights before I followed suit. He continued to cruise along at a clip of near eighty, with no sign of a destination at hand. I realized I was down to about an eighth of a tank of gas and cursed myself for not having filled up earlier in the day. Normally I'd always keep a full tank on a tail job, just in case, but I've gotten so damn rusty at even the simplest things that I forgot all about it. I had to hope the van driver wasn't heading a real long distance or I was screwed.

As luck would have it, the van's brake lights flashed after another couple of miles of high speed and the driver cut sharply into the slow lane as he came up on the Agua Dulce exit. I slowed as well, giving him time to make it down the exit ramp without crawling up his ass. I stayed close enough behind to see him take a left at the end of the ramp, and felt a surge of excitement when I saw the signs offering directions and distances. I hadn't been up this way in ages, but realized that the van must be following the sign that pointed the way to Vasquez Rocks Park.

He had to be heading for a film shoot.

Vasquez Rocks is a small park—not even a state park, as I recall, just a county affair—that you'd recognize in a minute if you saw it. It's probably been used in hundreds, if not thousands, of movies, TV shows, and commercials. We even shot a dream sequence from *Salt & Pepper* there once. It sits in the middle of a big nothing—Agua Dulce is your classic dead-horse town; the name's the giveaway—just brown hills and countryside in Escondido Canyon. The rocks themselves are a sight, though. They shoot up out of the ground at dizzying angles, like big granite teeth gone bad in an old man's mouth. At their peak they're not more than about two hundred feet tall, but they look pretty damn impressive when you're standing at the base of them. Or more important, when you frame them just right in a Panaflex viewfinder. The rocks are a natural film set, a veritable Monument Valley in miniature less than an hour away from the heart of Hollywood. The best set designer in the world couldn't do any better with a bottomless budget.

Laughing Boy had to be busy with a night shoot; there was nothing else up here and no other conceivable reason for one of their vans to be out this way. I kept a safe distance behind the van as he headed up the twisty road toward the Rocks. Topping a small crest, I pulled over and saw the van stop at the gated entrance to the park. I pulled a pair of binoculars out of the glove compartment. It was getting pretty dark, but I could still make things out. The access road had been cordoned off, and a couple of security guards shined flashlights into the cab. They waved the van on through, then drew the gate closed again across the road. I wasn't sure, because of the fading light, but it looked to me like the guards were armed with handguns.

There'd be no going in through the front door tonight.

Ten

I turned the car around to look for another, less obvious access point
into the park. Attempting to play the good PI, at first I drove with
my headlights off and ran right into a metal post on the side of the narrow road. The I tried driving with just the parking lights on and quickly
took out two more posts. I got out to inspect the damage, but it was so
goddamn dark I couldn't see, and not only did I have to turn the lights
back on, but I switched on the high beams as well. My front bumper
was a little bit scratched up, but given that the car was for shit anyway,
I couldn't get too upset about it. Like any true-blue Angelino, I've been
driving without insurance for years, so it's not like there was any hope
of making up some kind of claim for the damage. Deciding to hell with
the spy stuff, I drove back along the road with the brights still on. I managed not to hit any more posts, but couldn't avoid mashing something
small and furry that darted out in front of me from the brush. Roadkill
always sends a shudder through my system, and I was glad it was too dark
to see the mess I left behind, though I glanced in the rearview anyway.

I followed the winding road around what I thought were the rough
contours of the park, searching for another way in. I stopped to glance
at my Thomas Guide under the dash light, but no other park gates were
marked on the map as far as I could make out. As I came around what
I took to be the eastern edge of the park, I spotted a dirt road leading
roughly back in toward what I thought was the Rocks. I turned in and
immediately broke sharply when two armed guards sprang out from a
shack beside a locked gate. They quickly approached my car from either
side. It was too late to back out, so I decided to roll down the window
and play dumb.

"Hey," I said, mustering what I hoped looked like a goofy, gee-am-I-
ever-lost-what-a-dope smile. It's not actually all that different from my
regular look.

The guard who approached on the driver's side was big and obviously a pro. He kept a good four feet back from the window and didn't bend down to talk. He didn't actually put a hand on his gun—I couldn't tell for sure what it was, though it looked Glockish—but he let his fingers dangle lightly near the holster on his hip.

"Park's closed," he said. He had a square head with tiny, lobeless ears and an ugly scowl.

"I think I'm pretty lost," I said, still smiling. I had the map open on my lap. "Got off the freeway looking for a gas station and I can't seem to find my way back on."

I thought I saw a little of the stiffness go out of his posture, but he didn't come any closer. He nodded at his partner, who joined him over on my side of the car. The partner had a round, jolly face. The two of them reminded me of a set of Greek masks.

"Freeway's back that way," Comedy said, vaguely pointing. "Bear left at the fork, then straight on."

"Gee, thanks," I said, glaring off in the direction he'd indicated. "Don't suppose you fellows got a Porta Potti round here I could use?"

Tragedy shook his head once.

"Damn!" I said. "Never much cared for the bushes. All that poison oak and such. And I got to take a squat real bad."

"There's a Mickey D's a couple exits up," Comedy told me. He had hunched down a bit to talk to me. Probably figured no one in a Subaru could be that big a threat. Which is usually about right.

"Say," I tried, "what's going on here anyway?"

"Nothing," Tragedy spat.

"County guard all its parks this fiercely?" I asked, still smiling.

"Film shoot tonight," Comedy told me. It earned him an icy glare from his partner and he quickly stood up and took a step back.

"Should have known," I offered jovially. "Can't swing a dead cat in this town without hitting a film crew. What's the movie? Anybody famous around?"

"Closed set," Tragedy said. He stiffened up again.

"Gotcha. Well, golden arches, here I come."

I drove off slowly. The guards walked out into the middle of the road and watched my taillights. I continued along at a nice even pace around a few bends until I was sure I was well out of their sight, then pulled over and killed the lights.

Whatever the hell Laughing Boy was working on, they didn't want any prying eyes. There was nothing unusual about a closed shoot—even on location—but they were sure taking no chances about this one. Posting armed guards on a dirt trail out in the middle of nowhere meant one of two things: either they were filming something major and didn't want any press coverage—not an unreasonable likelihood for a Jack Rippen prestige production—or they were doing something they shouldn't be. It might have been as petty as employing some nonunion crew or shooting with minors after legal hours (God knows I had done it enough times in the old days), or maybe just Julia Roberts being persnickety, but then again, maybe it was something more. In either case, I had a hankering to find out.

I couldn't drive back past the Mask boys and was hesitant even to cruise by the main gate. I glanced through the dark toward the park. It was probably a two- or three-mile trek to the Rocks from where I was parked, across some fairly rugged terrain and a night as dark as a producer's heart. I considered blowing it off completely when, like a divine vision, the image of Rosa's long legs danced through my head again.

I pulled the car as far off the road as I could, grabbed a flashlight and the pair of binoculars, and made for the Rocks.

I hate nature. I really, really do. My first wife (don't ask) used to drag me out for hikes and nature walks all the damn time. I don't too much mind a nice stroll along the beach round about sunset, or even a quiet afternoon sauntering through the Huntington Gardens in Pasadena. But all that trudging up and down hills and along dirt trails to gawk at a bunch of dried-out Southern California flora amid the debris of Diet Coke cans and spent condoms never quite rang my bell. And don't even get me started on camping out. I'm strictly—credit rating notwithstanding—a five-star-hotel kind of guy. When you can pitch room service and shower massage along with your tent, I'll reconsider my position.

Which is by way of saying that the hike across the scrubland toward Vasquez Rocks was a little tougher than I had figured. The moonless night worked in my favor in terms of being seen, but it made the walk a living bitch. The ground was rough and broken with gopher holes and Joshua trees everywhere. Those trees look pretty as hell from your car window on the road to Vegas or on the cover of U2 albums, but they're mean on the skin when you walk into them in the dark. I repeatedly barked my ankles on jutting rocks and kept tripping over some creeping vine that looked to be out of *Day of the Triffids*. I even managed to stumble into a thin creek of stagnant, foul water—the eponymous Agua Dulce itself, more than likely—soaking my shoes and rousing what seemed like an entire colony of mosquitoes. I didn't even think we had mosquitoes in this part of the state, but this batch must have been shacking up with vampire bats, because they bit the living bejesus out of me as I continued on toward the Rocks, slapping at my exposed arms and face and cursing a trail of blue as I went. I could hear coyotes baying in the distance and hoped they were only after roadrunners. (It turns out, by the by, that roadrunners are disappointingly tiny little critters. I was crushed the first time I ever saw one out near Palm Springs, because they don't look a damn thing like the guy in the cartoons, and they sure as hell don't go "beep-beep.")

The landscape got even rougher and the grade steeper as I approached the Rocks proper. As I made my way around a pair of boulders, big as house-high hooters, I saw the glow of high-powered kliegs spilling out from beyond the next rise. I scaled the first tit and squatted down about on the nipple. I hauled my binoculars out of their case and scanned the tops of the surrounding rocks, but didn't spot anyone perched up high. I could hear the whirring chug of generators echoing out from the Rocks and the intermittent sound of revving truck engines. As I was about to shimmy down off the boulder and head in a little closer to the action, I heard someone trip and curse off to the right. I flattened myself against the still warm stone as footsteps drew nearer. Whoever it was stopped at the neighboring tit. I held my breath through a brief silence, then heard the sound of liquid splashing against the rock. I exhaled softly as the sharp scent of uric acid reached my nose. The whizzer drew up a wad of phlegm and spat as he shook off the last few drops, then hurriedly made his way back toward the shoot. I waited until his silhouette disappeared behind a crag before sliding back down to the ground. I hadn't realized I was quite so close to the set, and slowly backed off into the darkness to look for a more secluded approach. Like dogs marking territory, where one crew member goes to piss, others are sure to follow.

The only way I could figure to get a view of the shoot was to take on one of the tall rocks. I worked my way around the rim of tiered rocks that form the central section of the park, hoping that I would find a less trafficked approach to the set. I scaled a low ridge of boulders fairly easily, peering cautiously over the top as I reached the zenith. The nimbus of the heavy-duty klieg lamps was brighter here, though I still couldn't quite make anything out. I spotted a rough trail leading up into the next, taller ridge of stone and found a series of handholds conveniently carved into the semisoft surface. I remembered how I'd seen kids fearlessly scaling the rocks during previous visits to the park, though I'd never had the guts to venture up them myself. I saw, as I progressed easily up the ridge, that though the rocks looked steep, the sandstone was soft and gritty, making for easy purchase. Even so, I managed to slip a couple of times, scraping a fair chunk of skin off my right forearm in the process. The rough trail wove back and forth across the small ridge, taking me a little bit away from where I wanted to go, but it seemed smarter to follow the beaten path than risk forging my own way up and taking a serious fall.

I was huffing and puffing some by the time I made it to the crest of the ridge. I could make out the lights of the freeway a few miles back behind me and was a little stunned to realize just how high up I was. An even higher set of rocks, with a narrow apex that flattened out into a natural terrace, rose out of the ground directly across from me, but between me and the terrace was the massive oval of a stony, oblong bowl where the Laughing Boy crew were at work. The pale ocher rocks served to reflect the portable lamps such that the shoot was as brightly lit as the Dodger Stadium infield for a night game. As stifling as the day had been, it was quite cool up high, with a mountain breeze whistling through the crags. I felt a slight chill as the wind dried the cold sweat on my skin, and wished that I had thought to take a jacket with me.

I didn't have a great angle on the set itself from my position on the ridge. I could make out a humming generator truck and see the tops of the kliegs, but had to climb back down a couple of yards for a clearer view. I crawled up a hunk of boulder that jutted out of the rock face, and obscured the view, straddling it with both legs. As I carefully shimmied out toward the edge and looked down, my stomach suddenly lurched and I felt a wave of vertigo wash over me, I had to flatten myself against the stone, cheek to rock, and close my eyes to stop from losing my grip and my lunch. I was a good hundred feet above the surface of the basin, and caught a quick glimpse of the cast and crew scurrying across the rocks below me. For a second I thought I was going to throw up on them, but I quelled the nausea by lying flat against the rock on my stomach. I took a few very deep breaths and found that when I opened my eyes the vertigo had passed. Still on my stomach, I slithered out to the edge of the boulder and peered down. I was so high up that I couldn't make much out with the naked eye beyond the positions of the four big lights, some equipment trailers, and a camera rig, along with assorted crew members. I could tell it was a small crew—probably second unit—but nothing more. I got my binoculars back out, and using the rock to shield myself from view as much as possible, spied down on the shoot.

There was no set to speak of beyond the natural splendor of the rugged rocks. The action appeared to be centered around a squat mini mesa rising six feet out of the ground at the base of the higher rocks near the far end of the bowl. A series of multihued characters—Japanese or Chinese—had been painted on the ground all around the altarlike mesa as well as on the rock face behind it. A trio of crew members were huddled around the mesa, painting it as well. I scanned around the bowl for anyone resembling the unit director, but since virtually everyone wore beards and baseball caps, I couldn't make him. The opening of a door in one of the parked trailers caught my attention as another capped head briefly peered out, but it ducked back in too fast for me to get a decent glimpse.

I focused back on the action around the mesa. Only a couple of the crew members lingered around the rock, and I could see that they were drawing elaborate, flamboyant ideograms in a spiral pattern around the top of the mesa. I also noted, for the first time, that the crew themselves appeared to be mostly Asian: Japanese, I assumed. It struck me as very unusual, even if Laughing Boy was shooting product for the Japanese market; by and large, the Hollywood craft unions are as lily-white as the KKK.

I watched for about forty minutes as they continued to dress the set. In fact, they did little more than paint various characters and designs on the rocks and shift the lights and camera back and forth. I was getting a headache from looking through the binoculars for so long and finally put them away for a while. My attention must have wandered for a minute or two as I stared off into the clear night sky, because when I glanced back down at the set, the crew had mostly disappeared, except for the cameraman and his assistants. A group of heavily costumed actors had wandered out—from the trailers, I assumed—and took up positions around the mesa. I grabbed the binoculars again for a better look at the scene.

As I watched, a smallish Japanese man in a flowing, jet-black kimono was hoisted up on top of the mesa by two younger men, also Asians, also in black. The man had a thick black beard and mustache—the most facial hair I'd ever seen on an Asian—and wore a tiny black cap that resembled a sombrero that had shrunk in the dryer. The sleeves and hem of his kimono blazed with electric blue and red silk, and it was cinched at the waist with an extravagant red sash that practically glowed under the bright kliegs. As near as I could tell, he was barefoot under the kimono. He also wore two swords, one short, one long, tucked into the sash on his left side. He began to walk in a small circle around the rock, following the contours of the painted ideograms.

The two Asians who had lifted the man onto the rock were joined by two Caucasians in brown kimonos. The four of them took up equidistant positions around the mesa. Each of them was also outfitted with two swords, and they stood as still as the rocks themselves. I tried watching them for a while, and as far as I could tell, not one of them so much as blinked. Extras were never that disciplined when I was in The Business.

I looked up from the binoculars for a moment when I heard the squeaky hinge of a trailer door opening. Two Japanese businessmen in gray Savile Row suits emerged from the trailer, followed by an American with slicked back hair and a pinky ring. He *had* to be the producer, and I assumed the Nippons were his money men. They didn't approach the action on the mesa, but stood by the trailer watching silently. The two Japanese kept their hands behind their backs while the producer had his arms folded across his chest. At one point he glanced over his shoulder into the trailer and said something, but I've never been any good at reading lips.

I kept scanning the scene looking for the director, but no one seemed to be in charge of the shoot. The camera crew appeared to be filming without direction, but I couldn't spot a sound crew or even an AD on the set. And where were all the gaffers and gofers? The whole thing seemed awfully amateurish and chaotic for a Jack Rippen production. It suddenly struck me that this had to be a complete cowboy operation: nonunion. If word ever got out that Rippen was shooting nonunion right here on the rim of Hollywood, there'd be hell to pay. Certainly he'd have to kiss his big Yoshitoshi deal good-bye. Probably his ass, too. Potentially very useful information if correct.

Unless, of course, the Savile Row boys *were* Yoshitoshi.

I turned my sights back toward the mesa. The man on top—I got the idea he was playing a priest of some sort—had crouched down in the center of the spiral of characters. Even way up in the rocks I could hear him chanting in singsong Japanese, occasionally echoed by the others around him, but of course, it all sounded like Sid Caesar gibberish to me. As I watched, he drew the short sword out of its sheath and touched the flat of the blade to his forehead three times. Then he stood up and pointed it at each of the four men below—compass points?—and then touched the point of the blade to the rock and used it to etch a new character, which looked to me like a pair of birds in flight, into the sandstone. I thought I saw him look briefly in the producer's direction before raising his arms up to the sky, the sword still in his right hand.

As the kimono sleeves fell back, I saw that his arms were a mass of brightly colored tattoos. I couldn't see well enough to make out all the details, but got the impression that the pictures and characters on each arm told a story of some kind, beginning at the wrist and culminating somewhere I couldn't see on his shoulders or perhaps even his upper body. I tried to "read" the story on his left arm, starting with the picture of a hunched quasi-human figure, but he started waving his arms again and the images blurred. When he stopped gesticulating, he pressed the point of the sword into his left wrist—to a point right in the middle of the hunched figure—and traced a line down his arm with the sharp blade. Blood instantly began to spill from the wound, washing over the tattooed pictures in a flood of red. It was a brilliant effect, which I realized would look sensational on the screen.

Except: where was the effects crew?

Something was very wrong here. I watched as blood continued to spill down the man's arm. He slowly lowered it and directed the flow into the grooves of the character he had etched into the center of the rock. The bright red liquid sloshed into the bird shapes, giving them a menacing trace of life. I tried to focus in on the bleeding arm, looking for some sign of latex or a tube pumping the mix of Karo syrup and dye from a bladder secreted somewhere under the kimono.

No latex. No bladder. No syrup.

Real blood? Impossible.

"Fuck," I whispered, then slapped a hand over my mouth, afraid that the word had echoed.

I scanned over for a quick look at the suit brigade by the trailer. The Japanese continued to watch impassively, though the producer was tapping one foot nervously. I thought I could see the shape of another face peering out from the trailer window, but it may just have been a shadow.

When I looked back at the mesa I saw that a new figure had joined the priest. I hadn't seen where the actor came from, but he appeared so quickly that he must have been ducked down behind the rock, waiting on a cue.

He, at least I assumed it was a he, was outfitted in extremely elaborate effects makeup. The actor stood a good seven feet tall—wookie-sized, I thought—and looked even bigger in comparison to the small Japanese man beside him. His rippled, muscular flesh was a rubbery brown and gray, but the latex appliances looked utterly convincing, not at all like the cheap body costumes of bad monster flicks. Tufts of wiry black hair, like overgrown pubes, burst out of the skin on its legs and torso, and a fierce leonine mane flowed from his scalp, framing two ivory horns, each at least a foot in length. Matching ivory nails, more like claws, emerged from each four-fingered hand and three-toed foot. A thin golden anklet adorned his right leg, twinned by a thicker gold band on his left wrist. His pelvic region was discreetly covered by a thick blue sash, into which was tucked a redundantly phallic sword. Blood-red lips curled back to reveal a wide mouthful of savage white canines. His big eyes were as yellow as a geriatric smoker's teeth, the pupils glowing like hot coals.

Hot stuff indeed! H. R. Giger had nothing on this puppy: he was the best movie monster I'd ever seen.

The priest didn't seem to be bleeding anymore, which led me to reconsider how real the blood might have been. I decided I must not have been able to spot the effects rig from my queer angle. Everyone sort of stood there for a while without moving, the monster looming over the priest's stooped shoulders. I thought maybe they were reloading the camera—this had been an awfully long take—but the camera crew were curiously inactive. Maybe, I thought, they were after some sort of Stephen Bochco vérité thing here, though it hardly seemed appropriate style to the subject matter. But then *I* was only an actor, not an auteur.

I froze as the priest looked up, scanning the top of the rocks. I ducked instinctively, but he obviously didn't see me as he continued to scan the skies. Then he bent down and picked up what looked like a conch shell and put it to his lips. He blew into it, his cheeks puffing out like Dizzy Gillespie, and a low-pitched moan bassooned from the open end of the shell, echoing through the rocks. The priest lowered the shell and again looked to the skies.

I glanced up myself, but there was nothing to see but the dim stars and a flash of lights from a high-flying jet. I thought I heard a flapping of wings—an owl or a falcon, most likely—but I couldn't see any bird in the dark. Finally the priest looked back toward one of the trailers and gestured insistently with his bloody hand. The producer and the money men took a few steps closer to the mesa, but remained outside the shot. From across the set, two more robed Asians emerged from a trailer holding someone up between them. I didn't have much of an angle on them as they walked toward the priest, but I could tell it was a woman they were leading. She was clad in a magenta kimono just a shade or two darker than her Irish setter–red hair. The girl barely moved her legs, and the robed men were doing more carrying than escorting. I couldn't see her face, but the kimono only reached her exposed calves. She was barefoot.

The man on the girl's right stumbled slightly as he walked past the money men and into frame, losing his grip on the girl. The priest barked angrily in Japanese, but before the guide could grab her arm again, the girl got spun around and faced my general direction. Much as I wish I hadn't, I recognized her immediately.

It was Cheri: one of Rosa's missing hookers.

I had left the photo Rosa gave me in the car, but I was sure of the ID. She couldn't be more than sixteen, slim but sexy. I didn't have long to study her face, but it was clear to me that she was stoned or drugged. Her eyes were coin-slot slits and her pretty mouth hung open vacantly. I had a very bad feeling about things to come and was regretting—as I somehow knew I would—having agreed taking this job on.

The acolyte, or whatever he was, who had stumbled bowed deeply in the direction of the priest and monster, then resecured his grip on the girl. They brought her right up to the robed guard standing at the southern point of the mesa. The priest spat another word of Japanese and the guard stirred for the first time. He quickly but gently slipped the girl's kimono off while the two acolytes continued to hold her up.

I wasn't remotely surprised to see that she was stark naked underneath. Though I hated myself for noticing, Cheri had the pert, toned body of a teenager, her tits round and firm, her belly and thighs slender and smooth.

The guard placed his hands around the girl's bare waist and in a prodigious show of strength, hefted her easily up onto the mesa. She landed on her hands and knees and instantly fell flat on her stomach. Her impressive rear was aimed right at me, and despite the situation, I had to suppress dirty-old-man thoughts again.

I reckoned that this was what the action was all about tonight, and expected the camera to come in for the close-up work. But the crew never budged. I figured this for some Japanese porno-horror flick with the virginal white girl ravaged by the monster or demon or whatever the hell it was supposed to be. I still couldn't figure why in the world Jack Rippen and Laughing Boy would get involved with this kind of shit, but those questions could wait. One part of me didn't want to stay and watch the fuck scene—I don't think pornography is evil, just humiliating for participant and voyeur alike—but another part, the part that still stirred at the sight of teen twat, didn't want to go. And I thought that I *should* stay if I was going to give Rosa the full story.

The dirty old man and the detective outvoted the virtuous citizen. God help me.

The priest gesticulated and chanted, then knelt down and touched his forehead to the stone. The monster continued to wait behind him, though now its gaze was locked on the naked girl. The priest raised his head and held one palm up toward the demon, who took a step forward, reaching for its sash. I expected him to expose an oversized penis—I regard anything more than five and a half inches as oversized, by the way—but instead it unsheathed its sword, driving the tip through the center of the priest's upraised hand. I groaned slightly as I saw—*saw,* goddammit—the end of the blade penetrate the priest's flesh, and knew, much as I wanted to believe otherwise, that there were no special effects being employed here. I suddenly began to feel very ill and found myself praying that what I knew was about to happen would not happen.

The monster drew the sword back out of the priest's hand and used the bloody tip to etch a new ideogram into the stone—I thought it looked like an upside-down copy of the flying birds—then placed the sword down on the flat rock. The priest clasped his bloody hands together under his chin and bowed, again touching his forehead to the stone. All the others—the acolytes, the guards, even the producer and his cronies who were out of frame—similarly knelt and abased themselves. Only the cameraman remained on his feet, and even *his* assistants had their heads on the floor.

"What the fuck . . ." I mumbled, utterly mystified. What the hell kind of footage could they expect to get out of this?

The monster stepped over the supine priest, looming over the girl. She was still facedown on the rock, not having so much as twitched since being placed on the mesa. The monster spun her around, grabbing at her ankles. I felt sure he was about to mount her doggy-style, but he only dragged her back to a point at the center of the mesa and roughly flipped her over. I could see red abrasions on the soft skin of her breasts where they'd rubbed against the stone. He then picked his sword back up and touched the flat of the blade to his lips. He pointed the sword to each compass point, then used the tip to trace a bloody character into the girl's exposed abdomen. He must have pressed the blade in deep, because blood spurted out in volume, quickly obscuring the shape of the ideogram. As soon as he completed the character, he tossed the sword away and went down on his haunches over the girl. There wasn't even time to blink, much less shout a warning—though to whom I could have shouted, I don't know—before he dug his claws into the girl's flesh.

"Oh, Jesus," I cried, but I didn't look away.

The demon thrust his hands into the girl's belly up to the wrist. The gold bracelet on his left hand glittered in the kliegs amid the blood and gore. I felt my stomach seize up and I swallowed back a tongue of vomit that crawled up my throat. I think I may have whimpered again.

This definitely was not special effects. Rosa's young hooker was being disemboweled for the camera before my eyes. Jack fucking Rippen was shooting a snuff film in a county park.

The monster continued to root around inside the girl, who convulsed slightly, but had yet to make a sound. I prayed that she was already dead, but then I distinctly saw her eyes blink as the demon ripped a length of glistening intestine from out of the hole. The rock was covered in blood, and even the priest's black robe had been spackled with red, though he had yet to raise his forehead off the rock. The creature pulled more of the girl's bowel out of her tiny body, carefully wrapping lengths of it around his arm, like a phylactery, until it looked as if a flayed snake had devoured him to the left shoulder. Then he tore the soggy strip off with a flick of his claw, leaving a decidedly unhealthy length of gut protruding from the girl. She had to be dead by now, though I couldn't bring myself to focus the binoculars on her face to make sure.

The others all remained frozen in their kneeling positions as the monster nonchalantly rolled Cheri's body off the rock with a flick of his toe. She landed out of my sight—mercifully—though I could hear the splodgy noise of her landing even from the distance.

The monster slowly unraveled the length of bowel from his arm, starting at the shoulder. He inspected it carefully as he went, the way a doctor reads an EKG strip. He paused several times and seemed to nod approvingly to himself, as if satisfied with the quality of the girl's innards.

When it was all unlooped he spread it across the top of the rock in a spiral pattern that clearly mimicked that of the characters that had been painted onto the mesa. He then strode into the center of the spiral, careful not to tread on any of the intestine, and knelt down like the others, touching his head to the stone. His horns pointed straight at me, and damned if they didn't really look like they were really growing out of his scalp.

There was complete silence then, except for the omnipresent buzz of the generator and big lights. Insects fluttered through and around the kliegs, occasionally casting giant, Mothra-like shadows on the rock face, but there was no other movement. I didn't have a clue what they were all waiting for or why they would want to film any of this, if indeed the cameras were even rolling. I was afraid to move, though, for fear of dislodging a pebble or making any slight sound that might disturb the incredible stillness of the tableau. I did look up when I thought I again heard a flapping of great wings—perhaps even an eagle—but it was only some small stones tumbling off the opposite ridge, and there was nothing to be seen but the starlit sky.

When I looked back down, the monster had vanished. I hadn't heard him scrabble off the rock, but there was no trace of him around the set. As if on cue—well, it probably was—the others all raised their heads off the ground and started moving again. The producer and the money men bowed to each other, then went back inside their trailer while the priest was helped down off the rock. The camera crew began to pack up their gear, and the other crew members strolled back out and started striking the set. All but one of the kliegs got killed, leaving me in sudden but welcome darkness. I shimmied back down from the edge of my perch, deciding I'd better get out of there while the getting was good. I didn't want to risk stumbling over anyone as I slipped away.

That's when it struck me.

I wasn't sure at first, but I had to check before the crew got to it. I scrambled back out to the edge of my rock and turned the binoculars on the bloody mesa. The crew were still fussing with the equipment, and the various "cast" members had left the set. No one was anywhere near the rock.

But the string of intestine was gone.

It hadn't been there when I first looked back at the mesa after glancing up into the sky. I suppose the "monster" must have taken it with him, since I hadn't seen his departure either. But it struck me as especially weird. Maybe not weirder than everything else I had seen, but somehow disturbing.

I didn't have any more time to ponder. I slid down from the perch and followed the trail back down the rocks. I slipped a couple of times on the way, making what sounded to me like a frightful amount of noise, but obviously no one noticed. At ground level, I worked my way back around to where I'd first approached the Rocks. Despite the darkness and rough ground, I was too spooked by what I'd observed to hazard use of my flashlight.

Which is why I tripped over him.

At first I thought it was the dude in the monster getup and all but shit my pants. Even in the dim starlight I could see that there was something wrong with him, but then that he was very small. I flicked on my flashlight and he scurried away a few feet and then turned to face me.

The kid couldn't have been more than eleven or twelve years old and was obviously severely retarded. Though he wore a Dodgers cap, I could tell he had a narrow pinhead, microcephalic, I think is the polite term, with concave indentations on either side of the skull. His broad, flat nose was almost beaklike, an effect intensified by the birdlike nature of his tiny pink eyes. His face was hairy, too, with fuzzy yellow down that made me think of a tiger's fur. He wore a torn T-shirt, revealing scaly, mottled skin on his short arms, and webbed fingers on his stumpy hands. Thalidomide? He smelled like he hadn't been bathed in weeks, a thick, fishy odor that made me want to gag. My initial revulsion over his appearance was tempered my the sudden thought that he must have wandered off the Laughing Boy shoot. My fear that someone would come looking for him was tempered by a horrible idea about *why* they might have brought this pathetic creature out here. After witnessing Cheri's fate, I could only imagine what they might do with a deformed kid.

I flicked the light off of him and turned it on myself. "Hey," I said softly, and held out my hand. "Hey, it's okay."

The boy drew a step closer, bringing that awful rotten-anchovy smell with him. I had to suppress a gag.

"Hey there. Can you speak?"

He stopped and cocked his head to one side, looking more like a bird than before. Actually, he looked like some awful mutant from an eco-horror movie. Toxic Waste Boy, maybe.

"It's all right," I said. "Come with me."

And he started to screech.

It was a noise like a sackful of baby ducks dropped in a vat of hot oil. Or a warren of screaming rabbits played through a stack of Marshall amps. I glanced back toward the Rocks, no more than half a mile away, and though I didn't see anyone coming, knew that they had to have heard that glass-breaking sound.

"No! Kid! Sssshhhh," I tried, but it just got louder. I thought I saw a light flash over by the set, and opted, as always, for discretion over valor. I didn't like the idea of leaving the kid to the Laughing Boy scum, but I didn't see where I had any choice. I made one last effort to reach toward him, but his siren wail went up another ten decibels, so I hauled ass.

Incredibly, I made it back to the car without getting lost. I jumped inside and started the engine, but hesitated a moment before pulling out.

Though he was at least a mile away, I felt pretty sure I could still hear the kid screaming in the murderous night.

Eleven

I tried not to think too much as I sped back down the freeway and into town. I dredged an old Lou Reed tape out of the shoe box under the front seat and rammed it into the cassette deck, letting Lou's astringent guitar and antidulcet New York croon fill my head. I cranked the volume as loud as I could, until the vibration of the tinny little speakers in their mounts threatened to drown out the music.

It didn't do any good.

The picture of Cheri's disembowelment wouldn't go away. I feared that the image of the man in the monster suit unfurling and inspecting her guts with his bare hands, like so much sausage at the deli counter, would be with me for a long time to come. I kept seeing the vacant look on the girl's pretty face as he did it, wondered what they had done to her, shot her up with, that she could go through such horror without so much as a grimace or a squeak. And the others, faces buried in the dirt like ostriches—or like slaves, I thought—obeisant and unmoving. The arcane costumes, the sense of ceremony or ritual. Almost religious, in a perverse sort of way.

Yet all enacted for Jack Rippen's cameras.

People often talk about snuff films, but in all my years in The Business, I'd never known anyone who claimed to have actually seen one for him or herself. They're the stuff of urban legend, like vanishing hitchhikers and hook-handed killers. I even remember reading a feature in the *Times* about how they were a total myth, an invention of screenwriters and religious nuts. Yet here was Jack Rippen, one of the most powerful men in Hollywood, shooting snuff under the aegis of his own prestige production company. What with all that Japanese crap and the two Nips in the suits, I assumed it must be for export, but Jesus! Why would he do it? How much more money could it bring to a man who was set to pocket a billion dollars?

It all served me right, I suppose: never believe anything you read in the fucking *Los Angeles Times.*

By the time I got back to civilization—such as it is—I found that my hands were still literally shaking on the wheel. I knew I should just head straight home, pull the shades, crawl under a blanket for a few weeks, and try to forget everything I'd seen, but I didn't think I could make it. I pulled off the freeway in Studio City and stopped at the first bar I could find that didn't have its name stenciled in cutesy letters and a row of plants in the window. It turned out to be a sports bar—the yuppy, faux-macho equivalent of a fern joint—but I simply couldn't go any further without a bracer.

I marched up to the bar and ordered a double Jack and downed it in a gulp. My hands shook as I picked up the glass.

"More," I told the bartender, a little guy in a mustache and a Lakers jersey. The mustache twitched at me as he eyed my shaking hands, but he poured another glass. I drank it just as fast, which garnered me another twitch.

"Problem?" I asked.

He shrugged, put the bottle away, and started to walk back down the bar, but I stopped him with an order of a pint of Anchor Steam. He managed to keep his lip steady, but an eyebrow went up. Still, he didn't seem any too bothered about taking my money off the counter.

The bourbon didn't go down so good, but then it wasn't supposed to. I took a hefty gulp of the beer, a couple of deep breaths when I started to hiccup from the bubbles, then another gulp. The pint was half-drained, but I started to feel a little better. I continued to shake some and had to hold the mug with both hands. By the time the glass was empty and a replacement was on the way, I had the tremors under something like control. I swiveled on the stool and took a look around.

The place was littered with team pennants, network TV banners, sports photos, schedules and posters of all kinds, draped from every rafter and nook. Eight or ten televisions blasted different ball games from all corners of the room. The Dodgers and Mets, in extra innings from New York, played on the big screen. The sound was up on every set, creating an impossible-to-follow audio jumble. You'd hear a home run called, and by the time you found the right screen, they'd already cut to commercial. The jukebox played as well, though even if I could have heard it clearly, I don't think I'd have recognized the song. Some head-banging retro-punk thing; the kind of music that didn't make any sense to me the first time around when I was supposed to be young enough to understand it. Fortunately, it wasn't enough to overcome the cacophony of the competing stadium organ tunes. Da-da-da-DUM-da-dum . . . charge!

I took a less ferocious first sip of the second beer and started to feel somewhat human again. Amid a roomful of happy baseball fans, in the glow of all those cathode rays and neon Bud signs and the peppy sound of popcorn popping, the whole rest of the night seemed like a bad, impossible dream. Then the shakes started to build again from the inside. I fought them off with a bigger slug of beer and a turn back toward the Dodger game.

That's when I saw them.

It was crazy. It was nothing. They were perfectly harmless, I'm sure.

A group of middle-aged Japanese men in gaudy shirts and golf hats huddled around a table under a life-sized picture of Sandy Koufax. A couple of pitchers of beer sat in front of them as they toasted each other over and over and laughed. They were probably in town on business, relaxing for the evening over a few drinks. Or a bunch of tourists who'd wandered out of their Universal Studios hotel for a taste of American nightlife. God knows, they couldn't have looked any less menacing.

But then one of them saw me staring and caught my eye. He smiled and raised his glass—meaning only to be friendly, I'm sure—revealing a dragon tattoo on his upper forearm. The others glanced my way and raised their glasses, too.

I should have picked up my Anchor Steam.

I should have raised up my mug and toasted them back.

I should have thought nothing of it at all.

Instead, a convulsive shudder built up from somewhere deep in my belly—from my bowel, I greatly suspect. I started shaking worse than before. The bartender must have seen it, 'cause his mustache was twitching as he quickly came my way.

I didn't wait for him. I got up, fast, leaving my money on the counter, and ran towards the door. I heard the Japanese laughing at their table, heard their glasses clink as the televised stadium crowds roared in unison. I barely made it out the door and threw up violently on the sidewalk in front of the bar. A young couple about to walk in abruptly changed their minds and got back in their car.

I suddenly got racked by the chills and heaved up again. As I stood up I crossed my arms over my stomach, felt the perspiration on my skin, the sweat that had soaked through my shirt. The bile in my belly rose up again and I had to fight it down.

I stumbled back to my car, fumbled open the door, and fell into the front. I reclined the seat back and lay there with my eyes closed, sweating and shaking and seeing Cheri's belly ripped open over and over again in my head.

After a while, I don't know how long, somehow—I don't know how—I drove myself home.

Maybe if I hadn't been so shook up, I'd have noticed something was amiss. Or if I hadn't downed the beers and the pair of double JDs. But then maybe not, because the goons who were waiting for me knew their business.

The first one came at me as soon as I closed my front door. He grabbed my right arm and twisted it behind my back as I reached to turn the hall light on. I started to yell, but a leather-gloved hand clamped down over my mouth, and before I could even think to try and bite it, I caught a thunderous blow to the solar plexus which knocked all the wind out of me. If not for the iron grip on my face, I'd have doubled up on the floor right there. The first blow was followed by a rapid series of kidney punches that had me seeing razor-edged stars.

Only sheer, primal instinct prompted me to stomp down on the instep of the guy who was holding me. He didn't quite let go, though the stomp did loosen his grip enough for me to swing my left elbow back into him. I caught him solidly in the gut, and the gloved hand fell away from my face. But before I could take any kind of advantage, his partner sent me into orbit with a steel-toed kick to the balls.

I crumpled to the floor as bright, pinpoint fireworks exploded before me. The attackers immediately launched a series of hard kicks, connecting solidly with my head and back. I tried to cover up, but it was no good; whatever part of me I covered left another area exposed, and they took quick advantage. I tried curling into a ball and rolling away from the assault, but they just followed me as I spun across the hall and into the living room, lashing out with their feet as they went along. Marty Burns, human soccer ball.

It was dark in the house, but the living room curtains hung open. I usually close them at night, because the taco joint down the street,

Chimichang-Ra-La, has a flashing neon display that drives me crazy. Tonight, though, the neon glow provided the only means by which to catch a glimpse of my attackers. I saw that they were both Asian—Japanese, I had to figure—both small, but self-evidently strong. Between trying to cover my face and the stream of blood that dripped into my eyes, I didn't get a very good look at their features, but what I saw, I didn't like. They were expressionless as they went about their business, displaying neither pleasure nor malice, just resolute determination. Even through the pain and blood, something about their expressions seemed familiar to me. With a wash of cold fear, I realized that theirs was a look I'd seen before, on my old best buddy Joey the Jar.

That *really* scared me.

When I couldn't even cover up anymore, the assault came to a stop. One of the goons, slightly taller and with a shaved head, issued a final kick that caught me square in the chest. I heard the rib crack before I felt the pain. I prayed that my lung wasn't pierced, then decided that might be the least of my troubles. Curly stepped on my hand as he cautiously approached the living room window. He drew the curtains and it got very dark. At least, I assumed it was the curtains and not me. He tried to pull them all the way shut, but they wouldn't quite meet in the middle. They never do, they're cheap curtains.

Though it was dim, I could still make out the shapes of my attackers. Curly, the residual neon lighting his head up like an amber Christmas tree bauble, stood over me and planted his small foot on my chest. He applied gentle pressure, but I felt like an almond in a nutcracker as my damaged ribs scraped jagged edges. I coughed—big mistake—and tasted blood in my throat. I tried to spit it out, but ended up drooling it down my chin.

Meanwhile, Curly's partner, Moe, was idly rooting around through my stuff. I had no idea how he could possibly see, but it didn't sound like he was trashing the place too badly. He paused at one point as he was going over my bookshelf. I saw him pull something down. It glowed like Curly's head, and I realized he held my Golden Globe. He spat something in Japanese at Curly, who grunted in response. I found myself wondering if they were Don Siegel fans, too, regretting that I didn't have a picture of myself hamming it up with Toshiro Mifune.

Curly took his foot of my chest, and I managed to catch a breath in the brief respite, even wipe some of the blood off my chin with my sleeve. Just lifting my arm sent waves of pain through my ribs. I hurt everywhere and had to fight the desire to cough, but figured this might be my only chance.

"Listen," I whispered, raising my head, "maybe I can—"

Curly spun around and nailed me under the chin with his toe. The kick hefted me into the air, and I found I couldn't move at all when I came back down with a bone-rattling lurch. My mouth hung open and I tried to shut my jaw, but I couldn't seem to make it work. Little black whirlpools danced across my vision as I pissed in my pants. I tried to groan, but nothing would come out of my throat besides a raspy wheeze. I believe it's called a death rattle.

I heard something go *snick!* and saw a flash out of the corner of my eye. Curly came up behind me and hauled me by the arms to a sitting position, leaning me up against the base of the couch. I think it must have hurt, but the pain had become so overwhelming, so total, that I was beyond noticing anymore. He grabbed me by the hair and raised my chin. Looking up, I saw Moe approaching with a short sword held stiffly before him in both hands.

"Wha . . ." I tried to croak, but the word wouldn't form. Curly tugged again on my hair, further exposing my throat as the swordsman stepped closer. I saw him raise the blade up above his head, the reflected neon from Chimichang-Ra-La changing from cobalt blue to bloodred.

I closed my eyes.

I heard a muffled "Ooof," thought it was the blade descending toward my throat.

But the blow never came.

Curly suddenly let go of my hair, and I opened my eyes as I fell over sideways. Another tide of darkness washed across me as I made contact with the floor, but I fought to hold on to consciousness. Curly, his bald head bobbing like the bouncing ball in those old sing-along cartoons, was struggling with someone in the middle of the living room. At first I thought he was duking it out with his partner, but then I saw Moe on the floor, impaled through the throat with his own blade. I couldn't see the blood, but I could smell it; it must have made a mess, and bizarrely, I found myself thinking that now I'd never get my cleaning deposit back.

Curly seemed to be taking a thrashing in the fight, but I still couldn't make out his assailant in the dark. Whoever it was, he was quick and deadly silent. The only sounds came from blows struck on Curly's flesh. They were definitely battling martial-arts style, though the sound of the blows was nothing at all like the dubbed Naugahyde slaps of chop-socky movies. I heard Curly's pained gasps as each new thrust connected. Curly said something to his foe in Japanese, but the other only responded with his feet and fists. Curly went down hard several times, bouncing right back up only to take yet another blow to the face.

Finally, in some desperation, I sensed, Curly tried to get inside on his opponent and the two grappled like wrestlers. They danced farther backward into the living room, away from the light, where I couldn't make out anything beyond the vaguest of shapes. I tried to drag myself across the floor for a better view, but failed to make it more than six inches before quitting for the pain. I could hear them knocking items off my desk as Curly's moans grew louder. Glass smashed on the floor, followed by a loud, sudden, and terrifying crack. One of the two fighters collapsed to the floor with a thud.

Then there was silence.

I thought a saw a dark shadow disappear down the hall, but it moved with inhuman speed. Just then a car turned up the street, its headlights briefly flashing across my living room window. The glare was enough to illuminate the dome of Curly's head on the floor. The light faded quickly and my vision was woozy, but I'm certain that his neck had been twisted in an impossible way.

I tried again to drag myself across the floor, reaching a hand up to the couch to brace myself. It landed in something wet and sticky on the leather cushion and slipped off, sending me falling back toward the floor.

I think I passed out *before* my head hit the ground.

The sound of a garbage truck woke me up. At least, I thought it was a garbage truck; when the sound didn't go away after about ten minutes, I realized it was something in my head.

It was just after five-thirty in the morning when I came around. The sun hadn't quite risen yet, but the night was well in retreat and the pale gray predawn began to stick its fingers through the window. I was overwhelmed by the pain in my head and chest and gut. The taste of blood filled my mouth and throat, and my first attempt at a deep breath reminded me of the broken rib. Or ribs. It sure hurt enough to be a well-barbecued rack.

By the time I managed to haul myself onto the couch and the grating, garbage-truck whir began to fade in my head, the memory of the assault lit up my brain. With no small effort, I lifted up my head and forced myself to take a look around, wondering how I was going to explain the two bodies in my apartment to Rowan and Holloway.

But the bodies were gone.

The place was still a mess—I mean *more* of a mess than it usually is—with books and bric-a-brac strewn across the floor. There was a terminally large bloodstain, still tacky, in the middle of the carpet, and several smaller ones on various items of furniture. Tiny splotches of red spattered the glass on my framed poster of *The Man with the Golden Arm*. My wooden desk chair had been busted like kindling, and broken glass was sprinkled about the floor like morning dew.

But no bodies.

I slumped back against the couch and tried to piece together what had gone down. Someone had come in and taken out Curly and Moe for me. Taken them out of the fight and then literally taken their bodies out of my house. Why and how—not to mention *who*—I didn't have the faintest idea. My assailants never even told me what they were after—though it didn't take too much thinking to come up with an idea—they just attacked. I had to believe that meant there was some kind of contract out on me, which meant I needed to get the hell out to someplace where they couldn't find me.

But then, whoever had saved me might not know how to find me either. Not that I had a clue how he had found me to begin with. I had to believe that the attack on me was a consequence of what I had witnessed out at Vasquez Rocks. The fact that Curly and Moe were Japanese was the proof positive as far as I was concerned. Maybe the Greek-mask boys at the gate had written down my license plate number and they tracked me through that. Or someone else saw me take off after my encounter with the retarded kid. Either way, the finger pointed at Laughing Boy.

But then who would have been stalking the stalkers? Who would have let go down what went down at the Rocks, but then spend the effort to save my bony ass? And what did they do with the bodies that left the stains in my rug?

Oh, did my head hurt.

Summoning reserves of strength not drawn upon since my Hollywood partying days, I got off the couch and onto my feet. I swayed a bit, but managed to stay upright: one of my finest performances. Careful not to step on the bloodstains, I edged my way around the room, stumbling down the hall and into the bathroom. The sight that greeted me in the mirror wasn't a pretty one.

Polka-dot patches of dried blood matted my hair. My chin was also smeared with dry brown. I had one tennis-ball-sized bruise, all purple and black, under my chin, and another smaller one at my right temple, but my face was surprisingly intact, especially given how it felt. I washed my face and brushed my teeth, spitting out gobs of brown clots, and discovered a couple of loose teeth on the right side. With great care, I unbuttoned my shirt and groaned, half from the pain in my ribs, half at the ugly sight of a dozen purple bruises across my chest and torso. I gingerly pressed a finger to each of them, but found I couldn't fairly say which was the most painful of the lot. I found that the pain in my ribs remained just shy of excruciating if I didn't breathe too deeply. The fact that I could breathe at all suggested to me that the lung hadn't been punctured, but I knew I should get to a doctor before too long.

I was so absorbed in my misery that I wasn't consciously thinking about what had happened at that moment, but I suppose it all had to be bubbling away under the surface. I was still trying just to strip off, with the idea of slipping into a hot bath, when the notion struck me. I hadn't been thinking about it and then I was. It appeared with the suddenness and malignancy of a tumor and it wouldn't go away. It was more like intuition, really—or precognition—than conscious thought, but I was overwhelmed by it. Even the pain and the allure of a bath couldn't separate me from it.

I had to move.

I didn't even stop to find a clean shirt, just put last night's bloodstained one right back on. I did at least have the sense to grab a windbreaker and a baseball cap to cover my bloody hair, but that was my only concession to reason. I flew—well, quickly staggered—out of the house and across the street to my car. The panic in my stomach grew so fast and big that it pushed even the pain in my ribs out of my system. I drove like a madman, which is to say like a true Angelino.

The firemen were still on the scene as I pulled up across from Night Haven.

The crowd of observers was small for a fire, but then it was early in the morning. Mostly, the bystanders were hookers. Refugees from inside, I prayed.

I hobbled out of the car to the edge of the yellow police cordon that had been raised. I approached one of the firemen who was smoking a cigarette on the sidelines.

"What happened?" I rasped.

He looked me over and sneered. "You get mugged or you just a bum?" he asked.

I suppose I deserved it, but I was still fighting the panic. "What the fuck happened?" I yelled.

He tossed his cigarette—without stamping it out, I might note—and scratched his burly, unshaved neck. "Fire," he said.

"I can see that. But what *happened?*"

"Place burned down," he said, nodding. "Probably arson. Hey, you're not with *The Times*, are you?"

I looked down at my disheveled, filthy self, then back at him. "No," I said, *"Daily News."*

"Well, that arson thing was off the record, okay? I could get in trouble."

"Was anybody hurt?" I begged.

"Nah!" he said, lighting up again. I felt a little of the panic start to ebb. "Them cunts move fast. They all got out okay."

"What about Rosa Mendez?"

"Heh?"

"Rosa Mendez. She runs Night Haven."

"Nobody hurt's all I know. At least we ain't found no bodies. Don't know about the madam."

A wave of relief washed over me, and he must have noticed it. "You a regular?" he asked with a smirk.

"Say what?"

"You a regular john? Some of these young 'uns look pretty nice. What for hookers and all."

I tried to glare at him with contempt, but I was never very good at it in the best of times, and given my own recent activities, my moral-outrage battery was running a little low. So I just walked away.

I wandered down toward the corner where a group of Rosa's girls were standing around watching the action. One of them was still wearing her street outfit, but the others were clad only in pajamas. They all young and looked like refugees from a sleep-away camp. I recognized one of them as the girl with the flower tattoo I had met on my first visit to Night Haven.

"Hey," I said, approaching cautiously. They started to edge away until the girl, Debby her name was, recognized me. "Any of you seen Rosa?"

An anorexic blonde with a nose ring started to cry. One of the others embraced her in a gentle hug.

"Don't know where she is," Debby told me.

"Was she inside when the fire broke out?" I asked.

The girls all looked at each other. Debby answered for them: "Ginny and Tra-la say she weren't, but Coco thinks she was. I didn't see her last night, but I don't know. We scared."

They all looked close to tears. I felt the ball of panic start to bounce again in my belly.

"I'm sure she's fine," I said, but my voice wavered and the girls picked up on it. "I mean . . . the fireman said they didn't find any . . . That is to say, they don't think anyone was hurt." The anorexic continued to cry, and Debby sniffled herself. "Any of you see what happened? How the fire started?"

They all shook their heads. A roar came from across the street as another section of roof collapsed into the ruins of Night Haven.

"Place burned down," Debby said, her voice breaking. "Just burn right down."

Well, at least everyone was agreed on that.

Invocation (III)

A corona of hot light blurs the edge of the darkness, like some ever-present threat of dawn. It brings with it a cascade of fractured and confusing images of the strange, new world seen through a whizzing cascade of demons' eyes. Slowly, slowly, his ancient mind grapples to make sense of it, to bring it all together. To ready himself for the time when he will move upon it and within it. There are sounds, too: a constant, if distant, buzz of summoners' prayers and chants of invocation, the screams of sacrifices and the cackle of oni delight.

And there is a consciousness.

With the suddenness of a scorpion's sting, it is present and he is aware of it.

The one who will be: the human shell that awaits his pleasure, through which he will act and walk again upon the corpses of his enemies.

He reaches a piece of himself toward it through the blackness, grasping for the light and the taste of blood. The light flickers and strobes, confusing him as he tries to race across the slender connection. There are images within images, sounds on top of sounds. He cannot be sure of the trail down which the connection flows. He catches a glimpse of flames, a brief taste of charred meat. For an orgasmic moment he experiences the sensation of corporeality—the feel and flex of human skin and bone—as a searing heat laps the night sky.

Then it fades and is gone as the blackness returns. He wails his frustration as a silent scream when he finds himself back again in the darkness.

The time is not yet come.

But the light is that much brighter and his moment grows ever closer.

Twelve

It cost me nearly four hundred bucks to get my ribs poked, prodded, X-rayed, and taped up at a local clinic. That's what they call health-care reform in this country. The doctor, an Indian woman with an over-bite and a name I couldn't pronounce, confirmed that I had one broken rib and no punctured lung. She seemed pretty impressed by my bruises. But since I didn't have any gunshot wounds and I paid in cash, she didn't bother to ask any questions beyond the purely medical. She handed me a prescription for two months worth of codeine and sent me on my merry way.

Life in Hollywood.

The doctor did a pretty good job on the ribs, too. It still hurt like a banshee scream, but I found moving around a lot easier after the tape job. I didn't quite feel up for a session of Nautilus training, but then I wouldn't have under any circumstances. Given the extremity of the beat-ing, *physically* I didn't feel half-bad. Of course, the prescription, which I immediately filled at a discount drugstore, may have had some influence on that.

My mental state was something else again.

It had proven to be an unpleasantly eventful eighteen hours or so. Cheri's snuff-film murder at Vasquez Rocks. The Pearl Harbor reenact-ment at my place and the mysterious savior who broke it up. The fire at Night Haven and Rosa's disappearance. I was amazed to realize that I was more concerned about Rosa's well-being and whereabouts than any of the rest.

I tried, fruitlessly, to piece it together as I drove away from the clinic. At first I thought I shouldn't risk going back to my house, but I didn't have anyplace else to go. At the very least my clothes and money were still there and I'd have to pick them up. And I doubted that another as-sault was likely—certainly not in broad daylight—and not after what had happened to the first set of assailants.

Of course, I didn't actually know what *had* happened to them, though I was pretty sure they were dead, especially considering the kink in Curly's neck.

It all looked normal enough as I parked in front of the house. I sat in the car for a few minutes looking the place over, but everything seemed fine, down to the tattered copy of the *Times* tossed, as usual, into the shrubs by the front door. I sauntered up and opened the door carefully, letting it swing inwards. I stuck my head in, then ducked back out to grab the paper before going inside.

It looked clear.

I did a room-by-room search—that took almost forty seconds—to satisfy what I regarded as fully justified paranoia, though even I felt a little silly as I squatted down to look under the bed.

Nothing but dust bunnies and dirty magazines.

I found a lonely bottle of Henry's in the fridge, almost popped it open as I heard it cry "drink me" in a sad little orphan's voice, but swapped it instead for a big glass of orange juice and another codeine tablet. I sat down in the living room for a think, something I really had to start doing more of, but couldn't stand to sit there with the sight of blood still on the carpet. I picked up my newspaper, gingerly stepping around the stain, and sat back down at the dining table in my kitchen.

I quickly skimmed the front page, but of course, there was nothing in the early edition about the fire at Night Haven. I flicked the radio on and dialed up an all-news station. I listened though the traffic, weather, and sports for the next set of headlines, but they didn't mention Night Haven either, and when they started back in on the traffic I turned it off.

I hated to do it, but I picked up the phone. I dialed the 69th and asked for Sid. The switchboard knows better than to ask who's calling, which is a good thing. I didn't know if Sid would want to talk to me.

The extension rang six times before he answered with: "Teitlebaum."

"Hi, Sid. It's Marty Burns."

Dead silence.

"You still there?"

He sniffled. "I can't decide," he said. "Convince me."

I took a deep breath. "Night Haven," I said.

I heard *him* exhale. "What do you know about that, Marty?"

"Actually, that's what I was calling to ask you."

"I don't like this conversation. At all. What's going on here? Why are you asking about Night Haven?"

I didn't want to lie to him again, but wasn't prepared to come clean just yet. Especially on the phone. "Is Rosa Mendez all right?"

"What's that to you?" Sid shot back. "What do you know about it?"

"Listen, Sid, I drove by Night Haven this morning—"

"What were you doing there?"

"I . . ." I wasn't sure what to tell him. "I was looking for Rosa."

"Why? What's your involvement with her?" He was getting madder.

"She . . . she hired me," I told him.

"Bullshit!" he yelled. "I heard tell how she slapped you around the other night. Straczynski's still laughing about it, trying to get pictures. Why would she hire you after that? What for?"

"A couple of hookers—her girls, she calls them—went missing. She thought they might have been hanging with Long John's girl, the dead one. She's worried about them and thought maybe I knew something about where they might have gone."

"Do you?"

"That's not important now. If you want, we can meet later and I'll tell you what I have, though it's not much." That lie slipped out easy enough. "I just want to know if Rosa's all right."

I could *hear* Sid thinking on the other end of the line, weighing what to tell me. I heard another person talking to him in the office, judged it to be Straczynski from the tone, though I couldn't make out what he said.

"I don't know," he finally said. "I don't know if she's okay. We haven't been able to find her."

"No bodies at the scene?" I asked.

"No," he said. "You disappointed?"

"Far from it," I sighed. "Any idea how the fire started?"

"No. But I don't think I'd tell you know if I knew. I don't like this at all, Marty. This conversation is definitely NG. I want to see you. Pronto."

"I can't, Sid. Not right this minute. I'll . . ."

I froze.

"Marty? Marty! You still there?"

I held the phone in my hand, but I couldn't speak. Sid kept yelling my name, accompanied by increasingly fouler profanities, but I was riveted by an item in the paper. I'd thrown it on the table when I sat down, and the Metro section had slipped out of the bundle. I hadn't even glanced at it then, but now a headline caught my full attention: *Agent Found Mutilated.*

Beside it was a small photograph of Mickey Marvin, the cigar-chomping clown I'd run into at the Laughing Dog offices.

"I got to go," I whispered into the phone. At least I think I said it. Sid continued to scream my name as I hung up the receiver.

The story sat below the fold and was only two columns long. A homeless dude had found Marvin's body sticking out of a Dumpster in North Hollywood. The reporter trod delicately around the facts, suggesting that the corpse had suffered "dismemberment of a reputedly sexual nature." *The Times* is, as they never fail to remind you, a *family* newspaper.

Translation: Marvin's equipment had been hacked off, and I don't mean his cigar.

I read the story three times, but there wasn't much there. Marvin was tersely characterized as a minor talent agent, bottom-feeding around the edges of The Business. The cops had no leads, the story concluded.

I reckoned I might be able to provide them with one or two. But for the sake of my already tenuous health, I didn't know if I should.

In the end I blame it all on *The Times*. The article about Mickey Marvin raised the hackles, sure, but it was a piece in the Calendar section that really set me off. Another worshipful profile of Jack Rippen and his latest charity venture, some homes-for-the-homeless or legs-for-the-legless crap designed to make the Ripper look human. There was nothing unusual about the story; the Hollywood publicity machines spit them out like clockwork, and the suck-ups who run the Calendar section—a newsroom full of big-lipped slugs permanently affixed to the butt of The Business—run them with obsequious glee. A PR puff piece, pure and true, accompanied by a photo of Rippen as flattering as anything William Daniels ever snapped of Garbo or Dietrich. The paper's chock-full of such fluff, and normally I don't pay the stories any mind. They're just part and parcel of living in an industry town.

But today it more than rankled.

It made me furious.

Maybe I didn't exactly know the whys and wherefores of all that was going down around me—kidnapping, assault, murder, arson, just for a start—but it was clear that it all came down around Laughing Boy. Maybe Rippen didn't know a thing about any of it—*probably* he didn't—but that didn't mean he didn't have responsibility. I had no doubts about the link between Celestial Dog and Laughing Boy, and I had seen the Celestial Dog crew callously slaughter a young girl for the sake of a few feet of film. And I had to assume that Long John and his girl were taken out by Celestial Dog as well, maybe for knowing too much. Probably Mickey Marvin, too, though that was sheer conjecture on my part. Still, it wasn't exactly a Grand Canyon leap from that set of events to the failed attack on me and the successful torching of Night Haven. And to Rosa's disappearance.

I dug through the back of my bedroom closet and found the Armani suit. A bit out of style and a tad musty to the nose, but not bad-looking at all. It was one of my last remaining vestiges of better times, higher living. It cost more than a grand when I bought it all those years ago, and I couldn't remember the last time I'd put it on. A whole career's worth of memories, sweet and bitter, went with it like mismatched cuff links. Sometimes, when I'm feeling particularly wistful, I'll take it out of the closet and stroke the fabric. Pathetic or what?

The acts of dressing and undressing caused needles of pain to shoot through my chest, so I popped another tab of codeine. It left me feeling a little light-headed, but I thought the buzz might actually offer an advantage for what I was about to do. The suit had grown kind of tight around the crotch and midriff—or I had grown kind of loose—but I managed to squeeze into it without busting a seam. I didn't have a decent enough pair of shoes to do the suit justice, but even in scuffed, tasseled Florsheims, I thought I didn't look half-bad.

If you sort of ignored the purple and black bruises on my face.

I certainly shouldn't have driven, stoked to the gills as I was on codeine, but then wanton stupidity is half the fun of drugs, I've always believed. I managed to drive the car with reasonable aplomb as I cruised up Melrose, and only blew through one set of red lights. I nearly clipped a pedestrian as I turned up La Cienega, but if the bastard had any sense of self-worth, he wouldn't have been walking in L.A. anyway.

Above all else, Jack Rippen was famous for two things: first and foremost for being the most ruthless, successful, and hated son of a bitch in Hollywood; secondly, for eating lunch every single day in the same restaurant: Samizdat.

Samizdat is one of a group of ultrahip, ultraexpensive eateries owned and run by a Eurotrash couple named Klaus and Barbie Korzybski. They insist that those are their real names and refuse to change them. At least they recognize that the names are a tad . . . problematic, especially given the predominance of Jews in The Business, so they're conspicuous contributors to several major Jewish charities, and they turn up every year on the Chabad Telethon along with Jon Voight. In any event, their names don't seem to hurt business any. Agitprop in Santa Monica supposedly has the best eats of their three places, and Mao-Mao in Venice is the most expensive, but Samizdat is *the place* to be seen, thanks in no small part to Jack Rippen. It's where he hosts the biggest and gaudiest of the post-Oscar parties every year. At lunchtime the hoi polloi are permitted to litter the bar if they're well dressed enough, but no one who isn't someone *ever* gets a table. I've heard rumors that Rippen actually bankrolled the place, but his compulsive attendance is probably just an affectation. It simply contributes to the image that suits him.

I didn't waste my time with the restaurant's Versace-vested valets—there wasn't a pauper's dream that they would even *consider* parking a Subaru—but instead pulled off onto a side street and parked the car myself. Right off the bat it would mark me as hopelessly déclassé to walk into Samizdat off the street, but I was counting on the Armani to get me past the maître d' and into the bar. From there it would have to be pure swagger and bluff.

I caught a minor break when the maître d' was away from the door as I walked into the restaurant. I ducked quickly around the reception podium and into the bar area. It was slightly early for lunch, but the lounge was hopping. I felt like I'd walked through a movie screen and into *Bringing Up Baby* or *The Philadelphia Story* or some such. The customers all seemed to have wandered in from some other dimension, where jeans and sneakers and day jobs don't exist. No one in the bar looked to be over thirty—other than me, of course—with nary a midriff bulge or visible panty line in sight. Compared to what the rest of the men wore, my old Armani looked like an off-the-rack bargain-store special. Both the gentlemen and ladies sported flashier bridgework than the Golden Gate, and I couldn't remember the last time I'd seen this much cleavage outside of a Russ Meyer film. And all for *lunch!*

It brought a lot of old memories flooding back. When I used to fit in, be welcomed and feted at places like this. When all that cleavage and dental porcelain was pointing my way.

Now everyone seemed to be staring at my scuffed shoes—to the extent that they noticed me at all.

I squeezed in at the end of the bar nearest the dining room so I could scope out the action on the main floor. I hadn't yet spotted Rippen's table when the bartender cleared his throat at me.

"You in the right place, fellah?" he asked. He was eyeing the purple blotch under my chin. Thank God he couldn't see my feet.

"Spago, right?" I said.

He wasn't amused.

"It's okay," I told him, "I'm Danny De Vito's personal trainer."

"Huh," he said. It seemed to satisfy him. "Hell of a bruise you got there."

"Polo injury," I said, nodding. It appeared to confuse him.

"Ralph Lauren?" he asked.

"Yeah," I said. "He and Danny work out together. They're a couple of animals, I tell you." The bartender nodded as if that explained things. In the through-the-looking-glass world of Samizdat, it probably did.

"What can I get you?"

I considered the four codeine tablets I'd already swallowed that morning and thought about a Perrier and lime.

"Bourbon rocks," I said, laying a ten on the bar. He poured the drink and took the bill. He didn't bring any change.

All the old memories.

Although the bar area was rather small and close—the hoi polloi thing—the rest of Samizdat looked like it might have started out as a furniture showroom or perhaps an airplane hangar. The dining room featured an incredibly high ceiling that lent the restaurant an extravagant sense of open space, exaggerated by big skylights and a light aqua color scheme. The tables were big, few, and far apart; the waiters tall, numerous, and Teutonic. The chef had become famous for his novel blending of Mexican and Thai cuisines. It sounded kind of revolting to me—yumyai in a tostada shell: yikes!—but then I couldn't afford it anyway. And Samizdat had become so much the place to be seen that I reckon they could have served crispy turds in smegma sauce and garnered a praise-be-to-God from Egon Ronay for the effort.

I leaned out over the rail separating the bar from the dining room, but still didn't see Rippen around. The place had filled up in a hurry and I only spotted one empty table. It was on a slightly raised dais lit by a couple of hidden spots. It commanded an ideal view of the restaurant and couldn't be missed by anyone else in the place. It had to be reserved for Rippen.

"Looking for someone?"

The bartender had returned and was looking suspicious again. I sat back down and gestured for another drink. He didn't move.

"Danny's supposed to be here with Jack Rippen," I said. "Do you know when he usually arrives for lunch?"

The bartender looked at me as if I'd asked him if he knew what color the sky usually was. He crossed his arms and pursed his lips. "*Mr.* Rippen arrives promptly at 12:10."

"Well, there you go," I said, and slapped my hand on the bar. "That damned De Vito told me eleven fifty-five. Who can you trust nowadays?"

The bartender continued to scowl at me, but at last went ahead and filled my glass. Another sawbuck departed into the Nazi void.

At exactly 12:10 on the big Samizdat clock—the face was a photo of Mikhail Gorbachev; his strawberry birthmark blinked the seconds—Jack Rippen and his entourage made their entrance. Two beefy bodyguards wearing dark glasses and Goons 'R Us suits preceded his royal Ripperness, who was probably the least fashionably dressed person in the house. He wore a pair of plain khaki chinos and a red polo shirt with the Laughing Boy logo emblazoned where the alligator used to sleep. The Ripper strode in glancing through a sheaf of papers and never looked up as he paraded across the restaurant to his waiting table. Like a western town at high noon, everyone else in the place stopped in midmotion—some with satay nachos en route to waiting lips—and watched The Ripper accede to his throne. Rippen continued to stare at his papers as he sat, not even looking up when the maître d' placed a glass of clear liquid in his outstretched hand.

Like everyone else, I was so entranced by the Ripper that I hadn't paid any notice to the trailing members of the parade. A stunning young woman who I dimly recognized from some dreadful sitcom sat down on his left, and a man whose face I hadn't noticed—did I mention that the sitcom babe wore a white silk blouse and no bra?—sat down with his back to me. A team of waiters immediately began bringing plates of food, though no one in the party had been handed a menu. When Rippen finally looked up, he stared directly at me, but not surprisingly, I failed to register in his consciousness and his gaze quickly panned across and dismissed the room.

Although one waiter continued to hover near Rippen's table, there seemed to be a lull between courses. I figured it was now or never, put down the last of my bourbon, and got to my feet.

"Where's Danny?"

"Huh?" I said.

The bartender was peering over at Rippen's table. "I thought you said De Vito was supposed to be with him. I've never seen the little guy."

I dropped the empty glass onto the bar with a thud. "That rat bastard!" I said. "I'm going to find out where the hell that midget son of a bitch is!"

With that I stormed out of the bar and made a beeline for Rippen's table. I marched quickly and purposefully, though in truth, I hadn't worked out exactly what to do when I got there. I was counting on those old actorly improvisational skills to carry me through. Along with my anger.

Though I was focused on Rippen, who had returned his gaze to his stack of paper, I did notice the expressions on the faces of some of the other patrons as I stormed up the aisle. I'm certain I saw a few jaws drop and heard a glass crash behind me. Even the bodyguards appeared stunned by my boldness. They sat at a table at floor level, just below Rippen's platform, and simply watched as I whipped past them. I leapt up the two steps to the table and leaned down over the back of Rippen's lunch companion.

"Long time no see, J.J." I said.

I felt the man below me all but jump out of his chair, and the sitcom honey gagged on her prawn crackers and salsa, but Rippen slowly looked up at me. Before he had even fully taken me in, the bodyguards were on me, each grabbing me by an arm. The maître d' came running up the aisle in a nervous half crouch, trailed by two waiters. They looked like the Marx Brothers in *Room Service.*

Rippen looked good. No, not true: he looked spectacular. Even better than in his retouched publicity photos. Deep bronze complexion that was all sun, no tanning bed. Thick chest and muscular arms that rippled out of his shirtsleeves like suspension cables and attested to a personal trainer slightly more expert in his guidance than Danny De Vito's. Blue contacts and blinding white teeth that had to be caps, yet were expensive enough to look perfectly natural.

And the best hair transplant job I'd ever seen. I only knew it was plugs because J. J. Ripowitz had been balding when I'd known him more than twenty years earlier. No one else would ever guess. Rippen's hair put Paul Simon's plug job to shame.

Rippen had barely looked me over before he dismissed me with a slight jiggle of two fingers. His goons started hauling me away and the maître d' was well into a fawning apology when Rippen's head snapped back up and he took another look.

"Hold," he said.

Everybody froze. Me, too, though sandwiched by the bodyguards, my feet were barely in contact with the floor.

"Martin Burns," Rippen said, and waggled his fingers again. The goons hefted me back up to the table. The maître d' wavered between confusion and panic.

"How's it going, Jack?" I forced a smile.

"My God," Rippen said, though it sounded like he was talking to himself. "I feel like I've stumbled across an old grade school report card."

"A-plus, J.J.," I said.

"Nostalgia city," Rippen said, still shaking his head. He waved the bodyguards away and gestured toward the empty chair. The maître d' quickly pulled it out for me. "This is Martin Burns," Rippen said to his companions. "He's . . . he was . . . I don't actually know what you are, Martin."

"Just another stardust memory," I said, and sat down. I smiled and nodded at the young woman, who looked me over like a museum curio, then turned for the first time to the other man.

And nearly fell off the chair.

It was the producer I'd seen at the snuff shoot at Vasquez Rocks, the fellow with the Japanese money men who'd watched the killing go down. He showed no sign of recognition, but eyed me dubiously. I felt my heart start to race, but tried not to react.

"This is Karl Aldus," Rippen said, pointing to the producer. I grokked to the name from my visit to Laughing Boy. Aldus vaguely nodded. "And of course, you recognize Alex Gilbert."

The girl flashed a TV smile at me, then her mouth formed a big O and she gasped. "Hot enough for you?" she squealed, and grabbed my arm. "God, I *love* your show. It's so *retro.*"

She seemed so genuinely excited that I think I actually blushed as she beamed at me. Aldus continued to give me the evil eye, but Rippen flashed a tiny smile of his own.

"That's because it's twenty-five years old," he explained to her. I honest-to-God think she didn't know. Christ, what a town. "To what do we owe this . . . unexpected pleasure?" Rippen's eyes flicked on his goons as he emphasized "unexpected." I smelled an impending rise in the unemployment rate.

I looked over at Aldus and shuddered slightly as Cheri's image flashed back on me. He glared at me with undisguised hostility now, and the notion that he knew exactly who I was and that he was behind the assault on me suddenly took hold in my mind. I turned back to Rippen, who betrayed only amusement. I didn't know what to think about how much he knew.

"I'd like to discuss some business with you," I said. "It concerns Laughing Boy."

"Hmmm." The Ripper shrugged. "I can't imagine what. You're not *in* The Business, anymore." It wasn't a question, and you could hear the capital letters in the way he said it.

"Oh, you never can stray too far from the action in this town. But you know that."

"Let me see. I seem to remember reading something about you; one of those whatever-became-of things. You're a security guard now. Or is it a night watchman?"

"Private investigator," I said.

"Wow!" Alex chirped. "Neat!"

"Yes," Rippen said. "How very *Mannix* of you. You get that face working on a case?"

I fingered the bruise under my chin. "Aw, you know: no one and nothing gets in the way of Joe Mannix when his Peggy's in trouble."

"What do you want?" Aldus asked. He sounded like he needed to clear his throat.

I figured the direct approach was best: "I wanted to talk to you about Celestial Dog," I said.

Aldus inhaled sharply and his eyes went wide, but Rippen was good. Not even a blink. "Intriguing name. The title of your screenplay, I presume?"

I waited for the waiter to put a heaping plate of tiger shrimp soft tacos down on the table and depart. "It *is* a most interesting name," I said, "but I don't have a script to hawk."

"No way!" Sitcom Girl squealed. "Do you, like, *totally* not live in L.A.?"

I meant to ignore her, but the remark drew an unintentional double take. When I looked back at Rippen he offered an eyebrow shrug which rather elegantly said: "What can you do; she's a piece and it's a living." Aldus nervously played with his spoon.

"Actually," I continued, taking a sip from the glass of champagne that had almost magically appeared in front of me, "Celestial Dog is a production company. I believe they've been working on some . . . projects with Laughing Boy."

"It seems unlikely," Rippen said, "but then Laughing Boy is rather a large operation these days. I don't pay the details too much mind." He never took his eyes off me or broke his poker face. "Karl here manages the day-to-day . . . problems. Are you familiar with this . . . What was the name?"

"Celestial Dog," I said. "I can spell it if that'd help."

"I think it's a cute name," the girl said.

"Do we know any Celestial Dogs, Karl?"

"Never heard of 'em," Aldus growled. He had bent his spoon almost in half. You'd think Klaus and Barbie might spring for better cutlery.

"There you go," Rippen said. "Obviously you're mistaken."

"Obviously," I said. I started to get up. "Well, I did want to check with you before going to the police."

"Police?" Rippen said.

"Yeah, it has to do with the death of a guy named Mickey Marvin."

"Oooooo," the actress said. I don't know why.

"My, but you do travel in high circles," Rippen said. "Do we know Mr. Marvin, Karl?"

"We may have had some business," Aldus growled.

"Then perhaps we should discuss this in greater depth," Rippen said.

"Hey, you got the beer, I got the time," I said. I started to sit again, but Rippen held up his hand.

"Not now," he said. Any trace of mirth had fled his face.

"When?"

"Tonight," Rippen said. "We're shooting on the Sony lot in Culver City. It's only been there about fifteen years. Do you know it?"

"I think I can find my way," I said, swallowing the dig with as Ripper-like a smile as I could muster.

"I'll leave your name at the gate. We should be done with the shoot by ten o'clock."

"I can't wait," I said. I smiled at the girl, who crinkled her eyes at me, and I tried not to look at Aldus. I was no more than five steps down the aisle when I heard Rippen call after me.

"And get yourself some new shoes, Martin," he said. Loud enough for everyone to hear. "Or at least spring for a shine."

I tried hard to ignore the laughter as I crawled out.

Thirteen

The Samizdat tacos left me with killer heartburn. Or maybe it was just meeting Rippen that upset my stomach. In any event, I drove through a McDonald's for a large shake to ease the agita. It tasted, as always, like a blend of thirty-weight and vanilla extract. I had intended to get a real shake at Johnny Rockets, but when I got there I found that I couldn't bring myself to walk through the door for thinking about Long John's girl. Still, the McDonald's potion cooled the flames. And no one there made fun of my shoes.

I mused over the confrontation with Rippen as I drove. Aldus was a nervous Nellie, but the Ripper had been cool, not given a thing away. I couldn't even be sure that he actually knew anything about what Celestial Dog was up to. Still, why would he have agreed to meet me again if he didn't know that there was something less than kosher about the operation? I felt more than a little squeamish about a late night assignation with him, but reckoned I would probably be safe enough on the studio lot. Certainly no *less* safe than in my own damned house, as I'd learned the hard way. As I finished my shake and cruised east down Melrose through Little El Salvador, I considered the merits of getting myself a gun, and just as quickly dismissed the idea.

In Hollywood it wouldn't take more than ten minutes to find a reliable, untraceable piece for cash. Trouble was that the only time I'd ever fired a gun was in a movie, and then I was shooting blanks—in more ways than one. I played a crazed mutant in a schlocky sci-fi actioner called *Helltown U.S.A.* and almost managed to deafen Chuck Conners when I fired the piece off too close to his ear. The only other thing I can remember about that flick was how Conners used to sing the theme from *Branded* to himself all the time. By the end of the shoot the cast and crew knew all the words.

A fresh burst of heartburn, along with a prodding throb in the rib cage, hit me as I turned onto my street in Silver Lake. I found a spot right out in front of the house, but once again dallied in the car just to look things over.

Something didn't look right.

I tried mentally to run through my actions earlier in the day, after coming home from the clinic. I remembered the Japanese goons pulling the living room curtains closed last night as they roughed me up. I know I didn't touch them when I finally came around early in the morning, but I was sure—well, pretty sure—that I had opened them back up when I came home from the doctor.

The curtains were drawn shut now.

Nothing else looked amiss. No one was out on the street, and there wasn't even another car parked for half a block. I sat there drumming my fingers on the steering wheel, staring at my front window and trying to decide what to do.

"Fuck it," I said.

I tossed the empty shake cup under the seat and got out of the car. I went around to the back and opened the hatch, tossing the musty blankets and sweatshirts and frayed jumper cables out onto the grass. I pulled up the bottom panel and pried the thick metal jack handle out of its slot. It was half-rusted in and required some doing to free it. I'd never even used the thing. The one time I'd punctured a tire and tried to change it myself, I couldn't figure out how to make the damned jack work. I ended up driving all the way to a gas station, ruining a rim in the process.

I hefted the jack handle, gripping it tightly in my right hand. I thought about slipping around to the yard and going in through the back door, but figured that if anyone was inside, they'd already have seen me out front and wouldn't be surprised. Besides, the yard was too secluded; if I had to dash back outside in a hurry, it would be safer to make straight for the street.

I walked slowly up the path to my front door, keeping an eye on the living room window. I thought I saw the curtain stir as I mounted the single, concrete step leading to the door, but couldn't tell if it had really moved or if I was just paranoid. I switched the jack handle to my left hand and fished the keys out of my pocket. I slipped the key into the lock, then switched the metal rod back into my right hand. I turned the key until the dead bolt clicked, then pressed my ear against the door.

No sound.

I turned the knob and quickly kicked at the door with my right foot, taking a quick step back and raising the jack handle up over my shoulder as it shot open.

The hall was deserted.

I took a cautious step forward, jack handle poised to strike, and stuck my head quickly through the door to peer around the jamb. That's the way the cops always do it on TV, though they usually have a gun held stiffly out in front of them. I haven't got a clue if real cops do it that way, but it felt cool.

The hallway was definitely clear, so I walked in, leaving the door open behind me. I paused again to listen, heard only the omnipresent drip-splat of my kitchen sink. I proceeded to the living room door and repeated the Don Johnson–*Miami Vice* move to check out the room. All clear. No one at the curtains. I went on down the hall, feeling a little bit silly now, but performed the head-duck once more for the kitchen. Nothing but dirty dishes and fat roaches.

One room to go.

It was as I stepped on a creaky floorboard just outside the bedroom that the voice called my name.

I screamed, dropped the jack handle, and spun around. In precisely that order.

Rosa Mendez stared back at me, looking tired but awfully amused.

"So how'd you get in?" I asked. I found a couple of nearly clean mugs in the cupboard and boiled some water for instant coffee. Rosa sat at the kitchen table and watched me. If she noticed the roaches, she had the good grace not to say anything.

"Your locks are for shit," she said. "I've got a set of picks."

"Hmmph. That the kind of stuff they teach you in journalism school? Christ, *I* don't even have a set of lock picks. They're hard to come by. Where'd you get them?"

"One of my girls gave them to me and taught me how to use them. I think she lifted them off her pimp," she said. "And all the valuable stuff I learned, I picked up at Night Haven."

"Hope black's okay," I said, putting the coffee down. "The milk's gone to heaven on a sour rowboat."

"Fine," she said. I browsed the shelf for a snack, found a semistale package of Chips Ahoy cookies, and tossed it on the table. Then I sat down across from her.

"What happened to you?" she asked.

"What do you mean?"

She reached over and gently fingered my bruised chin, then touched the side of my head. It was sore, but it felt sort of nice.

"Shaving incident," I said, not wanting to get into it just yet. "What happened last night at Night Haven? Do you know?"

Rosa extracted a cookie from the pack and took a nibble. Her lip curled and she looked over both sides of the cookie, but went on eating it.

"Burned down," she said.

It's like a conspiracy, sometimes. I let it pass.

"Were you there?" I asked.

"No," she said. Then: "Yes. But not when the fire started." She put the cookie down on the table and stared at it. Then she started to cry.

There were no hysterics. No blubbering or wailing or fountains of tears. Just a few shudders and stuttered breaths. A rack of sniffles and a thin line of moisture down each cheek. I got the feeling she didn't cry very often. She certainly wasn't very good at it. I wanted to go over to her, comfort her. Hug her from behind and stroke her hair and say hush.

I sat in my chair and looked down into my coffee.

She got herself together in less than a minute. She grabbed the roll of paper towels off the counter and tore one off to loudly blow her nose in. She dabbed the tears off her face.

"I'm sorry," she said.

"It's okay," I croaked. I wanted to say more. "It's all right," I added. Pithy or what?

"It's just . . . Night Haven meant so much to me. I . . . It's like my baby. We've worked so hard and so long to make it happen. You can't imagine. And for it just to be . . . gone. It breaks my heart."

"I can believe it," I said. "But didn't you have a fire once before?"

Her head jerked up at me. "How do you know about that?" There was suspicion in her voice. I couldn't blame her.

"Sid mentioned it," I vamped. I didn't tell her about the research I'd done on her at the library. How impressed I was by her vision and determination. Her raw strength of purpose.

She nodded, but didn't look entirely pleased. "Yeah. We used to run out of a place on Ivar. It got torched by a pimp. You think there's a connection?"

I didn't know if I was ready to go into it all just yet. In fact, last night's fire was almost certainly my fault, at least indirectly. But I wanted to tell her in a way that wouldn't cast me so much as the villain. Which I wasn't. Sort of.

"I doubt it," I said. "I just meant that you've built from scratch before. Probably made it better than it was."

"I suppose," she sighed, "but I'm older than I used to be. Older and a lot more tired."

"I think you look pretty good," I blurted. She eyed me with some surprise but kindly let the remark pass. She made me feel like a high school kid. Criminy!

"What made you come here?" I asked. In part to change the subject, but as much because I honestly couldn't figure the answer.

She picked her cookie up and took another nibble. She bit out the chocolate chips, then ate the plain cookie bits. Then she swirled the coffee around in the cup, took a sip, swirled some more.

"I think someone's following me," she said.

"Who?"

"No idea. I couldn't prove it, but I'm pretty sure about it. I've felt it for the last couple of days."

"Did you tell the cops? Sid?" She shook her head. "Why in the world not? Even after the fire you didn't tell them?"

"I haven't spoken to the cops about the fire yet."

I shot to my feet, which hurt my ribs, but the action was instinctive. "Christ, Rosa. They're looking all over for you. If they find out you're here, they're going to fry my nuts with a blowtorch."

"You want me to leave?"

"I didn't say that, no. It's just . . . What are you hiding from?"

"Maybe you'd better sit down," she said.

The tears were all gone from her eyes, but a great deal of sorrow, I saw, remained.

Rosa was in the bathroom. I could hear her tinkling in the bowl—I hate that—so I got up and started cleaning the dishes. I didn't have any dishwashing liquid, but found an old Brillo pad under the sink. At first nothing but rusty water came out of it, but eventually I found a little bit of pink soap still encrusted inside. I scrubbed at the coffee stains on the mugs and considered what Rosa had told me.

"Night Haven's been in some trouble," she'd said. I'd taken her advice to sit, though I couldn't believe anything she had to say would be worse than what I had to tell her. Still, I was grateful for the extra stalling time.

"Money troubles," she went on. "It's not anything new, exactly, it's been a struggle from the very start, but things have gotten real tight of late."

"Any particular reason?" I asked.

"Oh, just a sudden conjunction of bad forces. We've always found a little bit of public funding for Night Haven, but it's controversial and the Republicans hate us, so I try to raise as much private money as I can. Then last year, I got wind that the new head of the City Council would be sympathetic to us. So I put in a grant proposal and it actually came through."

"How much?"

"A hundred thousand dollars."

"No shit?"

"It's not as much as it sounds like, believe me. With our outreach programs and all, it just about covered one year's budget. And that's only because we were paying a token rent on the building itself."

"How'd you manage that?"

"Oh, a little charm goes a long way when applied correctly."

I had no problem believing that.

"Like I say, public money sometimes has strings attached, but here they practically threw it at me, so I figured, what the hell. The problem is that it lulled me into a false sense of security. I mean, I've always been good at fundraising . . ."

"A little bit of charm," I said.

"Right. We've done well with individual contributors and even some pretty big corporate sponsors—a couple of condom manufacturers, actually—though they didn't always want the publicity. Anyway, I've always been pretty good at it, but I hate it like the plague. You can't imagine what you have to put up with to scrape together a few donations. With all the money and liberal guilt floating around this town, you wouldn't think it would be so hard."

"Yeah, well, in my experience, everyone's a socialist as long as it's with somebody else's money."

"Tell me about it." She nodded. "So I slacked up a little on the fund-raising when the money from the city started coming through. I figured I could always turn the charm back on when the need arose. But it arose a lot quicker than I expected."

"What went wrong?"

"Everything. The City Council made the grant payments on a quarterly basis, then decided they couldn't afford the grant after the second quarter. We tried to take them to court, but that's a joke. Technically, the case is still pending. Our trial date is two years from November."

"Oy," I said.

"I've always been careful with Haven's resources, squirreling enough cash away for emergencies. Just in case, you know?"

"So?"

"So that money got eaten up real fast. At the same time, the demand for services just keeps increasing. It seems like there are more girls out on the street all the time. As the city and the state keep hacking away at social service funding, more and more of the girls turn up at our door. We just got way overstretched. I went back out on the fund-raising trail, but suddenly the sponsors proved hard to come by. Conservative backlash. Or I don't know, maybe I'm not as charming as I used to be."

"Not a chance," I blurted. Rosa graced me with a tiny smile.

"For *whatever* reason, the money just dried up. By the end of the first quarter of this year, Night Haven was in the red for the first time. Almost twenty thousand dollars. People have always been good to me about extending credit and offering discounts and so forth, but when you start to fall a couple of months behind in your payments, suddenly even the best-hearted merchants want cash in advance. And I can't really blame them.

"Then to top things off, our landlord sold the building. He was real apologetic, but he has his own troubles to deal with. And the new owner isn't quite so sympathetic to the cause."

"He increase the rent?" I asked.

"By about fifteenfold."

"What? In *that* neighborhood?"

"Rumor has it that a big Hollywood restoration project is in the works. Probably a few years down the road—some millennial thing—

but the sharks are moving in on the real estate already. Anyway, on top of all the other problems, there was just no way I could swing that rent increase. And there wasn't even money to find a new location, to move. It looked like the only thing to do was shut down. And I would. Not. Do. That."

Her face took on a cold, hard look as she said the words. I could see that the very idea of closing Night Haven raised seething anger in Rosa's face as her eyes narrowed and her jaw clenched. She took a deep breath and her features relaxed again. She paused and swirled her coffee dregs, deciding how to tell me the rest of it. She kept her eyes on her mug as she resumed the story.

"I couldn't see any way out. The girls were scared silly that Haven would disappear, and frankly so was I. I networked like a crazy person, hit every contact I knew and twice as many I didn't for money. But I came up way short.

"Then an . . . opportunity presented itself."

"Uhhh," I said.

"One of the girls brought it to me. Ex-girls, really. She's a little older, but still in the life. I hadn't seen her in a while, but word got out that Haven was in trouble. I think she meant the best, that she just wanted to help. I'm sure of it really. She offered it in the only way she knew. And it seemed like too good a thing to pass up."

"Famous last words," I said. "What did you do, Rosa?"

"It was a coke deal," she said. She finally peered up out of the coffee.

"Oh, Christ."

"The girl's pimp was moving up and out into the Tunnel trade."

"Tunnel? I don't even know what that is."

"Oh, it's just this season's variation on crack. Some kind of super, synthetic cocaine apparently. A little more middle-class than crack, so there's big money."

"Are you out of your mind?" I asked her.

"I was. I was out of my mind. I just didn't see any other way out. And I couldn't let Night Haven die. But there's more."

"Oy," I said again.

"The deal was that I would mule a suitcase of this . . . crap up from Tijuana. Just pick it up there, drive it back over the border, and hand it over to someone. To my girl, actually. Nothing could be simpler."

"Except maybe quantum mechanics," I said. She ignored it. "How much did they promise you?"

"Ten thousand dollars. For a day's work. It would have seen Haven through for two months, maybe longer. Long enough to raise some other money."

She hesitated again and went back to reading her coffee grounds.

"I agreed to do it. I drove down south and collected the case. I didn't even have to hand over any money. The girl said they do that all electronically now."

"God bless the Internet," I said.

"I made the pickup easy as cake, but ran into a problem on the trip back up. Amazing bad luck really. I blew the head gasket on my car just outside of San Ysidro. I found a mechanic, but it's a two-day job. I had to stay the night."

"Uh-oh." I realized I was going to have to work more on my witty repartee.

"I tried to get in touch with the creep I was muling for, but I couldn't find him. I knew he'd freak when I didn't show up with the stuff that night."

"This is last night?" I asked.

"No, this was all a few weeks ago. Before you came to see me that first time. Let me finish. It wasn't until I got back to L.A. the *next* night that I found out why I couldn't get ahold of him: he'd been killed."

"Oh, fuck," I said.

"The pimp and the girl were killed in his apartment that night. Whether it was about the drugs or something else, I still don't know. But there I was with a suitcase fill of crack and no one to deliver it to. Also no money, because I was supposed to get paid on delivery."

"Natch'. What did you do?"

"What could I do? I took the junk back to Night Haven and stashed it away there. I . . . had thoughts that maybe I'd try to sell it myself. For the money."

"You *are* out of your mind. How could you even dream of getting away with something like that?"

"I know," she said. "I didn't do it. I just *thought* about it. The stuff has just been sitting there at Night Haven. But that's *got* to be what the fire was about."

"You think someone else knew you had the junk."

She nodded her head very slowly. "The last few days I've had a notion that someone's been following me. I can't be sure, it's just a feeling. I've been stalked before, you know."

"No, I didn't."

"Pimps, mostly. Upset 'cause I interfered with their trade. Messed with their merchandise, their money machines. I know the feeling and I'm sure someone's been after me. It *has* to be because of the drugs." She slammed her fists down on the table, jarring the cups. "How could I be so fucking *stupid?*" she shrieked. *"I* burned Night Haven down. My own stupidity."

"You don't know that for sure," I said.

"What else could it be?" she demanded. *"I* did it. *My* involvement. How can I go to the cops with that?"

She started to choke up, whether with anger, sorrow, or both, I couldn't tell, but it was then that she darted into the bathroom. A minute later I got up to do the dishes.

I hadn't yet told Rosa my story. I had assumed that the fire at Night Haven was a result of her contact with me, but it *could* well have been a consequence of her insane drug venture. I realized that I didn't have to tell her all that I had seen and learned, involve her in the Laughing Boy–Celestial Dog mess. If the fire at Night Haven didn't have anything to do with Jack Rippen and company, then I could be endangering her just by filling her in now. Not to mention how bad—how much worse, I should say—it would make me look in her eyes. And I didn't relish telling her about Cheri, even if it was what she had "hired" me for. I *could* forget all about the Laughing Boy situation. Let it all drop here and now and move on.

Rosa came back out of the bathroom. Her eyes were red and her pretty face looked puffy. She blew her nose in a wad of toilet paper. But she didn't look so much sad as tormented. With guilt, I imagined. Or maybe I was just projecting. It made the decision for me, at any rate.

"I've got a story to tell, too," I said. She looked up. "I think *you'd* better sit down for this one."

Fourteen

"I don't know, Marty," Rosa said.

I expected worse. A *lot* worse. I figured she'd explode when I told her all that I'd seen and done. Rosa let out a small sob when I told her about Cheri's murder, but otherwise she sat there at the kitchen table without saying a word until I finished my story. I thought she might get up and hit me again at the end, like at the police station the other night. Or simply get up and leave. I certainly wouldn't have blamed her. Hell, it's what I would have done in her position. But she just sat there, staring at her hands, not even moving.

"I don't know," she said again, with even greater sadness. Then: "You're assuming that these guys who attacked you are with Laughing Boy, right?"

"Or Celestial Dog." I nodded. "If there's even a difference."

"But how can you be so sure? You said they didn't see you up at the film set at Vasquez Rocks when they . . . you know."

"There was that little retarded kid who saw me, though it's hard to believe he could have identified me. And also the guards at the gate where I stopped. They might have taken down my license plate number. Given what was going on there, I'd be surprised if they didn't."

"Yes, but you said those men who beat you up were waiting for you when you got home. That doesn't seem like much time for whoever it was at Laughing Boy to put a contract or whatever out on you. It was what? A couple of hours? Less?"

"Something like that," I said. "But remember that I'd been poking around for a few days beforehand. Up in their offices in Burbank and then at the county clerk's office. Who knows what kind of monitoring they do? We're talking big money here with Rippen."

Rosa shook her head. "But even if all that's true, how did they connect you to me? And to Night Haven? I didn't tell anyone that I asked you to look for Cheri and Syd. Did you?"

"No," I agreed.

"So who could have made the connection? We only spoke that one day at U.C.L.A."

"But I did stop at Night Haven to pick up the photos of Cheri and Syd. Could be someone was following me. Especially if I pushed the wrong buttons up at the Laughing Boy offices. Raised the wrong eyebrow."

"You could have had any number of reasons to stop at Night Haven that day. Maybe you were going to see your girlfriend." I blushed slightly when she said that. If Rosa noticed, she was good enough not to say anything. "Maybe you were making a delivery, working on another case. Whatever. That doesn't seem like much of a reason to burn the place to the ground. What would be the point?"

"Maybe just to throw a scare into you. Just in case. Taking no chances. These guys obviously play very rough."

"I don't see it," she said, shaking her head again. "No, the connection to my drug fiasco makes much more sense to me. It's right *there*. The link to you is too tenuous. No matter how awful Laughing Boy is."

I didn't know if Rosa really believed what she was saying or if she preferred to believe it. Not because she didn't want to pin the blame on me, but because I had the feeling that the loss of Night Haven was easier for her to cope with if she could somehow take the responsibility for it onto herself. I had to admit that there *was* some logic to the case she made. And she *was* nuts to have agreed to mule the drugs. But then I was pretty goddamn desperate *not* to be the one to be responsible for everything.

"And, of course, I *did* hire you," Rosa added.

"What do you mean?"

"I hired you. Asked you, manipulated you even, to look into Cheri and Syd's disappearance. You said you didn't want to get involved any further, that you didn't like it. You wouldn't have done it if I hadn't insisted. So even if they did burn Haven down and attack you because of what you saw them do to Cheri, it would *still* be my fault."

Rosa *did* make it easy for me. And I always have taken it easy when it comes that way. But it just didn't sit right today. Not with her.

"I think you're being too hard on yourself," I told her. "And too soft on me. I stepped in the applesauce from the first, when I took Long John's money. I haven't handled any of this very well, been way over my head and out of my league from the start. So far there're at least three deaths as a result."

"Are you really going to meet with Jack Rippen tonight?"

I'd avoided thinking about it until she asked. I was definitely feeling hinky about the whole thing, but I was also angry. It was that anger, about what had happened at Vasquez Rocks, about the attack on me in my own place, that had given me the chutzpah for the confrontation with Rippen to begin with. And seeing Rosa like this—downhearted, guilt-ridden—made me even madder.

"Yeah," I said, deciding then and there. "I feel like I've got to follow this through now. Try and scope out what he knows. If only for my own protection."

"You think you're going to outsmart him or something?" Rosa asked. She didn't mean it to be a dig, but the incredulity of her tone stung me. I hadn't really thought about it in those terms; when I did, I saw her point.

"Seems unlikely, huh?"

She must have heard a bit of hurt in my voice, because she tried to cover. "No, I . . . I didn't mean it quite like that."

"It's all right. It's true."

"No. It's just that . . . Does it really make any sense to you that Jack Rippen would be involved in this kind of thing? I met him once, you know."

"Oh?"

"I didn't like him," she said.

"Yeah, well, take a number."

"I didn't like him," she went on, "but he impressed the hell out of me. He seemed to take a genuine interest in Night Haven when I told him about it—this was at some big political function for the state Democrats—and he talked about making a donation. Of course, when I tried to follow up, I got the big brush-off from one of his toadies, which is why I don't like him. But he does cut quite the figure."

"The question is: What else does he cut?"

"I just can't see him involved in murder and snuff films and pornography. It just seems too . . . stupid."

"I thought the same thing," I said. "But then why did he agree to meet me tonight? And why the hell was he breaking bread with that creep Aldus?"

"I don't know," Rosa said. "But it doesn't sound too smart, your meeting him all alone."

"Hey, doesn't-sound-too-smart is my secret Indian name. I'm one-quarter pure Hekawi, you know." She didn't catch the reference; obviously not a regular Nickelodeon viewer. "Besides, I've got a guardian angel."

"What do you mean?"

"Whoever it was who took out those two assholes who ambushed me."

"Is that really blood on the carpet?" Rosa asked, glancing back toward the living room. She shuddered when I nodded. "And you don't have any idea who might have saved you?"

"Not a fucking clue," I said. "Or even why."

"Weird, weird, weird. I just can't make sense of any of it."

"That's why I have to meet Rippen," I said. "I've got to at least try and find out what he knows. Otherwise, how can I ever feel safe sleeping in my own bed?"

She nodded, then rested her chin on her interlaced fingers. Neither of us said anything, just listened to the drip-drip-drip of the faucet.

"I'm going with you," she said after a while.

"Excuse me?"

"To meet Rippen tonight. I'm going, too."

"I don't think that's a good idea," I said.

"I don't care."

"And you've got other problems."

"What do you mean?" she asked.

"You've got to get in touch with the cops."

"But the drugs . . ."

"You don't have to tell them about that bit," I said. "But they're looking for you. As in worried about you, not suspecting you. At least Sid Teitlebaum is. And if you don't turn up, *then* they're going to start to wonder. And it'll get complicated."

"But what do I tell them?"

"You always tell as close to the truth as you can when you lie," I said. She snorted. "Trust me on this. It's the best way to keep your story straight. If they ask where you've been, you tell them you've been out of town. If they ask, you say it was a personal matter. You're not a suspect in anything, so they won't push it. Make up something simple if they do. Something that can't be checked. You needed to get away, clear your head, polish your crystals. Something totally *California.*"

She thought it over for a minute, then nodded her head.

"Have you been back there? To Night Haven?" I asked.

Rosa drew her arms across her chest and shriveled up a little. She nodded and shuddered. "I drove by. Saw the ruins. I talked to a couple of the girls on the sly. Just to make sure everybody got out okay."

"Shit! Then the cops'll for sure know you're back."

Rosa shook her head. "I told the girls not to mention that they saw me. They'd never narc me."

"Don't bet on it," I sighed. "You better call Sid right now. And the arson boys will want to see you." She nodded again. "I mentioned to him that I was working for you. Just so you know."

"Okay."

"If he asks about it, tell him the truth. That you asked me to follow up on the missing girls. Don't say a word about anything else. For God's sake, don't mention Rippen."

"I understand that, Marty. I'm not an idiot."

"I never said you were. But you're rattled. And that's when people say things without thinking. I don't know what's going on here, but I'm not ready to bring any of this to the cops just yet. Not even to Sid. At least not until I get a chance to talk with Rippen."

"What about Cheri?" Rosa whispered.

"What about her?"

"Shouldn't . . . someone know? What they did to her? The cops? Someone? What are we going to do about that?"

I took a deep breath and let it out slowly. "We're going to sit on it. At least for now."

"Doesn't seem right."

"I know."

"I don't like it."

"I know."

Rosa looked me square in the eye, suddenly looking alert and angry. "And I'm going with you to see Rippen tonight."

I held her gaze as long as I could. "We'll see," I said.

Rosa called Sid, who was relieved to hear from her and informed her that the cops did need her to come and give a statement about the fire. I listened as she told him the stripped-down version of her story. She spoke easily and confidently, never faltering. I thought it sounded completely natural. She asked me if I'd go down to the police station with her, and much as I wanted to do it, to offer her the support and hold her hand, I suggested that it might not be such a good idea. She nodded, but looked slightly disappointed. Perversely, that made me feel a little better.

We agreed to meet up again later in the day. Rosa was determined to see Rippen, and while I didn't know if I really wanted to bring her along, I was more than happy for the opportunity to spend some more time with her. Part of it was concern—I didn't want Rosa to be another body on my conscience—but a bigger part had to do with the undeniable way she was evolving for me from object of fantasy and infatuation to subject of affection. If the attack on Night Haven *was* a result of what I'd seen, I wanted to keep Rosa as close as I could. Or closer.

After she left, I took a little nap. Tried to at least. I dozed for a while, but I felt too nervous to really drift off. Every creak of the house and passing car raised my hackles. I felt like I had to brace myself for attack constantly. After an hour or so I gave it up.

I decided to clean up the living room. The mess wasn't too bad, all things considered, except for the blood. I kept skirting around it: putting books back on the shelves, vacuuming bits of glass from the broken picture frame, polishing up the old Golden Globe. Finally there was nothing left to do. The blood on the sofa, I hid by turning the cushion upside down. Even found fifty cents underneath. But the carpet was another matter. I tried using a wet cloth to rub the blood out, but it only smeared it around. I found some spray-on stain remover in the closet, but that just seemed to change the color of the stain. In the end I grabbed an old throw rug out of the bedroom and tossed it over the mess. It didn't go with the carpet or the walls, but it covered the blood. And it's not like I was expecting a visit from *House Beautiful.*

It probably wasn't the best of ideas, but that little old bottle of Henry's beckoned me to the fridge like the siren's song. I hadn't eaten anything all day other than the fateful Samizdat tacos and found I was hungry. I grabbed a noodle Cup-A-Soup out of the cabinet and had it for a snack with the beer. There was even a Fudgsicle in the freezer to top it all off. Ah, that's living.

I paced around the house for a while after that, thinking about the situation and trying not to think about Rosa. I wish I could say I was struck by an epiphany, or even a clever idea. But a half hour or so of pacing and worrying just left me a little more tired and a lot more confused. The only decision I made was to give Doug Hughes a call over at *Variety* and see what, if anything, he might have found out about the Rippen Entertainment deal.

I rang Hughes at the office, but he was away from his desk. He returned the call about ten minutes later.

"Moving back up in the world?" he said by way of greeting.

"I'm not sure I follow you," I said.

"Lunch at Samizdat with Jack Rippen? What gives, Marty? I thought you promised me any scoops."

"Christ! Doesn't take long for word to get around, does it? How did you hear?"

"Marty. We keep a stringer at Samizdat all day during business hours. *The Reporter* does, too. *Entertainment Tonight* has exclusive rights to the goddamn closed, circuit security cameras. Get real! Now, is the Ripper really planning a new feature version of *Salt and Pepper?*"

"What?!?"

"I hear it's you and Eve Plumb as the Salts and that Macaulay Culkin is a definite maybe for your old role, depending on whether Fox finally green-lights his *Underdog* project."

"Who told you this?"

"It's all over town, Marty. C'mon, give. Rippen's people are talking it up like crazy. Nickelodeon's supposedly going to announce that they're set to run the old shows *twice* a day starting next month."

I couldn't believe it. Why the hell would Rippen's PR machine be putting out a load of crap like that? "Listen, Doug: you want a scoop? This is utter bullshit. I didn't even have lunch with Rippen, I . . . Never mind that. I don't know anything about a movie. For Christ's sake, who in their right mind would *pay* to see a *Salt and Pepper* movie?"

"Whoa, chief, that's what I said back when Paramount announced the first *Addam's Family* flick."

"There's no movie, Doug. You can quote me."

"How much you holding out for?" he asked. "Don't get too cute with them, Marty. You're really just a novelty item. Rippen won't think twice about finding someone else if you get haughty on him. It was only lunch."

"I did not . . . Douglas. Did you find out anything about Laughing Boy? The Yoshitoshi deal?"

He laughed. "You're asking me? *You* just had lunch with Jack the Ripper."

"Is that a 'no' then?"

Hughes cleared his throat. "Okay. Be that way. Laughing Boy *is* part of the Yoshitoshi deal, but Rippen signs on with the parent company as an independent producer. Apparently it's written up as a secondary deal on top of the Rippen Entertainment buy-out."

"Why would they do that? Didn't you tell me that they're already getting Rippen?"

"Probably just a tax dodge of some kind. Maybe it defers some money, would be my guess. It's all in the accounting, you know. The contracts for this are probably thick as a phone book."

"Anything else?" I asked.

"You mean about Celestial Dogs?" he teased.

I nearly dropped the phone. "What did you hear?" I whispered.

"Well, it was strictly OTR . . ." Hughes said.

I puzzled over that a second. "One-touch recording?" I asked.

"Off the record," Hughes said. "Get a grip, Marty. Anyway, word I hear is that *Celestial Dogs* is going to be Laughing Boy's first big project under Yoshitoshi."

"Celestial Dogs is a *movie?*"

"Yuppers. No one will say anything more than that it's going to be *Gone With the Wind, The Sound of Music,* and *Independence Day* all rolled into one spectacular ball."

"What the hell does that mean?"

"It means B-A-L-L-S. The Ripper wants everyone in town to know that even if he did sell out to the Japs, he's still *the* player in town. He's going to do it with this film. Though no one could explain to me what the crazy title is supposed to mean."

"Fuck," I mumbled.

"What's that?"

"Nothing, Doug. Listen, thanks for the info."

"Whoa, podner. When do I get the lowdown on your deal with the man?"

"I'll . . . I'll get back to you," I said.

Hughes was still spitting questions as I hung up the phone. I didn't much like what he'd told me. Rippen was being careful to cover his tracks. The *Salt & Pepper* rumor would explain our encounter in Samizdat. In two days it would be forgotten, just another high-concept project that never got off the ground.

Celestial Dogs had to be some kind of cover as well. It was a name that stuck in your head, and Rippen needed an easy answer if any questions about Celestial Dog got asked. He couldn't take a chance that I'd mention it to someone and have it connect back to him. I'd bet every meager penny I had that there were no paper links between Celestial Dog and Laughing Boy. If somehow the snuff outfit ever came to light, Rippen had a response: Gee, what a terrible coincidence, but we're producing a movie with that name. Don't know anything about a seedy production company. We'll have to change the name of the movie now.

Not that I thought there was a chance there would ever actually be such a movie.

I wondered again what in the hell Celestial Dog really referred to.

Fifteen

Rosa arrived back to my place just after six o'clock. At 6:04:17 to be exact. Not that I was watching the clock or anything. She just stood there on the front step when I opened the door. Her hair was mussed and her shoulders slumped. She looked ashen. Defeated.

"You want to come in?" I prompted when she didn't move.

She looked up at me, then started to cry.

"Hey," I said. "Hey, hey."

Her frame heaved up and down as the tears flowed, but other than the odd sniffle, she cried silently. I looked over her shoulder onto the street. My neighbors from across the way were unloading groceries from their car. They stopped to watch us.

"C'mon," I said, taking her elbow. "Come inside." She offered no resistance as I led her through the door. Once inside, she fell into my arms and really let go.

She held me around the waist in a death grip, her teary face wedged into my armpit. (I found myself worrying because I hadn't used any deodorant that morning.) She was out-and-out sobbing now. I had to grit my teeth because the pressure against my ribs hurt, but I wasn't about to push her away. For one thing, I was too surprised; but for another, I was pleased that she *was* holding me like that. I immediately felt aware of that pleasure, too. Not because I liked seeing Rosa unhappy, but because here she felt able to turn to me when she was.

"I'm sorry," she croaked. She started to pull back, but I didn't let her go. She left a glob of snot on my sleeve. If I kept a scrapbook, I probably would have mounted it.

"I'm okay," she said, pushing against me a little bit harder. I released her this time. "God, I'm sorry about that."

"It's all right. What happened?"

She fished a tissue out of her pocket, loudly blew her nose, and then stuffed it back in her pocket. She dabbed at her eyes with her shirtsleeve.

"It's just . . . everything. I just came back from Night Haven. God, Marty, it's awful. There's nothing left at all."

She walked past me into the living room and sat down on the couch. I pulled the desk chair over and sat right across from her.

"Somebody died, Marty."

"What?" I said. "Who? Sid told me no one got hurt."

"One of the girls. Lisa. They didn't find her right off because she was down in the basement. They're not supposed to go down there. Part of the building collapsed on her." Rosa started to sob again.

"I'm sorry," I said. It felt horribly inadequate.

"I barely even knew her, you know? She wasn't around much. But that's not the point. I just . . . I feel like this is my fault, too. Like I've got blood on my hands."

"Don't talk crazy."

"Why? Why is it crazy? What if the fire is connected with the drugs? Isn't it my fault? Didn't I just as good as kill that poor kid? She was fifteen years old! What am I going to do?"

She started crying all over again. Crying for herself, I realized. For the guilt and the fear that this was something she'd be haunted by forever.

"You can't think that way," I said. "For one thing, we still don't even know if the drugs and the fire are actually connected. She could be another body on *my* head." Rosa looked up at me when I said that. "But even if they are connected, that doesn't make it your fault. You can't take responsibility for other people's actions."

"But they're *my* actions," she insisted.

"No. You didn't set the fire. The bastard that did is the one who's responsible."

"But . . ."

"No 'but.' If you follow every action down a trail of causality, everyone is responsible for everything. If the girl hadn't been a hooker, she wouldn't have been in Night Haven. If her daddy hadn't been a bastard, she might not have been a hooker. If the building had been better constructed, the floor wouldn't have caved. For want of a nail, the kingdom was lost and all that."

"That doesn't make me feel any better," Rosa said. But she'd stopped crying.

"What about the police?" I asked.

She shook her head. "They were real nice. They never even asked me too much about where I was."

"Good. I figured."

"I saw Sid, too. He was really sweet. I felt like a shit 'cause I knew I was lying to him. Or not telling him the whole truth, anyway."

"Yeah, I know that feeling."

"He's mad at you," she said, her eyes growing wide. "I mean really pissed. He seemed to calm down a little when I told him that you really were working for me, but he said I should steer clear of you if I had any sense. I think you might want to talk to him."

"I'm afraid that'll have to wait. How come you aren't taking his advice?"

"Huh?"

"Steering clear."

She shrugged and for the first time since coming in, offered something like a smile. "I don't know. I think I trust you. But that's crazy."

"Crazy like a herring," I agreed. She almost laughed at that. "They didn't find the drugs," I said, hating to change the subject. Her face sobered up.

"No," she said. "I don't think so. Nobody said anything, so I assumed they burned. The place really went up."

"That's a relief." That didn't sound so good, but Rosa understood what I meant. Just then her stomach let loose with a temblor of a rumble. She flushed beet-red and I managed not to laugh. "Hungry?" I asked.

"No. I mean, I didn't think so. But yeah, maybe I am."

"Why don't we go grab some dinner. A little fortification before we meet with Rippen."

That perked her up. "I *told* you I'd go with you."

"In for a penny . . ." I sighed.

It proved to be a disastrous decision.

After my Samizdat lunch, I wanted some real food for dinner. Since we had to meet Rippen in Culver City, I drove us out to the marina and a barbecue joint tucked away in the corner of one of those ubiquitous minimalls. The place is a little family operation with the best ribs and chicken around, and side orders of candied yams sweeter than jelly apples. And not even all that expensive considering the neighborhood. I ordered the short ribs while Rosa went for the honey-barbecued chicken. The restaurant isn't licensed, but it's okay because they serve up homemade lemonade in big jam jars with free refills. There's nothing better for taking the edge off the heat of the hickory sauce.

I didn't say anything to Rosa about the yams until the waitress put the plate down on the table and she dipped her fork cautiously into the bowl. I wanted to watch her unguarded expression when the confected concoction touched her tongue. Sure enough, her face lit up like a baby's at its first taste of chocolate. She took another forkful and eased it into her mouth, masticating with—and I admit I was only projecting here—orgasmic glee.

"Wow," she said.

The waitress, who had been hovering nearby in anticipation, said, "Damn straight!" and winked at me as she scurried off to the next table.

We ate the meal in relative silence, exchanging the odd comment about the delights of the food, but otherwise wrapped up, each in our own thoughts. The conversation only really got going after the plates were cleared away and dessert and coffee appeared (peach cobbler for Rosa, pecan pie à la mode for me).

"So how *did* you end up here, Marty?" Rosa asked her coffee.

"I took the Marina Freeway off the 405 and took a left onto Min-danao, then—"

"That's not what I meant."

"I know what you meant," I told her.

"Sorry," she said, and visibly tightened up. That wasn't what I intended.

"How'd you end up running Night Haven?" I asked. "I can't believe that when you were a pretty little girl you dreamed of growing up to run a halfway house for hookers."

"No," she said with a little smile. "Not hardly. But then I wasn't a *pretty* little girl."

"Come *onnnn*," I said.

"No, it's true. I was a horrible, gangly kid. All knees and elbows. I was a, uh, late bloomer."

"Good things come to those who wait," I said.

"I dreamed of being a dancer. Of course. Like every other little girl in America."

"England, too, I think. And maybe Canada. And possibly Uzbekistan and Upper Volta."

"*Every*where," Rosa said, and laughed. "But I was such a klutz, I couldn't even bring myself to tell anyone. I remember that my mom once asked me if I wanted to sign up for a ballet class that they offered at the local Y. I was so embarrassed about the way I looked and moved that I told her I wasn't interested and ended up taking ceramics instead. My best friend took the dance class and told me all about it every week. I'd go to the library and read about famous dancers. Once I snuck over to the gym and watched the class through an open window. Then I ran home and cried and dreamed about it. Just dancing across that rotten old floor in the Y. Not even dancing for real. Pathetic, huh?"

"No," I said. "It's quite sweet actually." The waitress came and topped off our coffees. "So you were the bookish type then?"

Rosa nodded and ran a hand through her hair. I looked hard, but couldn't find a trace of that gangly girl.

"Yeah," she said. "Though I wasn't all that brainy in high school. I was a real nonentity. My dad was a sociology professor at the University of Chicago."

"That where you grew up?"

"Uh-huh. There's a real tradition there of *active,* practical work. It dates all the way back to Robert Park, you know?"

I made a face and shrugged my shoulders.

"Well, it does. So that's probably where I get my do-gooder streak. My dad died while I was in college, but I think he'd really have approved of my work at Night Haven."

"What's not to approve? What you do is brilliant. How many people would be willing to do it?"

"That's nice of you," Rosa said, "but you'd be surprised. Some people think it's like working with lepers. Like it's an infection that can be transmitted like the common cold. Or AIDS."

"Like the wise man said, 'There's a lot of bastards out there.'"

"Amen," she said, and raised a mini toast with her coffee cup. I could tell she was thinking about the fire again. She tried to change the subject.

"It must have been pretty wild growing up in Hollywood," she said, emphasizing "wild" ever so breathlessly and pinning me with The Look.

The Look is something every actor even remotely famous comes to know. It's a combination of jealousy and awe, leavened with just a hint of contempt—because, after all, you *are* "show people"—that eventually appears in the expression of every civilian who imagines The Business to be what it claims to be and not what it actually is. The Look is a result of seventy years of fairy stories and tabloid fantasies—from Fatty Arbuckle on—about the lurid life inside "the dream factory." The truth doesn't matter, can't be impressed on those outside. Just like the multitudes who refuse to believe that Freemasons are nothing more diabolical than a bunch of boring old farts with funny hats and a silly handshake, legion are those who assume that life in Hollywood is an endless stream of blow jobs, convertible cars, and designer drugs.

So who am I to set the record straight?

"Some if it was wild," I said. I don't always like to think back on that time. I *do* it all the time, but I don't always *like* it."

"Yeah?" she said. The Voice.

I leaned back and thought about it for a minute. As the memories came back on me like a Samizdat taco, I realized that some of those days *were* an endless stream of blow jobs, ragtops, and cocaine. I must have smiled.

"What?" Rosa said.

"It was a surreal life," I told her. "I mean, it *was* every fantasy come true in a lot of ways. But there are some things that should only be fantasy. The realization, the living of them . . . it's just not right. It's perversely stultifying. In retrospect, I would trade it all to have been a bookish kid who came out of school with a degree. Or who just had a chance to go to college."

"Oh, come *on!*"

"I'm not saying I would have traded it at the time. I was having a lot of fun. But we're talking hindsight here. And that hindsight gives me the benefit of seeing where it's all brought me. You did ask how I ended up where I am, after all."

"I know," she said. The Voice was history.

"The thing of it is: in some ways I don't know if my childhood—or adolescence—was that different from some of your girls." Rosa looked up sharply. I could see an angry rebuke forming on her lips. "Wait, wait, wait. I'm not casting myself as the victim here. That's too easy. But that doesn't mean I wasn't used. Or taken advantage of."

"Wasn't the acting your choice?" Rosa asked.

"I honestly don't know," I said. "It just kind of happened. I didn't have a show-biz mom or get pushed into the business against my will. I was just a California kid—and I wasn't a late bloomer, by the way—who fell into it. You know, the old legend of getting discovered at the drugstore has some truth in it here. It's no way to *get* into the business if that's your goal, but people get discovered in funny places and when they're not look-ing for it. It happened to me on the beach in Santa Monica. A casting agent was there with his girlfriend, and I just *looked* right for a part he was casting. He could have been a pimp or a chicken hawk or some other brand of scumbag. Fortunately—or not, in the long run—he was for real and worked for Columbia. The rest of it just happened."

"That's a long way from a pro's life on the streets, Marty."

"I'm not saying it's the same," I said, "but it wasn't as different as you might think."

"I don't—" Rosa started, but I cut her off.

"I didn't have a pimp, but I had an agent. He didn't keep me in line with a bent wire hanger, but he kept me in line just the same. There's all these laws that theoretically protect child actors, but most of them are bullshit. It was even worse back in the sixties. I was popping dexies like Judy Garland to stay awake for late shoots. The fucking producer would feed 'em to me like Hershey kisses. Manny Stiles, sitcom genius."

"Huh?" Rosa said.

"Nothing. You know I lost my cherry when I was thirteen years old? To a forty-year-old costume designer. I maybe didn't know it at the time, but if that's not exploitation, I don't know what is."

"That's terrible," Rosa said. But she said it in The Voice and was slip-ping back into The Look.

"You don't see it, do you?"

"What?" she said.

"Everything goes in Hollywood because no matter how bad it is, it feeds some part—maybe some dark but essential part—of everybody's fantasies. As soon as you hear it's show biz, it passes out of the real and into some fairyland of unfettered imagination. Like there are no conse-quences for the people on the other side of the tube or the screen."

Rosa looked offended. "I said that it's terrible, Marty. I hear what you're saying."

"You hear it, but do you really get it?"

"I can understand that you were exploited. But even if you didn't re-alize it at the time, what about your parents? You weren't some kid aban-doned to the streets by an abusive father or a junkie mother."

"That's true." I nodded. "And like I say, I enjoyed it at the time. I never told my parents about a lot of the shit. I covered up pretty good. But that doesn't mean it didn't take a toll.

"I remember when I was fourteen. I still had some friends out of The Business. One afternoon while my parents were at work, I dared three of them to come by my house and check out my new life through a window. I left the curtains open on purpose. When they got there I was going at it with two girls, maybe seventeen, eighteen years old. A couple of wannabe actresses who were so stupid, they'd fuck a kid because he told them he could get them an audition. You must know the type."

"Yes," she croaked.

"When I saw my buddies watching through the window, I put on a big show. Made sure they got their money's worth. To this day I can remember the looks on their faces the next time I saw them. An almost religious awe."

"And?" Rosa prompted me.

"And after that, none of them ever talked to me the same way again. But not how I had intended. And I couldn't understand why. One of them, a guy named Andy who was my best friend, I offered to get a couple of girls for him, thinking that would make things better. He never spoke to me again after that."

"That must have been awful."

"But don't you see? It became easy come, easy go. 'Cause there was always another girl to boff or dexie to pop. And then when *Salt and Pepper* took off, when everyone was saying 'hot enough for you' . . . oh, man! I was a fucking monster."

"I still don't see . . ."

"But you know what the worst part was? What it is?"

It was a rhetorical question, but I waited for an answer. I got it in the form of a whispered "what?"

"The worst part was that that was the peak."

"The peak of what?"

"Of my life, Rosa. That was it. The high point of my life. All I could ever hope to be, to make, to have, came when I was sixteen years old. And I knew it as soon as it started to fall apart, when *Salt and Pepper* got the ax. Suddenly the girls weren't quite so willing and the pills started to cost me cash. People on the street didn't run up and ask if it was hot enough for me. They pointed at me and whispered to each other and then nodded sadly. 'Oh, you mean *that's* him? What was his name again?' I could practically hear them say it. And I felt like your girls must feel. I felt like a whore past her prime, with nothing to look forward to but saggy tits and memories of dreams that will never come true. Burned out before I was old enough to legally vote or take a drink. Just another in the endless series of Hollywood's shooting stars.

"And that's how I ended up here."

Rosa looked at me with great sadness. I'd seen her bestow the same look on some of her girls. I didn't much like it, but I realized that I'd been asking for it, pleading for it, with my story.

"I'm sorry," she said. And seemed to mean it.

"But am I bitter?" I said. Rosa looked at me warily until I smiled. Then she grinned along with me.

"Let's go see the Ripper," I said. "I got twenty-five years of pissed-off stored up here. Might as well take it out on that rat-faced son of a bitch."

Rosa took my arm as we walked out of the restaurant.

You know how wherever you go when you're on vacation or traveling or whatever and you have to stay at some discount motel someplace—one of those chain motels with the TV bolted down and the blurry flower painting over the bed and a greasy, out-of-date yellow pages in the dresser drawer that you end up reading 'cause there's nothing on TV and what the hell else is there to do other than look at the blurry flowers—how every one of those motels seems to have the exact same guy working behind the desk and he always has bad teeth? Almost like the factory that stamps out the prefab motel building kicks one of these dudes out with every thirty rooms manufactured?

Well, it's the same at studio lot gates.

I don't know how it works, but for as long as I've been entering lots—and we're going on thirty years now—no matter the studio or which part of town, the same old guy seems to be manning the booth at the gate. He's about a year shy of retirement, with a cancerous, cadaverous look, wearing an ill-fitting uniform and a tarnished toy badge. The cap always rides too low on his head, weighing on his hairy ears, and he always doffs it when he talks to you, revealing a bald pate with a few scraggly yet dandruff-laden tufts of gray-white hair.

Where do they find them? There aren't *that* many studios. Is there a family of these guys somewhere, like ten identical brothers? And why are they always old? Don't they have to start out young? Or was some glamour cast by Carl Laemmle in 1914 freezing these poor brothers forever in time into their lot as guardians of the gates of filmdom?

And why, oh why, are they always named Pete?

"Evening, Pete," I said, pulling up to the gate. I didn't even bother to glance at his name tag.

" 'Lo," he said. They always say that. "Help you?"

"I'm here to see Mr. Rippen. Marty Burns."

"Have to check," Peter said, and wandered back into his booth. Like he couldn't have anticipated this and brought his little clipboard out with him. Like I just drove up to say hey. He fumbled through some papers, stopping intermittently to take a leisurely sip of coffee from a Winchell's Donut go-cup. You'd think he was sorting through the Watergate papers in the national archives in there. Finally, stopping first for another sip of joe, he ambled back out.

"Yep," he said. "Studio Seventeen-A. Just follow the road around there to the right." That's the only instruction I've ever received from a Pete, perhaps the only one they're programmed to offer. I considered that the Petes might actually be animatronics built by the Disney people. I suggested all this to Rosa as we drove slowly up the studio lane. She didn't understand at first, then the lightbulb lit.

"Ah! You mean like waiters in Chinese restaurants," she said.

I told her that was the general principle. She turned around to catch another glimpse of Pete, but he'd wandered back inside his little hutch. I wondered how far he was actually able to stray, and imagined that he'd just shut down if he moseyed too far from his magical lair.

We snaked around the massive lot, though we barely saw a soul as we drove. Occasionally someone would beep from behind, then zip around us in one of those little electric golf carts. I could have sworn I saw Rosanne behind the wheel of one of them, but it was dark and her face gets surgically rearranged so often that I couldn't tell for sure. Finally we saw some arrows pointing the way to Studios 15–20, so I parked in the closest lot I could find and we followed the path.

The walkway widened out into a huge concrete courtyard between two hangar-sized studios marked 15-B and 16-A. The yellow light outside 16-A was spinning away, warning that shooting was in progress and no one was to enter. The other studios looked deserted, and I didn't see anyone else around until Rosa tugged at my arm and pointed in the direction of a dark corner of the courtyard.

"What's that?" she said. She sounded a little nervous. In fact, the shadowy, empty lot felt more than a little spooky. I think it was the unnatural quiet of the place. Though it's smack-dab in the middle of Culver

City, the production buildings are far enough removed from the street that the omnipresent traffic roar is barely a whisper in the distance.

I didn't see anything at first, then gradually made out a shape lurking at the corner of the active studio building. It stood very still, but looked too big to be a person. I thought it must be a mannequin or a prop until I saw it move as we made our way across the courtyard. It turned around and I saw a longish tail flail out behind it, heard it swish through the air like a cracking bullwhip. I immediately flashed back on what had transpired at Vasquez Rocks, the "monster" I had watched pull Cheri's guts out through her belly. I halted in midstep, reaching out and jerking Rosa to a stop in the process. The creature turned again to watch us, it's eyes seeming to glow in the dark. I didn't like this at all.

The creature stepped out of the shadows and into the brighter but still dim light of the courtyard. I heard Rosa gasp as its shape and substance were revealed to us. It was reptilian in shape, well over six feet tall, with scaly silver skin that was moist and sticky. Its two foreshortened arms tapered into multiclawed fingers with nails sculpted out of steel. It shambled as it moved, not looking quick at all, but with eyes that indeed glowed coal-red in the night, and crescent teeth.

Glowing eyes?

The tension drained out of me before it even spoke.

"Yo," the creature yelled, "any of you guys got a light?"

It was, of course, an actor in special-effects makeup. What else would you expect on a studio lot? As he came up to us I could see his real eyes through a small gap in the creature's neck. The man inside looked as sweaty as the creature outside.

"I left my lighter on the set," he said, pointing at the studio with his tail. "Can't get back in until they finish the shot."

"Sorry," I said, "don't smoke."

Rosa shook her head, still admiring the costume.

"Just as well, I guess," the creature said. "Every time I light a stick I'm afraid all this latex is gonna go up, take me with it. Gotta get me some of them damn patches."

He shambled back toward the shadows to wait at the studio door. I looked at Rosa and she looked at me. We simultaneously broke out into laughter. Rosa was laughing so hard she actually had to squat down for a minute until it passed. I had to offer her a hand to get her back on her feet.

"Show biz," I said as she wiped tears out of her eyes.

. . .

Studio 17-A sat at the end of the pathway. There was no activity outside the big building, but a couple of golf carts were parked in marked spaces just beside the main entrance. No sign of Rippen, though it was only just after ten. We sat down in one of the carts to wait. Rosa watched me closely.

"What?" I said. "I got a booger hanging out my nose or something?"

"Just wondering how you feel."

"I'm fine. Why?"

"Just being back in the middle of . . . this," she said, waving her hand back and forth. "Doesn't it feel a little weird?"

I looked around at the dark studio buildings and shook my head. "Not really. It's been an awfully long time. And I really did swear off it."

"No regrets?" Rosa asked.

"No, hey, plenty of regrets. Enough to fill a jumbo jet. I'd be a liar or an idiot not to wonder about what might have been. Where I *could* be today given a break or two, a different tumble of the dice. But it's not like I hear the cameras calling to me anymore. That's . . . another life."

"Is it really?" I glanced at Rosa, but she was staring up into the sky. "One of my girls—one of the first ones I ever met, actually—she got out of the life after a couple years. Most of 'em don't, but she did it. Went to Cal State L.A. part-time, got herself a degree and a job as a paralegal downtown. She ended up marrying a lawyer. House in Monterey Park, a kid, the whole nine yards."

Rosa paused, still watching the sky. "But?" I said.

"But I saw her not too long ago. At one of those dos I'm always having to attend. We made like we didn't know each other when someone introduced us, but then I ran into her in the ladies' room and we got a chance to talk. She told me all about her new life, and I told her how happy I was for her. She smiled and nodded and all, but then she lowered her voice to a whisper and said, 'But you know, sometimes I miss it.' She meant the life. I couldn't believe it, but she said it was true. As horrible as most of it was, she said sometimes she longed for the excitement of it. The sense of living on the edge, she called it. She did add that she'd never go back, but that sometimes she liked to walk down Santa Monica Boulevard and see it all. That it gave her a rush."

"Criminy!" I said.

"That's what I thought, too. But I wonder about it. You keep saying how you identify with the girls, how you see your life as not so different. I just wondered if you didn't feel like that coming back here. Just sort of smelling it again from the outside."

Just then we heard a noise from inside the studio, like a piece of equipment being dropped. It saved me from having to respond to what Rosa said. Or to think about it too hard. I glanced at my watch, saw it was almost twenty past ten.

"Maybe we should just go on in," I said. Rosa agreed, so we got up.

At first I thought that the metal door was locked, but it was just heavy and stuck and finally swung open after a mighty tug. It looked awfully dark, but after a cautious step in I saw that lights were on farther inside. Rosa followed a step behind me, closing the door with a resounding clang. I didn't see anyone, but the big studio space was divided up into several sets, separated by floor-to-ceiling scrims and backdrops. I called out a questioning "hello?" as we wandered inside, but there was no response.

Rippen, or whoever, must have been shooting a western. The first set was a classic frontier saloon complete with sawdust on the floor, wagon-wheel chandelier, and a rickety upright piano in the corner. I grabbed an empty sarsaparilla bottle off a table, and damned if the heavy leaded glass didn't look and feel authentic. Rosa spun slowly around the three-quarters set, taking it all in, a big smile on her face, like a tourist at Universal Studios. Though the illusion was spoiled by the presence of two big Panaflex cameras at the open end of the set, the art design was stunning.

"Better than Disneyland," Rosa said. I had to admit to feeling a tiny jolt of frisson myself.

We walked on through to the next set, which I took to be a western schoolhouse, each tiny desk graced with a small chalkboard and primer. Rosa inspected a picture hanging on the wall behind the teacher's desk.

"What is it?" I asked, walking up beside her.

"This? I'm pretty sure it's a picture of Henry James."

Then I remembered reading about this production in the *Times*. It was, indeed, a Rippen shoot, for something he called an "alternate-history western." Some kind of goofy story in which Henry James became president of the United States and started a war against the Russians who had settled in and claimed California. I think the article mentioned that Robert Towne was directing. I only remembered it because it sounded so completely crazy to me—it had to be a Laughing

Boy project—but the *Times* had gushed about the screenplay (surprise, surprise).

I had wandered off the dressed set to fondle one of the cameras when we heard another crash. It sounded like it came from the next set over. Rosa and I looked at each other, and I again called out a "hello," again with no response. Rosa came up beside me and grabbed on to my arm. Together we walked across a dark area of the studio and toward the lights of the last set. I tripped over a spool of gaffer's tape, but Rosa stopped me from falling. We came around the rear of a heavy backdrop and onto the set of the town church, a modest A-frame with perhaps ten rows of pews and an altar graced with a large crucifix.

Standing at the pulpit, staring up at the jumbo Jesus-on-the-cross, was another dude in a monster suit. I didn't remember reading anything about Rippen's western having a horror element, but it certainly sounded like Laughing Boy's style.

"Excuse me," I said, and cleared my throat. "We're looking for Jack Rippen."

The actor turned around at the sound of my voice. He wasn't as big as the guy we'd met outside. In fact, the makeup didn't look like it belonged to a guy at all—there were definite tits, monstrous as they might be—though the costume looked so heavy that I assumed there had to be a man underneath. As a special effect, it was even more impressive than the cigarette guy. It—or she—stood about my height with linebacker shoulders and earthy brown skin the texture of tightly packed mud. The flesh was layered in ridges that moved independently, like scales, forming a kind of mail or armor. The torso tapered into a narrow V supported by stubby but muscular legs that were double-hinged at the knee. Its large feet were broad, flat, and three-toed, its hands long, thin, and clawed.

The mask was the masterpiece, though. The massive forehead and bald pate was bony and limned with thick red veins. The bulging, deep-set eyes, immense ears, and absent nose lent the monster a cadaverous quality, accentuated by a mouthful of oversized, yellow teeth jutting over thin red lips. The creature had no chin, and the bottom part of the jaw looked hinged to the rest of the head, like a gator's. God alone knows how many hours it took to attach all those appliances, but the final effect was truly dazzling. I was thinking maybe I'd have to go see this movie when it came out.

"That's *great,*" Rosa said, echoing my own assessment. "But you must be hot as blazes in there."

Then it attacked.

Just like that, moving with otherworldly speed. I never saw anything other than a blur as it leapt down the aisle toward us, screeching a high-pitched wail as it came. Despite the speed with which it moved, its smell reached me first: a thick, feral odor—part excrement, part sweat, all animal. The smell of farms and zoos and circus menageries.

Then the creature hit me.

One second I was standing beside Rosa, the next I was on my ass halfway across the set. I cracked my head against the naked concrete floor, sending tendrils of darkness snaking across my vision. All the wind had been knocked out of my lungs, and my already sore ribs punished me severely as I tried to take too deep a breath. I raised my head, felt pain shoot down my neck. Rosa hadn't moved; she just stood there staring back at me, her jaw gone slack and her eyes wide. I saw her gaze dart up from my face, caught another whiff of that animal smell, and then I was hurtling backward, knocking the prop pews over in a domino effect as I tumbled.

In all honesty, I would have been content to lie there in my misery if not for Rosa's frightened squeal. I managed to get back to my hands and knees in time to see the monster—and I now definitely thought of it as such—lift Rosa up by the scruff of her neck and examine her. Rosa half screamed, half gagged, and kicked out at the creature, landing a solid-looking blow to the tit. The creature responded by running the claws on its free hand across Rosa's face. The thin, dark lines began to bleed instantly, enveloping Rosa's soft features in a dripping red grid. The creature touched a bloody claw to its lips, then tentatively traced a fresh gouge in Rosa's throat. The blood again began to flow, but thankfully it didn't look like it severed the carotid.

I looked around for a weapon, pulling a broken two-by-four out of the rubble of one of the pews I had trashed. It had split at one end, tapering to a sharp, stakelike point. I clutched it like a spear and, with a jungle yell of my own, charged the creature.

It looked my way and simply let go of Rosa. I saw her crumple to the ground with another squeal, but continued my charge. The creature didn't move until I was within striking distance, then executed a lightning spin to duck under my spear and plow into me with its powerful frame. I felt a bony, sharp shoulder catch me midriff, instantly reversing the direction of my charge. Then it stood up, lifting me off the ground. I was balanced, for a moment, like a seesaw on its broad shoulder. The smell, in close, was overwhelming, like a wet dog that had rolled in raw sewage. I reached out to steady myself and grabbed a handful of its coarse flesh. It was warm—hot even—and as I already knew somewhere in my heart, *not* made of latex.

Then I was flying.

The creature didn't even bother to follow my landing, though it surely heard it as I knocked over a camera. I felt a trickle of blood running down my lips and had a bad feeling that I'd just busted my nose. As I tried, and failed, to get up, I tried to determine what else was broken.

Rosa screamed again, which did get me scrambling. I saw, though, that it was a scream of fury and that she was attacking the creature with something in her hand. It made a spitting noise, like a bongo drum, and I realized she held a nail gun. She must have found it on the side of the set. She was firing nails at the creature, which howled in pain with each muffled thunk! The creature actually started backing away—I cheered as one nail ripped right though the back of the monster in a cascade of dark ichor—then stopped.

Rosa had run out of ammo.

The creature realized its advantage immediately and again, moving too fast to follow, jumped on top of Rosa with one mighty leap. Rosa fell backward and bounced off the altar. The giant crucifix fell off the wall and crashed down on top of the two of them. It stopped the creature for a second, but then it easily tossed the martyred carpenter aside. I saw it raise a claw high above its head. I couldn't see Rosa on the floor, but I heard her scream as the claw descended.

And then again.

I tried to yell to distract the creature's attention, but all that came out of my mouth was a molar, jarred loose by my impact with the camera. I looked frantically for another weapon, saw nothing at all. I spotted a power junction box on the wall nearby and, out of sheer desperation, scrambled over to it and threw every switch.

The keys and spots on the set came on all at once, with blinding intensity. The creature rose off its haunches and let out a screech against the glow. It raised one arm up over its eyes and picked me out in the dark just beyond the edge of the illuminated set. It started toward me.

I saw it move this time. Maybe it was the lights, maybe the angle. Maybe just the knowledge that a cruel death was racing straight for me.

I saw it accelerate at me up the now rubble-strewn church aisle. I saw the sinewy muscles in its legs as they pounded up and down, heard its yellow nails click on the concrete floor. I saw the thick saliva dripping off its teeth, the raw fury in its eyes. It just got bigger and bigger as it roared down on me. I even saw Rosa stir on the floor behind it and felt a brief sense of victory, knowing that at least it hadn't killed her. Yet.

It was just about on top of me when, with a glass-shattering squeal, it fell over amid a shower of dark liquid. It knocked over the last pew as it fell, but I couldn't figure out what had tripped it up.

Then I glanced back toward the aisle and saw its leg, still moving, on the ground in a pool of its foul blood.

A Japanese man with long, flowing hair in a silky gray kimono stood just to the side, holding a gleaming silver sword stiffly out in front of him, angled roughly at the creature. I had no idea where he'd come from.

"Huh?" I stammered.

The monster tried to stand, fell over once, then balanced itself in a crouch using its arms and remaining leg. Blood continued to pour from its severed limb. The swordsman never took his eyes off the monster, but altered his posture slightly, adjusting the angle of the sword as the creature rose. The two stared each other down. It appeared to be a standoff, though I didn't see how the creature could hope to outlast the swordsman given the amount of blood it was losing. I had the feeling the creature was about to charge when a voice called out from across the set.

The swordsman didn't look, but both the creature and I did. Another Japanese man, in black denim jeans and a black T-shirt, approached the wounded monster from the other side. He, too, held a sword and barked several short words in Japanese, though whether to the creature, the first swordsman, or me, I had no idea. Nor did I have a clue what he said.

The appearance of the second man seemed to make the decision for the monster. With surprising agility, given its wounds, it leaped over the pew and at the first swordsman. All I saw was a blurry flash, like Luke Skywalker's light sword without the hum, and the creature's head flew from its shoulders.

The head went one way and the body tumbled another. A geyser of blood erupted from its neck, but incredibly, not so much as a drop touched the swordsman, who held his pose as the creature collapsed. It wasn't until the second man came up beside him, a broad smile playing across his face, that the swordsman sheathed his blade, first wiping the blood off on the dead creature's cooling flesh.

The two men then glanced my way. I smiled. The man in black grinned back at me, but the man in the kimono had the look of granite. Then I remembered Rosa.

As I turned up the aisle, I saw that a third man, also Japanese and also dressed in black but with a gun tucked into his belt, was already bent over her, tending to her wounds. I limped to the altar and saw that Rosa was semiconscious, moaning and covered in blood. Her eyes were squeezed tightly shut and she rocked her head from side to side. The man was gently dabbing at her wounds: a series of razor slices across her face, neck, and torso. One slash of the creature's claws had torn her blouse, exposing a breast. It had rent the flesh around the nipple, and a tiny pool of blood had formed atop the globe. It made me wince in sympathy as she shuddered as he sprayed the wound with a can of plastic skin.

I squatted down beside her and took her hand. She opened her eyes, which were glassy and filled with tears. I tried to smile at her, but it seemed to make things worse. The other black-clad man came up behind me.

"We go now," he said. He pointed at Rosa and me. "You come."

"Okay," I whispered.

What, was I gonna argue with him?

Sixteen

I wanted to help carry Rosa, but barely managed to keep up with our mysterious saviors as we fled the studio building. The Kimono Kid led the way while one of the men in black—the one with the pistol, not the sword—carried Rosa easily in his arms. I followed them out through a rear door that had been pried open from the outside. The second man in black brought up the rear.

The swordsman, his hand resting on the hilt of his blade, his eyes darting around like tumbling dice, proceeded to a black Acura sedan parked just up the road. He waited at the rear while the man with the gun got behind the wheel and his partner gently deposited Rosa in the backseat. He gestured for me to get in, and the three of us sat in the back, Rosa propped up between us. With the engine started and the car already moving, the swordsman got in on the passenger side. Rosa whimpered beside me, and I tried to take her hand, but she pulled away with a subvocal squeak.

The driver roared down the narrow studio lanes, heading for the nearest exit. As we approached it I saw that a heavy chain secured the high metal gates, barring the way. If the driver noticed it, he didn't regard it as an obstacle. He revved up into fourth and pointed the nose of the car at the center of the gates. I closed my eyes, felt the crunch, heard the crash. And we were through, heading east on Culver at a rapid, but not unduly conspicuous, clip.

I had a million questions in my head. So many that I didn't even know which to ask, where to start. I settled for the most obvious.

"What the hell was that back there?"

The driver glanced at the swordsman, who was eyeing me in the rearview mirror. I saw him nod all but imperceptibly and then the driver nodded a little more forcefully to the man sitting in back with me.

"*Yamamba,*" he said.

"My mama?" I asked.

"*Ya-mam-ba,*" he repeated slowly. "Very bad. Not nice."

I'd figured that last bit out for myself, but it didn't exactly answer my question. "*Yamamba,*" I echoed.

"*Hai.*"

"*Yamamba* High. Is that like where you went to school?"

"*Hai.* Yes. Is *yamamba.*"

Well, this was going along just swimmingly.

"*Hai* means yes," Rosa said. I glanced down at her. She was still huddled up, but her eyes were open and a little more focused. "Christ, Marty, haven't you ever read any James Clavell?"

"*Shōgun*—pahhh!" the driver spat. Bad enough every bag lady has a screenplay, every hack in this town is also a critic.

"What is *yamamba?*" I asked. "What does that mean?"

The man in back spoke in Japanese to the driver. He said something to the swordsman, who nodded again.

"Demon," the driver told me. "Lady demon. Very not nice."

A lady demon, I thought. Well, that seemed as good an explanation as any, I suppose. My head hurt.

"Who—" I started.

The swordsman spat a couple of words out, the first I'd heard him utter. He had a voice like oily gravel. I couldn't understand what he said, of course, but I didn't need the others to translate it for me.

"Shut the fuck up" sounds pretty much the same in every language.

Rosa finally let me hold her hand as we were driven north on Robertson under the Santa Monica Freeway. Traffic was light and only the gaudy neon of the countless taco stands, doughnut shops, and burger joints challenged the darkness. I was tempted to try another question as we drove through the quiet of Beverly Hills, but the eyes of the swordsman in the mirror never seemed to leave me, and I couldn't quite find the nerve to articulate anything.

The driver kept going north right on up to Coldwater Canyon. He turned off the Canyon pass about a half mile into the hills onto one of those anonymous winding roads with a terrifyingly steep grade that leads up toward rich-people heaven. I hadn't been up in this area since I'd left The Business and fell out of contact with the kind of people who can afford the big glass and stilt houses with the best views of the city. Rosa had closed her eyes again and I thought maybe she'd dozed off, but I felt her squeeze my hand tight when the car took one of the steep mountain turns a little too fast.

The driver followed the twisty road to the top of the hill. The night was relatively clear and the twinkling lights of the L.A. basin below looked magical, almost fairylike. Like every old whore, Los Angeles is much prettier in the dark. It almost looked too good to be real; more like a Spielberg special effect than the city I knew and lived in.

We turned off onto a posted, private road covered over with a tunnellike thicket of vegetation. At the end of the thicket we came to a concrete wall with a steel gate. Two guards, both Japanese, stood at either side. One wore a kimono and pair of swords, the other black denim and cradled an Uzi. Both had long black hair, though the man with the gun wore his in a ponytail. They both looked hard as Chinese algebra. Or Japanese fuzzy logic.

The man with the Uzi opened the gate by hand. The dude with the swords seemed not to pay us any mind at all, but kept his eyes on the road behind us. As we slowly drove past him through the gate, I tried to study him through the window and thought I saw tattoos on his fingers and neck.

We continued slowly up the drive toward the now visible mansion. It looked vastly older than the other houses I'd glimpsed in the area, almost Victorian. Although there are lots of great, if dilapidated, Victorian houses downtown, dating from the once-upon-a-nineteenth-century time when South Central L.A. was the place to live, I didn't think anything of the like had been built up in the hills. This was a monster of a house, though, three stories tall with arching gables and a crow's nest that surely afforded one of the truly brilliant views in all of Southern California. Looking around, it seemed to me that we were atop the highest of the Hollywood Hills, with even Griffith Observatory and the Hollywood sign below us and off to the east. I couldn't begin to imagine how much this property must be worth. Somehow that thought made me a little more nervous about the identity of our "hosts."

We came to a stop at the end of the driveway, which traced a small circle leading up the front door. Another pair of guards held station on the wooden porch. The driver got out and opened the door on my side, while the man who rode in back with us helped Rosa out on his. The swordsman was already out of the car, surveying the darkness. One hand always, it seemed, rested on the hilt of his sword.

"Nice digs, huh?" I said to Rosa. She nodded, looking as scared as I felt. I would have said something comforting if I could have thought of anything.

One of the porch monkeys opened the front door—it wasn't locked—then resumed his post without exchanging a word with the others. Rosa and I were led into the house and directed to sit on a backless wooden bench just inside the front door. The swordsman kept us company while the men in black disappeared down the hall. The walls were barren of decor, and nothing gave any indication that the house was *lived* in. Even the grand staircase visible at the end of the foyer seemed to trail up into a cold darkness.

"What do you think?" Rosa whispered to me. I glanced at the swordsman, but he was a statue.

"I haven't got a fucking clue," I said. "How you feeling?"

"It hurts," Rosa said. She touched the scars on her face. She was a right mess, with her torn clothes and dried blood. But the bleeding all seemed to have stopped. "It hurts a lot actually. I feel like I went ten rounds with O.J. Does it look really bad?"

I was about to lie to her, but my face answered her before my brain could. I ended up nodding sadly.

"I thought so," she said.

We sat there quietly for a minute, Rosa fingering her face and me prodding with my tongue at the space where the tooth had come out. My ribs hurt, too, not that anyone asked.

"What did they mean by 'lady demon'?" Rosa suddenly said.

"Huh?" I said. But I had heard her.

"The *yamamba* thing. 'Lady demon,' he called it."

I tried to look nonchalant. "Probably just an awkward translation of some sexist Japanese phrase. You know, like 'bitch from hell' or 'cunt on wheels.' Pardon my French."

"Could be," Rosa said, nodding to herself. "You really think so?"

I took a deep breath. "No," I said, letting it out.

"Me either," Rosa said. She looked up at the swordsman. "He cut its head off."

The swordsman continued to ignore us. I didn't have a clue if he understood us or not. "He did," I had to agree. "He definitely did that."

"It's pretty amazing that we can discuss it so calmly like this, don't you think?"

"I'm impressed." I nodded. That seemed to take care of the conversation for a while.

"Marty," Rosa started, but whatever she wanted to say was interrupted by the return of one of the men in black. It was the driver. He beckoned us to our feet, and I had to help Rosa to stand.

"She needs to get to a doctor," I said, but he only held up his hand. "A doctor. Do you understand?"

"We take care. Now you come." He gestured again. There didn't appear to be a lot of choice.

Rosa was okay once she made it to her feet. She followed the man in black, and the swordsman followed behind me. The driver flipped on a light and led us up the stairs, down the second-floor hallway past a row of closed doors, and up another steeper and less opulent stairway to the third floor.

The third floor at least had a lived-in feel missing from the downstairs part of the house. The hallway was adorned with large Japanese prints in bold colors with flowing brushstrokes. I was only able to glance at them as we went by, but they all seemed to depict warriors engaged in battle with a rogue's gallery of ugly monsters. I tried to stop and take a closer look at one featuring a figure that bore an unsettling resemblance to the creature I'd seen kill Cheri, but the real-life swordsman behind me urged me on with a not-so-gentle prod of his finger.

We were ushered into a room at the front of the house—it must once have been the master bedroom, though no bed now stood in it. Large bay windows offered a genuinely breathtaking view of the city. The room was bare except for a set of swords hanging on one wall and a few cushions scattered atop a mat in a loose circle about a low table on the hardwood floor. The swordsman indicated for us to take our shoes off before entering the room. Rosa kicked her shoes off right away, but I grumbled a bit as I unlaced my Hush Puppies. My socks had holes in the toes, which made me feel very self-conscious. I'm sure the swordsman noticed, because for the first time a smile nearly cracked his otherwise stolidly solemn expression.

An elderly man waited for us in the room. He stood with his back to us, hands clasped behind him, staring out the window. He didn't turn around when we came in. He wore a somber, blue kimono and a matching skullcap. Long gray hair flowed from beneath the cap and was fastened with a gold ring into a ponytail. The swordsman bowed deeply to the man's back and retreated to the doorway. He took up a position just outside, one hand, as ever, ready to take up his sword.

"I don't especially like your city," the man at the window said. His accent was thick, but he was reasonably comprehensible. He only battled with his els and r's a little bit. "Though it can be very pretty in the night."

"Nobody really likes it here," I said. "Or they don't admit to it if they do."

The man turned to face us. He was short, probably average for a Japanese, but solid-looking. He had a high, round forehead verging into a receding hairline, and a thick gray beard and mustache. Studying his features, I decided he wasn't as old as I first thought. The gray hair made him look older, but I guessed he was no more than about fifty. Still, I'm lousy with people's ages, especially Asians. He let his hands drop to his sides and bowed slightly to us. *His* socks didn't have holes in the toes.

"And how are you feeling, Miss Mendez?" he asked.

Rosa jumped slightly on hearing her name, but recovered fast. "I've been better," she said. "But then *yamamba* always disagrees with me."

I thought I saw his lip turn up under his thick facial hair and he nodded, but didn't respond.

"Who the *fuck* are you?" I blurted.

That definitely brought a little smile. "Minamoto Yorimitsu," he said, and bowed again. Well, dipped his chin an inch, anyway. I must have looked puzzled, because he repeated his name, slowly. "Is that useful to you, Mr. Burns?"

"Don't mean a thing," I said.

"Nor should it." Yorimitsu gestured toward the cushions on the floor. "Please, won't you sit?"

Both Rosa and I groaned and grimaced a bit as we sat down Indian-style—Japanese style?—on the pillows. I noted that Yorimitsu moved across the room with gazellelike grace, lowering himself to the cushion the way a silk hankie falls in a light breeze. Almost immediately, a door opened on the other side of the room and yet another man in black came in carrying a wooden tray with festive teacups and a pot. The server had big, meaty hands, but poured the tea with remarkable delicacy, starting with Rosa. I got the feeling that some ritual was being observed in the serving, but damned if I knew what it was. No explanation was offered and the man quickly departed, silently closing the door behind him. Yorimitsu seemed to be waiting for us to drink first. Rosa mimed a toast with her cup and took a tiny sip.

"Lovely," she said. "Jasmine." Yorimitsu nodded.

I don't know Earl Grey from Joel Grey, but I took a slurp. The hot liquid went straight for my missing tooth, lighting my eyes up like three sevens on a one-armed bandit. I clasped a hand to my mouth, spilling half the tea out of my cup before I could put it down. Yorimitsu didn't look pleased, but he handed me a cloth napkin from the tray and used another to blot up some of the mess.

"Nice," I croaked. "Little bit hot."

Yorimitsu bowed again and almost cracked another smile. "We will have someone see to your mouth as soon as possible," he said, then turned to Rosa. "And to your wounds."

"How do you—"

He held up his hand. "In time. First, I believe we should speak."

Rosa and I exchanged a look and a shrug. Then we both nodded. The ball was in his court.

"Do you have any idea what you have involved yourself in?" he asked.

I started to say something smart, thought better of it. "No," I said. "I don't think so."

"I don't think so either. Tell me, Miss Mendez, Mr. Burns: are you spiritual people? Or merely religious?"

The question took me aback. "Huh?" I said. Rosa shook her head.

"Americans, American Christians especially, call themselves religious—often violently so—but they are not spiritual, I think. They also call upon God very often. Always thanking him or cursing him—'God damn it' is to me the epitome of the American idiom. Along with 'motherfucker.' "

The profanity sounded funny in Yorimitsu's mouth. I had to suppress a giggle.

" 'God bless America,' you like to say, too, yes? Your politicians, your president says it all the time. 'God's country' is another phrase I have learned here. As if this could be the only one. As if only America has God looking out for it. Like only America has freedom, you seem to think."

"They're just expressions," I said.

"Which is exactly my point. You are a people who lay claim on God, who lay claim on religion and belief. But does that make you a religious people?"

"What does this have to do with what's happening here?" Rosa asked.

"And an impatient people," Yorimitsu said. "A mark of great immaturity."

"Goo-goo, ga-ga," I sniped. Rosa elbowed me in the side, which hurt. Our host ignored it.

"Japan is a very spiritual country. Even if it is not so religious in the way Americans prefer to understand."

"What's the difference?" Rosa asked.

"Religious people believe," Yorimitsu said, holding up a finger in a pedantic way. "Spiritual people also believe, but more than just believe. Spiritual people *feel* as well."

Yorimitsu paused to take a sip of his tea. He cradled the porcelain cup in both hands, as if drawing water from a stream. I picked my own cup up and took a cautious sip. It had cooled enough for me to imbibe carefully.

"The spirituality of Japan takes on many forms and guises. Shinto, Buddhism, Confucianism, Taoism, have all found a place in the hearts of the people of Japan. And not just a place, but a concord, a—" he searched for the phrase "—a *modus vivendi*. The many sects and cults and *faiths* coexist in a shared feeling of spirituality and not the—" another mental word-search "—the *balkanization* of belief."

"Who. Are. You?" I said.

"My name is Minamoto Yorimitsu," he said slowly, as if talking to a child. "I am *yamabushi*. And I am *oyabun* of the *Kakure.*"

"How's that?" I said.

"What is important for you to understand is that only we stand between you and the hand of Jack the Ripper." He smiled for real this time, though most of it still disappeared into his facial hair.

"Hot enough for you, Mr. Burns?" he asked.

God, I hate this town.

I didn't like being separated from Rosa, but she said it would be all right. I don't think the guy who looked me over was a real doctor. I tried asking him outright, but if he understood English, he didn't let on. And it's not like I could look at the diploma on the wall. In any case, he did a pretty good job retaping my ribs, though he was none too delicate about it, and he gave me some herbal crap for the pain in my mouth. It smelled like swamp water, but tasted like lemon, and damned if the throbbing in my mouth didn't ease within a couple of minutes of drinking the stuff.

Comparing notes about bedside manner, Rosa and I decided that the same Silent Sam attended to us both. She said it hurt like a queen bitch when he scraped the plastic skin off her wounds to treat and disinfect them, but that she, too, had been given some kind of herbal concoction that quickly helped to assuage the pain. Except Rosa said that hers smelled like lemon and tasted like swamp water.

We were led back upstairs into a small dining room. The floor-high table had been laid for three. A steaming bowl of white rice stood in the center, surrounded by artfully laid plates of sushi and a heaping tray of vegetable tempura. We were directed to sit. I assumed Yorimitsu would be joining us, but suddenly found I was too hungry to stand on formalities. I've never much gone for the raw fish and seaweed thing, but piled up the tempura and rice and started shoveling it in my gob. I had to chew on my right side, but I didn't let it slow me down. Though Rosa was a little less animalistic in her approach and showed no qualms about the sushi, she wolfed it down pretty well herself. I was starting on seconds when Yorimitsu finally came in, followed by another of what I realized were the many Men in Black, this one carrying a tray with sake. He waited for Yorimitsu to sit before he started serving, starting with the big boss. I've never been in love with sake, either, but the warm rice wine just hit the spot. The servant left the bottle, bowed and went out of the room, closing the door behind him. As he did, I noticed that our swordsman friend continued to stand guard just outside.

"D'Artagnan out there got a name?" I asked.

"Pardon?" Yorimitsu said.

"The dude with the sword." I nodded toward the door.

"Ah! Benkei."

He said the name again slowly, and I repeated it until I pronounced it correctly. The key was not stressing either syllable over the other. "He saved our lives," I added, saying it as a slight question.

"Your well-being is paramount to our plans, Mr. Burns. Twice now Benkei has intervened on your behalf." I must have looked puzzled, because he added: "At your home the other night. Against the two *Goryō-dō*. That, too, was Benkei."

"*Goryō-dō?*" I asked. But before Yorimitsu could answer, another of the interchangeable Men in Black entered, bearing a fresh pot of tea. He poured, bowed, and left.

"Hey, Benkei!" I yelled through the open door. The swordsman glanced inside, but held his poker face.

"This a no-girls-allowed deal?" Rosa asked after the door closed again.

"Pardon?"

"There don't seem to be any women about."

"Ah," Yorimitsu said. "We are a brotherhood, yes."

"We being the ka-ka whatever," I said.

"Kakure," Yorimitsu corrected. *"Kakure.* We are an ancient order."

"Order of what?" Rosa asked.

Yorimitsu folded his hands in his lap and stared down into his sake. I got the feeling that he was trying to work out for himself how much he needed to tell us.

"In Japan," he began, "it is said, there are eight million gods who live in *takama-ha-gara* and *naka-tsu-kuni;* in heaven and earth. The gods of Japan, the *kami,* are like the seasons, like the tides; they come and go, wax and wane."

"They don't sound very powerful," Rosa said, "very godlike."

"Yes and no," Yorimitsu replied. "The power of the gods rests not only with the gods, yes? It is also in the belief in the gods. In the depth of the *feeling* of those who believe."

"And you feel you believe in lady demons?" I asked.

"I think you have learned for yourself the wisdom of such belief, Mr. Burns. You surely have seen that disbelief is not itself a satisfactory defense for the unbeliever."

"So what is it exactly that your sect believes in?" Rosa asked.

"We do not regard ourselves as a sect exactly. The meaning of *Kakure* is . . . 'the hidden ones.' "

"Hidden from what?" Rosa said.

Yorimitsu smiled. He looked back and forth between Rosa and me. "Do you know much—anything—of Japan?"

"Seven Samurai," I said. *"Yojimbo.* I think I read *Rising Sun.* Or maybe it was *Disclosure,* I can't remember now."

"Not really," Rosa said, giving me a look.

"This, of course, is not a surprise. Americans are very good at holding opinions, but not so interested in learning facts." He seemed to wait for some rebuttal from me, but I had none to offer. "As I mentioned to you earlier, Japan is a culture of many religions and faiths. Most adhere to either Shinto or Buddhism. Many of the youth—the *shinjinrui,* too much under the American influence—now have no faith whatsoever, which is worst of all. But also there are those like ourselves. Whose beliefs are considered . . . esoteric, but whose faith is strong because it must be."

"Esoteric in what way?" Rosa said.

"It is not easy to explain to one who does not understand even the most basic about our land. But within our own culture we have long been considered *murahachibu.* Outcast. It is the curse which set us on our path, but also it is our strength. And now our mission."

"What were you cast out of?" I asked.

"The *Kakure* dwell on the island of Kyushu. You know this island?"

We both shook our heads. So did Yorimitsu, but for a different reason. He glanced at the table, then poured some rice onto an empty plate. He prodded it with his chopstick, until it formed what even I recognized was the general shape of Japan. He pointed at a small island he'd sculpted at the southern tip.

"This is Kyushu. It is one of the four main islands that form Japan. Tokyo is here—" he pointed to the middle of the biggest, central island "—on Honshu. Kyushu was a place of refuge for those seeking escape from the tyrannies of the Honshu shogunates in what you would call the Middle Ages."

He erased the rice picture by tapping the edge of the plate.

"There are some who claim that the origins of *Kakure* can be found even in the *Kojiki,* the great book of the ancient world. That it was with the violent birth of Ama no Zakogami that *Kakure,* too, was born. Others believe that the order was founded by the great warrior Yoshitsune. All that is sure is that the name *Kakure* did not appear until the reign of Tokugawa. *Kakure* always had its basis in a mixture, a coming together of different aspects of Japanese belief. Shinto, shamanistic Buddhism, Shingon. Later, even some aspects of Christianity. But its very heart, its soul, can only be found in *Shugen-dō.*"

One of the Men in Black—monks, I wondered? monks with guns?— came in to clear away the dirty dishes and bring a fresh bottle of sake. I wanted some more, but already felt a little light-headed. I thought it was important to try and follow what Yorimitsu had to say.

"In a land of so many gods," Yorimitsu said, "not all will be benevolent. Some, though not so many, are actively malefic."

"Can't you just not believe in them?" Rosa said.

"Ahhh, but there are always those who benefit by the belief in evil. It is because of those that *Kakure* came to be and continues to exist. The struggle of the gods, the struggle of good and evil, is a war of belief."

"So who is it who believes in the evil?" I asked. "Who are you at war with?"

"As I said, the *Kakure* have long been outcast. The reward of those who believe in evil is power. And it is that power which has cast us out. And against that power which we struggle.

"Once the evil and the good were one. They still are, of course, as must they always be. But the evil will not recognize this, which is to the advantage of the good."

That sounded like fortune-cookie mysticism to me, and it must have showed, because Yorimitsu tried to explain.

"*Shugen-dō* is a magical path—a way—to knowing. It is descended from the way of *yamabushi,* the holy men of the mountains."

"You said before that you were *yamabushi,*" Rosa said.

"Yes, the *yamabushi* and the *yama-no-hijiri* were Japanese mystics. They found a path to enlightenment through an austere life in the mountains. Mt. Yoshino was the most holy of these places, and it was to them and the spirits that dwelt there that these faithful men dedicated their lives and energies."

"Spirits?" I said. "Like pixies? What?"

"You see," Yorimitsu said, "this is what I cannot so readily make you to comprehend. Spirit has much deeper meaning in Japan than in the West. You have your Holy Ghost and your Devil and your Jesus . . ."

"He's not my Jesus," I said.

"But you do not share the Japanese acceptance of *bakemono.* The world of the spirits, of those who have passed on or have always been."

"You mean ghosts," Rosa said.

"Ghosts, yes, but not just the *yūrei,* the ghosts of those who have died; also the *yōkai,* those who never were."

"I don't follow you," I told him. "And I don't understand your point."

"My point is about the nature of belief. In Japan it is readily accepted that spirits exist. That they dwell with us, visit us, take interest in our lives. Spirits of our ancestors, to be honored and remembered, and spirits of other forms: human, animal and . . . just other. Some to be honored, some to be feared."

"Gods," Rosa said.

"Some are gods, yes. Some are demons."

"Yo mama," I muttered. Yorimitsu gave me an odd look and I shook my head.

"The *yamabushi* worshiped the spirits of the mountains," he went on. "Their mission was one of enlightenment. But in their studies they had experience of the darker spirits as well. And because they were only men, some were tempted by that darkness and the power offered to them for their fealty. Their ways became debased as the dark powers, the gods and the demons, exerted their will upon them. Such power is a terrible thing.

"The *yamabushi* split into factions. There were those who mastered means of opposing the dark powers: the *Shugen-dō,* the *Nembutsu,* the *Onmyō-dō.* And then there were those who took succor in the power of darkness: *Goryō-dō.*"

He paused for some sake. I decided to join him, thinking maybe light-headed was the best way to deal with this after all.

"The battle between these factions has raged for centuries. It is a fight always in the shadows, away from the light of reason. Those who follow the way of *Goryō-dō* are strong and their allies are fierce. For the demons battle with them: the *kappa,* the *yamamba,* the many *oni.*

"And the *tengu.*"

I didn't much like the way he said that last bit. The word hung ominously in the air above us, like the smell of rotten eggs. "What exactly is a *tengu?*" I asked.

Yorimitsu scratched his beard. "It is an inexact translation, but the closest to say in your language would be 'Celestial Dog.'"

I spilled the rest of my sake.

Seventeen

I hate futons, that they've become so popular. I hate that you can't read the *L.A. Weekly* to check out what movies are playing or which hot-sex line to call without being assaulted by ads for futon stores. I hate that where twenty years ago no one would have dreamed of sticking some lumber and a ratty pad on the floor and calling it a bed, now, because it's a futon, that makes it all right. I hate looking at them, I hate sitting on them, and I really hate sleeping on them.

I was lying on a futon in one of the second-floor bedrooms of the *Kakure* house. Benkei had shown us to our rooms, Rosa's right across the hall from mine. Yorimitsu had invited us to spend the night, or as long as we wanted, under *Kakure* protection. It was the same kind of invitation you get from the Internal Revenue Service every April. Not a lot of choice.

I tried enticing Benkei into conversation. I asked him about his swords as an icebreaker, but he wouldn't have any of it. He opened the door to my room, walked in himself for a quick inspection, then pointed at the futon. He offered a minute bow of the head as he closed the door behind him. He'd done exactly the same for Rosa.

I was hurting and exhausted, but sleep wasn't on the agenda. I had too much on my mind, too much to think about from our conversation with Yorimitsu. My head was spinning with talk of Japanese names and places, legends and myths. I had to find some way to come to terms with the seemingly insane, irrational notions of good and evil, gods and demons. It was all as crazy as the proverbial soup sandwich. It had to be.

And yet . . .

Yorimitsu had gone on to explain that the Celestial Dogs, the *tengu*, were the most awful of the demons allied with the followers of *Goryō-dō*, those with whom Yorimitsu's people had been struggling, apparently with very mixed success, for hundreds of years. *Tengu* magic, in fact, lay at the heart of *Goryō-dō* belief. Although the *Goryō-dō* thought themselves to be masters of the *tengu*, Yorimitsu clearly saw them as dupes of an in-human power they didn't truly understand.

"The *tengu* are very ancient," Yorimitsu said, "Celestial Dogs born of the very heart of *Susa-no-o*, storm god brother of the sun goddess *Amaterasu*. The *tengu* cannot be mastered by men, and their realm lies beyond the perceptions of even the wisest of sages. And the *Genyosha* are not so wise as they think."

"*Genyosha?*" I said. "Now, who are they? Help me out here."

"The *Genyosha* are among the worst of the modern-day children of *Goryō-dō*," Yorimitsu explained. "It is how they are now known in the world, though they have had many names in the past. *Machi-yakko*. *Hanafuda*. In the end it is all the same. The rose is a rose, yes?"

"So they're all *Goryō-dō?*"

"*Hai.*"

"And how in the world does Jack Rippen figure into all this?"

Yorimitsu took a slow, deep breath, let it out before speaking.

"The *Genyosha* are *yakuza*. Do you understand this term?"

"Japanese mafia?" I asked. Rosa closed her eyes and rubbed her temples.

"Mafia is an American notion." *Errrr,* I thought, but let it pass. "*Yakuza* are criminal organization, true, but also much more than just that. Like *yamabushi*, there are different *yakuza*. Different families—different *oyabun*, fathers—and different beliefs. Some *are* just petty criminal: drugs, prostitution, gambling, etc. Some not so petty.

"But *yakuza* fingers reach deep into Japanese history and culture. In Japan, business and government are like one. This has caused many problems in recent years—you have no doubt read of the scandals, the parade of governments brought down—but still it is the way we continue to live, the way we know. *Yakuza* touches business, touches politics, touches everything. All for the end of power, but not all as criminal."

"But Jack Rippen—"

"Please," Yorimitsu said, gesturing patience to me with his wagging finger. "The *Genyosha* is the most dangerous of the *yakuza*. Their roots can be found in *yamabushi* discipline, in the *Nembutsu* ascetics who studied and prayed with my own ancestors in the mountains of Honshu and later of Kyushu. You have heard, perhaps from movies, of the *yakuza* custom of *yubitsume*, of cutting off a part of the finger as an act of contrition to their *oyabun?*"

We both nodded. I flashed on the stubby-fingered Japanese man I'd seen in the Laughing Boy office that first time. Little bells rang.

"This was originally a *Nembutsu* ritual—practiced among the *yama-no-hijiri* of Mt. Yoshino—a means of testifying to the fervor of their belief. A ritual that has been usurped and corrupted by the *yakuza* over the years, just as so much of the belief structure of *yamabushi* has been corrupted by those of the *Genyosha* who turned toward *Goryō-dō*.

"Whether it was a desire for power which led to the alliance between the *Genyosha* and the *oni*—the demons—or whether it was the influence of the demons that fostered the creation the darkest societies of the *yakuza*, it is not for the likes of me to know. But it was a relationship which served both sides very well. For *yakuza* power and influence has grown and spread, and the demons have survived thanks to the force of the *yakuza* belief. This is a relationship which continues to prosper to this day. A relationship with which *you* now must come to terms."

"Why me?" I said. I meant it rhetorically.

"Karma?" Yorimitsu said. I think he meant it as a joke. No one laughed.

"You still haven't actually explained what this actually has to do with us," Rosa said. She sounded weary.

"The *Genyosha*, and thus the *Goryō-dō*, reach deeply into the power base of corporate Japan. Many corporations are subject to *yakuza* influence. Not all are even aware of the extent or even the existence of this influence. *Genyosha* works with great subtlety, practiced over the years of living in the shadows of power, manipulating without being noticed. Touching without being felt.

"Different *yakuza* families invest their interests in different ways, in different businesses. This investment is both material and spiritual. The *Genyosha* have fingers in many bowls—even the so-called *Aum* cult who poisoned the subway in Tokyo were an arm of *Genyosha*—but the main focus of their efforts is Yoshitoshi International."

"Bingo!" I said, the lightbulb flashing over my head.

"Much, I believe, has been made in your country about the advance of Japanese influence in your business affairs. There has been also a great deal of propaganda about Japanese takeover of American companies and American property. It is a mystery to us how it can be that he who sells his house can complain about the one who buys it, even while he counts his money from the sale. If a Japanese corporation buys into the United States, it is because the opportunity is put out before it. We have always been an opportunistic and entrepreneurial people. This is a trait which, as I understand, Americans celebrate in their rhetoric. But it would seem only if it is *they* who are allowed to take advantage of the opportunity."

"Americans are funny that way," I muttered.

"I am afraid that I do not see the humor," Yorimitsu said. "Your Mr. Jack Rippen has provided opportunity to Yoshitoshi. It was, as you say, an offer too good to refuse?"

"But did Rippen know the can of worms he was opening?" I asked. Yorimitsu raised a puzzled eyebrow. "I mean to say, he didn't know about the *Genyosha* influence."

"Of course he did," Yorimitsu said. "Jack Rippen is himself *Goryō-dō.*"

"Fuck," I mumbled. I've heard lots of people refer to Rippen as the devil incarnate over the years, but how many would believe that he really was allied with the powers of darkness? All right, stupid question. I glanced at Rosa, but she seemed to be drifting. I couldn't tell if it was denial or mere exhaustion.

"Yoshitoshi already has many investments in the United States, but they—and through them *Goryō-dō*—are anxious to gain a more substantial foothold in your culture."

"How do you mean?"

"In Japan we view the world in a much more integrated, more holistic way than do you in America. We don't separate business from pleasure, for example. We have, too, a very different notion of public and private lives and the space between the two. In America a businessman buys a company to break it into pieces and sell the parts for a quick gain. The Japanese businessman buys the parts and seeks ways to weave them together to form a greater whole. You look to the near future, the short term, the . . . lowest line?"

"Bottom line," I said.

"*Hai.* We look to the far future. Not just business but also culture. *Goryō-dō,* too. They see opportunities here in America. Not today, maybe, not even tomorrow. But a far distance down the road. They see the whole beyond the parts, within the parts. If you invite corporate Japan—Yoshitoshi—into your land, you do not take just the part. With it comes criminal Japan—*yakuza.* But also, because all are of a piece, comes spiritual Japan. *Genyosha. Goryō-dō.*"

"And *Kakure?*" Rosa asked. She *was* paying attention.

"*Kakure,* as well." Yorimitsu nodded. "We, too, must look to the future. Whatever happens here in Los Angeles is but a piece of strategy, a move in a game that has been played over many, many years. My slightest actions today will echo before me and be magnified many times in the years to come. And in ways that I may not expect. If I do not carefully consider these actions, how can I even imagine what will be the consequence of those echoes ten years, fifty years, one hundred years later?"

"I could never think that way," I said, shaking my head. "It's too much, too overwhelming."

"That is why you are not *Goryō-dō*. You are not *Kakure*. But you are here and you are in very great trouble."

He had that right enough, I thought, squirming on my futon. Thinking over all that had happened, I wasn't even sure how things had ended up as they had. A little greed, a little lust, *a lot of stupidity.* Life had turned into some crazy Rube Goldberg machine, sending me higgledy-piggledy up this chute and down that ladder. Some tiny gear in the center of things had turned and suddenly I'd been launched headlong into . . .

I still didn't know what.

Twisting around, I managed to find a not entirely uncomfortable position when someone rapped lightly on the door. I shot bolt upright as the door opened and Rosa stuck her head in.

"Marty? You awake?" she whispered.

"Can't sleep."

"Me either," she said, and walked on in. She was wrapped in a delicate kimono with a flower pattern. As she was briefly framed in the doorway, I could see her form outlined beneath the silk in the hall backlight. As she closed the door, I thought I also caught a glimpse of Benkei patrolling the hall, hand on sword.

I swung my legs off the edge of the futon as Rosa sat down beside me. She sat close enough that I could smell the exhaustion and perspiration on her, though we didn't quite touch. Her arms were crossed over her stomach, wrapping the kimono tight around her, though it wasn't particularly chilly in the house. Yorimitsu had offered me a kimono, as well, but I felt too damn silly to put it on.

"Are you religious at all?" Rosa asked.

"I like those little white socks the Catholic school girls wear," I said. It earned me another look. "No, not at all. My dad was vaguely Jewish and my mom wasn't much of anything at all. You?"

"My folks had their Catholic moments, but they were never all that devout or anything. Me and my sister had to go to Sunday school when we were little, but I think that was just so my parents could stay home and screw on Sunday mornings."

"No, I never went to Sunday school or anything like that as a kid. I was too busy acting, mostly. It's pretty hard to be a believer if you're in The Business, though God knows there's more than enough worship to go around. But I don't think it's the kind that'll count come Judgment Day. And, I don't know, it's been a long time since I've even thought about that kind of stuff. A long time since I've believed in much of anything at all."

"My sister's real religious," Rosa said.

"Yeah?"

"Uh-huh. It didn't happen until she became an adult—actually, it was after she lost a baby—but then she really went all the way. Some sort of Catholic cult thing."

"I thought all of Catholicism was pretty much some sort of cult thing," I said.

"Yeah, well, that's the way I feel, too. But she takes it to heart. Really serious about the battle between God and the Devil and the influence of evil on the earth. She'll talk about angels the way other people talk about TV stars or baseball players. We're not very close."

"It's crazy stuff," I said.

"Is it?" Rosa looked up at me. Neither of us had bothered to put the light on, but I could see a dim glow from the window reflected in her wide eyes. "Can you still say that it's so crazy?"

Despite all that had happened, all that we both had been through, Rosa raised the one point that I'd deliberately avoided thinking about. I'd listened to Yorimitsu's story about the *yakuza* and the *Goryō-dō* and demons the way you might listen to a screenwriter pitch a project at a story meeting. But I hadn't really come to any terms with it. I hadn't taken an option out on it yet, so to speak.

"I'm not saying I buy it all," I said.

"But what do you buy? Jesus, we saw that . . . that thing at the studio. It attacked us! I felt it, smelled it. God, I've never smelled anything like that before."

I nodded along, remembering the sheer monstrousness of the creature's odor.

"Do you still think that was just some guy in a rubber suit?" she asked.

"No," I had to admit. "That was something . . . else."

"And what about what you saw out where they killed Cheri? The monster on the rock and the little kid. What did Yorimitsu call it?"

"A *kappa*," I said. After Yorimitsu told his story, I'd briefly described for him what I'd seen at Vasquez Rocks. He said that the ritual must have been an invocation to the *tengu*, that the girl's entrails were offered up as an enticement to the *tengu* by the *Goryō-dō* priest and the lesser demon I had observed. He nodded along as I continued the tale, showing no surprise until I mentioned the retarded child I'd encountered.

"*Kappa*," he whispered, and the way he said it sent a chill down my back. He explained that the *kappa* is a particularly nasty demon, something like a vampire, but usually only found near water. He was clearly perturbed to learn that its like had been raised in California.

"Yeah," Rosa said, emitting a little shudder beside me. "I had a feeling you really got to him when you mentioned that."

"Me, too," I said. "I don't like to think about what that means."

"I wish now that I *was* more religious."

"What do you mean?"

"I feel like it might offer me more protection somehow. Like I could hold up a cross or sprinkle some holy water and ward away the demons."

"Probably wouldn't work anyway," I said.

"Why not?"

"Wrong belief. Like in that movie, *Fearless Vampire Killers,* I think it is. The villagers hold up their crosses to ward away the vampire, but it doesn't work because the vampire's Jewish."

"That's silly," Rosa said.

"Is it? What would Catholic holy water mean to a Japanese *tengu?*"

"Maybe the belief would be enough," Rosa said. "Maybe that's all that matters."

We sat silently for a while in the darkness until it struck me exactly what underlay the conversation we'd been having.

"So you believe they are demons?" I asked softly.

She hesitated, but not for long. "I think that's as good a name for them—whatever they are—as any other. And I'm worried that they're something that a couple of unbelievers like you and me don't have any protection against."

"There's always Benkei," I said, nodding toward the hall.

"I'm afraid that won't be enough, either," Rosa whispered.

I don't know how it happened after that. We were sitting there in the dark: talking, philosophizing, worrying.

And then we were lying there in the dark: kissing, cuddling, groping.

With our various injuries it wasn't easy. I had to touch carefully around her injured cheeks and breast. She had to shift delicately on top of me because of my cracked ribs.

In the end we found a way.

It wasn't the best there'd ever been. No explosions or fountains of light or bullet trains zipping through tunnels to the accompaniment of the 1812 Overture. Just a couple of tired and frightened people finding comfort and escape in each other's weary arms. It was nice.

As soon as it was over, thoughts of demons and spilled entrails and odd little Japanese men with big swords again rushed into my head, but they didn't feel quite so menacing.

We fell asleep holding on to each other.

And woke together with a frightened start.

Yorimitsu rushed into the room. In the hall I could hear people yelling in Japanese and running up and down the stairs. Yorimitsu stood in the doorway for a moment staring at us. Rosa rushed to drape herself with the kimono while I fumbled for my pants. Yorimitsu had an odd expression on his face—almost a leer, I'd have to say—as he watched us pull our clothes on, then he stepped into the room, closing the door behind him. He didn't turn on the ceiling light, but Rosa flicked on a small lamp beside the futon.

Yorimitsu looked odd. He wore the same kimono as before, but his long hair was a mess, and from the sight of his beard, it looked as if he'd came straight from a pie-eating contest. His face was flushed and he was breathing, almost gasping, through his open mouth.

"What's happening?" I asked, trying to get my shoes on. Rosa had slipped on her kimono, but still shielded herself behind me.

"Must go," Yorimitsu creaked. His voice sounded rusty, as if some piecrust were still caught in his throat.

"What's wrong?" Rosa said.

"Goryō-dō," he said, and smiled oddly as he said it. For some reason I noticed the ivory whiteness of his teeth. "Must go."

I stood up and pulled Rosa off the cushion after me. She held tightly on to my arm.

"Go where?" I said. Something didn't feel right about this. "Why?"

Something pounded against the door. I jumped and Rosa gasped, but

Yorimitsu didn't even turn around to look. Instead he took a step closer to us, his grin widening as he strode.

"Danger. Must go," he said.

Another blow struck the door from outside as the furor in the hall grew louder, more confused. Yorimitsu continued to come toward us, and I found myself stepping back away from him without exactly knowing why. Rosa's grip on my arm grew tighter.

"Go now," he said, his voice like a bag of broken glass. As he moved more fully into the lamp's circle of light, I saw that something had happened to his beard. What I thought was food caught in the hair was the beard itself. Much of it was matted, and some of the hair had been yanked out. The strands that were left looked like rusty steel wool. The skin of his face wasn't just flushed, but appeared scalded or burned. His hands, too, were red and raw, with rough folds of skin peeling away.

"Jesus, what happened to you?" I croaked.

And then the smell hit us. Rosa must have noticed it first, because she nervously whispered, "Marty." And then I smelled it, too; that same inhuman odor exuded by the demon that assaulted us at the studio.

Another blow ripped the door off its hinges. Yorimitsu spun around at the sound of sundered oak and came face-to-face with . . .

Yorimitsu!

I felt my jaw literally go slack at the sight. Rosa gasped, dropping my arm. I reached back towards her, but grasped nothing but air as I gawked at the impossible sight before us.

The deformed Yorimitsu threw back his head and cackled at the sight of his double. The other took a hesitant step into the bedroom, but was cut off by Benkei, who leaped in front of him, sword in hand. Benkei started to charge, but stopped as Yorimitsu number two barked a command in Japanese. I saw several other men in black peering in from out in the hall.

The Yorimitsu in the room with us shrieked a word in Japanese. I saw Benkei and the others turn their heads and close their eyes. A second later I understood why.

The deformed Yorimitsu threw up his hands, and his kimono literally shredded off his body. By the time the torn silk landed on the floor, Yorimitsu was Yorimitsu no more. His body puffed out, like an inflatable raft, or one of those crescent rolls that comes in a cardboard tube. He just expanded.

One second the body wore Yorimitsu's face, the next it had the blood-red features of a demon. The nose grew long and thin, like Pinocchio's, coming to a beaklike point, and the cheeks swelled, pulling the mouth into a deathlike rictus revealing sharp, scimitar teeth. Its eyes grew wide and suddenly seemed to glow a fearsome yellow. The beard and mustache, or what was left of it, dropped away entirely, but the hair on its scalp visibly grew until it dangled to the middle of the creature's strapping back.

And out of that back sprouted two immense wings with long feathers black as topsoil and red as fresh-spilt blood. Spadelike claws had sprung from the tips of the demon's long fingers and splayed toes. I glanced up from those toes and noticed its stubby, scale-encrusted penis stood erect, a viscous yellow fluid oozing from the tip. It looked me straight in the eye and I suddenly knew, without being told, that this was a *tengu*.

The Celestial Dog.

I felt my knees go weak, but Rosa grabbed my arm again, helping to prop me up. I could hear her hyperventilating—or perhaps just sobbing—behind me as the *tengu*'s wings unfurled and the demon unleashed a raucous shriek that would have soured milk still in the cow. Yorimitsu, the real one, screamed something at it, but the *tengu* only laughed. Well, it flashed its teeth at him, anyway.

Benkei again took a stride toward the creature—its noxious smell now filled the room—but the tengu was faster. It hurled what looked to me like a some kind of ball, though I never saw where it came from, right at Benkei's face. The ball glowed as it flew through the air and ignited like a magnesium flare as it made contact with Benkei's flesh.

Benkei screamed—if I hadn't heard it with my own ears, I'd not have believed it possible. He fell to the floor, his sword clattering away.

The *tengu* emitted another screech of laughter.

I felt Rosa try to tug me a step farther back away from the monster, but there was nowhere left to go. The *tengu* sensed the movement and turned toward us. Another swordsman rushed into the room, but Yorimitsu held him back. The *tengu* never even turned around.

One second the creature was in the middle of the room, the next it was on top of us. I felt a rough claw grab me about the waist and lift me off my feet. I heard Rosa scream as the *tengu* picked her up under its other arm. I tried to turn toward her, but my head was wedged against the creature's side and I couldn't move. The smell was overwhelming, raw decay, and I started to gag. I heard Yorimitsu yelling again from the doorway, but to no apparent effect. I could feel the demon's chest expand with each heavy breath it took, its scales scraping off swatches of my skin where they abraded.

The *tengu* twisted. I tried kicking out, but my legs merely flailed in the air. My arms were pinioned inside the creature's iron grasp. By straining I could just barely see in front of me. The creature turned toward the window and began to run. I heard its wings start to flap, hot air rushing up into my face. I saw the window coming closer, closer.

I felt my forehead impact with the glass as the demon burst out through the second-story window. The blood immediately began to pour down my face and my vision went all blurry.

I was able to savor the impossibility of human flight briefly before everything went black.

Eighteen

I saw her body before I noticed the blood.

I was drenched in it.

As I tried to rouse myself and crawl toward her, I found I couldn't move the fingers of my right hand. I thought I'd broken it until I realized that the fingers were just caked together with dried blood. As I prised them apart, little shards of brown peeled away. My shirt clung to my chest and back, spattered with tie-dye patterns of dark crimson. I felt cold, but it took a few seconds before it registered that I was naked from the waist down.

My crotch and thighs were literally painted with blood.

I reached for my cock, carefully pried it loose of the tatty nest of pubic hair. I ran my hands up and down my body, feeling for wounds, relieved not to find any. The blood couldn't be mine.

Then I looked across the room again at the body sprawled facedown behind a ratty old couch. I didn't have a clue where I was, except that it obviously wasn't the *Kakure* stronghold. Which apparently wasn't all that strong. I could see the backs of her legs, naked and smeared with blood like my own, but not the upper half of her body. "Rosa," I groaned—or maybe whimpered—but managed not to vomit as I got to my hands and knees.

My head was pounding, the vibrations reverberating down into the gap where my tooth had been knocked out. I touched my forehead and felt another long scab of dried blood. I remembered the feeling as it had made contact with the window when the *tengu* burst through. The flesh was soft, mushy to the touch, and I winced.

I fell back on my ass.

Through a curtained window I could see that it was day. A thin line of bright sunlight pierced the curtain, dividing the room in two. It appeared that I was in a one-room house or cabin. The wooden walls and floor were roughly finished, the scattered furniture cheap and utilitarian. A small kitchenette occupied one corner, a king-sized bed, the sheets also drenched in blood, the other. Various stuffed animal heads glowered down at me from the walls, and a shotgun dangled over the fireplace mantel. A hunting cabin, I reckoned. I'm clever at figuring things like that out. Detective, you know.

Rosa, I thought again, and tried to get to my feet.

There hadn't been a trace of movement from her, and it suddenly struck me that though I was breathing heavily, no sound of life could be heard from across the room. I felt the panic rise in my belly, and a chill deeper than the cool morning air ran through me. I wobbled to a half crouch, propping myself up against an old chair, but then had to pause again, resting my aching head on the seat cushion.

I was deathly afraid to cross the room.

I took a series of slow, deep breaths, reminding myself that the time I was wasting might be the seconds that made the difference in saving Rosa's life if all this blood was hers.

All this blood. If it was hers, the seconds wouldn't make the slightest bit of difference.

I raised myself to a standing position, wobbled a bit, but didn't fall over. As I stood, I could see the deep pool of blood that she was lying in. I groaned again—and froze—knowing what it had to mean.

I took a half step when the front door burst open. All I saw was the gun pointing at my chest.

"Freeze, motherfucker!" the cop screamed. He edged warily into the cabin, his partner behind him also with his gun drawn and pointing at my head.

"Okay," I said.

"Down on the floor!" he yelled. "Now, asswipe!"

I sort of wanted to explain to him about the effort it had just taken for me to get off the floor and up to my feet, but I didn't think he'd be interested in hearing it. As it happened, there wasn't all that much keeping me upright, so dropping back to the floor was none too difficult. As soon as I was down, he was in the room and on top of me, one foot planted painfully on my back.

"Move and you're dead," he said.

"Oh, fuck!" I heard from across the room. "Oh, this is some sick fucking shit."

"Dead or alive?" the cop standing on me asked.

"You gotta be kidding, Johnny," the other said. I could hear the choke in his voice and felt the pain. "This is butchery here. This is . . . Fuck, I think I'm gonna puke."

"Steady, bro. Don't taint the scene."

"I'm all right. It's just . . . fuck."

"Come over here then. Cuff this motherfucker."

I couldn't see much other than floor, but I heard the second cop march across the room. I saw his feet go past as he stepped over me and the first cop took his foot off my back. Cop number two yanked my arms behind me and slapped cuffs on my wrists, giving my sore ribs a good workout in the process. I heard his partner, John, walk across to inspect the body. Then I heard him gasp.

"Jesus, God," he whispered.

I could hear a siren approaching in the distance now. I craned my neck to look out through the still open front door and caught a glimpse of woods and the front end of a patrol car parked out front. A steel toe caught me roughly in the side.

"Move again and you're dead, freak," the cop growled. He crouched down beside me and laid the barrel of his .38 against my cheek, the bore pointing into my eye. "I would love to blow your brains out. Please give me a reason."

I wanted to curl up into a ball from the pain, but I was too scared even to blink. I could feel the gun shuddering in the policeman's nervous hand and knew that he was quite serious about his threat.

The sirens were just outside now, and I heard a couple of car doors slam. Out of the corner of my eye I saw two plainclothes cops walk into the room. They hadn't taken more than a couple of steps in when they both froze. They looked at me, then at the cop standing by the bloody corpse, then back at me.

"Christ," one of them said. The other just breathed hard.

"Lieutenant," the cop named John said. "You see this shit?"

"Man, what a number," the lieutenant said. There was silence as they stared at the body for a while. Then they walked back over to me.

"Get him up," I heard the other detective say. The patrolmen each grabbed an arm and hefted me off the floor. I slumped as they dragged me to my feet, but the cop who'd threatened me continued to hold my arm until I found my balance.

The two detectives were middle-aged and paunchy. The lieutenant had a bulbous nose and cauliflower ears; the other had droopy eyes and glowered at me over half glasses. They were all glancing at my exposed and bloodstained crotch. I don't think my penis had ever shrunk so small in my entire life. Not that I'm that blessed to begin with.

The detective with the glasses ran his gaze back to my face. "I know this asshole from somewhere," he said.

The others all looked me over again. At any minute I expected one of them to poke me in the ribs and ask: "Hot enough for you?"

"Yeah," the lieutenant agreed, "he does look familiar. What's your name, scum?"

"Sandy Salt," I said. What the hell, maybe he didn't have cable.

"Don't ring a bell," the lieutenant said. "You?"

His partner shook his head. "No, but I know I know this creep."

More vehicles pulled up outside, including an ambulance. A couple more suits came in, one carrying a black medical bag. The man with the bag immediately strode over to the body.

"Ah, Christ!" he wailed. He shook his head sadly.

"Why the fuck'd you carve her like that, you sick fuck?" the other detective asked me.

I felt numb, dead inside, as I heard the doctor fumble with the body behind the couch. He cursed intermittently.

"Why?" the detective asked again, poking me hard in the chest.

"Didn't," was all I could say, staring down at the ground. The tears started flowing from my eyes.

"Awwww," John the Cop said, "little freak feels bad now that he's caught."

"I didn't do it," I said again, starting to sob this time.

"You didn't do it," the lieutenant mocked, shaking his head. "And I suppose that's just ketchup on your dick, huh? Taco sauce?"

I was out-and-out crying now. I couldn't seem to get any kind of control. "Rosa," I sobbed.

"Was that her name?" the lieutenant yelled. "Was that the poor girl's name? Look at me!"

I couldn't raise my head. The cop did it for me, grabbing me by the chin. "C'mere, freak."

Still pinching my chin between his fingers, the lieutenant tugged me across the room to where the body lay. I closed my eyes tight as we rounded the end of the couch and the body came into view. I felt a slap on the side of my head. It sent a wave of painful vibration through my missing tooth, but it barely penetrated the numbness I felt inside.

"Look!" the cop screamed, slapping me again. "Look at what you've done!!"

I opened my eyes, but stared at my own feet. I could see her toes, pointing up now at the edge of my vision. The nails were spattered with drops of blood. The ones that hadn't been pulled out.

The lieutenant grabbed my hair and yanked my head up, forcing me to see it all.

My gaze went up her legs, barber poles streaked with red, past the ruins of her cunt and belly and the chewed, bloody expanse of emptiness that had been her oh-so-lovely chest. Her neck had been torn out as if by a wolf (or a demon, a voice said from somewhere deep inside).

Her face hadn't been touched, though. The mouth was twisted in pain, the eyes wide with the horror of death.

Incredibly—at least to the cops—I stopped crying and started to laugh. I couldn't help it, much as I tried, awful as it was.

It wasn't Rosa.

The lieutenant's name was Estevez, and his partner's name was Gil, though I never found out if that was his first name or last. They let me sit there for ages, with tears in my eyes and my dick hanging out, without asking me any more questions as a parade of cops, coroners, and forensics guys paraded through the room. At one point John the Cop, filling in some salmon-colored form on a clipboard, asked the ME what the cause of death was. The coroner studied the cop, scratched himself under the chin, and burst out laughing. John the Cop's face turned the same shade as his form, but he finished scribbling without asking any more questions.

After the coroner left and the forensics team set to work, Estevez and Gil came and sat on either side of me. They watched while one of the rubber-gloved investigators carefully scraped blood samples off of my legs, chest, and penis—none too gently, I might note—and onto little plastic slides which he dropped into glassine evidence envelopes. Even with the gloves on, the officer showed visual distaste at having to handle my privates. I was tempted to tell him that he wasn't the first to ever make that face while doing so—in fact, I'd once gotten the same look from Tina Louise—but didn't think the timing was right.

"Want to tell us why you did it?" Estevez said after the forensics guy finished up and he'd read me my rights again because John the Cop couldn't remember for sure if he'd done it, which he had.

"I didn't kill her," I said.

"Okay." Estevez nodded. "Then who did?"

I'd been thinking about what to say the whole time I'd been sitting there. I came up with various scenarios approximating what had happened that didn't require mention of *tengus* and demons and sword-wielding Japanese cult members. None of them sounded any less crazy than the truth. In the end I decided there was only one sensible answer given the circumstances.

"I want to see a lawyer," I said.

"Why do you need a lawyer if you didn't kill her?" Gil asked.

I kept my mouth shut.

"Funny way for an innocent man to act, don't you think?"

"I want to see a lawyer," I repeated.

"What about poor Rosa there?" Estevez said. "What about what she wants? Think she wanted some asshole to carve her up? To yank her guts out through her tits?"

"Her name's not Rosa," I said before I could catch myself. I clamped my lips shut and tried biting my tongue.

"So what is her name?" Gil asked. I bit harder and stared at the floor. "Can't you at least tell us that? Maybe she's got a mom, a kid, whatever. A family that's worrying about her even now, praying that she's all right. Don't you think they have a right to know what's become of her?"

He sounded so goddamn reasonable. Not even mad. "Her name's Syd," I said, not knowing how my tongue got loose. I'd recognized her from Rosa's photo as the other missing hooker, Cheri's pal. "She was a prostitute."

"Whore, huh?" Estevez said. "I bet you're the kind of guy who doesn't much like ladies who spread their legs for money. Am I right? Unless, of course, it's your money. That why you cut her?"

I bit my tongue again.

"Uh-huh," Gil picked up, addressing his partner. "I can't really blame him. I fucking hate whores, too. Goddamn slags who give up God's gift to any trash with a couple deuces in his pocket." He looked at me. "Makes me mad. Make you mad?"

I kept silent, not returning his gaze.

"Yeah, it makes me mad. You just want to do something about them, don't you? You just want to make 'em stop. Just stop, that's all. Just teach

205

'em right from wrong. That's probably what you brought her out here for, right? Thought you could teach Syd there a lesson. Maybe scare her a little with the knife. I bet you didn't mean to go quite so far. Perfectly understandable."

They both seemed to be waiting for me to say something. A couple of the forensics guys were listening, too.

"I want to see a lawyer," I said.

They kept at me for a while, going on about whores and lessons and generally trying to schmooze me into saying something stupid, but I just kept repeating the same line.

"I want to see a lawyer," I said for about the twentieth time before they gave it up.

"Okay, scumbag," Gil finally said, "you'll get your lawyer. Your limousine awaits."

They dragged me to my feet just as the ME's people started to haul Syd's body out. She almost broke in half as they zipped her into a body bag and carried her out. Gil started to march me out after her, but Estevez stopped us.

"He can't go out like that," Estevez said, pointing to my crotch. Gil rolled his eyes and walked out to a patrol car. He rooted around in the trunk until he found a pair of orange prison pants. They were covered in oil with a suspicious brown smear on the ass, but I put them on gratefully. I wished I could have washed the blood off, but I wasn't about to ask the cops for any favors. Especially one I knew they'd never grant.

As they refastened my handcuffs and led me out the cabin door, I saw that we were indeed out in the sticks somewhere. The cabin sat on a small parcel of land up near the top of a hill. A two-lane road wound past the property about fifty yards up an unpaved drive, and the nearest neighbor was a good five hundred yards away. Nevertheless, a small crowd had gathered at the base of the drive, mostly kids on bicycles, but a good dozen adults, too, craning their necks at the cherry-tops for a glimpse of the action. The insignia on the door of the police car identified it as belonging to the San Bernardino PD, which suggested we were up somewhere in the San Bernardino Hills, a good eighty miles or so east of the *Kakure* house in L.A.

"We out near San Berdoo?" I asked, looking around.

The two cops exchanged a glance. "Course," Gil said. "Where you think?"

"Near Big Bear?" I asked. Big Bear is a popular mountain resort for

Angelinos. Lots of outdoorsy activities of the sort I've always loathed.

"About a dozen miles back that way," Estevez said, pointing over his shoulder. "You saying you don't know where you are?"

"Fucker's working on his insanity defense already," Gil grumbled.

I shook my head, but didn't say anything more. Estevez waved to the cops who'd first found me, John and his partner. As they approached I saw from their name tags that John's last name was Flaherty and his partner was Lopez. Estevez wanted them to drive me back to the police station in San Berdoo. I think it was supposed to be some kind of reward, but neither of them looked all that thrilled with the assignment.

Lopez assisted me into the back of the patrol car, "accidentally" banging my head into the roof as he shoved me in. I thought he was going to get in back with me, but he only slid in long enough to refasten the cuffs through a steel bar set in the roof. He checked it by giving a brutal yank on my wrist, then got out, slammed the door, and took the shotgun seat. Flaherty already had the engine rumbling and slowly accelerated up the driveway as soon as Lopez closed his door. He turned the squelch up on the radio and hit the flashing lights, but mercifully laid off the siren except for a quick blast as we approached the crowd standing at the end of the drive.

As we crawled through the rubbernecking throng, I tried to stare back at the excited gawkers, but found I couldn't keep my head up. I tried to imagine what it would be like if I were actually guilty of something, then realized that I *did* feel guilty, though indirectly, about Syd. And Cheri.

And whatever in the world had happened to Rosa.

As Flaherty drove past the bulk of the crowd and started to speed up, I managed to raise my eyes for a glance out the window. I saw an angry old man, several teeth missing, pointing at me and snarling as best he could with his pink-white gums. A fat lady stood beside him, her dull eyes wide, shaking her jowly head at the very sight of the likes of me. I felt like a monkey jacking off in a zoo cage and started to turn my eyes back to the filthy squad car floor when his presence registered in my head. I craned my neck around and stared him eye to eye.

The little retarded kid I'd stumbled over at Vasquez Rocks: the creature Yorimitsu had chillingly referred to as a *kappa*.

With its long, scraggly hair and deformed, oblong head, it looked perfectly harmless. But as we caught each other's gaze, I saw the intelligence in its eyes: the mirth and the hate.

It started to do a dance, a jig from one leg to the other. Its Dodgers cap bounced up and down off its concave head as it danced and flashed a spike-toothed grin. No one else seemed to notice it, or pay it any mind if they did.

"Hey!" I yelled as we drove past it. I spun around as best I could to keep it in view as we headed down the road. "Hey!"

"What?" Lopez said, glaring at me. "Turn around, asswipe!" he ordered.

I wanted to explain it all to him. That it was the *kappa* they should be after, not me. I started to point toward the tiny creature, but it was already disappearing in the rear window, a little bouncing dot in the distance.

"What's your fucking problem?" Lopez asked.

"Nothing," I said. "Nothing."

"Then face front and keep your pie-hole shut."

I did what I was told.

The countryside was pretty, but completely unfamiliar to me. I'd been in San Berdoo on business plenty of times—a more miserable city does not exist on the North American continent, with the possible exception of Scranton, Pennsylvania—but had only been up in the hills once before for a winter shoot in Big Bear for a Juicy Fruit commercial. As we cruised up and down through the hills on the windy road back toward the city, I tried to think through my situation and what I had to do, what I could possibly say.

I couldn't come up with a damn thing.

I also found my thoughts turning repeatedly back to Rosa. Where could she be? The *tengu* had us both as he flew—Jesus Christ! the motherfucker grew wings and flew!!—out the window. Was Rosa still alive? Or had the *tengu* saved her for a special treat? Was he—if it was a he— eating her? Fucking her? Turning Rosa into a demon?

Could such a thing even be possible?

Could *any* of this actually be possible?

As I continued to turn events over in my mind, something in particular bothered me. I realized it had been gnawing at me all along, but hadn't articulated itself to a degree to enable me to ask. It did now, though, so I did ask.

"Hey," I said to the cops, "how'd you know to find me at the cabin?"

I saw Lopez glance at his partner, who eyed me in the mirror, then shrugged. "Phone tip," Lopez said.

"From who?"

"Anonymous."

Rippen? It had to be. Or one of his cronies. But why? Why not just waste me, leave me to the *tengu*'s less than tender mercies, like Syd or Cheri (or Long John and his girl for that matter)? They could easily have disposed of me, but they must have a reason for wanting me alive. The cuff tugged on my sore wrist as the car took a sharp curve, and I knew that was the answer.

I was the fall guy, the answer to any lingering questions about the rash of bodies, from Long John and his hooker to Mickey Marvin, that had washed up on the streets. I had a nasty feeling that the resources of Rippen Entertainment were working even now to manufacture the evidence that would somehow link me to all the murders. Rippen, after all, was a master at packaging and selling improbable plots. The only thing missing was David Lynch in the director's chair and Henry James in the White House.

Knowing The Business as I did, I imagined Rippen would probably secure all the rights and produce a TV movie out of the deal. I could practically see the network promo for it already: *Hot Enough for You?: The Salt & Pepper Murders*.

I was casting the movie in my head when I heard Flaherty curse and jerk the car to a halt. A big old Cadillac sat jackknifed on the narrow road in front of us, its nose pointing dangerously out into the oncoming lane. A sharp, blind turn in the road loomed no more than fifty yards beyond. Anyone driving along the other way would be hard-pressed to avoid broadsiding the stalled vehicle. At first it appeared that the car had been abandoned, but then I noticed a figure slumped over the wheel. The cop saw it too.

"Heart attack?" Lopez said.

"Asshole *better* be dead," Flaherty replied. "If he's sleeping, I'm gonna kill him."

Flaherty backed the patrol car up a few yards and left the lights flashing. "Stay with him," he said, and got out of the car.

Flaherty kept a wary eye on the road in front of him as he walked up to the jackknifed Caddy. Lopez opened his door and half stepped out of the patrol car as his partner bent over to peer into the other driver's window. Flaherty kept glancing over his shoulder at the road behind him, but Lopez yelled that he'd warn him if he saw anyone coming. I saw Flaherty knock on the window, but the slumped figure didn't respond. Flaherty reached for the door handle and tugged, but the door didn't open. I heard him curse again. Lopez stepped out of the car and took a step toward his partner, but Flaherty gestured for him to stay with me. Lopez halted, leaving the front door open. He stood watching with his hands perched on his hips, the little finger of his right hand brushing the butt of his holstered revolver.

I glanced behind me as Flaherty strode quickly around to the passenger side of the Caddy. There hadn't been much traffic on the road, but I was amazed that no one at all had come along from either direction. The only sounds were the chirps of birds in the woods and the odd blip and squawk from the police radio.

Flaherty tugged at the door handle on the passenger side of the Caddy, but it, too, was locked. The window on that side was partly open, though, so the cop stuck his arm through and fumbled around for the lock. He had to twist around sideways for the release, and I saw his lips move as he delivered a stream of curses with the effort. He must finally have found it, because he smiled and gave a thumb's-up to Lopez with his free hand. He carefully withdrew his arm from the window gap and pulled at the handle. The door swung open and he leaned inside.

As Flaherty crawled in and reached toward the slumped driver, the sound of a car engine came up behind us. I saw Lopez turn around and start to walk back, holding his arms up over his head for the car to slow. As he walked past my window I saw his eyes grow wide. He started to shake his head violently and lowered his arms in front of him, frantically crossing his hands in a warding-off gesture. I turned around in my seat and saw a black sedan coming up fast. Though I couldn't make out the driver through the darkly tinted windshield, I saw that he wasn't going to stop in time. I tried to brace myself against the front seat, but I couldn't get much leverage because of the way I'd been cuffed to the post.

Lopez's agonized "No!" was drowned out by the roar of the crash.

The impact jolted me off the seat, the handcuff yanking me back down just as fast. A line of blood trickled down my wrist where the edge of the metal cut into my skin, and I smacked my head against the roof again. The fingers of my cuffed hand went a little numb and I felt a twang in my shoulder, but it wasn't quite dislocated. A drop of blood plopped into my eye, though, and I knew I'd reopened the wound on my forehead.

Lopez just stood there for a moment with his head in his hands. I imagined that he was seeing the mountain of paperwork that doubtlessly now awaited him. He drew himself up with an audible sigh and his face went stern as he stormed off toward the driver of the black car. It suddenly struck me that there would be real trouble if a car came up the other way around the blind curve, and I nervously glanced to the front.

Flaherty was gone. As was the figure who'd been slumped over the wheel.

"Uh-oh," I said.

I turned back around in time to see Benkei dispatch Lopez with a single blow to the side of the head. The doors of the black car were all shut, and I didn't have the slightest idea where he'd come from. The cop went down like a cold beer on a hot day. Benkei touched a finger to the cop's neck, then grabbed Lopez under the arms and pulled him off the macadam and into the shaded brush at the side of the road, well out of harm's way.

The back door of the patrol car squeaked open and Yorimitsu's hairy face dropped into view.

"Konnichi wa," he said with a bow and a smile.

"Hi," I said.

I may not know my James Clavell, but I sure as hell understand a friendly greeting when I hear one.

Nineteen

Yorimitsu explained the situation as we sped back toward Los Angeles in the Caddy. One of his many Men in Black drove, with Benkei again grabbing the shotgun seat. He had a nasty bruise on his forehead from where the *tengu* had dealt him the blow, but otherwise appeared uninjured. The two cops, both unconscious, the patrol car, and the other damaged vehicle were left behind without further mention. I tried to ask Yorimitsu how the *Kakure* had set up and accomplished the ambush, but he waved the question off as though it were an inconsequential detail. Like questioning Picasso about his brush-cleaning techniques.

"Do you know where Rosa is?" I asked him.

He turned to look full at me in the Caddy's backseat. The edge of his lip curled up a bit under his mustache, and his eyes went hard and narrow. I didn't like the look one bit; it reminded me of the expression I remembered seeing on a vet's face as a kid when he told me my dog had to be put down. Or Manny Stiles's expression when he announced *Salt & Pepper* had been canceled.

"Miss Mendez is in very grave trouble," he said. "She has been taken by the *Goryō-dō.*"

"Taken where?"

"The creature that breached the defenses of our house to assault you—the shapeshifter—was a very powerful demon. This is the *keshin.*"

"Not a *tengu?*" I interrupted. Like I knew what I was talking about.

"*Tengu,* yes. But very strong. *Tengu* are mountain creatures, yes? The holy mountains—Yoshino, Hiko, Hatsuse, Atago—sit in more than one realm. You understand?"

"Not exactly," I said.

"Mountains emerge from the earth, yes? They exist at many levels."

"You mean altitudes?"

"Heights, yes, but just as the mountain exists both in the earth and the sky—two realms—so, too, do they hold their place in *Naka-Tsu-Kuni,* the Central Land, the plains where men walk, and in *Shide-no-yama,* the gateway to *gokuraku* and *jigoku.* The realms which are beyond. *Tengu* are the lords of the mountains, yes? And *keshin,* what came for you cloaked in my skin, is lord of the *tengu.* "

"So it's a mean motherfucker."

"You understand correctly. We had no idea such a creature had been summoned here. The *Goryō-dō* have achieved a greater degree of enfranchisement than I had thought possible in so short a time."

"All the nuts roll to California," I muttered.

"Pardon?"

"Old joke," I said, "not funny. So what about Rosa?"

"Your Miss Mendez has been taken, it is my belief, to fulfill a part in a ritual to be acted out tomorrow night."

"What do you mean ritual?"

"You witnessed such a ritual yourself. You described it to me."

"You mean the snuff shoot at Vasquez Rocks?" I yelled, grabbing the sleeve of Yorimitsu's kimono. Benkei turned around in his seat, but Yorimitsu shook his head at him. "They're going to kill her?"

"It would not be exactly the same as you observed, but yes, her sacrifice will be a central aspect of the ritual."

The memory of Cheri's disembowelment flashed across my mind's wide screen. I pictured Rosa splayed out on a rock as the *tengu* plunged its claw into the soft skin of her trim belly. I felt sick.

"But why?" I croaked. "If the *tengu* lord is already here . . ."

"The *keshin* unfortunately is here, yes. But there are mightier demon lords which can yet be summoned forth. It would be necessary, essential, to the *Goryō-dō* to bring such a creature among them in order for them to make complete their presence here."

"But why now? What's happening?"

Yorimitsu barked a command at Benkei. The warrior bent down and picked something up off the floor and handed it over the seat. A copy of the *Times.* Yorimitsu folded the page back and handed it to me. I shook my head when I saw it was the business section until the headline caught my eye: "SEC Approves Rippen Sale to Japanese."

"But what—"

"The timing of this event is not coincidental," Yorimitsu explained. "Tomorrow is *Obon,* Japanese festival honoring the spirits of the dead. The official signing of the paperwork between Jack Rippen and Yoshitoshi will take place tomorrow. And tomorrow night the *Goryō-dō* will summon Shuten Dōji."

All the Japanese words and names were starting to make me dizzy. I dropped my head into my hands. "I don't understand," I said.

Yorimitsu drew a deep breath before speaking. "Shuten Dōji is the fiercest of the demon lords. It is incredible, even to me, that the *Goryō-dō* will dare to summon him to this place. Never before has such a rite been attempted out of Japan. It is a measure of *Goryō-dō* confidence in their strength here and of their belief in all future inviolability. Shuten Dōji played a part in the last great battle between *Goryō-dō* and *Kakure*. It was many centuries ago, but still the legend is told with fear and wonder, among even those who do not believe in the myth.

"The legend tells of how the virgin daughter of the mighty Lord Kunimasa and her handmaidens were kidnapped by the demon forces of Shuten Dōji and brought to his stronghold atop Mt. Ōe. Kunimasa was greatly distraught and entreated the services of the warrior Minamoto no Yorimitsu—" I jerked my head up at the name "—of whom I am, indeed, a namesake, to retrieve his daughter. Yorimitsu agreed to take on the challenge, and for three days he prayed to the spirit of the great warrior Shōki, the demon queller, for his blessing. Yorimitsu and a band of his greatest swordsmen began their quest to Mt. Ōe. Along the way, Yorimitsu was aided by the *yamabushi, Kakure* priests, and directed to the lair of the demon lord.

"Outside the stronghold, the party encountered one of the handmaids, washing blood from a silken kimono in a mountain stream. The maid informed Yorimitsu that Shuten Dōji was serving human flesh to his demon hordes and that Lord Kunimasa's daughter was next to be sacrificed. Yorimitsu and his men snuck into the fortress and, with the help of the spirit of Shōki, vanquished the demons, cutting off the head of Shuten Dōji and capturing many lesser *oni*. These were returned to Lord Kunimasa to be slowly tortured to their deaths."

"So if this Shuten Dōji was killed, how can he be back?" I asked.

"This story is legend, yes? Legend is truth and half-truth, mixed to make a better story, for proper lessons. 'When legend and truth are as one, teach the legend,' the *Kakure* say. Such as Shuten Dōji can never be entirely destroyed so long as the belief in him remains. *Goryō-dō* exist and believe. So does Shuten Dōji. If the belief is strong, so will be the demon lord."

"And Rippen and the *Goryō-dō* think they're strong enough to bring him back?"

"The completion of the sale of Jack Rippen's company is the sign they have been awaiting. They choose the first night of *Obon* to conduct the ritual, for it is the time of prayers to the spirits of the dead, and the gateways between the realms are open. It is when the power of belief is at its greatest."

"And Rosa?" I said, but I had a feeling I knew the answer.

"She is to be served up as sacrificial invocation, *homa,* to Shuten Dōji. Her living flesh will be served to the newly reborn demon lord."

"Fuck me," I said. It was too much to handle. Then a thought occurred to me. "But you said Yorimitsu, I mean the other one, vanquished this Shuten Dōji dude in the legend, right? And he saved the girl."

"He triumphed over the demon lord, that is correct."

"And saved the girl."

Yorimitsu turned and looked out the window. We were approaching downtown L.A. on the westbound Santa Monica Freeway. The smog was so thick, I could barely make out the monolithic Arco towers.

"Yorimitsu?" I prompted.

"In the legend, the party was too late to save the maiden. She had been violated and her liver devoured by the demons. Yorimitsu retrieved only a lock of her hair and returned it to her grieving father." I thought I heard a catch in Yorimitsu's voice. As if it had been *his* fault or something. "The warrior offered to surrender his own life in reparation for his failure, but Lord Kunimasa forbade this sacrifice."

"Well, that's a hell of an ending," I snarled.

"It is not a . . . Hollywood ending, no," Yorimitsu said. "But in it lies the moral of the tale."

"And that is?"

Yorimitsu turned back to face me. "That neither good nor evil, darkness or light, is ever entirely victorious in the eternal contest. In the story, as in life, there is always a point of balance, and all we can hope for in our own actions is to find some way to maintain that precarious equilibrium."

I thought about that for a minute. "Phooey!" I said.

Yorimitsu nodded. "It would not make for such a good movie," he agreed.

I sat alone on the floor of the empty room.

Yorimitsu led me straight there when we got back to the *Kakure* house in the Hollywood Hills. To meditate, he said, and insisted I sit on the floor. *Za-zen* was the word he used, and he said it the way an agent talks about gross participation points.

I don't know from meditation, it just bores me. Lots of people have tried to impress me with the wonders of it over the years, yapping on about serenity and inner peace and harmony and all that crap. I can still remember when personalized mantras were the hot thing in California, every bit as essential a seventies accoutrement as paisley-patterned silk shirts and flared pants. At one time I went out with this model—this was before the age of "supermodels," though she could sure enough leap my tall building in a single bound. She was in thrall to some maharishi or Bhagwan or whatever the hell the sappy swami called himself, and she *lived* for transcendental meditation. She insisted that it gave her better orgasms. In a sense she was right, because she'd meditate and do yoga in the stark raving nude while I watched, and it always made me horny as hell. I don't know if *her* orgasms were any better, but mine were pretty nice. I started to explain this to Yorimitsu, but he just pressed a finger up to his lips and whispered, *"Za-zen."*

So I used the time to think.

Which was okay, because I had an awful lot to think about.

Back in the car, when I'd asked Yorimitsu what he planned to do about Rosa, he looked at me funny and scratched his beard à la Toshiro Mifune.

"That is, in large measure, up to you," he said.

"What do you mean? What can I do?"

"Just as Minamoto no Yorimitsu challenged Shuten Dōji in his keep on Mt. Ōe, so will the *Kakure* mount an assault on the *Goryō-dō.*"

"You know where they are?" I asked.

"Hai. Your Mr. Jack Rippen is in possession of an estate in the hills north of the city. The *Goryō-dō* will carry out the ritual there."

"You mean Ripperland?" I said.

"Ah, yes. I believe it is colloquially referred to in that manner."

Ripperland was Rippen's extravagant retreat in the Santa Barbara Hills. It was originally built in the thirties for Irving Thalberg and is supposedly second to nothing for unfettered luxury. Not to mention its ocean view. Rippen holds an infamous Halloween bash there every year for the top crust of the Hollywood elite, and it was all over the news when he lent the stead out to Madonna for her most recent wedding-cum-circus. Needless to say, I've never been anywhere near the place, which is officially known as Heaven's Gate, because of the view. But I've never heard anyone call it anything other than Ripperland.

"You're going to waste Ripperland?"

"With your help," Yorimitsu told me.

I got tired of sitting on the hard floor and started pacing the empty room. I counted the number of steps across, then the number down. When I got tired of that I counted the number of steps it took to walk the perimeter. I tried to make all the numbers square, but I must have miscounted somewhere. I kept pacing until it came out right. This *zazen* stuff was all right.

Yorimitsu had explained that the *Kakure* anticipated a tough fight. The *Goryō-dō* were more deeply established in California than had been thought and had raised a number of demons to aid them. The mortal *Goryō-dō*, he added, were keen fighters of their own accord. Furthermore, Rippen and his circle would no doubt be anticipating and ready for the possibility of a *Kakure* attack, especially once word got out about my escape from the police.

"So what have we got going for us?" I asked.

Yorimitsu offered me a funny little smile. I know it's terribly politically incorrect, racist even, to use the adjective "inscrutable" to describe an Oriental, but frankly there is no better way to characterize the look on Yorimitsu's face.

"Shōki," he said.

Shōki, Yorimitsu told me, was a famous Japanese warrior and destroyer of demons. It was Shōki to whom the original Yorimitsu prayed in the tale of Mt. Ōe. Apparently the Shōki legend dated back well over a thousand years. He was a kind of avenging spirit, an "arbiter of hell," vowed to an eternal crusade against demons. A Japanese Zorro.

"So Shōki's a dead guy," I said.

Yorimitsu shook his head. "This is not the right attitude," he sighed.

"I'm sorry. I just don't understand."

"Shōki is a spirit, neither alive nor dead, except in belief. Like Shuten Dōji, he may be summoned, invoked to service."

"Okay . . ."

"But none of us may serve as receptacle for him."

"Why not?" I asked, though I was still having trouble with the basic concept.

"We are not of this land. California is an alien place to us. To raise such a spirit as Shōki requires one who is bound to the soil. To the spirit, the soul of the land."

"Soul of the land? In California?" Yorimitsu nodded. "Well then, how can the *Goryō-dō* raise the spirit of Shuten Dōji?"

"They have Jack Rippen, you see. He is connected to the land. He will be the vessel for the demon lord's return."

"Fuck!" I spat.

"But we have you," Yorimitsu said.

"Huh?"

"You are of the land. I understand you are even a native Californian, is that not true?"

"Yeah, I was born up in the Valley."

"So much the better." Yorimitsu nodded. "Your Mr. Rippen—" I wished he'd stop ceding ownership of the Ripper to me "—is not actually of this place. He is from . . . Cleveland?"

I didn't have a clue where Rippen was born, but I didn't make him for a local. "Could be," I said.

"If you are willing," he went on, "you could be the receptacle for Shōki in this place. He would act through you."

"And how would this work, exactly?" I asked.

"A ritual will be performed. The ceremony is arcane but not difficult. You would be required to be prepared with the *hannya-shinkyo*. It is a ritual of *harai*. Of purification."

"What? Hanna Schygulla? Would it hurt?"

"*Hannya-shinkyo*. No physical pain, no. You would be required to drink *yomogi*. Mugwort."

"I don't know what that is," I said.

Yorimitsu glanced out the car window, searching for the word. "Wormwood?" he said.

"You mean like in absinthe?"

"Very similar, yes."

I'd always wanted to try absinthe, which has, of course, been illegal for decades because of its supposed god-awful effects on the brain; I wasn't sure if these were quite the circumstances I'd been waiting for. "Is that all?"

Yorimitsu's expression suddenly turned very scrutable. Not at all happy. "No," he said. "There is one other thing. You would have to believe."

"Believe in what?"

Yorimitsu scratched his beard again. "I have been considering this question very carefully in my own mind. It is my feeling that the strength of the *Kakure* belief in Shōki would be enough to summon him to this place. But for his spirit to enter you would require a greater devotion."

"I don't know if I can believe in Shōki," I said. "It's . . . too fast, too weird. Too *too.*"

"I understand. But you must tell me, and with complete honesty now, do you believe in anything?"

Do I believe in anything? What a thing to ask! I mean, that's the existential fucking question, isn't it? Truth is, I don't much like thinking about it because it means thinking about the past. Belief, I've long thought, is a luxury of the naive. According to the old war-movie cliché, there are no atheists in foxholes, but I think that's just the dull, surface truth. Scratch a hardened veteran, of Vietnam *or* Hollywood (and pity those poor bastards who worked on *Apocalypse Now*), and you find a lost soul. I know mine took a permanent hike the day I blew off my mother's fortieth birthday party to judge the 1970 Miss Nude Redondo Beach pageant.

I flashed back on having this conversation with Rosa—Christ, was it just the night before? It felt like ages—to indeterminate end. I thought about God and Christ and religion and found myself shaking my head. I thought about America and politics, Hollywood and movies, moms and apple pies and shiny new Chevrolets. And I came up blank.

Then I thought about Rosa.

"I believe I love Rosa," I said softly. I couldn't believe I was saying it. I hadn't said it, even thought it, that squarely until that moment.

"Are you absolutely sure?" Yorimitsu asked.

Who can ever say yes to that question?

"Yes," I told him.

"Very good," he said. "Then, perhaps, there is a chance."

I was still pacing the floor of the empty *Kakure* room, thinking about my belief, when the knock came on the door. Before I could respond, the door opened and Benkei stuck his head in. He looked up at me questioningly, but didn't say a word. I still didn't even know if he spoke any English.

I stared at him for a moment. His features didn't look as hard as usual, and somehow that scared me about what was to come. As I stood there, I ran it all through my mind again in a microsecond. Then I nodded and walked toward the door.

"Let's do it," I said.

"All right!" Benkei exclaimed, and slapped me on the back.

Benkei led me upstairs to a small bathroom. He indicated that I was to remove my clothes, which I did, and pointed to the filled bathtub. I got in, feeling more than a little self-conscious, found the water was comfortably warm. One of the Men in Black came in, sleeves rolled up, and knelt down beside the tub. He picked up a white cloth and began using it to wash me. I started to protest, insisting I could do it myself, but Benkei got all huffy, so rather than make a fuss, I let him wipe me down. I had to draw the line when he tried to scrub my nether regions, but I think he was relieved, too.

Another man came in as I stepped out of the tub and dabbed me dry with a big, fluffy towel. Benkei continued to supervise, growling and pointing out bits that had been missed. I expected to be given a kimono to wrap myself in, but Benkei simply took my hand and led me, naked, into the adjoining room.

I was directed to sit on a tatami mat in the middle of the floor. An elderly man, somewhere between sixty and three hundred, with a beach-ball head and shaved eyebrows, sat down beside me on a squat wooden stool. He held a delicate paintbrush in each hand, with a half circle of various-colored inkwells at his feet. He looked me over—a bit disdainfully around the pelvic region, I thought—then dipped the brushes, one into black, the other into carmine ink. He then started painting Japanese characters on my flesh, using both hands at once. It was an awesome display of ambidexterity, as every character was ornate and flawless. His hands moved so quickly, from flesh to inkwell and back again, that he seemed almost machinelike. The brushes tickled a little as he dabbed the characters on me, but I wasn't in a laughing mood. He began at a point over my heart and had quickly painted the words all across my chest and back.

The painting was all part of the *harai,* the purification rite that Yorimitsu had told me about. The words, he had explained, were from a sacred text called the *hannya-shinkyo,* and they served to make it possible to open me as a receptacle for Shōki and ward off any evil spirits that might be tempted to enter me at the same time. The sacred characters would have to be painted over every part of my body.

And so they were. I again raised a hackle or two as the bald artist began to dab away at my cock and balls, but I glanced at Benkei, who raised a finger, and before I knew it, the artist had moved on to my thighs. I had to stand so he could paint my buttocks and the backs of my legs, and though I felt a bit cold standing there, I also felt a slight charge start to run through me. Whether it had something to do with the sacred words, or was just power of suggestion, I didn't know.

The artist was thorough; before he was done, he insisted on painting the soles of my feet, under my arms, and between my fingers and toes. I glanced down at myself, at the text of my body, and exclaimed a loud "huh!" at the sight of the rainbow spiral of delicate characters radiating out from the center of my chest. Adding one final character to each eyelid, the artist sat back down on his stool and screwed the lids on the ink jars to announce that he was done.

Benkei looked me up and down and nodded. With a hint of awe, I thought. He didn't touch me, but indicated I should sit back down on the mat. A Man in Black helped the artist gather his things and they left the room together. It was just me and Benkei, but neither of us said a word.

Finally Yorimitsu walked in, followed by a dozen kimonoed *Kakure*. I thought some of them might have been Men in Black, but couldn't tell for sure. They set candles up on the floor at four equidistant points of a circle and sat down around me on the mat. Yorimitsu was garbed in a flowing azure kimono embroidered with gold, and black Peter Pan boots. On his head sat a matching tasseled cap, which actually looked sort of silly, though I wasn't about to tell him. He held a wooden goblet with both hands and knelt down in front of me. A sword dangled from an ornate leather scabbard at his waist.

"Are you ready, Martin-san?" he said.

"Yeah," I squeaked.

Yorimitsu belted out a series of chants in Japanese. It was all gibberish to me, of course, though I was pretty sure I could pick out the name "Shōki" several times. The circle of *Kakure* around me would occasionally sing a response to his chant, though they were no more intelligible to me.

Yorimitsu handed me the cup.

"Yomogi," he said. "Drink."

I took the cup in both hands, as Yorimitsu had instructed. The wood felt warm and smooth, as if fitted to my touch. I looked down into the cup. It held an acrid green liquid the consistency of pineapple juice, with particulate matter swirling inside. It smelled slightly bitter with just a hint of licorice or anisette. I raised the cup to my lips, paused to glance at Yorimitsu, who was carefully tracking my every gesture even as he continued to mutter a singsong Japanese litany under his breath. The *Kakure* brethren muttered with him, eyes closed, hands clasped to form a circle around me. Yorimitsu nodded at me but didn't break his chant.

I put the cup to my lips and took a slug.

The *yomogi,* or absinthe or whatever it was, tasted even more bitter than it smelled. And really strong, like Bacardi 151 or grain alcohol. Or paint thinner. I've been there, I know.

Yorimitsu had told me that I needed to drink the whole measure in one go—no problem, I was sure, for an old chugalug champ like myself—but I didn't think I'd be able to do it once I tasted it. The thick liquor didn't go down so easy, with the little bits of whatever-it-was sticking to the roof of my mouth, making me gag. I started to lower the cup, but caught sight of Yorimitsu's widening eyes. I shut my own and forced back the rest of the slop.

At first it felt like I was pouring lye down my throat as a line of fire raced down my gullet and exploded in my stomach. I could feel the sweat pouring out of me as I swallowed. But as I forced myself to drink, I remembered what Yorimitsu had told me: Think about Rosa, he had said. *Believe.*

I formed a picture of Rosa's face in my mind as I gulped the *yomogi.* And curiously enough, the stuff started to taste a little bit better. I've never been a big licorice fan—as a kid, I always sucked the pink candy shell off my Good 'N Plenty, then spit the licorice bit out—but I found the anise taste almost soothing, like cold water dousing the fire in my system. By the time I reached the bottom of the cup, the *yomogi* didn't seem any worse or more harsh to me than a shot of ouzo or Sambuca. And with not an unpleasant little aftertaste.

I was dimly aware that the chanting had grown in intensity as I drained the cup. And as I opened my eyes I saw that the *Kakure* were all standing around me, hands still joined, singing at the tops of their lungs. A soft, wavering light filled the room, but when I looked at the candles, there wasn't a flicker to be seen. In front of me Yorimitsu had drawn his sword, a massive, silver-blue blade with an intricately inlaid hilt of gold and jade. He held the sword above his head, the blade angled toward me. I wanted to flinch, to duck away, but I found that I couldn't move. I tried to close my eyes as I saw him raise the blade back to begin the killing stroke, but I was unable even to blink.

Everything happened in slow motion; I don't know whether it was due to the haze of the absinthe or the terror of the moment. Maybe a little of both. But I saw the silver blade inch backward, then forward, cutting the air with a sound like high-tension wires crackling in ozone. I saw the raw concentration in Yorimitsu's eyes, the tension in the muscles of his arms and hands as he impelled the blade toward me. As the shining silver drew closer, I could see the other *Kakure* reflected in the mirror of the steel, their arms raised high, breaking the circle, their mouths open wide as they shrieked in some weird religious ecstasy.

The blade passed by my ear, with a sound like a falling tree. I felt the slightest tug at the side of my head and saw a lock of my hair tumble toward the floor. As it ever so slowly fell to earth, I was pulled to my feet and felt myself bathed in a radiant glow, as if caught in a spotlight's beam or encased in an argent cylinder. I couldn't see through the light to Yorimitsu or the *Kakure* or the room, but I could see *in* it.

Flecks of gold, much like the particles in the *yomogi,* swirled around me in the light. It felt like I was standing in the middle of a cloud of pixie dust.

I could hear crashes, chimes, and tinkles; the delicate shattering of finely tuned crystal and the banging of elephantine gongs as the swirl of flakes intensified. I wanted to stick out my tongue to capture a morsel, like winter's first snow, but I was still utterly paralyzed. Though I couldn't move, tears flowed from my eyes at the spectacle.

It was the most beautiful thing I'd ever seen.

I caught a glimpse of something dark darting in and out among the flakes, thought it was my hair, then caught sight of *that* closer to the floor. As the lock of hair touched the ground, the light exploded in my head in a pinwheel swirl of silver fireworks.

And it was over.

I blinked and realized I could move again, but not fast enough to stop me from collapsing onto the tatami mat. I landed awkwardly, but was more stunned than anything else.

Yorimitsu still held the sword in one hand, but quickly extended the other to me, helping me back to a sitting position.

"Are you all right, Martin-san?" he asked.

"Hai, okagesama de," I said. *Yes, thank you very much,* I somehow knew it meant. I looked up into a grin so broad, even Yorimitsu's bushy facial hair couldn't conceal it.

"What the fuck?" I said. The Japanese for it came into my head almost immediately.

Twenty

I kept wanting to look over my shoulder. It felt like someone was standing just behind me, watching me all the time. The kind of paranoia you feel walking a city street in a neighborhood you don't know just after dark.

But it—or should I say *he*—was all in my head, of course. Literally.

After Yorimitsu sent the *Kakure* brethren out of the room, we had a brief conversation. All in Japanese, with Yorimitsu showing great deferentiality and rarely meeting my gaze. I understood every word, though I didn't say any of it. I mean, it was my lips that were moving, my voice echoing, my hands gesturing.

But it was Shōki who was speaking.

I could feel it all. That was the really weird part. It was a little like being deeply drunk—and after chugging a cup of *yomogi*, who's to say I wasn't?—so drunk that the rational part of your brain recedes to a point in the back of your head where it's nothing more than a tiny voice coming in on a staticky shortwave frequency. The voice that usually tells you: "Boy, are you going to be sick tonight, asshole!" and which is so easy to ignore until it's proved correct.

When Shōki wanted to speak or act, *I* became that voice. When he was quiescent, the voice was him.

Yorimitsu quickly left me—us?—alone. I tried to engage Shōki in mental conversation, but it didn't quite seem to work that way. I found myself thinking in English and Japanese, not always sure whose thought was whose, which language came first. It was a little bit like a battle, though not painful or unpleasant, and I wondered if this was anything like what schizophrenics felt. Or multiple-personality types.

I saw things, too. Things Shōki had seen and done. Wondrous, terrible, impossible things:

I saw the dark palace of Emma-o, in the Land of the Dead, with its silver and gold towers encrusted with rose-colored pearls and glittering precious stones; soul-ships carried the spirits of the departed into the Death Lord's cold embrace across a luminescent black sea.

I saw the *hyakki yakō,* the Parade of a Hundred Demons, dancing down a sleepy village road running just ahead of the creeping dawn sun.

I saw a massive plain of battle. Ten thousand warriors in armor, swords drawn, blood flowing, fighting for the glory of the *tai-shōgun.*

I saw a young woman, kimono parted, her skin like honeyed porcelain, lying amidst an endless field of blossoming chrysanthemums, giggling.

And so much more.

But even as I was dumbstruck with the wonder of it all, I felt Shōki's no lesser sense of awe over things I have known: the arc of a rainbow over the Golden Gate at sunset; the sprawling, imposing steel towers of Manhattan viewed from the top of the Empire State Building; the feel of a Porsche convertible tearing down the San Diego freeway at 165 mph; a bronze goddess with silicone breast implants bobbing in the foamy Malibu surf.

We "exchanged" memories like that for a while, oohing and ahhing in our own ways over the splendor of the other's experiences. It seemed to me that I was the luckier one, recognizing that Shōki had stored up not merely one lifetime's worth of memories, but generations of experiences he had come to know through both his own eyes as well as through those he had inhabited. My paltry and pathetic life seemed a meager trade for such wonders, but though we didn't exactly share all our thoughts or personalities, I got the distinct feeling that he felt the same way: grateful, as he always was, for the gift of another's vision and point of view.

In the end, I didn't win the "battle" for control so much as I felt Shōki retreat somewhere into the back of my consciousness. I sensed some regret in his action, as if he longed to take full control, but also an awareness of the necessity of his backing off if we were to proceed. When I finally got to my feet, I still felt a bit woozy, a little drunk, but I also felt Shōki there to help straighten me out, prop me up. It was undeniably unnerving, but also oddly comforting to have him with me. As I got dressed and went out to look for Yorimitsu, I realized that I'd never felt so confident—so strong in body and spirit—in my entire life. Not even as a cocky kid riding on top of the world as a TV star.

I liked it.

Yorimitsu loitered out in the hall, pacing with his hands folded behind his back. Benkei, as always, stood within sword's reach.

"We . . . I'm going out," I told him.

"You cannot," Yorimitsu said. "Too dangerous!" He was still having some trouble looking me in the eye.

"I think we . . . I'll be okay," I said. The assault on the *Goryō-dō* wouldn't go down until after dark. It would take us a couple of hours to drive up to Santa Barbara, but that still left three or four hours of dead time until we would need to get ready. And I knew that Shōki was anxious to see Los Angeles for himself, as it were. I couldn't tell for sure, but I had the feeling that Shōki had not been . . . *invoked* for quite some time. He seemed quite fascinated by the inventions of the modern world.

Yorimitsu started to object again, but Shōki cut him off with a command in Japanese. The language was a little stronger than any I would have used on the *Kakure* leader, but it succeeded at stifling any further discussion. Yorimitsu went a little bit pale, but bowed deeply and backed away.

Shōki started to exert control again and automatically reached for a sword that hung on the wall, until I stopped him with a thought. He was confused, but quickly grasped the fact that people don't walk down the streets of Los Angeles with swords dangling from their belts.

At least, *most* people don't.

Still, I found myself—I think it was me—reluctantly accepting a Glock from a Man in Black at Yorimitsu's urging. I double-checked the safety and stuck it in my waistband. I also donned a leather jacket to hide the gun. I started for the door, but Yorimitsu called me back.

"Martin-sama," he said, gesturing at my face and hands.

I looked down, saw the multihued Japanese characters that had been painted across my skin. I touched my cheeks, realized the characters were painted over all my exposed flesh.

"Can I wash this off?" I asked.

Yorimitsu violently shook his head, his eyes wide. I sensed Shōki's thought that it would be a very bad idea indeed.

"Hmmm," I said, "maybe we'll just stay in the car then, take a little motor tour of the scenery."

Yorimitsu didn't look happy about it, but he directed a Man in Black to hand over a set of keys to an inconspicuous Nissan. He and Benkei followed me out to the car.

"Please be careful," Yorimitsu said. Benkei nodded behind him.

I nodded, but then Shōki said something to the pair in Japanese. I probably didn't get it exactly right, but the way I translated it was: "Take a chill pill."

Shōki was going to like this town.

I felt an unaccustomed but welcome serenity as I drove down out of the Hills and over toward Hollywood proper. I wondered if this was the tranquil feeling that Yorimitsu told me I was supposed to get out of *za-zen*. It was nice.

I felt Shōki in the back of my mind, taking in the lay of the land as we cruised up the trafficky streets. Near as I could tell, he accepted this strange new world in relative stride. I sensed the odd hint of excitement from him, especially at the sight of women in short shorts and halter tops—I think maybe Shōki was something of a ladies' man in his more corporeal days—but all in all he handled the situation better than I would have in his stead. I mean, if such a thing were imaginable, much less possible.

In fact, I was able to marvel at my own tranquil acceptance of the incredible events that had taken place, suspected that it was Shōki's presence that itself accounted for much of my equanimity. My whole world, everything I thought I knew, understood, believed, or failed to believe in, had been turned inside out in a matter of hours. Before all of . . . *this* had happened, I'd been an avowed agnostic (an admittedly hedged bet to begin with) who couldn't even abide talk of the "what's your sign" variety, much less mumbo jumbo about gods, ghosts, and demons. And now here I was easily accepting that I'd been possessed by the spirit of a dead Japanese warrior, in the service of some ancient and secret religious cult, preparing for a battle royal against the forces of darkness.

I thought I could hear Shōki laughing inside me as I pondered it.

I was still worried about Rosa, but somehow Shōki made it easier for me to deal with that as well. Yorimitsu had convinced me that she would be fine until the ceremony to invoke Shuten Dōji was complete. And from Shōki I felt a determination, or rather a conviction impelled with a kind of strength and certainty unlike any I had ever known in my own life, that Rosa could and would be rescued. And although that conviction bolstered me, reassured me, the weaknesses of my own character and a lifelong cynical world view left a nagging doubt and worry that even Shōki's supernatural influence couldn't entirely overcome.

I tried to ward the worries off by playing tour guide. It's a little strange doing it for yourself, but I could tell that Shōki was enjoying it as I described the landmarks and landscape that I usually took for granted driving around Los Angeles. Shōki seemed to have much freer access to roam around my thoughts and memories than I did in his. Whether it was because he had greater experience at this manner of weirdness than me, or simply because of a fundamentally stronger personality and decidedly superior mental abilities, I didn't know. This less than equal reciprocity disturbed me some, but I did occasionally glean flashes of Shōki's inner self, and the little bits I saw were either incredible or terrifying enough that I considered it possible Shōki was actually protecting me by limiting what I could know of him.

Though wary of making myself unnecessarily conspicuous—several drivers hazarded frightened expressions as they looked my way while paused at stoplights—I thought that Shōki deserved as full a treatment as I could give him on his brief visit to the city of angels. My favorite taco stand is a little run-down shack on a grubby site near Normandy and Seventh, so I took a right on Wilshire and headed over that way. It's not a great neighborhood, but I figured my guest should get a good look at both sides of L.A. life while he was here, and since the route would take us through Beverly Hills along the way, I saw it as the grand tour.

I don't think Shōki was impressed as I briefly detoured up Rodeo Drive. It added to my respect for him, because it's never much impressed me, either. I wouldn't live there even if I had the money, as I once did. I remember the parties at swank Beverly Hills addresses in the old days, and not a one of them was ever any good. People who choose to live in Beverly Hills are people whose ideas about class and style are shaped entirely by price tags: that's why it's full of nouveau riche geeks and pistachio-chomping Iranians. There's probably more truth in *The Beverly Hillbillies* than even my perky friend from the SAG office ever suspected in her doctoral dissertation.

I pulled up at the curb across the street from Romero's Tacos. I didn't see any customers at the taco stand or anyone coming up the block, so I dashed out of the car and over to the little wooden shack.

You're in for a treat, my friend, I thought, and tried to summon an anticipatory mental image of one of Romero's unbeatable Mexican pastrami burritos. I can't be sure, but I think Shōki performed the equivalent of licking his lips at the prospect, and I was halfway across the street when the woman's screams caught our attention.

A small, elderly Mexican lady with an armful of plastic grocery bags stood halfway up the stairs to a dilapidated garden apartment building. Two teenaged Latinos flanked her and a third glared down at her from the top step. A beat-up sign above the door identified the property as Casa Del Sol, but it looked like the sun hadn't shone on this particular parcel of real estate for quite some time.

As I turned to look, I saw the two thugs on either side of the woman each grab an arm, while the third pointed at her purse. She tried to fight them, hold on to her shopping and purse and keep her balance all at the same time. The bag of groceries toppled out of her arms and fell down the stairs. A head of iceberg lettuce rolled down the sidewalk and into the street, stopping almost at my feet.

We were on the move before I knew what was happening.

Shōki ran toward the action. (I wish I could say I had something to do with what followed, but in all honesty, I was nothing more than a passive observer inside my own body.) He mounted the steps in two great strides and reached for the nearest of the thugs, grabbing the kid by his slick ponytail. The kid yelped with surprise, but before he or his companions could react, Shōki kicked out at his knee and yanked back on his hair. Something snapped—maybe knee, maybe neck—and the kid was down.

The second thug shoved the old lady out of the way. She fell off the concrete steps and landed on the dead grass, losing the rest of her groceries. The last of the thugs pulled a blade out of his pocket and charged down the steps. Shōki whirled around and lashed out at the second kid with an open-handed thrust to the solar plexus. The kid groaned and doubled over, but Shōki grabbed him by an oversized silver death's-head belt buckle and lifted him up into the air.

The kid rushing down the stairs must have seen it coming, but he had too much momentum to put on the brakes. Shōki hurled his hoodlum buddy right at him, propelling the kid directly onto the point of his partner's outstretched blade. He screamed as the knife went into his back and the tip burst out through the middle of his chest. The weight of the impaled Latino was too much for the kid with the knife, and still entwined, the two of them tumbled roughly down the steps, bones breaking as they went. The were deathly still when they landed at the bottom.

Shōki turned to the woman, still lying in the grass, watching in horror.

"Ogenki des ka?" he said.

She looked terrified, then as she saw the Japanese characters painted on my face and heard the strange words, looked merely confused.

"Are you okay?" I repeated.

She started to nod her head, then she pointed at the words on my flesh. I touched my fingers to my cheeks, then examined them. The paint appeared to have a run a little in the sweat we'd worked up. I hoped it didn't affect Shōki.

"*Qué está?*" she asked.

With the three kids lying in a bloody mess around us, there wasn't time to explain (as if I *could* explain). I sensed that Shōki had retreated back to wherever it was in my head—in my soul?—that he was residing.

I decided that a general retreat was definitely in order.

I ran back to the car and pulled away as fast as I could. I considered what I had done to those kids, that I may well have killed one or more of them. Not that I felt any great sympathy for them, but what had transpired, the way Shōki completely took me over without my being able to exert the slightest will, was frightening in the extreme. No matter how chivalrous his motives.

I had forgotten all about the taco stand, but as the sight of the little shack disappeared in the mirror, I caught another flash from Shōki.

I think he was disappointed about missing out on that burrito.

*I*nvocation (IV)

The invisible wind begins to swirl around him. Shuten Dōji feels it tugging at his essence. What was once a fuzzy blur at the edge of the darkness has now intensified and blossomed into a searing crimson incandescence that melts away the blackness that is the prison of his long exile. The wind grabs at him, reaching deep inside him with a thousand taloned fingers to draw the demon lord toward the hot, red star burning at the center of the light.

The blood rites are almost complete. The chain of sacrifices and ceremonies has been perfectly realized. Though he yet has no true tongue or throat, Shuten Dōji can taste the blood. Though he has no belly, he is sated by the prodigious volume of digested flesh and bone. As the power grows greater within him, as the wind-between-the-worlds impels him toward the gate that seals the realms, he aches for his long-lost physicality, longs for the sensation of wearing human skin once more.

A crystal bell peals and the crimson light grows brighter still, until even Shuten Dōji has to shield his multitude of eyes from its power. The final summoning has begun, his human shell nearly made ready for the experience of his majesty: for Shuten Dōji's possession.

The wind blows stronger behind him, lifting him toward the blinding glow. The voices of invocation sing their discordant prayers and the demon wind howls its counterpoint response. Shuten Dōji is in the light now, indistinguishable from it. The crimson heat is formed of his own blood and that of the human sacrifices from which he has drunk. The raw heat of the light and might of the wind rip open the gateway.

Shuten Dōji prepares to cross when the light blinks. The wind dies and the summoning voices miss a beat and grow silent.

The gateway closes in front of him. The demon lord howls his anger, then stops and sniffs at the returning darkness.

He hears another song, a distant and harmonious chant. Veins of black rip through the crimson light, which dims around him. The wind reverses direction, pulling him back toward the shards of darkness.

He reaches out with his essence, opening wide his every eye to see all that can be seen.

Another gateway has opened.

The Other has passed through.

Shuten Dōji's anger gives way to resignation and just as quickly to mirth as he considers what has transpired: his ancient foe will be waiting for him, summoned, like Shuten Dōji, from a realm beyond. Thus has it ever been, and so must it always be.

He would not really have it any other way (not that he really has the choice).

The wind swirls, dies out, then builds up again as the summoner's chants begin anew. The force returns and pulls him once more toward the gateway. The black tendrils fade, darkness receding as the crimson light grows again in strength. The bloodlust builds up within him as somewhere in the realms between a crystal bell tolls.

Shuten Dōji prepares himself anew. His anticipation—his desire—is even greater than before.

One final sacrifice and the blessed, cursed flesh will be his.

Twenty-One

A fresh Santa Ana kicked up in the early evening. It rattled the windows of the *Kakure* manse at the top of the hill, sending brown palm fronds swirling through the air like paper airplanes. I sat up in the crow's nest, watching the magenta sunset over the ocean—the rich color the surest sign of another heavy-pollution day—chased by the magical twinkling of lights coming on across the city as darkness fell. The basin seemed like an immense pinball game to me, the cars darting back and forth like steel balls bouncing off bumpers and triggering a light show of targets, lanes, and bonus points. Pretty.

Considerable activity took place in the house below me. People kept coming and going as a veritable legion of Men in Black drove off in dull cars, laying the groundwork for what was to come. Yorimitsu had said little about any specific plan for the assault on the *Goryō-dō*, and I didn't ask. Benkei continued to hover close by, and though Shōki exchanged a few brief words with him, to which Benkei responded with uncharacteristic verbosity, I paid him little mind. Benkei and all the others, even Yorimitsu, had a hard time meeting my eye since the Shōki ritual went down, even when it was clearly *me* talking. It's not like there could be any confusion: I continued to speak in English, while Shōki always used Japanese. Though we understood each other, I still couldn't make sense of the Japanese until it came filtered through Shōki. It was all a little— hell, *a lot*—disconcerting, but I found I was getting used to it.

As I sat and stared at my city, I thought again of the Latino gang-bangers we'd beat up (or killed?) over by the taco stand. I was still disturbed by it, but considered whether I could afford such feelings given what lay ahead. Though I wasn't clear on the details of the *Goryō-dō* assault, I understood that no one would be playing by Marquess of Queensberry—or Shōgun of Honshu—rules. All of the *Kakure* had spent at least part of the day meditating; on their deaths, I understood. It startled me to learn that none of them were overly anxious about the prospect—the impending battle was something for which they'd evidently been preparing for a very long time—but *I* sure as hell was scared to death. I wasn't about to back out of it, not with Rosa's life, maybe even more than just her life, hanging on my actions, but I couldn't reconcile myself to things quite so readily.

I tried to communicate with Shōki about it, but found it hard to connect. He, too, seemed to be mentally girding himself—with his mind or mine?—and didn't care to be disturbed. I did briefly get through to him with my fears: both about what we had done to the Latino youths and what we might have to do to Rippen and his mob. The response, I sensed, was one of puzzlement that there could be any concern over the likes of those who would attack an old woman, and steely resolve about the conflict to come. As I should have realized, Shōki, not in any sense truly alive, had no fear whatsoever of death. For one who had trod the very soil of the Land of the Dead, what terror could the release of mortality hold? Shōki was not tethered to his existence by anything so fragile as flesh and blood, but rather by the ethereal and thus less immediately dispatchable force of collective belief.

I should have been able to take some comfort from him, but I did not. There should have been solace in the notion, the seeming proof positive, of existence above and beyond human mortality. It could be argued, of course, that I had been granted that most cherished of all possible gifts: a glimpse into the afterlife, a denial of oblivion.

Yet I still didn't know if I entirely believed. I was *sure* I believed in Rosa, knew that it was that belief that kept me going.

As to the rest: I reckoned the night would provide all the answers.

I rode up north with Yorimitsu, Benkei, and a Man in Black driver. We set off with one other car in front of us, a new Lexus that, except for color, was identical to our own. It contained four more *Kakure,* and our driver kept us less than a car length behind it all the way. We cruised up toward Santa Barbara on Highway 101 at a leisurely pace. Full darkness had set in, and the road was relatively quiet. The winds had grown in intensity and sent the odd jolt through the car. Benkei, riding up front, would squint at the driver every time it happened, but Yorimitsu wasn't bothered.

Both Benkei and Yorimitsu clad themselves in kimonos, and each bore the two swords of *bushi,* the warrior. Yorimitsu expected me to wear a

kimono as well, and though I tried it on, I felt too damned silly. I settled for a Man in Black costume: denim pants and T-shirt and black shoes
that seemed to stretch themselves to fit the shape of my foot. Kind of a
cross between slippers and Air Jordans. I sensed that Shōki was a little
discomfited by the outfit—he went for the kimono look big-time—but
he was flexible.

And I had a sword.

Yorimitsu presented it to me just as it was time to go. He didn't touch
it himself, but laid a long, polished ebony case at my feet, bowing as he
opened it. Inside, packed in chrysanthemum petals, lay the blade.

"Ummm, couldn't I have a gun?" I asked him. "Glock? Ingram? Hell,
I'd settle for a Saturday night special."

Yorimitsu shook his head, then dipped his chin, indicating that I
should pick up the sword.

I carefully brushed aside some of the flower petals to reveal the hilt.
The sword was quite magnificent. The hilt was gold and nacre, etched
with a complicated series of characters and lightning bolts. The steel blade
itself was flawless, polished as bright and clear as the finest silver. My own
nervous reflection in it seemed a disgrace to the perfection of the steel.

It was also a good four feet long and looked like it weighed a ton.

"It's really nice," I said, "but I can't even carve the Butterball on
turkey day without making a mess. I don't think this is for me."

Yorimitsu bobbed his head again, a little more sternly. I sighed and
let my hand fall on the hilt.

Shōki took over. He drew the sword out of its case and whipped it
above his head. He knew this blade, had wielded it before. This was not
just a sword but *the* sword: *Kusanagi-no-Tsurugi* was its name, and it was
a slayer of demons. The sword had been forged for Susa-no-o, the God
of Storm himself, its perfect metal folded ten thousand times until its
tensile strength could sunder raw diamond. Its perfect balance was a joy
to the wielder's hand, its honed edge a black line of death to any foe. It
sang as Shōki slashed it through the air, all the room's light seeming to
rush to embrace its pure argent grace.

It clunked to the ground as Shōki handed it over to me.

Yorimitsu winced as the edge of the blade chewed a rut in the hardwood floor. I tried to yank it out with both hands, but the sword was
back in the stone, and I was no young King Arthur. Shōki had to yank
it out, and I managed to get a firmer grip this time as he departed. Using
both hands, I was able to heft the sword almost to my waist. I held it

stiffly out in front of me, like a big metal dildo. I felt more than faintly ridiculous.

"Nice," I said.

Yorimitsu looked a little bit worried, but he didn't say anything. His two swords dangled at his waist.

"Don't I get a scabbard?" I asked, pointing at his.

"It cannot be sheathed," he told me.

I started to ask how come I only got one sword—not that I wanted another or could handle the one I had—when Shōki answered the question for me. Carrying two swords was *bushido,* the way of the samurai. Shōki had very deep respect for *bushido,* but he himself predated the code by some years. He was not samurai, he was not anything other than Shōki. And he'd always only carried the one sword.

The sword, along with the others, had to be left in the trunk as we drove. While swords may be the weapons of true warriors, there's simply no room for them in your modern luxury sedan. The driver had an Uzi, though, and Benkei cradled it in the crook of his arm as we drove. Yorimitsu had still not told me what the plan was, so as we passed through Thousand Oaks I thought maybe it was time to ask.

"We fight," he told me.

"I figured that," I said, "but what's the plan to get in? There must be some kind of strategy, right?"

"We attack," he said.

"Uh, but won't they be waiting for us? Expecting it?"

"Very likely."

"Then how do we get around that?"

"We fight," he said. I could sense Shōki nodding his approval in the back of my head.

Hell of a plan, I thought.

In fact, the *Kakure* had the situation scoped out a little more keenly than Yorimitsu let on. Whether he was trying to be humble, inscrutable, or was just jagging my wires—though in no other respect had he struck me as a wire-jagging kind of guy—I never entirely figured out.

It was nearly eleven o'clock by the time we crossed the Santa Barbara city line. A thin sliver of moon provided dim light, but away from the overwhelming glare of the L.A. basin, a litter of stars could be seen sparkling in a clear black sky. With the windows cranked down I could smell the salt air of Santa Barbara Bay, a once beautiful natural harbor long since sullied by rows of gray steel oil rigs jutting out of the surf like rusty needles in a blue pincushion. As we crested a small hill I could see red and white lights on the rigs blinking in the distance. Even they didn't look too bad at night.

We followed the lead car off the main highway just before the main part of town. Santa Barbara is a rich shopper's wet dream, the downtown district chockablock with self-parodically twee restaurants and over-priced boutiques. In fact, it's what I think of as an "eeky" kind of town, where every other shop features "unique" or "mystique" in its name, where every battered old piece of crap is labeled and priced as "antique," and where if you aren't rich, white, and gorgeous as a movie star, you're bound to be up shit's creek. It's pretty as hell, no denying, and definitely the place to hang out if you're in the market for stuff like designer soap or black-currant-scented candles, but also the kind of place where you half expect the cops to move you along if you can't produce an American Express gold card on demand.

We followed a curvy two-lane road up into the hills at the edge of town. As we came over the top of one hill and down again through a small canyon, Yorimitsu pointed up to the left. I hunched down to glance out his window at some lights atop the highest peak in view. I could tell that a large, white house sat at the top, but we were too far to make out the slightest detail.

"Ripperland?" I asked.

Yorimitsu nodded. I could feel Shōki stir in the back of my head at the sight, and his hand instinctively reached out for a sword hilt that wasn't there. Benkei shifted his grip on the Uzi, and even the driver cleared his throat.

As we neared the base of the Ripperland summit, the road forked: the main road continued on through the pass while a second, single-lane road branched off and up the hill. The lead car turned up the secondary road toward the estate, but we didn't follow. I shot a glance at Yorimitsu; he didn't return it, still playing coy—close to the kimono, you might say.

The driver followed the road around the hill at a leisurely pace that added to the tension inside the car. When I glanced again at Yorimitsu I saw that his eyes were closed and his lips moved slightly, either in meditation or silent prayer. Up front, Benkei held a white-knuckled grip on the gun, while the driver nervously started to tap his fingers on the wheel until Benkei stopped him with a growl. I was amazed at how calm I felt, no more than a mild bowel twinge of nerves, and had to attribute it to Shōki, though I couldn't sense anything much of my "guest" at the moment. If not for my own uncharacteristic calm in the face of adversity, I wouldn't even have known he was around.

The driver turned off the road and onto a dirt trail that you had to know was there even to notice. The Lexus complained some as it bounced along, the scraping of its undercarriage on the rocks raising hackles and gooseflesh, not to mention repair bills.

We came to a stop as soon as we were out of sight of the main road. Benkei and the driver jumped out and ran around to the rear, while Yorimitsu and I slowly got out of the back. It was pretty damn dark, but I could see that we'd stopped at a point at which the dirt trail angled steeply up the hill. No way the Lexus could handle that kind of terrain. I couldn't see Ripperland from this side, nor even the top of the hill in the darkness, but I made it a good fifteen hundred feet to the summit, and as Benkei and the driver unloaded the ebony sword case, I prayed that we weren't going to have to hoof it.

My prayer was answered by a hoarse call in Japanese from the bushes. Benkei had his own long sword in hand, but he lowered it as a pair of *Kakure* emerged from the brush. They exchanged a few words with Yorimitsu, but I was too busy struggling with the sword to pay much attention. I used both hands to heft it out of its box. As soon as I touched it, I felt an electric spark from Shōki. For a second, as the sword was raised up into the air, I thought I'd lost control again, but the feeling quickly faded. The sword felt heavy, but not as bad as before. I found I could manage it by resting the edge of the blade against my shoulder, like a rifle. I almost cut an ear off when I shot a glance to my right upon hearing the start of an engine, and decided to rest the *flat* of the sword on my shoulder.

Yorimitsu called my name and indicated I should follow him into the bushes. Waiting there was a black, four-wheel drive vehicle with an open top. The *Kakure* who'd driven us up got behind the wheel, and Benkei gestured for me to climb into the back.

As I walked around the side of the vehicle I saw the decapitated bodies.

The four of them were clad in black, but a different variety of uniform from that worn by the *Kakure* minions. And none of them had worn their hair long, as did all of Yorimitsu's men. The head of each had been neatly severed—actually, the closer I looked, the more I realized it wasn't all *that* neat—and then laid upon the victim's chest. I assumed it had been done with a sword. Even with a stiff Santa Ana rustling the trees, the sickly scent of blood ran thick in the air, and insects swarmed and buzzed about the tacky corpses.

"*Goryō-dō?*" I whispered.

Yorimitsu nodded. I saw him smile, flashing his teeth.

It made me shudder.

Yorimitsu followed me into the back of the Land Rover, while Benkei claimed his usual shotgun seat. Two of the *Kakure*, who'd evidently dispatched the *Goryō-dō,* came with us as well, hopping up onto the running boards on either side of the vehicle and holding on to the roll bar. The driver backed us out of the brush and started up the steep dirt road. He left the headlights off, though a canopy of trees blocked even the slight glow of the moon crescent, and I don't know how he managed to follow the trail. The weight of the six passengers effectively nullified any suspension the car might have had, making for a tooth-jolting, ass-pounding, bone-crunching ride up the rutty path. At times the road narrowed so severely between the thick trees that the men on the running boards had to lean inside to avoid getting crushed.

The road flattened and smoothed out about halfway up the hill, and as we broke out into a clearing I could see the lights of Ripperland above us. I thought I heard an odd sort of buzzing noise, but couldn't tell if it came from the house or from somewhere in my head. I shot a glance at Yorimitsu, who peered up toward the house and nodded.

"It has begun," he said.

I thought about Rosa and felt another twinge in my gut. I tightened my grip on the sword. It seemed to bring Shōki closer to the surface and calmed me down. Like taking a hit of bourbon.

"Hadn't we better hurry?" I asked.

"There is time," Yorimitsu said.

The driver slowed as we approached another thicket. The men on the running boards jumped off and jogged along beside the car. Benkei stood up in the front, bracing himself against the top of the windshield with one hand, the Uzi clutched tightly in the other.

"What is it?" I whispered.

Shōki heard it first and stood up, sword at the ready. Benkei was almost as quick, aiming the barrel of the Uzi up at the sound. It started as a whistle, like a bomb falling, and turned into a scream as it drew closer.

The shape plunged out of the sky, a dart of blackness against the night's paler gloom. Shōki swiped at it with the sword as two yellow eyes became visible, and a moment later Benkei fired a controlled burst from the Uzi. The shape suddenly changed trajectory away from the vehicle, barrel-rolling off to the right. It cackled as it turned and two claws shot out, grabbing one of the Kakure who'd jumped off the car, carrying him up into the night. The man's screams Dopplered away.

Everyone had a weapon in hand, awaiting further attack, but all was still. Shōki raised his sword as the whistling sound again broke the silence. The shape again plummeted out of the sky, heading straight for the Land Rover. It didn't veer this time, but Shōki held back his stroke and barked an order as he leaped out of the vehicle. The others quickly followed.

The eviscerated body of the snatched Man in Black landed smack-dab on the middle of the hood, crushing the front of the Land Rover. A geyser of boiling water and hot oil burst out of the engine. The smell of blood and burning flesh filled the air.

Then the demon attacked again. Silently this time, flying just above ground level like a radar-avoiding plane, only the yellow glow of its eyes giving it away.

That was enough.

Shōki pivoted and dropped to one knee as the creature reached for Yorimitsu. As its claw snatched the cap on the Kakure leader's head, Shōki plunged his sword upward, twisting his wrist as he thrust. The creature screamed, its veiny, batlike wings flapping madly as it struggled to disimpale itself from the great sword, or at least pull the blade from Shōki's grasp.

Not a chance.

Shōki stood up and whipped the sword down with a flick of his wrist, dashing the flailing demon against the earth. Dark grue, smelling like sulfur, poured out of the jagged gash in the creature's belly, searing the grass below. Benkei and the others quickly joined the fray, slashing at the demon with their own blades. It continued to screech and wail, not giving up the ghost until it had practically been hacked to bits. Even then it managed to raise its malformed head and spit something at a Man in Black. The demon's sputum caught the Kakure on the cheek, his flesh smoldering where it touched. The man started to scream, but Benkei immediately was on top of him, short sword in hand. He used the point of the blade to dig under the man's skin and slice the affected region away. Blood gushed down the stricken fellow's face, but at least he stopped screaming.

"What was it?" I said, poking at the still spasmodic bits of demon with Shōki's sword. He'd retreated again, but I felt him very close to the surface, and the answer formed in my mind even as Yorimitsu said it.

"*Shikome,*" he said, and from Shōki I knew that this was yet another of the many demon servant/masters of the *Goryō-dō.*

The *Kakure* who'd been spat on started moaning again as he clutched his cheek. Benkei hovered over him, but even in the dim light I could see that one whole side of the man's face had turned black. The wounded man had sunk back to his knees and appeared to be shivering or maybe convulsing. Yorimitsu and the remaining Man in Black walked over to him, and I followed. The man had dropped his head and buried his face in his armpit. Benkei reached down and grabbed him by the hair, raising his infected cheek for inspection. Yorimitsu shook his head and looked at Benkei, who in turn looked at me.

I didn't understand, but Shōki did. Without a second's hesitation he strode around behind the prostrate *Kakure* and raised his sword.

With one neat, two-handed swipe, the man's head rolled off his shoulders and landed facedown in the grass. His body remained upright for a few seconds, blood furiously pumping out of the neck, before it, too, tumbled into the dirt.

"Jesus," I said, looking down. The blood still dripped off the heavy sword in my hand.

Yorimitsu wandered over to inspect the ruins of the Land Rover. The body of the *Kakure* who'd been dropped from the sky had turned black from the heat of the engine, and wisps of steam continued to rise from under the hood. Yorimitsu reached out to shut the still open eyes of his dead comrade, briefly cupping his hand over the man's face.

"Come," he said, glancing up at Ripperland. "We walk."

Much to my surprise, we made it up the slope without further incident. The climb was steep, but not all that difficult. Yorimitsu struggled a bit, at times, reminding me that he was not a young man, but he insisted on taking point. I had the feeling that he'd been waiting for this night for a very long time, his whole life for all I knew, and he was determined to face it head-on and in the lead. Benkei guarded the rear.

At the top of the hill, the path we followed led to the edge of a large meadow effectively forming Ripperland's immense backyard. Some of the meadow was taken up with gardens, and several metal sculptures dotted the lawn—even in the dark I recognized the exaggerated lines of a Giacometti figure—but there was no real cover between our position and the rear of the house. Lights were on all over the three-story mansion, and one wing was illuminated by the reflected blue glow of a swimming pool. The buzzing in my head seemed to grow louder now that we were in sight of the house, and I felt Shōki exerting greater will to help shake it off.

"Now what?" I asked.

Yorimitsu rubbed his temples with his fingertips. I wondered if he felt the effects of the buzzing noise as well.

"We wait," he said.

"What for?"

"Shuten Dōji," he whispered.

Huh! I thought.

The longer we waited, the worse the buzzing became. I had Shōki to help shield me from it, but Yorimitsu was holding his head in his hands. Neither Benkei nor the remaining Man in Black seemed to be affected.

"What is it?" I asked Yorimitsu.

He forced himself to hold his head up. I could read pain in his eyes. "The *Goryō-dō* are opening the gateway between the realms. When it is fully open Shuten Dōji will attempt to come through."

"Shouldn't we get a move on then?"

"Soon," he said. He grabbed the wrist of the Man in Black and looked at his watch—a Swatch, yet—and nodded his head. "Soon."

I couldn't tell which came first; perhaps it happened simultaneously: a sudden dramatic increase in the intensity of the buzzing and a body flying out through the big glass windows in the back of Ripperland.

"Hai," Yorimitsu said, still supporting his head with one hand. The other held a sword. The four of us charged across the lawn toward the house, Benkei now leading the way.

Assorted yells and the sound of steel clanking against steel grew louder as we approached the rear of the mansion. More glass broke as combatants burst through the ornate French doors leading to the redwood sun deck around the pool. Two men dressed in black, one *Kakure,* one *Goryō-dō,* flailed away at each other with swords. One of the *Kakure's* arms hung limply at his side as he parried fierce blows from Rippen's goon. The

Kakure was backed steadily toward the edge of the pool. We were too far away to help him, but Benkei ran toward the pair anyway. Just as the *Goryō-dō* prepared to deliver the killing blow, the Man in Black dropped his sword and produced a dagger, seemingly out of thin air. Before his foe could deliver the stroke, the Man in Black thrust up into his belly with the dagger, tossing the *Goryō-dō* over his shoulder and into the water in the process. Without wasting a moment to even catch his breath (not to mention one-armed), the Man in Black picked his sword up and dashed back into the house through the broken door.

"All right!" I cheered. Shōki echoed the sentiments.

"Come," Yorimitsu said, and ran toward the house.

Bedlam beckoned inside: the keenly appointed halls of Ripperland dripped blood and grue as men and demons squared off in a fantastic battle royal. Though the occasional burst of automatic-weapons fire sounded from somewhere in the house, all the *Kakure* and *Goryō-dō* warriors fought it out with swords.

Benkei had already entered the fray, coming to the aid of a wounded Man in Black fighting off a tiny, three-eyed demon that attacked him from a tabletop in the massive dining room. The creature whirled like a dervish, spinning its razor talons like a buzz saw. It had disarmed the *Kakure,* but Benkei came up from behind and sliced the legs off the table with a swipe of his sword. The demon leapt up into the air and grabbed on to a hanging Tiffany lamp with one claw. But before it could start to spin again, Benkei slashed away at it, cutting the creature almost in half. The demon screeched as its rotten innards slopped to the floor, but Benkei quickly silenced it with a final sword thrust through the head.

I felt Shōki's urge to take over and join the battle, but Yorimitsu put a restraining hand on my shoulder and Shōki backed off. Benkei came running back toward us, getting in the odd slash at *Goryō-dō* warriors as opportunities arose. I had no idea where all the Men in Black had come from, but I assumed that it was a consequence of the ceaseless activity that had gone on at the *Kakure* house during the day. I couldn't help but wonder, wading through the carnage, how many men had already been sacrificed to get this far.

Yorimitsu nodded at Benkei, who led us through the mayhem, across the dining room and down a wide corridor. As we came into a large hall near the front of the house, we encountered another melee of clashing fighters. Benkei immediately began hacking away at the nearest *Goryō-*

dō, rending the man from neck to navel with a stroke. A particularly pained scream caught my attention as a *Kakure* warrior stumbled backwards out of an adjoining door and fell to the floor almost at Yorimitsu's feet. He landed on his back, arms flung over his head. A gaping hole, big as a cantaloupe, had been gouged out of the middle of his chest. A second later, a horned demon—the same seven-foot, intestine-ripping son of a bitch I'd seen kill Cheri at Vasquez Rocks—came roaring out through the doorway, something red and wet sticking out from between its lips, blood running down its chin. It charged as soon as it saw us.

Yorimitsu had his sword in his hand, but Shōki was faster. Yorimitsu yelled, "No," but it was too late. The demon slashed out with his own sword. Shōki parried the blow, deflecting the edge of the demon's sword into a Mondrian on the wall, shredding the canvas. Shōki dropped down and executed a spin on the balls of his feet, swiping at the demon's legs with a sweep of his sword. The demon hurtled the blade, yanking his own out of the wall and bringing it down at Shōki's head.

Shōki ducked under the cut by dropping onto his back. He followed through by kicking out at the demon, catching it heavily on the side of its double-jointed knee. The creature's leg crunched and caved underneath it. It tried to use its sword as a crutch to stop from falling, but Shōki swiped at it as he sprang back to his feet and the demon went down. It rolled over its own blade, roaring as the edge of the steel cut into its flesh. It tried to get up, but Shōki easily hamstrung its good leg as he leaped over the rolling demon. The creature managed to grab Shōki's ankle and tried to pull him down, but another backhanded swipe of the blade severed the taloned hand at the wrist. The creature screamed its fury, only to be silenced forever as Yorimitsu drove his short sword up under the demon's chin and on through. The point of the blade formed a third horn at the back of the demon's head.

"Goddamn!" I said, watching the light go out of the creature's eyes.

"We must hurry now," Yorimitsu urged. "They will know you are here."

I wasn't sure what he meant, but no sooner had he spoken than the buzzing noise ratcheted up in intensity. Yorimitsu almost doubled over in pain, and only Shōki kept me upright. There was a kind of electric current in the air that made my skin crawl and my fillings vibrate. The buzz got louder, its pitch growing higher, until it climaxed in a sound like a collapsing mountain of glass. Even the other combatants must have felt it, because there was a sudden lull in the fighting. Benkei used it to hack apart a couple of *Goryō-dō* fighters and then the battle was joined again. I looked at Yorimitsu, who forced himself to straighten up.

"Shuten Dōji," he said. "He is come."

Twenty-Two

I followed Yorimitsu up the stairs, with Benkei covering our rear. We trod over bodies on the steps and in the hall, both *Kakure* and *Goryō-dō*, dead and alive. Though I'd never been in Ripperland before, I had no problem knowing which way to go: the electric current in the air seemed a tangible thing, growing stronger, almost pulling at us the closer we got to Shuten Dōji. As we turned a bend in the hall a phalanx of fresh *Goryō-dō* fighters came running at us. Shōki charged right into them, mercilessly hacking away flesh with bloodlust relish, the corridor walls quickly spackled with red as Yorimitsu and Benkei joined in. When the quarters drew too close for effective use of the long sword, Shōki flailed out with fists and feet, snapping bones and breaking spines. When the last remaining *Goryō-dō* tried to retreat in fear, Shōki caught him from behind, wrapping an arm around the man's head. With a quick jerk of the shoulder, the fighter's neck popped like a flip-top soda can, his bowels evacuating themselves as he died.

Yorimitsu came up beside me, pointing to the sword, which Shōki had dropped during the fight. I picked it up, still struggling with the weight. I stared at the blood on my hands and marveled at the carnage around us. I had been nicked or slashed a good half dozen times, but of course, Shōki hadn't even felt it. It hurt *me,* though, as blood oozed from wounds on my arms and legs. My knuckles were swollen and bleeding and it felt like I'd broken a toe. I had to struggle just to hold on to the heavy sword. Benkei, I saw, had also suffered some nicks and one serious-looking cut across his left cheek—a flap of skin drooped down like badly hung wallpaper—but Yorimitsu was unhurt.

"There," he said, pointing at a set of double doors at the end of the hall. It was obviously what the fighters had been guarding. I held up my hand and felt the strength of the current pulling towards the doors. I half expected Shōki to retake control; when he didn't, I took a deep breath and followed the pull, hefting the sword back up to my shoulder. Yorimitsu and Benkei followed at my heels. I don't know if they thought they were following me or Shōki, or if it made any difference to anyone at that point.

The electricity reversed itself and became a palpable deterrent force as we approached the doors. Benkei had fallen several steps behind and was leaning far forward as if walking into a gale-force wind. Yorimitsu fared slightly better, but he, too, was slowed by the current and had to hunch his shoulders and turn his face away to impel himself forward. I was better able to move, but only slowly, like wading through mud or swimming in molasses. I managed to grab hold of the knob, but couldn't manage any more.

Shōki had to open the door.

The force was dispelled as soon as I stepped inside. The large room was lit by hundreds of flickering candles lined up neatly around the perimeter. The space was big enough to house a movie theater, which I realized was what it must be: Rippen's private screening room.

Some of the seats had been removed, but the flawless silver screen glistened in the candlelight. A dozen or more vintage movie posters—along with a few decidedly nonvintage Rippen-produced numbers—dotted the walls like the Stations of the Cross. At the front, on either side of the big screen, stood a glass display case, each containing but a single item: an Oscar, lit almost ethereally from within. Some of the candles were scented, but through the sandalwood and lilac I caught the faintest trace of a deeper, more redolent smell: buttered popcorn.

The chapel of St. Cecil the De Mille.

Dense lines of tiny Japanese characters had been painted up and down the walls between the framed posters and in spiral patterns across the floor and ceiling. Shōki could read them, of course, and I understood that they were ritual invocations to Shuten Dōji. Shōki quickly cast his gaze away, lest I be corrupted by them.

The *Goryō-dō* cabal sat in the middle of the room, surrounded by a second circle of candles. I recognized Aldus and the two Japanese money men from Vasquez Rocks among the six in the circle.

In the center, squirming naked on the floor, his body covered head to toe in a swirl of painted characters, lay Jack Rippen.

Only now, I knew, it was Shuten Dōji.

He flopped around on the floor, a gleaming sword beside him. Apparently the demon was still trying to come to terms with Rippen's body (and a part of me noted with some glee that the long-held rumors about

Rippen's limited physical endowments were all too true). He looked up at me and I saw the awareness and the hatred in his eyes, but he couldn't yet muster sufficient control of his new human form. The *Goryō-dō* circle closed ranks to protect him in his moment of vulnerability, but none of them carried a weapon and I felt Shōki's bloodlust rise to the surface.

I heard a clamor behind me and turned around to see Benkei and Yorimitsu battling it out in the hall with a new group of *Goryō-dō* fighters led by the little *kappa* I'd already encountered twice. I had to resist an urge to go back and help them, but knew that this was the moment to dispatch Rippen and his demon host. I felt Shōki start to take over when I was distracted by the plea.

"Marty . . . ?"

In the corner of the room, trussed up like a Christmas goose, was Rosa. She looked small and scared, still wrapped in the torn kimono she'd been given by the *Kakure*. Her eyes had a faraway, drugged look, but she half smiled at me through her fear. I couldn't see any obvious injuries and I instinctively took two steps in her direction.

Which was one step too many.

Shuten Dōji charged, sword in hand. Shōki was fast, but not fast enough. He got his sword up in time to parry the worst of the blow, but the demon's blade skipped off and deflected into Shōki's left shoulder. I felt Shōki briefly wink out as Shuten Dōji brutally wrenched his blade out of the meat of my upper arm. I thought I might pass out from the pain, thought I heard a hoarse yell from Rosa, but then Shōki returned.

Shuten Dōji windmilled his blade before beginning a savage series of thrusts and slashes that had Shōki moving backward on the defensive. The demon wielded a shorter, lighter sword that allowed for quicker movement. Shōki struggled to parry the flurry of strikes, suffering two more cuts to the left side that drew spurts of blood. The smell of blood seemed to drive the demon to a deeper frenzy, but it proved his undoing as he stumbled over a row of burning candles.

Shōki took quick advantage of the clumsiness, beginning a fierce offensive of his own. The great sword was lightning in his hands. One of the *Goryō-dō* cabal tried to throw himself at Shōki's feet to unbalance him, but Shōki executed a half turn and cut the man's face in half even as he skipped over him. The others in the cabal hurriedly retreated to a far corner of the room, led by Aldus.

Shōki continued to press the attack, steel meeting steel with a din like ramming battleships. Shuten Dōji stumbled again as he retreated, and

Shōki got inside his defenses, slicing a chunk of painted flesh out of Rippen's upper thigh. The demon lost his blade and howled as he fell over, screaming like a slaughtered lamb, but as Shōki raised the sword for a killing stroke, Shuten Dōji directed a stream of hot piss from his dangling cock straight into Shōki's eyes.

Shōki blindly slashed out with his sword as he backed away, wiping the urine out of his eyes with the back of his free hand. The demon got to his feet quickly and charged headfirst. He ducked under Shōki's swipe—just; it cost Rippen some of his expensive hair plugs—and plowed into Shōki, driving him into, and right on through, the rear wall of the screening room. The combatants tumbled into a sumptuous study with big bay windows looking out over the rear of Ripperland. Men could be seen battling on the lawn, but it was impossible to make any sense of who might have the advantage.

Shōki still held on to the great sword, pummeling the demon's face with the heavy hilt, but the quarters were too close for any more effective use of the weapon. Shuten Dōji raked at Shōki's eyes with his claws and tried to soften Shōki up with a flurry of blows to the groin and midsection. Shōki managed to reverse out from under the demon's grip and pinned one of Rippen's legs under his weight, grabbing at the demon's foot and twisting with all his strength. The bone snapped like a twig and the demon howled again, but simultaneously kicked out with its free leg, landing Shōki a solid blow to the side of the head. Shuten Dōji quickly followed with a series of kicks to Shōki's hand, until the warrior dropped his sword. The demon dove for it, but Shōki recovered fast enough to kick out at the sword, sending it shooting across the floor and under a leather divan. Shuten Dōji scurried after it, dragging one twisted leg behind him, but Shōki reached for the damaged leg and gave it another brutal twist, forcing shards of bone out through the tanned skin of Rippen's ankle.

The demon screamed its fury at the injury. Shōki didn't let go this time, but picked Shuten Dōji up by the injured leg and whirled Rippen's body around in an airplane spin. The demon's head smacked into a wall with a thud, leaving a brown smear across the pine paneling. Shōki continued to whirl the demon through the air, as if winding up for an Olympic hammer throw, finally flinging him loose toward the big bay windows. The demon screamed as he hurtled through the air and burst through the glass in an explosion of crystal shards.

Shōki dashed to the window in time to see the demon roll off the balcony and fall to the sun deck a story below, redwood planks splintering under the force of impact. Shōki hopped the balcony rail in a move and lowered himself off the edge, knees braced to absorb the impact of the fifteen-foot drop to poolside.

The end of a metal pole caught Shōki midriff as he turned to face his foe. Shuten Dōji used the pool skimmer like a spear. A second, powerful thrust broke the skin and Shōki was impaled on the end of the pole. He tried to pull it loose, but the demon saw his advantage and rammed the metal rod deeper into Shōki's flesh. As the warrior tried to grab the skimmer with both hands and free himself, Shuten Dōji jerked the pole to the side, forcing Shōki off the deck and into the deep end of the pool.

I swallowed a lungful of the chlorine-heavy water as I struggled to get back to the surface. I could feel the pain of the pole still stuck in my side, but all I could think of was air. The pole was pushing me down, but it slipped free as I struggled and touched off the pool bottom and back to the surface, gasping as my face broke free of the water.

No sooner had I snatched a breath than the pole caught me on the side of the head, sending me back under. I saw black, or maybe it was just my blood in the water, but managed to hold on to consciousness. I bobbed back to the surface and sucked in another mouthful of air before Shuten Dōji hit me yet again, sending me back under.

I tried to get to the surface, but the pole was jabbing me in the chest, holding me under the water. I tried to swim down deeper to get out from under it, but only lost more ground. I couldn't seem to dislodge it or counter the pressure from the other end.

Shōki, I thought in desperation, *where the hell are you?*

I don't know if it was him or not, but with darkness descending, I managed to twist free of the pole and claw my way back up for air. As I broke through the skin of the water, I saw Rippen—I mean Shuten Dōji—laughing at me, his little red pecker hard as rock candy. I reached out again for Shōki, but there was no trace of him in my head. It was then that I caught sight of my hands and saw that the Japanese characters on my skin had run. I ran my hand across my cheek and it came away covered in ink.

"Oh, shit," I said.

Shuten Dōji must have sensed that Shōki was gone. He started playing with me, poking lightly at me with the end of the skimmer and hopping up and down as he cackled with joy. The bones in Rippen's shattered leg rattled and splintered further with every hop, but the demon danced on without a care. I was aware of the sound of steel on steel around us, not to mention the pain in my side, but I was afraid to take my eyes off the demon. I suspected that the rest of it wouldn't really matter much now that Shōki was gone. The *Kakure* didn't stand a chance without him.

Shuten Dōji caught me with another harsh poke to the side of the head, sending me back under the water. I tried to swim over toward the edge of the pool, out of his reach, but he pushed me back out into the center and jabbed me with a series of short, hard blows to the head and chest. Blood swirled around me, forming pretty, fractal patterns in the water. I felt myself getting light-headed as the demon pushed me under again and I gagged on another mouthful of water.

What saved me again was just dumb luck—the only kind I've ever really known. I'd drifted back toward the edge of the pool. Shuten Dōji directed me with the end of the pole, planning, I think, to put an end to things once and for all. I felt myself slipping back under the water, and certain that I wouldn't have the strength to come back up this time, I reached out for a Donald Duck inner tube bobbing in the pool. I missed it, but I grabbed the filter hose by mistake.

I held on tight as Shuten Dōji pushed me back under. He didn't realize that he was standing on the other end of the hose.

I saw him drop the pole and teeter at the edge of the pool. His arms shot up and the smile ran away from his face. He tipped forward, then back, and just about caught his balance, but then he tried to rest his weight on the injured leg.

It couldn't take it.

The demon fell face-first into the water, landing with a big belly flop. Even as he flailed about, I could see the ink dissolving off his skin and swirling away into the chlorinated water. He tried to make it back to the edge and drag himself out before the characters faded completely, but I grabbed for the skimmer and used the net to snag his head and pull him back into the pool.

When he broke surface again, I was looking into the extremely pained and vexed face of plain old Jack Rippen.

"Cocksucker!" Rippen screamed at me. I poked him in the mouth with the skimmer. Hard. He went back under and came back up spitting water. I jabbed him again. Harder. Then half a dozen more times, till his face was a bloody mess and he spat teeth along with water.

Rippen bobbed below the surface with a furious flail of arms and working leg. He briefly made the surface, and I was about to poke him again, but he went right back under.

It was only when I saw his broken leg pop up through the water that it struck me that, despite owning an Olympic-sized pool, the Ripper didn't know how to swim.

I tossed the skimmer aside and instinctively started toward him. His head broke surface and I saw terror in his eyes as he gurgled another mouthful of water. The ink on his cheeks had smeared like blackface, so that in his wild panic, eyes bulging, he looked like some old racist Hollywood portrayal of a comical "Negro."

I was still a quarter length away from him when Rippen managed to snag on to the Donald Duck float with one hand. It briefly went under with him, but popped back up to the surface, bringing the Ripper along for the ride. He gagged as his mouth found air, vomiting water and bile. The float was none too strong or steady, and Rippen's grip weak at best. I saw him suck in a quick breath before slipping back under the surface. He broke top again just as I got within reach.

He swallowed another desperate lungful of oxygen as he flailed out for me. I drew back as he caught and just as quickly let go of my arm. He grabbed on to Donald again, flipping the bird over as he went under yet again. As he came back up he managed to throw his arms over the rounded upside-down bottom of the float and rested his chin on top of it. He gagged and spit water again, but stayed afloat this time.

He wasn't even looking at me; his cheek lay against the rubber float, his eyes closed as he desperately sucked in air. Blood trailed behind him from his ruined leg, swirling around the pool, lit from below by the underwater lights. It drifted into patterns, perhaps only in my mind. I saw Cheri and Syd. Long John and his girl. Even Mickey Marvin and his foul cigar.

I saw Rosa.

I reached over and popped opened the air valve on the float.

The hissing noise caught the Ripper's attention. He started flailing again, accelerating the rush of air out of the float in the process. He tried to resecure the valve, but in his panic he snapped the whole thing off.

Donald drooped like a failed soufflé.

The Ripper started to scream, but whatever he had to say was drowned out, literally, by a sudden intake of water. He managed to break surface a few times as he struggled. Once he even grabbed hold of my arm as I floated nearby. I didn't move, didn't pry at his fingers or try to shake him loose.

When he let go it was of his own doing.

I don't know how long it took him to drown. Quite a while, it seemed to me. Not long enough in some respects. After a while, he just sort of stopped struggling. He floated up to the surface, facedown, like William Holden in *Sunset Boulevard*. When the body started to drift toward me, I swam away, but kept my eyes on it as I backstroked to the edge of the pool.

Just in case.

As I reached out for a ladder up to the deck, I realized it had grown quiet around me. The sound of clashing swords had faded, replaced by the chirps and clicks of crickets and cicadas. I thought I heard some commotion in the main house, but I couldn't see inside from where I was. I glanced up at the broken windows through which Shōki and Shuten Dōji had tumbled, but saw no activity there either.

Then I saw Rosa running across the deck in my direction. She looked ragged, her kimono torn and soiled, but I don't think anyone ever looked so good to me.

"Hey," I said as she came to the edge of the pool and leaned over me. "Come here often?"

She smiled, revealing a set of yellow, talonlike fangs. Her pink skin shriveled before my eyes, revealing the scaly red countenance of the *tengu* shapeshifter beneath. It raised a clawed hand to swipe at my throat when the staccato burst of an Uzi exploded above and behind us. Dark ichor spilled from a jagged line of holes that blossomed across the demon's torso. It roared its pain.

Over my shoulder I saw Rosa, the real one, standing on the balcony, Uzi braced against the rail. She fired another long burst, tracing a second line of bloody holes in the demon's flesh. Wings sprouted from the *tengu*'s back, flapping madly, as it prepared to take to the air. I saw the muscles in its thick legs bunch and coil as it crouched to spring. I saw its feet leave the ground even as a movement from the side penetrated my peripheral vision.

Benkei screamed like an avenging angel as he swung his flashing sword in a perfect arc. The *tengu*, I believe, never even saw him. Its head rolled cleanly off its shoulders and splashed into the water behind me. A spume of black ooze exploded out of the stump of the creature's neck. The body tottered on its feet, then fell backward.

The last thing I remember was the demon's still-beating wings coming down toward my head, forcing me under the water.

Twenty-Three

S id Teitlebaum's stubbly face hovering over me was the first thing I saw.
"I know this ain't Heaven," I croaked.

"Private room in Cedars," he told me. "Next best thing."

"Huh!" I said. "Who's paying?"

"Not to shvitz. It's covered."

"Hey," a softer voice said, "come here often?"

I blinked a couple of times until Rosa, standing at the foot of the bed, came into blurry focus. I tried to lift my head, found that it hurt, then realized I had a cervical collar on.

"Am I okay?" I asked, trying to look myself over. One tube snaked into my arm, another led under the covers in the direction of my crotch.

"I don't know." Rosa smiled. She came up beside me and took my hand. "How do you feel? Can you remember anything?" She squeezed my hand hard as she said *remember*. I took the hint.

"Umm, not exactly. How long I been out?"

"About eighteen hours. You needed some minor surgery on your side there. Where you got stabbed."

"I don't remember," I said, staring into her eyes. She nodded at me and patted my hand. "I guess I'm still a little groggy."

"I'm not surprised," Sid said. "You had quite the night. Quite the week to hear Rosa tell it."

"Do tell," I said. What the hell was going on here?

"I'm sure it will all come back to you," Rosa said. "I mean how you rescued me from the *yakuza* kidnappers and helped break up Jack Rippen's snuff-film operation."

"I did that?" I squeaked.

"Fucking A," Sid said. He looked at me with no small concern. "Maybe we should get the doctor."

"Would you, Sid?" Rosa said.

Rosa waited until he left the room. "It's a long story," she said. "You'd better play dumb for a while. Just 'remember' that you were working with the Japanese police to crack the Celestial Dog–Laughing Boy connection and that they kidnapped me when you got too close."

"Japanese police? What are you—"

Sid came back with an intern just then. Sid and Rosa went out in the hall while the doctor looked me over and filled me in on my condition. The major thing was the hole in my side. There'd been a bit of kidney damage, but nothing that wouldn't heal. Other than that, just some bruises and cuts. I'd be out of the hospital in three or four days, he said.

Rosa came back in by herself, but before I could ask her any more questions, Sid stuck his head in the door.

"You up for a couple more visitors?" he asked.

I glanced at Rosa, who nodded her head yes. "Sure," I told him, "the more the merrier."

Sid came in, followed by two Japanese gents. They looked vaguely familiar to me.

"Hello, Martin-san," the older of the two said. They both bowed.

"Ummm," I stammered.

"Marty, surely you recognize Inspector Yorimitsu and Detective Benkei," Rosa prodded.

"Inspector . . . ?"

"I am pleased to see you are looking better," Yorimitsu said. He was clean-shaven and his hair had been cut short. Benkei, too, had been shaved, though a large bandage was affixed to his cheek and he had one arm in a sling. Both wore dull gray business suits and ties and looked very uncomfortable.

"Yeah," I said, fighting a smile, "how you doing there, *Detective?*"

"All right!" Benkei said, and smiled back at me.

"We must be returning to Fukuoka this afternoon," Yorimitsu said, "but we wanted to say good-bye and to thank you again for your assistance with the Jack Rippen affair. Your help proved invaluable. I only regret that you suffered such grievous injury on our behalf."

"Anytime," I said. Then I suddenly flashed back to what happened in the pool. "Rippen . . ."

"Dead," Sid said. "The scumbag. Imagine: all that money and still he couldn't keep his fingers out of the dirty business. Japanese mafia yet. He got what he deserved. Thanks to Yorimitsu."

"Yorimitsu?"

"Regrettably, it was necessary for me to shoot him."

"Shoot? Rippen?"

"Yes. The body, sadly, was lost to the fire."

"Fire?"

"Ripperland," Sid said. "Whoosh!"

"No shit?"

"You okay, Marty? You look a little dazed."

"I think this is a little too much, too soon," Rosa said. Thank God. "I think he needs to rest for a while."

"Of course, you are right, Miss Mendez," Yorimitsu said. "We will take our leave."

"But I was hoping to get a chance to talk some more with you," I said. "We had such . . . interesting times."

"Alas, that will have to wait. But I am certain that we will have further opportunity to converse in the future."

"I'll be waiting."

Yorimitsu bowed to each of us and walked out of the room, Benkei at his heels. He didn't look right without his sword, but he flashed me a quick thumb's-up on the way out.

I got the feeling that Sid wanted to talk to me some more—I could imagine there were lots of unanswered questions; I sure had plenty—but Rosa shooed him away. She got chased out herself by a nurse, who zapped something lovely and strong into my IV.

I fell asleep within seconds.

There were indeed lots of questions to be answered, not to mention formal statements to be given, to the LAPD and to the cops in Santa Barbara and San Bernardino. Fortunately, I spent enough time rehearsing with Rosa in the hospital to get the story straight. And given that I'd been cast as some kind of hero, the cops—even the San Berdoo crowd who had me pegged for Syd's murder—cut me quite a bit of slack.

Yorimitsu had set the stage for the main part of the tale—and it was a whopper—and since we all sang the same hymn, it went down okay. Rippen, it was told, set up Celestial Dog to produce porn and snuff for a rich clientele in the Far East market. As a result he got hooked up with the Yaks who effectively ran Yoshitoshi, and through them arranged his big stock deal. I stumbled into it via Long John and then Rosa, as a result of their concern over girls who had disappeared in the snuff operation. In the course of investigating Celestial Dog I met up with Yorimitsu, running a hush-hush investigation for the Kyushu police over here. I got ambushed and framed for Syd's killing until Yorimitsu sprang me from the San Berdoo cops. Rosa was kidnapped in an attempt to blackmail me into turning over the evidence I had on Rippen, but together with Yorimitsu, we freed her and wasted Rippen and, oh yeah, Ripperland in the process. The Yaks had been exposed, killing the Laughing Boy–Yoshitoshi deal, leading to a major scandal involving Yoshitoshi in Japan. There was talk another government might fall. I got hurt in the scuffle at Ripperland and ended up in the hospital. End of tale.

Got that?

The cops clearly didn't like it all. The San Berdoo boys were especially unhappy about the kamikaze raid on a couple of their own. Yorimitsu explained it away as being necessary in order to save Rosa. I shrugged when they asked me about it and told them that's what Yorimitsu told me, as well. Since Yorimitsu provided solid evidence of Rippen's involvement with Celestial Dog and the Yaks, everyone was satisfied in the end. More or less.

"But what about all the bodies at Ripperland?" I asked Rosa when we were alone. "The demons and the *Goryō-dō* and the *Kakure?*"

"All gone. The *Kakure* pretty well polished off the *Goryō-dō* and took all the corpses away. They burned the demons up in the house fire at Ripperland."

"Pretty amazing," I said. Rosa agreed. "But no more amazing than you with that Uzi."

"Benkei did the hard part." She blushed.

"Where'd you learn how to shoot like that anyway? I wouldn't even know where the safety was on an Uzi."

"Just the kind of stuff you pick up working the streets of L.A.," she explained. "You should see me with a straight razor or a set of 'chuks."

I didn't ask.

The story was huge, of course. Rippen's death hit the town like a 7.5 on the Richter scale. I was safe in my hospital room—the Fukuoka police picked up the tab, by the way—but the animals in the press were waiting for me when I was discharged. I dodged them at the hospital, but was besieged when I tried to go home. I only stayed long enough to grab some clothes and Long John's cash from the freezer. Then Rosa and I hotfooted it across the border to recover on a Mexican beach. We drank cheap beer, ate hot food, and screwed ourselves silly on the dirty sand.

The media glommed on to us after three days.

I found a stack of messages and telegrams waiting for me when I got back home. Half of them were heartfelt thanks for my involvement in the Ripper's demise, half were offers for parts. Everybody, it seemed, wanted the rights to my life story: the networks, cable, even (a joke, surely) Laughing Boy. The dollar figures were staggering. Nickelodeon had started showing *Salt & Pepper* three times a day, and video sales were through the roof.

The public, it seemed, couldn't get enough of me.

In the end I gave the exclusive interview to Doug Hughes at *Variety*. I had better offers, but figured I owed him. He even managed to sell that old interview I'd given him for his book. And Random House snapped up the manuscript for big bucks.

I had offers to sign with all the big agencies, but in the end I turned them down. I called Kendall Arlo at SAG and asked if she'd be interested in looking after the offers for me. She was flabbergasted at first, but the idea grew on her. I'm her only client right now, but fifteen percent of me—at least at the moment—is a lot more than she was making at the Screen Actors Guild. And she drives a pretty hard bargain.

After a lot of soul-searching, I decided to take the plunge back into The Business. I can't believe it sometimes, but then I've seen a lot of unbelievable things lately. I know I said I'd sworn off acting forever, but I feel like a different person now. I *know* I see the world in a vastly different, a more wondrous, way. Though I've learned that there are horrors beyond any I'd ever feared, I've also been shown that there are splendors beyond any I've ever imagined. I feel stronger, braver, recharged.

Hell, maybe I've still got some of Shōki inside me. In fact, I'm sure of it. I wonder, though, if he—wherever he is—ever thinks about that pastrami burrito.

Rosa and I see still see other, but I'm not sure about our future. She's rebuilding Night Haven, bigger and better than ever, of course, and she's back fighting the good fight. We're trying to make a go of things, but it's tougher than I thought. Maybe I've been on my own too long. I know I'll always love her, but there's a residual darkness that gets conjured up between us. We do have fun, yet sometimes I think that even with all she's done for me, I expect *too* much from her. Having made her the object of my belief—or having *had* to do so; I'm still not sure which it is— it's hard to see her as just a person again. I think maybe there are good reasons why people only go to church once a week. We'll just have to see, I guess.

Just the other day, thanks to Kendall Arlo, I signed a contract for a new series with Fox. It's a PI thing, naturally, with me ostensibly playing myself: another hard-boiled detective walking the mean streets of L.A. It's called *Burning Bright* and I'm exec-producing, too, which doesn't mean shit except I get some extra cash for the credit. What the hell.

The Fox people are really excited about the project, and to be honest, so am I. More than I ever would have dreamed.

No sooner were the contracts signed than the PR guys cornered me for a chat. They wanted to get my input on their proposed promotional theme for the new season. *Burning Bright* is the main attraction, and they want to position everything else around it. I could see they were nervous approaching me, and when I saw the catchphrase they pitched, I understood why. I was a little peeved at first, but then I saw the humor in it and told them it would be okay. We shoot the first promo next week.

There'll be a montage of clips for all the new shows. And then my bit: It'll be me standing on the beach at Malibu, a bikinied babe on either arm, a knowing glint in my steely eye. The camera will zoom in tight and I'll ask all my adoring fans the question they've waited so long to hear once more:

"Hot enough for you?"

About the Author

J. S. Russell was born in New York City in 1961. He attended Cornell University and the University of Southern California, from which he received a Ph.D. in communications. He has worked for a private investigators agency in Los Angeles and as a media researcher and editor. His short fiction has appeared in a variety of magazines and anthologies, including *Midnight Graffiti, Splatterpunks, Science Fiction Review,* and *Still Dead: Book of the Dead 2.* He moved to England in 1993, and lives in London with his wife.